# BENEATH A SKY OF STONE

## E.B. TOLLEY

# BENEATH A SKY OF STONE

## E.B. TOLLEY

woodhall press

Woodhall Press | Norwalk, CT

woodhall press

Woodhall Press, Norwalk, CT 06855
WoodhallPress.com

Cover design: Asha Hossain
Layout artist: L.J. Mucci

**Library of Congress Cataloging-in-Publication Data available**

ISBN 978-1-960456-23-6     (paper: alk paper)
ISBN 978-1-960456-24-3     (electronic)

First Edition
Distributed by Independent Publishers Group
(800) 888-4741

Printed in the United States of America

*This first book is dedicated to my children:*
*Odin, Thorin, Linnea, and Aksel, without whom*
*this story would never have been written.*

# 1

## Into Darkness

Darkness is relative. What most humans think of as pure darkness is rarely so, since there is always some kind of ambient light coming from somewhere, even if it's just faint starlight. It is a rare occasion when a person is plunged into such darkness that their eyes can't eventually adjust, and they are forced to stumble blindly in whatever direction they are facing.

To understand true darkness, one must venture underground. True, there are some caves in the world that display rare and magnificent lifeforms that exhibit the same bioluminescence that can be found in the nightmarish entities that lurk in the depths of oceans, but most cave systems have only the light that humans take in with them. Should these lights be extinguished, the explorers gain a knowledge of what darkness truly is. True darkness is not just the absence of light. True darkness weighs upon the observer (if darkness could be observed). It is sensed and felt by the body as well as the spirit, and plays upon the mind until the observer even has difficulty determining which way is up. To many, such darkness is reprehensible and should be shunned at any cost. To others the darkness holds a fascination, a lure into unknown regions that may or may not hold danger but that certainly hold adventure.

The cave system stretched for several kilometers, according to the maps. The party was small, about a dozen or so, all equipped with bright LED headlamps on their helmets and each holding another bright flashlight of one design or another. The cavern they were passing through was exceptionally large, measuring at least three hundred meters end to end and nearly fifty high at the tallest point. The group had spread apart into smaller teams, examining various fascinating mineral deposits.

"What kind of rock is this?" Ryan Shaw asked, indicating a large formation that resembled mounds of melted wax.

"That's called flowstone, and it happens when water runs down and deposits minerals, like when it drips from the ceiling and forms stalactites and stalagmites." Sam Morris smiled to himself. It wasn't often that he felt smarter than Shaw. Shaw was one of those people who was always interested in—and was consequently reading about—everything. It was amazing how much knowledge he had stored inside his brain. When it came to exploring caves, though, Shaw was pretty green. He'd hardly been underground anywhere, so it seemed to Morris like the perfect getaway for Shaw.

"How deep are we here, anyway?" Shaw asked, looking around. Their group had been walking, crawling, sliding, and squeezing around the caves for several hours. His muscles were starting to ache from the unusual physical activity.

"Oh, I'd say about two hundred fifty, three hundred meters or so." Distance and time were always difficult to determine in the

7

underground. Morris chuckled. "I doubt we'll pass the record for the deepest mine in the world."

"Why? How deep is the deepest mine?" Shaw asked.

"It's a gold mine in South Africa, and it's almost four kilometers deep now. I guess it gets really hot in there. They have to air-condition the place."

"Four kilometers . . ." Shaw couldn't imagine people working that deep in the earth in the crushing, stifling heat. This cave was actually quite cold, but Morris had told him the deepest anyone had gone in this cave system was four hundred thirty meters. Definitely not far enough to feel any of the deep earth's heat.

"Here, I want to show you this," Morris said, his dark skin making him almost disappear in the shadows. "I saw it last time I was here five years ago." The rest of the group was nearly out of sight at the far end of the cave, almost one hundred fifty meters away, but their voices could be heard clearly due to the unusual acoustics.

"Knowing your sense of humor, it's probably a rock formation that's grown into a rude shape," Shaw said sarcastically.

"Funny you mention it; there is something like that in another cave system I visited last year, but we'll have to go see that another time. This is pretty neat. It's just a little further on down this short tunnel."

Shaw followed Morris, scanning carefully to make sure his footing remained solid. Sometimes the cave floor could be quite slippery. He didn't fancy having to be carried out with a broken leg . . . or worse. After a few minutes, Morris stopped, and Shaw could feel a breath of warm air coming from somewhere.

"Is that warm air?" he asked. "Where's it coming from?"

"Down there," Morris answered, pointing at the floor ahead—or rather where the cave floor *should* have been.

Shaw moved up beside Morris and gasped involuntarily. Not five steps ahead was a massive hole—thirty or more meters across—opening into blackness. A glance above showed that the hole was part of

8

a channel—continuing upward out of sight. A faint trickle of water between their feet showed that the erosion was ongoing.

"Whoa. How far down does this go?"

Morris laughed. "I don't think anybody knows. We dropped a few glow sticks last time I was here, and we never saw them hit the bottom. It's a long way; I know that much. The warm air you feel is rising from down there, closer to the mantle."

"Are we even supposed to be over here? The guide told us to stay close."

"Yeah, we're fine. I've never gone any closer than this. The guy that dropped the glow sticks was tethered to an anchor we installed in the wall over there. I wouldn't want to fall down there. That's a one-way ticket."

Shaw looked again at the gaping hole in the earth's crust and felt a wave of vertigo.

"Pretty amazing, eh?" Morris looked over at his best friend.

"Yeah, actually. I mean, I know it's just a hole in the ground, but it's kind of scary that it's so deep. How would something like this form?"

"You know, I'm not sure. Could be an ancient volcanic lava tube or just a lot of erosion. I'm no geologist; I just picked up a bunch of stuff over the years of spelunking. Let's get back with the group. They're probably ready to get going."

"Sounds good to me." Shaw wouldn't admit it to Morris, but he really didn't like heights, and the hole yawned wide, hinting at the untested depths below.

Morris began to walk back up the short tunnel to the main cave. Shaw took a step, then realized that he hadn't gotten a picture. Getting as close to the hole as he dared, he took a few pictures with his phone then shoved it back in his jacket pocket. Shaw turned to see Morris waiting for him.

"Finished?" Morris prodded. "Come on."

"Yeah, I just wanted a—"

Suddenly the cave was rocked by a huge jolt. Both men were knocked from their feet as stones and debris came crashing to the floor. Screams from the other cave explorers were drowned out by a deafening roar. Then a blast of hot air shot out of the crevasse.

The floor continued to shake. Small rocks, mud, and water began to slosh past Morris and over the edge of the abyss. Already soaked, Morris scrambled to his hands and knees and managed to crawl out of the mouth of the tunnel and the deadly flow. He turned to make sure that Shaw was still behind him and his heart stopped.

Shaw was gone.

# 2

## Anarchist Troubles

At first glance, the pub looked like the quintessential English pub, right down to the large carved sign over the door that advertised it as the "Capering Goat" in brightly painted red letters as well as a picture of said goat in the act of capering in a manner in which an intoxicated person would have considered incredibly humorous and nearly everyone else, incredibly offensive.

Upon closer inspection, the building had an air of shabbiness about it that made most passersby, if they hadn't been warned away by the sign, decide they might feel better about having a drink in another part of town. The pub stood on a quiet street lit by gas lamps, four of which were burnt out and a fifth that had simply given up and fallen over.

There were rusted metal garbage bins out front of the pub that looked like they hadn't been emptied in recent memory, and it was a strange fact of science that the contents of one of the bins had briefly found sentience and had quickly decided it had been a bad idea.

The windows in the pub appeared to be frosted glass; however, this effect had been accomplished entirely by accident due to a gradual buildup of grease and dirt over the years. The slate roof tiles were cracked and uneven, uncannily resembling the unique dental characteristics of the proprietor.

This was exactly what the owner and proprietor, Mr. Paracelsus Brown, wanted. As the head of a particularly violent group of anarchists, Paracelsus Brown needed as much secrecy as possible, and having the pub in a massive state of disrepair served his purposes nicely.

On this evening, Paracelsus Brown had gathered his group together to celebrate their most recent attack, and to plan their next. Only a few days before, they had dealt a serious blow to the ruling government, and they wanted to keep up the momentum. Plus, they had to keep their promise to their mysterious new benefactor. If it hadn't been for him supplying both funds and explosives, they wouldn't have enjoyed such success.

"I want to start off with congratulating all of you," Paracelsus Brown began, looking around the room at his fellow anarchist "soldiers." An odd lot, to be sure, but they were all loyal to the death and fully committed to the cause. "Taking down that power plant was a major victory for us, and one the ruling class will never forget!" Brown paused to allow his eclectic group to raise a cheer that caused the windows to shake and more than a little dust and debris to fall from the ceiling. He smiled, enjoying the adoration from his fellows. He went on: "But now, we have to continue our battle against the government and let them know they can't afford to ignore us or our agenda any longer. We will be heard!"

Another cheer went out from the assembled crowd, which numbered nearly forty in the small stone pub. Many of them were already quite intoxicated, and they were all in such high spirits that they would have cheered even if Brown had said they were about to be attacked by the very government they felt so invulnerable against.

Individually, most of the assembled group were good, hardworking, decent people, though idealistic and feeling disenfranchised. Unfortunately, as happens with human beings in general when grouped together with a charismatic speaker, the condition of "none of us is as dumb as all of us" happens, causing most of the assembled crowd to perpetrate things they would never dream of doing alone.

In this case, they had planned and executed a bombing of a large power plant in the town of Thaw, which had dealt a major blow to the current government. This latest action would definitely make the prime minister sit up and take notice, though they were in denial about what sort of notice the prime minister would take. All of their previous attacks had been minor in nature: an arson here, an assassination of a government official there. In this case, though, thirty-seven people had been killed, with another fifty-two injured, not to mention the tens of thousands of people who had to do without electrical power for the foreseeable future. No, the prime minister would take notice.

Paracelsus Brown allowed the cheering to die down before going on. "My friends, we begin this very night in planning our next great venture. We cannot rest on our laurels; we need to keep the fight going; we need to keep them on their heels!"

Another loud cheer rattled the filthy windows, including one window sporting a very small spot that had been surreptitiously wiped clean inside and out earlier in the day, and through which someone was watching through a tiny periscope.

Brown continued, "Our next target is the prime minister's seat of power itself!" This last revelation had the effect of sucking all the sound out of the room. More than a few drunk anarchists suddenly found themselves feeling a lot more sober than they had felt just a few seconds ago, and quite a bit less drunk than they would have preferred to be at hearing what their next target was. Brown, sensing the feeling in the room, lowered his voice. "I know, I know. It will be dangerous, more dangerous than any target we've attempted in the past. But I promise you it will be necessary, and the most worthwhile target we could ever hope to attack."

Paracelsus Brown continued with his speech, completely unaware that many shadows had detached from nearby buildings outside and converged on the Capering Goat. Brown, ever the prudent leader, had stationed three cleverly concealed sentries outside the pub, each of which had been quickly and quietly disabled by three even more cleverly concealed persons dressed entirely in black.

As Brown's speech began to ramp up once again, one shadow that had been watching the proceedings through the surreptitiously cleaned window turned and nodded to the other assembled silent shadows. They all began to move quickly and soundlessly, some of them into positions on either side of the front door, others into similar positions around the back. One of them began to affix a small charge to the front door.

"As you all know, we have a new benefactor, who was instrumental in our success at the power plant and who is assisting us with our future endeavors," Brown said. "Though we don't know this person's true identity, we are certain of his willingness and ability to help us in our cause. We can only hope that, whoever he is, he will allow himself to be known soon so that we may know to whom we are so indebted—"

The steel-and-glass front and back doors exploded inward nearly simultaneously, sending fragments in all directions. Those who had been standing close to the doors were cut down instantly, as was Paracelsus Brown's rousing tirade. Many of the assembled anarchists immediately began to draw weapons, but they were too slow to fight back the flood of government agents that streamed into the small pub. Any person who held a weapon was quickly shot down by the agents' incoming fire. In the panicked scramble of the drunken anarchists to find an exit that wasn't blocked by black-jacketed agents, many anarchists were killed by the wild firing of their own people.

Within a space of twenty seconds, the only two anarchists left standing were Paracelsus Brown and a teenage boy who had been recruited recently and whose name Brown hadn't bothered to learn yet. The boy was so drunk that Brown wasn't sure what was still holding him up, and it was clear that the boy didn't know what was happening as agents took hold of him and placed a set of heavy manacles on his wrists.

Brown, on the other hand, did know what was happening.

An agent with extremely dark skin, almost black, with her tight black curls tied into a severe bun, approached him, leveling a large rifle at his chest. "Paracelsus Brown. I am Special Agent Adebe. You're under arrest for treason, murder, conspiracy, and inciting crime and disorder," she said.

Brown smiled. "Is that all?" he asked.

"It'll do, for a start," Adebe replied. "Turn around and place your hands behind your back, sir. If you don't comply, you'll wish you did."

Brown laughed. "Well, if you insist . . ."

As Brown turned slowly around, he quickly reached his clenched left hand up to his mouth and then swallowed what he had placed on his tongue. He immediately began to choke and gag.

Several of the agents surrounding him ran forward in an attempt to pry whatever it was out of his mouth.

"Dammit, he's swallowed something!" Adebe screamed. "Hennessy, grab his throat! It has to be poison of some kind!"

Hennessy, the closest agent, had already grabbed Brown's throat in an attempt to close it off and prevent the poison from going any further, but it was clear from the sounds Brown was making that it had been too late the instant he had closed his mouth.

Brown, his lips turning blue and his eyes bulging and rolling back in his head, sagged to his knees then onto his side as Hennessy and the other agents grabbed hold of him. Brown thrashed about for several seconds as foam began to spray from his mouth and nose.

15

He soon stopped twitching, and the agents released his body. Agent Hennessy stood up and faced Adebe.

"It's too late, ma'am. He's gone."

Adebe nodded. "It wasn't your fault, Hennessy. He was probably dead before he even swallowed it. Take charge of the cleanup here; I need to give an update to the director."

Special Agent Ama Adebe had to step over several bodies that littered the floor. From the look of things in the Capering Goat, there were precious few survivors among the anarchists, a testament to the accuracy of the agents. Two agents had been wounded, one with a bullet through her leg and another with one in his buttocks. His mates were already giving him a hard time about it. None of the agents had been killed, which made Adebe very happy. She would have been happier if they had been able to capture Brown alive, because she was certain that none of the others would have known much of anything.

The war had ended decades ago, before Adebe had even been born. The conflict, however, had never abated. The two opposing armies still remained, their fortifications squatting on the land, forever facing each other in mutual distrust and hatred. The soldiers sat idle, watching their enemies, waiting for attacks that never came.

The same was not true for the intelligence services. For the agents on both sides of the divide, the war continued. It would ebb and flow, sometimes going years between taking lives. But lives it took. Agents on both sides would be caught occasionally; if they were lucky, they would be killed quickly.

The recent trend of using criminals and anarchists as proxy agents and soldiers was still unusual to many of those involved, but the idea, whoever's it had been, was genius. These proxies were ordinary citizens of their respective nations and required far less in terms of support and training. They could blend into the background of their society because they *were* the background. Should they be caught, they could only reveal what they had been told by the agents who controlled them, which was little to nothing. All that was required in most cases was money, and the agents on both sides had access to plenty of that.

Thus, the conflict had transitioned slowly from open warfare to espionage and assassination, and then on to terrorism.

Exiting the ramshackle pub, Adebe approached an area of shadow that was somehow darker than the surrounding shadows and snapped to attention.

"Stand easy, Agent Adebe. Your report?" the shadows said.

"Well, sir. Two of our agents wounded, none killed. Looks like nearly all the anarchists are dead or dying, but we will likely have half a dozen or so able to talk."

"What about Brown?"

Adebe shook her head. "Took a poison pill of some kind, sir. He was dead before we could act. Bloody Tricians."

"Unfortunately, we still have no evidence that the Tricians are involved," the shadow said. "Though we all know they are. Damn. I shall give my report to the prime minister. Will you require anything else from me before I go?"

"No, Director. I can handle the scene from here. I'll have a full report for you by morning, sir."

"Thank you. Excellent work, Adebe. This was not an easy operation, but you pulled it off splendidly. Give my regards to your people."

With that, the shadows didn't change at all, though the lead agent got the distinct impression that the presence in the shadows had disappeared. She never could figure out how the director did it, but the man was as silent as a ghost.

# 3

## Mr. Spall, Director of Special Branch

The prime minister's office was built entirely of polished marble. The floor, the walls, pillars—even the vaulted Gothic-style ceiling—appeared to have been carved from inside a giant block of white marble. Most of the furniture was carved out of stone as well, with the exception of a beautiful wrought-iron and bronze bookcase and a similarly beautiful carved walnut desk that dominated the center of the room.

Prime Minister Whitley sat at the desk in silence, inspecting what appeared to be a thin sheet of metal with writing on it. There was a small stack of identical metal sheets sitting on one corner of the desk next to a polished brass lamp. On the other corner of the desk, a large instrument resembling a massive gramophone squatted like a mechanical toad with various gears and levers sticking out at all angles and a large bronze bell at the top.

Bartholomew Whitley was in a solemn mood. He felt as though he had aged far too much during his time in office. His dark brown skin was showing more wrinkles every day, and his formerly jet-black hair was betraying a lot more gray than he would have liked. As the leader of the Republic, he had a lot on his shoulders, but recent events had caused his stomach ulcers to have a party once again. This time, it felt like they had invited friends and family over and had decided to use his stomach as a piñata. Thank goodness his third and final term as prime minister was almost up. He felt as though another five years would kill him. As he sat in his comfortable leather chair, he became aware of a presence in the room that had not been there previously. The presence was only detectable to the prime minister because one corner of the room had become more silent than usual, and he had been expecting it. He broke the silence.

"Ah, Director Spall. As always, you never cease to amaze with your uncanny ability to avoid people's notice. How long have you been standing there?"

A dark shadow in the corner of the room suddenly resolved itself into the shape of a human being. Nothing had changed in the lighting or position of anything in the room; the man just somehow became visible when he wished to be. The man to which Prime Minister Whitley was speaking was unusually tall and dressed almost entirely in black. He remained immobile; however, his eyes were constantly moving throughout the room, peering into shadows as though looking for things that weren't there.

"Several minutes, sir. You wished to see me?"

"Indeed so. I have a new assignment for you, but before we get into that, I need to know how the raid went. Did you locate all of them?"

"Every one of them, sir."

"And did they surrender?"

"No, sir; though the raid was over in the space of twenty seconds, so I doubt that any of them could have surrendered if they had wished to. They fought back, as we both expected, and there were few survivors. The leader, Brown, swallowed poison to avoid capture."

19

Whitley nodded his head solemnly. "Blast; I hoped we would get lucky on that one. We needed Brown alive."

"I agree, sir. We still have no evidence that the Tricians are helping them, and I seriously doubt that any of the surviving anarchists will have any useful information at all. I have agents combing through everything at the Capering Goat, and they will inform me the instant they find anything at all."

"Good, though I think we both know they won't find anything. Whoever has been pulling these anarchists' strings lately is a master manipulator. Not even a whisper of who it might be, but it's clear from their attacks that someone is pulling the strings."

"Indeed, sir. I have to agree."

"Yes. Well, to the current business. I have an important mission for you, Spall. One that I trust only to you."

"The surfacer?"

"Yes, the survivor from the surface. I understand that he is in extremely poor shape; however, the doctors are optimistic. From all appearances, he seems to be a genuine survivor. Naturally, I am very suspicious."

"As am I, sir."

"Of that I have no doubt. You are a naturally suspicious man, Spall, a trait which, like your ability to avoid detection, makes you invaluable to this office. In this case, I wish for you to take charge of this man and befriend him."

Spall looked at the prime minister for a moment before replying with a confused expression. "Befriend, sir?"

"Yes. I know the term is somewhat unfamiliar to you, but that is what's required in this circumstance. I need to know if he is as he seems, and if he can be trusted. Our enemies are not above placing a spy into our midst using such a ploy. Of course, if he is not a spy, he will contain a wealth of valuable information. My hope is that he may possess knowledge that could aid us in settling this conflict once and for all."

Spall nodded. If the survivor was as he appeared, there was no telling how advanced his society had been. Even the slightest technological marvel could provide an edge against the Tricians. This surfacer, as people were already calling him, may very well hold the key to stopping the endless conflict that had cost so many lives.

Spall appeared to come to a decision. "As you wish, sir. I shall . . . befriend this person as requested. Perhaps I shall introduce him to Schlenker as well, sir?"

Prime Minister Whitley smiled slightly. "Yes, I think Schlenker will be invaluable in obtaining useful information from him. Just remember to be cautious. While you are obtaining information from him, ensure that he is not doing the same from us. Schlenker is always working on 'interesting' things and talking about them ad nauseam. And you need to be more respectful of his butler."

"I give respect where it is warranted, sir."

"Yes. That is all, Spall. Do not let me detain you."

Spall turned quickly and left the room as silently as he had arrived, a feat that never failed to surprise Prime Minister Whitley. He was there one second, and then he wasn't.

The hospital was not unlike any other hospital found anywhere in the world. The floors shone, despite the evidence of a lot of heavy traffic over the years. There was the faint smell of antiseptic in the air everywhere one went. There were nurses' stations at regular intervals, filled with files, charts, and the usual overworked and underpaid medical personnel. The only details that set this hospital apart from any other were that the floors and walls, like the prime minister's office, were made of solid stone, and the medical equipment was archaic and built from metal rather than plastic. The doctors and nurses came and went, treating patients and each contributing to the efficiency of the entire facility, giving the impression of a gigantic beehive. This bustle throughout the long corridors went unnoticed by Spall as he walked from station to station, hallway to hallway, on his way to a large set of closed doors clearly marked "Secure Wing. Access Restricted to Authorized Personnel Only."

Spall pressed a brass button, polished bright by countless fingertips, on the wall next to the door. An alarm could be faintly heard through the doors.

"Name?" Came a tinny female voice from the speaker a few seconds later. It sounded like the speaker was talking through a long metal tube.

"Spall. Secret Service," came the reply.

"Please enter and show your identification at the nurse's station."

A buzzer sounded and Spall was admitted through the doors into the hall beyond. An officious-looking Chinese man in a white doctor's coat approached him with a nervous air. The doctor was not short; however, next to Spall he looked positively tiny.

"Ah, Mr. Spall. You have arrived to check on our patient?" the doctor asked, avoiding the gaze from the tall man, who towered over him. From a bystander's perspective, it looked like a child was dressed in a lab coat, playing doctor with an adult.

"Yes," Mr. Spall replied. "His condition, Doctor Chan?"

"Well, as you know, he was found by the patrol at the foot of the glacier, badly injured. Nearly the same spot where many of the others have been found, but this man was very lucky; he is the only one to have been found alive—"

"Yes, I am aware of the circumstances," Mr. Spall interrupted. "His condition and your prognosis?"

"My apologies, sir. Yes, he is alive, though very badly hurt. Both femurs broken, the right one in four places. Right humerus broken above the elbow, left shoulder dislocated. Six broken ribs resulting in a punctured lung, and a skull fracture with subsequent minor brain swelling, which is the cause of the coma." The doctor rattled off the diagnosis and awaited Mr. Spall's next question. Doctor Chan preferred to speak as little as possible in the presence of Mr. Spall.

"His recovery?" Mr. Spall continued, scanning the room further and appearing to take no notice of the doctor's nerves.

"I suspect that he shall be in the coma for some time; several weeks at least. Following that, he should make a full recovery physically, though it will take some months, and he may have a limp for the rest of his life. He is very strong, though, and he looked to be in excellent health prior to his . . . fall. I cannot foresee any difficulties in repairing his injuries. As I said, he is very lucky." The doctor removed a white handkerchief from his breast pocket and wiped his brow with it before folding it neatly and fastidiously placing it back where it came from.

Spall finished looking around as though satisfied that all was in order, then fixed Doctor Chan with a piercing gaze from his dark blue eyes, making the poor little man feel very small indeed. The doctor recoiled a little then mentally admonished himself for doing so, telling himself (not for the first time and certainly not the last) that he was perfectly safe from harm by Mr. Spall. Mr. Spall was the head of the prime minister's security after all, and he would not do anything terrible if not provoked. At least the doctor hoped that was so.

"Thank you, Doctor." Mr. Spall said at last. "I shall go. One last thing, however. Upon his awakening, I am to be informed immediately, and he is to be told nothing regarding his current whereabouts or situation. Understood?"

Doctor Chan nodded in the affirmative and smiled weakly. Mr. Spall turned abruptly and walked out of the corridor and through the security doors, allowing them to close behind him. The doctor visibly relaxed. He did not dislike Mr. Spall, but the tall man did make him very uncomfortable. Although he couldn't imagine many people who would be comfortable in Mr. Spall's presence. *At least he could make some more noise when he walks*, thought the doctor. *It's unsettling how he can just drift silently through the halls like a ghost.*

# 4

## The Surfacer

It was nearly seven weeks after the conversation between Mr. Spall and Doctor Chan that the subject of that conversation finally awakened from his coma.

The man in the hospital bed groggily opened his eyes, after which followed a period of confusion. There was pain throughout his body and, in many places, intense pain, but over all of this was the confusion. *Where am I? What is this place? What's happened to me?* As the view of the room became clearer, it was obvious that he was in a hospital and that he was badly injured, but the memory of what had happened to him was gone.

He slipped in and out of consciousness, with vague memories of the hospital staff coming in and out to attend to him. He would often awaken feeling intense pain and a crushing weight and would then see a nurse enter the room. After that the pain would drift away and carry him with it into blackness. At times he tried to speak, but when he did finally get the words out, the nurses and doctors seemed not to hear him. Finally came a day when he became fully conscious and was able to get a clearer picture of the room and his injuries.

The first thing he noticed, before even opening his eyes, was the feeling of pressure. It felt to him that he was being squeezed on all sides, almost as though he had dove too deep in a swimming pool. The air itself felt heavy and ... somehow ... thicker, making breathing difficult. He opened his eyes and gazed blearily about until he was able to focus on himself and his surroundings.

Both of his legs were in full plaster casts, as was his entire right arm. His left arm seemed fine except for some dull pain deep in the shoulder joint. His ribs hurt on one side, but the worst pain was the splitting headache that seemed as if there were a tiny person inside his skull, trying to simultaneously force his eyes from their sockets and split the back of his head open with a hammer.

The nurse entered a short time later and looked very pleased to see him awake. "How are you feeling today, Mr. Shaw, sir?" she asked, her British accent echoing slightly in the large stone-walled room. "I'm very happy to see that you're fully conscious. I'm Nurse Diaz, and I'll be taking care of you throughout your stay with us. How is your pain right now? Do you think you might need some more medication?"

As she was speaking, she picked up a small flashlight from a nearby drawer in a cast-iron hutch and flicked it on. Despite its small size, the light was intensely bright to his right eye and agonizingly bright to his left as she checked his pupils. Seemingly satisfied, she replaced the flashlight in the metal drawer, which then slid closed noiselessly on well-oiled rollers.

"Well, I must have been having fun to have woken up in the hospital like this. What happened to me?" he asked, noticing that the nurse's smile diminished. The nurse took out a small hand mirror and gave it to him before replying. Shaw looked in the mirror, expecting the worst, and was surprised to see that his features were nearly unchanged from his last memory. The largest change was that his walnut-brown hair had been shaved off at some point and had returned in a fuzzy way that reminded him of puppy fur. His gray eyes looked normal, except that his left eye looked much more dilated than the right one. He had a bandage along the left side of his head above the ear, under which his headache seemed the strongest. His handsome face looked normal to him, at least. The nurse began to talk as he inspected his reflection.

"Well, sir, I don't know all the details, but it seems you had a very bad fall from somewhere. I'll have to get Mr. Spall in to tell you more. Do you not recall anything from your accident?"

"Nothing. The last thing I remember is sitting on a plane with Morris; everything after is just . . . gone."

The nurse looked puzzled. "A plane?"

"Yeah, a plane. An airplane."

"Oh! Yes, of course . . . an airplane," the nurse replied hastily. "My apologies, sir. I just . . . didn't understand the word spoken in your accent. I shall go inform Mr. Spall that you have awakened. Please excuse me."

"Wait, where am I? Is Morris okay?" Shaw asked.

The nurse seemed not to have heard his questions and left the room quickly. Shaw lay on the bed, even more confused than before. He had seen the momentary confusion in the nurse's face when he mentioned the airplane, as though she had no idea what he was talking about. She had made a good attempt to hide it by claiming to have heard the word wrong, but he could see that the word was still unfamiliar to her.

How could she not know what an airplane is? How could anyone not know what an airplane is? Of course she seemed like someone who would pronounce the word "AE-ro-plane," but that still didn't explain the nurse's reaction.

The room was very odd too. Everything was made of old-fashioned materials. The intravenous solutions were contained inside glass bottles rather than plastic bags, the bed was made of cast iron with a white enamel finish, and the walls and floor were made of polished marble. The lights were sturdy incandescents, but with clear glass rather than frosted, and housed in large metal reflectors. Everything looked brand-new and spotlessly clean, but bought in an antiques shop.

His contemplation of the room was stopped abruptly by the arrival of a very tall, large man of perhaps thirty-five to forty-five, dressed in an excellently tailored black suit and carrying a black hat. His hair was shaved down to almost nothing, and his dark blue eyes glimmered as he scanned the room after entering. His pale complexion was clean-shaven and excellently groomed, but what drew Shaw's gaze was a long blue stripe tattooed straight down across the left side of his face, beginning at his hairline, covering the left eye, and disappearing beneath the high collar of his white linen shirt. If it weren't for the shaved head and unusual tattoo, he'd look like he had stepped out of the early 1900s. The man entered the room, ducking his head to avoid hitting the top of the doorway. He stood near the foot of the bed and studied Shaw for a few seconds before speaking in a deep English accent.

"You may call me Mr. Spall," he began. "I work for the government here as the director for the Special Branch of the Secret Service. We know from your personal effects that your name is Ryan Shaw. You were badly injured and have been in a coma for seven weeks. You are very lucky to be alive."

Shaw regarded Spall for a moment before replying. "Yeah, that's me. I sure feel lucky right now."

Mr. Spall nodded. "Excellent. Your cognitive functions and language skills appear to have fully returned, as Doctor Chan predicted. How *are* you feeling, physically?"

Shaw moved his limbs as best he could, groaning a few times from the pain that still lingered almost everywhere. "Not bad, considering. It feels like I was hit by a truck."

"Yes, I imagine you will have considerable pain for some time. Fortunately, the medical staff here is excellent."

"Yeah, it looks like they managed to put me back together pretty well. All the pieces are here, anyway."

Spall glanced down at Shaw's many plaster casts and bandages. "Indeed. The doctor tells me your casts will be removed in a few days' time." Spall stopped momentarily, as though considering how to best approach the next subject. "Tell me, Mr. Shaw," he continued, "do you know where you are right now?"

Shaw shook his head slowly. "Well, the easy answer is that I'm in a hospital, but where the hospital is, I have no idea. I assume I'm in the UK from everyone's accents, but I honestly don't remember anything about how I got here. I know I must have been in a bad car or plane crash, but when I try to think back, it's all blank. My last memory is sitting in a plane on my way to a . . . vacation, I think. Did the plane crash? Is that what happened?"

Mr. Spall, much like the nurse, betrayed a miniscule expression of confusion when Shaw mentioned the plane, but the expression vanished as quickly as it had appeared. It would have passed unnoticed if Shaw hadn't been watching carefully for it. Spall went on: "No, I can only assume that your 'plane' did not crash, though I confess that I am unfamiliar with the word. You have suffered a fall from a tremendous height, one that no other person has survived to date."

Shaw looked even more mystified. "I fell? From where? Can you just explain where I am and how I got here? What city is this? What country?"

Mr. Spall thought for a few seconds before appearing to come to a conclusion. "Very well, Mr. Shaw." He paused then began to pace slowly back and forth across the room at the foot of the bed. "I am afraid that you are not in any city or country you have ever heard of."

Shaw scoffed, wincing at the slight pain in his newly-healed ribs. "There's no way. I can use the internet, and I still own a globe *and* an atlas. I might not have heard of your city, but I can guarantee I've heard of your country at least. Unless—" Shaw stopped, thinking. "Unless your country is so new that it didn't exist before my accident."

Spall continued slowly pacing the room. "No, my country has existed for well over one hundred years, but I assure you that you have never heard of it. Maps and atlases only display the surface of the Earth. We are not on the surface—"

"Hang on," Shaw interrupted. "Are you trying to tell me that we're *underwater*?"

Spall paused in his pacing. "No, we are not underwater, Mr. Shaw—"

"Just call me Shaw. None of this 'Mister,'" he interrupted again, his impatience growing. "So we're not underwater. Where are we?"

Spall resumed pacing the room. "In our current position, we are more than seventeen kilometers below the surface of the Earth, deep inside the crust."

Shaw looked incredulous. "We're . . . underground?"

"Seventeen thousand, eight hundred, and eleven meters, to be precise, yes."

Shaw sat up in his bed, wincing at the effort. It took some time to form a sentence. "Do you realize how insane you sound?"

"This must come as quite a shock," Spall remarked. "In this instance, though, I am not insane, nor am I lying. We gather from your equipment and belongings that you were on an expedition of some kind, most likely exploring a system of caves; you must have fallen into a deep crevasse. You have come more than seventeen kilometers into the Earth's crust, which is where we currently stand."

Shaw sat in his bed following Spall's remarks, searching Spall's face for any sign of humor. Spall maintained his piercing gaze as the information sank in, and one look into those eyes told Shaw everything he needed to know. Spall was not lying.

"So I'm underground right now? You're telling me that we're in an underground city halfway into the Earth's crust?"

Spall nodded. "Precisely. You are in Echo City, population one and a half million, capital city of the Republic of Inner Earth. We were founded in the surface year 1898. We just celebrated the 125th anniversary of our descent into the underground last month, as a matter of fact. Our 'New Year's celebration' so to speak. We call it Founding Day."

"What? What the hell is going on here? You want me to believe that there've been people living underground for more than a century and nobody on the surface has any idea? This is ridiculous! It's impossible." Shaw sank back into the bed, suddenly exhausted. He still felt the intense pressure all around him. It was so hard to breathe. Then it started to dawn on him why. He originally thought it had been an effect of the pain medication he was being given, but his mind was quick in spite of the drugs. It was the air pressure. Seventeen kilometers below ground level. Of course the air pressure would be greater. But how much greater? It had to be a lot, but Shaw couldn't guess.

Spall went on calmly. "I am here to deliver the facts to you, Shaw. I cannot force you to believe them. I have been tasked to act as your liaison until such time as you have recovered from your injuries and adequately acclimatized yourself to your new surroundings. The fact that you are here at all is nothing short of a miracle." Spall delivered his sentences in a very calm, precise manner, as though his patience was infinite. He reminded Shaw of a Vulcan from *Star Trek*: logical and somewhat cold. He didn't seem overly comfortable with conjunctions, either.

Shaw didn't feel like arguing. For one thing, his pain level was increasing. The sheer effort of breathing the thick air was tiring him out as well. His diaphragm and lungs felt exhausted, as though he had just run a marathon. He shut his eyes, took a deep breath, and calmed himself. After a few seconds, he opened his eyes again and spoke. "Okay, I'll do my best to keep an open mind. I have so many questions, though. Can you tell me how I came to be here?"

Spall looked at Shaw's intravenous tubes before continuing. "I shall answer all your questions; however, I should have the nurse check your status. You look as though your pain is growing worse."

Spall left the room, and Shaw realized that he couldn't hear Spall's footsteps as he walked to the nurse's station. *Strange*, Shaw thought. *He's unusually light on his feet for looking like a pro football player.*

Spall returned a moment later with Nurse Diaz, who was dwarfed in comparison. She bore a large syringe, which she used to carefully inject a fresh dose of painkiller into one of Shaw's intravenous tubes. The tubes, he noticed, just like those on the surface, were made of some type of clear plastic, which made him feel strangely more at ease. It felt odd that such a small detail should have such an effect on him. Despite the room being arranged and furnished like any other hospital room Shaw had ever been in, the construction and materials that surrounded him made the entire scene seem utterly alien. It was intensely comforting to have something familiar to focus on for a moment.

Nurse Diaz finished and left the room after noisily scratching a few notes on his chart, which looked like a plastic clipboard, but the pages seemed wrong somehow. It was difficult to see the chart from his vantage point on the bed, though. He was glad he had managed to get a nurse with a decent bedside manner, at least. He suspected that if Spall was his doctor, the giant would have delivered the injection right into his arm with the frighteningly large needle. Within seconds, a wave of warmth washed over Shaw as the medication began to soothe the pain away.

Spall began to speak once again after Diaz finished and left the room. "You were found, very badly injured, at the base of a cliff several caverns up from here. You had landed in a pile of scree and ice, which evidently saved your life. We have routine patrols around that area, and one of our men spotted you. You were given what aid they could and then immediately brought here. You are very lucky they found you when they did, and that one of them had advanced medical training. It was assumed that you would succumb to your injuries, but you surprised everyone."

Shaw felt that he was very lucky indeed, though that might have been the drugs taking effect. He was suddenly feeling much better about everything. "Alright. I must have fallen from somewhere on the surface, or maybe a cave? I was planning to go spelunking with my best friend, but I don't remember the trip or anything." Shaw paused, thinking. "Was anyone else found with me?" he asked, dreading to hear the answer.

He had been best friends with Morris for longer than he could remember. They had first met in the army when they shared a bunk during basic training. Later, they were lucky to be posted to the same regiment and even got deployed on the same peacekeeping rotation. Eventually they both had grown tired of the army and had joined the police. They didn't manage to get the same patrol squads, but they were still able to hang out on their days off. Morris had even agreed to be Shaw's best man at his wedding. The thought of Morris having fallen as well was agonizing.

Spall shook his head. "No, you were alone."

Shaw sighed, relieved. Morris was a good spelunker; he was probably fine. His thoughts turned back to his own situation.

"I still can't remember anything more recent than a couple of weeks ago. Or, a couple weeks before I arrived here. I guess it's been a couple months already."

"Yes, the doctor informed me that you would likely have no memory of your fall, but that the memory may return in time. It is possible that it may never return. You were given the best doctor in the city who specializes in head and brain trauma, and he is very seldom incorrect."

Shaw nodded. With his headache dissipating, it was a lot easier to absorb everything. "How many people are there down here in the underground?" he asked, changing the subject. He wanted to learn more about where he was. How he had gotten here was irrelevant at the moment.

"Over ten million, spread throughout many caverns and cities," Spall replied.

"Ten million? How did they all get down here?"

"We started in 1898 with more than fourteen thousand people. Five to six generations of people expanded their numbers."

Shaw took a shaky breath, still struggling with the thickness of the atmosphere. It was like breathing soup. The painkilling medication, whatever it was, had driven away his pain and the headache, but it was really starting to affect his thinking. He decided to ask the question that had been clawing at the back of his mind for several minutes. He locked eyes with Spall.

"Can you get me back to the surface?"

Spall had been waiting for this question and dreading it more than any other. As blunt as he could be at times, he still didn't like to give bad news. His face took on an uncharacteristically sympathetic expression as he answered Shaw's question.

"No." Spall shook his head. "I am afraid that we cannot return you to your home. Such a thing would be impossible for many reasons. You are here in Inner Earth forever."

# 5

## New Surroundings

Shaw lay in his bed for some time, looking (and hoping) that he would see some sign of a joke or humor on Spall's face. He could see that Spall was telling the truth, but his brain was feeling muzzy from the meds, and he had difficulty in accepting the facts.

"I wish you were joking, but I can see you aren't," Shaw said at last.

Spall shook his closely-shaved head slowly while keeping his eyes locked on Shaw's. "I work for the government. I have little use for a sense of humor," he said matter-of-factly. "You will agree that this is neither the time nor the place for joking. I am perfectly serious. You are in Echo City, capital of the Republic of Inner Earth. You will not be able to leave. No route to the surface can be found. Many have searched and failed. The old ways our ancestors used to descend were sealed more than a century ago and were not recorded. This place is now your home."

Shaw, feeling positively loopy at this point, still examined Spall for any sign of trickery, not fully comprehending that there was none.

"What kind of home is this place, then?"

34

Spall strode over to the far wall and opened a set of heavy curtains that looked woven out of thin metal wires, revealing a large glass window framed in steel set into a channel in the stone windowsill. Spall opened the window, which slid noiselessly on rollers, and then walked back over to Shaw's hospital bed. The sounds of a city could be heard through the open window. Traffic, people shouting, even the occasional car horn, though instead of the usual *honk!* sound, Shaw could hear an *awooga!* that reminded him of old movies.

"You will have to see for yourself," Spall said as he pushed the heavy wheeled bed over to the window. The glass intravenous bottles clinked together gently, swaying against their metal support as the bed was moved against the wall. Sitting up as he was, Shaw was able to see out the large window, and the sight that met his eyes was extraordinary, banishing all doubts about whether Spall had been joking.

What Shaw noticed immediately was a greenish-blue beam of light emitting from the top of a very tall tower in the center of a massive city. The beam cast a glow over the entire scene, making everything appear to have been carved out of huge blocks of greenish stone. Following the beam upward, Shaw caught his breath as he realized that the beam was striking the upper surface of a cavern, thousands of meters above. He could even see clouds illuminated as they passed near, and occasionally through, the light, which astonished him further.

There were many visible stalactites; some joined stalagmites on the cavern floor, forming huge stone pillars hundreds of meters across, interspersed among the buildings and houses below. The cavern ceiling was perhaps three or four kilometers above the floor, and the far end of the cavern stretched away into nearly impenetrable blackness.

"Good lord!" Shaw exclaimed in spite of himself, feeling dizzy. The more he looked, the more he noticed and the more incredible the scene became. "Are those clouds? Like, regular clouds?"

Spall looked out at the cavern ceiling as another cloud passed into the light beam and was neatly bisected by it.

"Oh, yes. There is sufficient moisture in most of the larger caverns to occasionally have weather, though rain happens for only a few seconds at a time. You had clouds on the surface?"

Shaw nodded, too overwhelmed to comment on what seemed to him such a ridiculous question. He looked closer at the city below the inexplicable clouds floating silently above.

The city appeared to occupy one end of a long, narrow cavern; the narrowest he could see from his vantage was perhaps fifteen kilometers or more. It was impossible to tell how far the cavern went into the darkness beyond. Here and there Shaw could see clusters of lights sparkling away into the distance, suggesting the presence of smaller towns and settlements along the cavern floor. Looking closer at the city ahead, he could see scores of tiny streetlamps and lighted windows, with illuminated billboards and signs everywhere. He could see multitudes of tiny vehicles moving along the brightly lit roadways, their headlights driving the shadows away. And the people. There were throngs of people walking everywhere. The scene could have been found in any major city on Earth, except with everyone dressed in fashions that seemed more in keeping with the early 1900s. Tall buildings of steel and stone reached for the cavern ceiling, casting long shadows across the landscape that radiated away from the bright greenish-blue beam. A glance at the nearest cavern wall, perhaps seven or eight kilometers away, showed that even the sides of the great cavern had been tunneled and hollowed out; tiny lighted windows shone here and there in orderly rows pointing toward the ceiling.

It seemed that the hospital was perched on a large hill of rock at the outer edge of the city, looking down on much of the terrain. A closer look showed that many of the stalagmites, columns, and even a few stalactites on the cavern ceiling must also have been hollowed out, as they too were dotted with lighted windows.

All of this was too much for Shaw. Looking up at the ceiling of the cavern, several kilometers above, he was overcome by a severe feeling of vertigo and nausea. The room and window seemed to sway, and Shaw's vision began to close in as though he were looking through a dark tunnel. Shaw could feel himself beginning to pass out, and he began taking deep breaths to slow his heart rate and calm himself. The medication certainly wasn't helping. He closed his eyes and counted his breaths—in for four heartbeats, out for four more. After a few minutes more he opened his eyes again and looked at Spall. The tall, pale man was studying him closely with the same calm air he had demonstrated throughout their conversation, though there was also some concern in the stoic features.

"So that's Echo City?" Shaw asked.

"Indeed."

"Yeah." Shaw swallowed. "Great. What's the green laser coming from the top of that building?"

"'Laser'?" Spall tested the unfamiliar word on his tongue. "Unusual word. If you are referring to the beam of energy projected from the top of Government Spire, that would be the quake shield."

"Quake shield?"

"Yes. It was created several years ago by a colleague of mine, actually. It prevents the cavern ceiling from collapsing in the event of an earthquake."

"Do earthquakes happen often down here?" Shaw was suddenly anxious in spite of the drugs. He normally wasn't claustrophobic, but he didn't like the thought of being buried alive under several kilometers of rock. The crushing air pressure was horrible enough.

Spall shook his head. "No. That was why this cavern was chosen for the capital city. We have very little geological activity here. The quake shield is simply there for . . . insurance, one might say."

"So your friend built a force field that can protect the city from falling rocks?"

"Yes and no. The quake shield strengthens the rock face, making it impervious to disintegrating or cracking under even the most terrible earthquake, should one ever occur here. It essentially prevents the rock from fracturing and falling in the first place." Spall considered for a moment. "'Force field.' An interesting term. I shall have to mention it to my colleague; he often names his inventions with ridiculously long and overly complicated titles. His description of a simple bedside table would fill a small novel. I will introduce you to him once you are well enough to leave the hospital. He invented and constructed your breathing apparatus in just five and a half hours."

Spall indicated a strange contraption squatting on a nearby wheeled cart. He recognized some rubber hoses and a face mask, but the rest of it was beyond his understanding. There were lots of tubes and cylinders with what looked like a heavy collapsed tent, rolled into a neat bundle.

"I was hooked up to that?" Shaw asked. "What for?"

"After repairing your injuries, the doctor realized that your body was unable to breathe in our atmosphere due to the intense air pressure, and that you could die just from that. Your lungs and diaphragm were nowhere near strong enough. My friend built that contraption to provide you with air at a reduced pressure to ease your breathing as you healed. The doctor was able to turn the pressure up and slowly acclimatize you to our atmosphere over the weeks you were unconscious."

Shaw continued to breathe deeply, more cognizant of the thicker atmosphere than ever. He was glad for the medication. He was feeling a lot of emotions that he wasn't used to. Claustrophobia, loneliness, despair, anger, and denial were all trying to fight their way to the surface. Suddenly he sat bolt upright and vomited loudly into his lap. He was thankful that he hadn't eaten anything recently; all that came out was stomach acid and bile.

Spall turned silently and opened the door to call for Nurse Diaz, who arrived after a few seconds. Seeing Shaw's state, she turned and glared at Spall with a frustrated look.

"Mr. Spall, sir, I understand that you have a job to do, but the doctor and I both warned you not to upset him. He's still my patient, and it seems that you've given him too much to deal with for the moment. He hasn't even been awake for two full days yet, and he needs his rest."

Seeing the tiny blonde nurse telling off the gargantuan Spall helped calm Shaw somewhat. It was like watching a wolverine keep a grizzly bear at bay simply by sheer force of will and a snarly demeanor. The nurse walked over and began to clean Shaw up by changing his blankets.

"It's a good thing you had your blankets up. Otherwise I'd have had to change you as well as your bedding, Mr. Shaw," Nurse Diaz said, much more gently and sweetly than she had addressed Spall.

Shaw blushed and smiled crookedly. He thought of how many times the nurses must have changed and cleaned him while he was unconscious; the thought made him blush harder.

"There you go, Mr. Shaw. Now you just rest easy now. If I were you, I would tell this Mr. Spall to leave," Nurse Diaz said as she finished up and glared at Spall again.

Spall, knowing when to remain silent in the face of an angry medical professional, said nothing and smiled in a way that suggested he had seen people smile before but hadn't quite mastered the technique himself.

Shaw gathered himself and once again slowed his breathing down. "No, I'm alright, I think. Just the drugs. I'm not used to them. They sure take the pain away, though."

"Very well." Turning to Spall, in her most authoritative tone the fearsome nurse instructed: "If I come in here again to find him in such a state, I will take you by the ear and physically throw you out of here, Secret Service agent or not. Do you understand me, Mr. Spall?"

Spall nodded. He had to respect the nurse for her assertiveness; she meant exactly what she said, and she was confident that she could (and most likely would) do it.

"Yes, ma'am. I will take greater care with him in future."

"See that you do."

With that, Diaz left and shut the door behind her, leaving them alone once again.

"I apologize for giving you so much at once," Spall resumed. "I have neglected to take into account everything you are facing. The difference in our settlement alone must be a tremendous adjustment for you."

"It's alright. It was a lot to take in, that's all. I think my injuries and the drugs are making it worse, though. I think I'm okay now. Gonna be a lot of culture shock for me, I think." Shaw took a deep, shaky breath as he wiped his forehead.

"Culture shock…" Spall mused. "You have many interesting phrases."

"So do you. So that tall building is what? Government Tower?"

"Government Spire, we call it. It will likely be our first stop once you are well enough to leave the hospital. The prime minister is most anxious to meet you, as are many of our citizens."

"You make me sound like a celebrity," Shaw exclaimed, a slight look of distaste on his face.

Spall nodded. "You are the first person to arrive alive from the surface since the Republic was founded. Naturally, we attempted to keep your arrival secret to prevent a media circus, but of course that meant the news spread even faster than if we had not tried to hush it up. People are … predictable in that way."

Shaw chuckled a little. "It's like that where I'm from too."

Spall nodded in agreement. "Once the population heard the news that a survivor from the surface had been found alive and was recovering, there was a great deal of interest and considerable speculation. Everyone wishes to hear of your life on the surface."

"Everyone?"

"It is as though you have traveled here from another world completely alien to ours. Our history of the surface ends abruptly in 1898.

Everything after that is a mystery to us. For various reasons, much of the population believed there would be no more human life on the surface. Despite our locating the bodies of those who have fallen from the surface over the years, there are many who disbelieve that any civilization exists there at all. You are proof that much of that thinking was wrong."

"How many others have fallen down here ahead of me?"

Spall considered. "I cannot say. I expect the number to be in the dozens. Perhaps hundreds."

"I guess I am pretty lucky to be alive," Shaw said, not feeling very lucky.

Spall nodded, seeing Shaw's expression. "Quite so. You may not feel it now, but your being here is a miracle. There are many who think this as well, as you may be able to provide information on what has happened on the surface since the founding. The historians alone will likely wish to question you for months."

"That's the most frightening thing you've said to me yet."

"I don't doubt it. Our historians are easily the least-interesting people I have come across."

"It's the same on the surface. Except for my accountant. My accountant has the personality of a potted fern."

Shaw snickered at his own joke, then grew silent. He realized that he suddenly wished to see his accountant more than anything. The sudden knowledge that he would never again see any of his family and friends hit him like no physical force could have.

Spall noticed the sudden change in Shaw's mood and decided it was time to leave him to absorb all he had learned.

"I am truly very sorry for everything that has happened to you, Mr. Shaw. And I understand what you are going through."

Shaw was suddenly angry. "You what? How could you or anyone down here understand what I'm going through? I'm down here in the dark with no way out. I'll never see my family or friends, my home—even the sun—ever again! Everything I ever knew or ever was is gone now. I might as well have died on the surface and then been reborn down here."

Spall nodded, a melancholy expression crossing his features. "Much of what you have said is true, Mr. Shaw. But you are wrong about one thing. Though I have never seen the surface, I do understand what you are going through. I am perhaps the only one in this entire city who understands." He paused, resuming his usual stoic demeanor. "I also understand that you will need some time alone and that I have stayed too long already. Do you have any questions for me before I take my leave?"

Shaw sat in his bed, looking closely at Spall. Again, there was no sign of deceit. Spall was telling the truth about understanding. He sagged into his blankets and let out a loud sigh.

"No, I think I should rest now. You've given me a lot to think about."

"Very well. If you require anything, do not hesitate to ask. The nurses and doctors will notify me immediately, regardless of the hour."

"The hour? Do you still use the regular hours down here without days and nights?"

"Oh, yes. Some things remained unchanged from the surface, Mr. Shaw. Good day. I shall return tomorrow."

Spall turned and left as silently as his own shadow. He passed the nurse's station on his way out of the hospital's secure wing and tipped an imaginary hat to Nurse Diaz and the other medical personnel hard at work. He walked out of the hospital and caught a taxi to Government Spire to report to his boss. It was always entertaining to see how long he could stand there without the old man noticing him. It had become something of a game with the two of them. Spall was not looking forward to breaking in a new prime minister once Whitley's tenure was over.

# 6

## An Interview with Spall

"I'm very sorry this happened to you," Nurse Diaz said to Shaw later that same day after he had awakened from a long nap. "I can't even imagine what you must be feeling."

Shaw was propped up in bed once again, and his eyes kept returning to the window, once again concealed by the heavy metallic curtains. His conversation with Spall seemed almost like a horrible dream—like the one he had just awakened from, where he was tied to a hospital bed and being cut in two. Fortunately the hospital dream had been just that, but the revelation that Spall had delivered to him was certainly not in his imagination. If it hadn't been for the pain he suffered from constantly, it would have been much easier to believe it was all in his mind.

Shaw breathed a heavy sigh. "To be honest, *I* don't even know what I'm feeling right now. It still seems like it's not real, even though I know it is."

Diaz nodded. She had seen grief in many patients over the years, and denial was always the first thing she witnessed. People, for all their differences, inevitably clung to hope in terrible circumstances, even when every molecule of their being told them what the truth really was; they had to take the time to convince themselves.

"It *is* real, Mr. Shaw. I wish for your sake that it wasn't, I really do. Your physical wounds will heal quickly, but the emotional trauma will take longer. If you need anything, even if it's just to talk about something, don't hesitate to ask."

Shaw sighed again. "Thanks. I'm definitely not there yet, but I know I'll have to start sometime."

Diaz smiled again and patted Shaw on the hand before turning to leave.

"Could you open the window before you go?" Shaw asked. "I know it sounds weird, but I feel . . . claustrophobic . . . in this room. For some reason the thought of having more air outside feels better."

Diaz pulled open the curtains and slid the window open partway. The noises of the city could be heard echoing through the opening as the greenish light of the quake shield made a spot on the wall opposite.

"Thanks," Shaw said as Diaz walked out and closed the door, leaving him alone with his thoughts.

The next day, Spall visited Shaw in his hospital room as he had promised. He had brought with him a large book, which appeared to be quite heavy. Once Spall had set the book down with a metallic thud, Shaw realized why it looked heavy. With the exception of the plastic cover, the entire book was made of thin sheets of metal.

"Are all your books made with metal pages like that?" Shaw asked.

"Of course. At least most of them. Some are made from pyrox, which makes the pages much lighter, of course."

"Pyrox? What's that?"

"It is short for pyroxylin. The name encompasses a variety of synthetic compounds, most derived from petroleum. The cover of this book is pyrox, as a matter of fact."

Shaw looked more closely at the book. "Oh, we call that stuff 'plastic' on the surface. Huh. So no paper, then?"

"Paper does exist here in Inner Earth, but it is prohibitively expensive, as is anything made from wood."

Shaw realized that many things that were taken for granted on the surface would seem extraordinary in the underground. Of course trees would be nonexistent in the caverns, except for small numbers in well-lit greenhouses. Shaw had so many questions.

"I guess trees aren't common here. How do you people grow food?"

"We have several caverns committed solely to farms and food production using artificial light of one kind or another. You will see the Grand Cavern one day soon, and the light source there is miraculous. Aside from light, however, our ancestors were also forced to bring a large amount of soil from the surface to plant in. Many caverns were barren rock. They also spent many years developing plants that would grow with minimal soil."

Shaw was amazed at the amount of work that had gone into building a society underground. They even had to engineer the soil.

"Sounds like you could use hydroponics," he noted, realizing for the first time just how much knowledge he might have of everyday surface things that would be revolutionary underground. *This society has truly evolved independent of any surface influences*, he thought.

Spall raised an eyebrow. "We often use a type of growth called 'solution culture,' where plants are grown in nutrient-filled liquids without soil. It may be the same as your hydro . . ."

". . . ponics. Yeah, it sounds like it. Just a different name. So what's that book about?"

"This book is a history textbook of Inner Earth, as taught to our students. It may answer many questions you will no doubt have about our world. Doctor Chan informs me that you will not be able to leave the hospital for some weeks yet. You're nearly due to have your casts removed; however, you will still require a lot of care. Reading this book may be preferable to staring out the window."

"Yeah, I have a lot of questions, but not all of them are about this place."

"I am here to answer as many questions as I am able."

"Can you give me more details about how I came to be here? I still can't remember anything."

Spall nodded. "As you wish, though there isn't much more I can tell you that I didn't already say yesterday. Due to some circumstances, which I will detail later, we have a regular patrol through the area you were found in. Known as the Hawthorne Sea, it is an underground glacier spanning hundreds of kilometers. One day several weeks ago, our patrol located some surface debris. It happens on occasion in some areas where cracks are still open to cave networks far above. Incidentally, we have a sizable collection of mysterious items for you to identify for us. On this occasion, you were found nearby in a pile of scree and broken ice, badly injured but alive. It seems as though you had struck a slope on the glacier, which slowed your descent; then the scree broke your fall, as difficult as that is to believe. The patrol that found you happened to have a medical officer with them who was able to stop your bleeding and stabilize you enough to transport you to a medical facility. You were brought here, where you remained in a coma until two days ago, when your brain swelling had reduced sufficiently. That is all we know. We will have to wait for you to regain your memory so that we will know more."

"I've been trying to remember, but it's just not coming. Doctor Chan told me to be patient."

"Yes, no doubt you will have a long road of recovery ahead of you," Spall agreed. "Many of us are curious about your life on the surface. Are you able to remember much of that?"

"Oh, yeah. I can remember everything up to a few weeks ago. I was on a plane in January; I remember that much."

Spall considered for a moment then gestured for Shaw to continue. "Tell me about yourself."

"Well, I was raised on a small farm. I was the second of four kids—three sisters and myself. After I graduated from school, I joined the army as an engineer. I enjoyed that job."

"I imagine," said Spall. "Did you serve in combat?"

Shaw shook his head. "Not really. I was a peacekeeper in a couple of conflicts, but I was never directly involved in any fighting. I was mostly clearing land mines and booby traps and then supervising demining operations."

"You were a soldier in a war zone, but you didn't fight?"

"Nope. Things are a bit different up there now. No more huge armies battling it out for dominance. It's mostly small countries fighting each other, and a bunch of civil wars. We would send peacekeepers to act kind of like police to keep everyone from fighting and killing civilians and other noncombatants. Sometimes it worked; sometimes not. Rwanda and Somalia were pretty bad. Anyway, I got tired of clearing mines and unexploded ordnance, so I left the army after a few years and joined the police."

Spall inclined his head. "You were a police officer?"

"Yeah. Our police service had over two thousand officers, so it was pretty big, I guess. I've been there for more than thirteen years now. Patrol, training, some detective work in Homicide and Robbery."

"It sounds like a very interesting line of work," Spall remarked, an expression of approval on his face.

"It is. Or was." Shaw sighed. "Looks like I'll be needing a new line of work."

"We may be able to assist you with that. I am certain your knowledge of investigative techniques from the surface will be very useful here, as will your military experience. The surface tools and other devices we have recovered over the years appear to be quite advanced to us. There are many items that we cannot identify."

"I'll have a look at them for you when I get out of here. You said yesterday that some things were the same. You still use the hours of the day like we do, but what about the days of the week?"

"Our days of the week and months of the year are the same, with the exception that all of our months are thirty days in length except January, which is either thirty-five or thirty-six depending on the year. It made calendars easier to keep track of."

"That actually makes some sense. Do you still keep track of the years like we do?"

Spall shook his head. "That is where we have no doubt deviated from the surface. We count our years from the date of the founding of the Republic. The current year is 125. That would make your year . . . 2023?"

"Yeah."

"I think our ancestors would be surprised that the surface is still populated," Spall admitted. "They predicted a war to end all wars within twenty years of their leaving the surface."

Shaw scoffed. "They weren't far off. The First World War started in 1914 and lasted until 1918. It was between England, France, Russia, and the United States on one side; Germany, Austria-Hungary, and the Ottoman Empire on the other side. There were a lot of other countries involved, but those were the main ones. I don't remember exactly how many people died, but it was in the millions. Everyone called it the Great War at the time. The fighting was mostly in Europe, but just about all the major powers of the world took part. It was pretty bad."

"Before you called it the Great War, you called it the First World War. There have been others?" Spall, normally not an easily excitable person, was betraying his interest in the history of the surface. He had heard the names of many of the countries on the surface in history classes, and had even examined the gigantic globe of the surface world slowly rotating in the Echo City Museum of Natural History, displaying the countries and landmasses in polished bronze against the dark gray steel of the oceans.

"The Second World War happened from 1939 to 1945. It was between Germany, Italy, and Japan on one side; England, France, Russia, and the United States on the other. This one used much more advanced weapons and tactics, and there were a lot more casualties. Over fifty million, I think. The fighting was global that time. Europe, Africa, the Pacific—just about everywhere."

Spall shook his head, incredulous. "Such a loss of life is unimaginable. Who won those wars?"

"The Germans and their allies lost both times, but I'd say that nobody really won."

"Yes. It would seem so. Has the fighting continued since?"

"Sort of. There've been a lot of smaller wars and battles since, but nothing involving the entire world. After World War II, the two major superpowers, the Soviet Union and the United States, began to form big alliances against each other, with spying, an arms race, and a lot of mistrust. We called it the Cold War, and it lasted for decades. It's still kind of going on now. The United States and Russia (the former Soviet Union) still don't trust each other. Both still have a lot of nuclear weapons."

"Fascinating," Spall remarked. "You will have to tell me more about your surface history later, especially those 'nuclear weapons.' I can see that you need more pain medication."

"I'm alright; it's just this leg; still hurts like crazy. My ribs aren't much fun, either, but that might be worse because of how hard it is to breathe down here. And my headache is still here all the time. I'm actually glad I was in a coma for so long. I can't imagine what it would have been like with all that pain. At least my bones had started to heal by the time I woke up."

Spall nodded agreement as he walked to the door to summon the nurse.

Nurse Diaz entered the room, casting a glare in Spall's direction. She administered more pain medication to Shaw and then left. She clearly did not approve of Spall's visits. Once Nurse Diaz had gone, a short, round gentleman in a brown tweed jacket and carrying a polished aluminum top hat entered, smiling. He had an enormous gray beard and mustache, making Shaw think of Santa Claus on a day off. He even had rosy cheeks.

"Ah, Professor," Spall addressed the jolly-looking little man. Next to Spall, the newcomer looked even shorter and rounder. "Shaw, this is Professor Turnbull, dean of Historical Studies at Echo University. He has kindly offered to tutor you in our history over the next several weeks. Of course he would very much like to hear as much history of the surface as you can recall."

"Professor," Shaw said, visibly relaxing with the fresh medication taking effect. "It's a pleasure to meet you."

"Likewise, my good man," Professor Turnbull said, shaking Shaw's hand gently. His words were pronounced with perfect elocution in what sounded to Shaw like a German or Austrian accent; Shaw couldn't tell. Shaw felt that he could probably listen to the professor for hours.

"So you get to steer me through that huge textbook Spall brought?" Shaw asked, jerking a thumb toward the heavy volume.

Turnbull beamed. "Of course! No doubt you have many, many questions about our little world down here, and I certainly have a great many questions about the surface. I have taken leave from my position at the university for the next several weeks so that we may meet every day, if you would be willing to tolerate me for that long."

"Oh, it shouldn't be a problem, except for Nurse Diaz. If I don't get my proper amount of rest, she'll probably throw you out by the scruff of your neck."

Professor Turnbull laughed a loud, deep, jolly laugh, once again giving Shaw visions of elves and reindeer.

"The nurse certainly has an air of business about her, doesn't she?" the professor remarked. "I shall do my best to ensure that I don't tire you out, and please don't hesitate to tell me when you need to stop or take a break. Are you well enough to begin now, or would you prefer that I return later? I may even return tomorrow, if you are not feeling well today."

Shaw adjusted himself in the bed. "No, I think I'm just fine now. The medication's kicked in, so I should be pretty comfy for the next few hours."

"Excellent! Well, settle in. I shall begin with a condensed history of the Republic of Inner Earth and the settling of the Great Caverns."

# 7

## A History of Inner Earth

Shaw sat in silence, listening to Professor Turnbull.

"In the surface year 1892," Turnbull began, "a large number of respected scientists, doctors, engineers, inventors, and chemists began to see great trouble in the world. Wars were being fought on larger and larger scales, with higher and higher death tolls. The nations of the world were still building empires, which put them on a collision course with one another. It was becoming clear that the final result would likely be war on a global scale, with the potential to eradicate all life on the surface. This was unacceptable to those learned people. A summit was called among the most influential of these men and women, where they discussed what they could do to forestall this danger."

Turnbull paused long enough to take a sip of water before continuing. "The conclusion was that the coming war was inevitable. The learned ones were too few and could not exert enough influence on their respective governments to counter the growing unrest across the globe. So they made a decision to abandon their respective civilizations to their fates and attempt to construct a new civilization elsewhere, one based on reason, wisdom, and learning. Some wanted to find a location that was wild, unclaimed. But nowhere could be found that would serve their purposes. There wasn't a place in the world that was unclaimed or undisputed by at least one government, and even if there were some available space, war would eventually find them and consume them regardless.

There were several dreamers in the group who believed it would be possible to build a great ship and travel to the stars, but they hadn't even discovered the secret of flight, so travel through the great void of space would of course be impossible. It was finally decided that the group should find a secret location underground and form their civilization there. They adopted the motto that you will see inscribed on the doors to Government Spire: 'Pax in Tenebris Lumen Praefertur in Bellum.' It means 'Peace in the Dark is Preferable to War in the Light.' Once the decision was made, it fell to several leading geologists to find a suitable settlement location.

It took several years for them to find what they were looking for. Naturally, they wished to find a place deep enough that no excavations on the surface would uncover it. It must be far from any active volcanic or earthquake-prone areas, and there must be a large area for people to live, grow crops, and expand. By 1896 they had found what they were looking for. I really can't tell you where the entrance to these caverns was, as that information has been lost to our past."

Shaw sat forward in his bed, a look of incredulity on his face. "Out of everything I've heard in the last few days, I still find that to be one of the most difficult to believe. You're telling me that nobody remembers how their ancestors got down here? There has to be an entrance somewhere."

Turnbull shook his head. "As I said, that information has been lost. It was a stipulation of the founding members that nobody should attempt to leave our cavern for the surface, lest the governments on the surface attempt to lay claim to our settlements and thus bring their wars down here. The entrance was sealed off with high explosives shortly after the settlement of the first cavern. All settlers agreed to never reveal the location of the entrance to their children, and to my knowledge that promise was kept. There is also a rumor that many of the upper caverns were booby-trapped to prevent people from seeking an exit from Inner Earth. These rumors are completely unsubstantiated, of course, but the majority of our population believes them. Several expeditions have searched for a way out—against the law, of course—but none has returned."

Shaw settled back, an unsatisfied look on his face. "So I really am stuck down here," he said, a look of despair crossing his features.

"I'm afraid so," Turnbull replied apologetically, a sympathetic look turning his jolly features sad. "I take it you were harboring some hope that we could get you back home?"

"Yeah," Shaw answered simply, defeated.

"I'm truly very sorry about everything, Mr. Shaw," Turnbull said. "I had assumed that Mr. Spall had explained that to you already."

"Oh, he did," Shaw said. "I just kept hoping he was . . . well . . . wrong."

Spall shook his head slowly, offering Shaw an apologetic look. Spall looked genuinely sorry for Shaw's predicament as well.

"Would you prefer to have some time alone, Mr. Shaw?" Turnbull asked.

Shaw shook his head. "No, I'll be fine. You can go on. You were saying they were looking for a good site for their first settlement?"

"Indeed so. Once an appropriate site was found, all the original leaders were informed. The preparations had been ongoing during the search for the site, so everything transpired rapidly. During the intervening years, all the leaders had secretly been slowly identifying and recruiting other people who were of a similar mind and inclination to help settle the new world. In all, more than fourteen thousand people entered the first cavern between 1896 and 1898. Once all was ready, the cavern entrance was sealed permanently, and the building of our civilization had begun. The year 1898 was renamed year 0 for all inhabitants of the caverns."

Shaw sat forward with a slight wince and interrupted. "Hang on. How exactly did fourteen thousand people—especially so many of them respected scientists, doctors, and their families—just up and disappear in the space of two years? Wouldn't someone have noticed? Not to mention all the equipment, food, animals, supplies—everything you all would have needed down here. I've never heard anything about a lot of important people disappearing back then."

Spall stepped forward and spoke as Turnbull took a drink of water. "We do not know all the subterfuge that was employed, but we do know that many of the original settlers were on a ship that had been commissioned to transport a large number of the founders from Europe. The ship was reported to the authorities as lost in a storm, and all aboard were presumed dead; however, the ship arrived at a secret destination intact. I understand that this same ploy was used several times; however, there must have been many other people who carried out their own 'disappearances.' We only have journal entries from some of the founders to provide us with many of these details."

Turnbull nodded. "Once the first cavern was settled, exploration and settlement of the cave system continued for many years. As soon as an area was well settled, the people would find another and expand into it. Then they would abandon the caves at higher elevation and seal off the routes. The thinking was to gain as much distance from the surface as possible. The Miner's Guild developed methods of detecting caves and caverns through solid rock using sound waves, so tunnels were bored and dug to connect thousands of caverns and settlements throughout the Earth's crust. There are now more than ten million people living in underground caverns all around the world. The highest elevation that anyone still lives is only seven kilometers deep. The cavern we are in is nearly eighteen kilometers deep, and there are others where the heat from Earth's mantle can be felt through the ground, making settlement nearly impossible."

"That's something I don't understand—" Shaw interrupted, confused. "On the surface, our deepest mines are maybe three or four thousand meters deep, and the heat is so intense they have to air-condition the mine shafts. How is it that we're not roasting this far down?"

Turnbull looked momentarily confused himself. "The surface has not heard of the Hasegawa Effect?"

Shaw shook his head.

Turnbull smiled and went on. "The Hasegawa Effect was first studied and quantified by one of our most esteemed geologists, Professor Hasegawa, more than a hundred years ago. Originally from Japan, he found that Earth's crust exhibits many strange characteristics the farther down one goes. There are pockets of the Earth where the gravitational pull is slightly greater or lesser, where magnetism is incredibly strong or simply doesn't work at all, and even where water flows upwards. Past a depth of roughly five kilometers, it was found that the crust transmits heat upward at an incredible rate, allowing much of the deeper crust to cool. This is also aided by cracks throughout the crust that are open to the water from Earth's oceans, which absorb much of the heat and transfer it out to the depths of the sea."

Shaw's eyes widened. "There are tunnels open to the oceans?"

Turnbull nodded, seeing where Shaw's thoughts were taking him. "Not tunnels, I'm afraid. All the water systems we have detected have proven to be little more than cracks in the crust, many of which lead for hundreds of kilometers. To reach an ocean, and then the surface, we would have to bore through these cracks for decades. In any event, we dare not bore into these cracks without flooding the entire underground. The water pressure alone would be hundreds, if not thousands of atmospheres. There are caverns that are flooded, and even some that have huge oceans and lakes in them, but none have been found that would allow an expedition to get far."

Shaw slumped, his momentary hopes falling once again.

"I am not a geologist," Turnbull continued, "so I cannot explain much further regarding the Hasegawa Effect, but it certainly makes the crust livable. Our neighbor to the south, Ünterreich, is four thousand meters below our depth; their city is bisected by a river of flowing lava, but their cavern is not much warmer than ours."

"Ünterreich?" Shaw asked. He thought for a moment. "Is that German for 'Under Kingdom?'"

Spall's features hardened perceptibly, Shaw noticed. It was as though a shadow had passed over his face. Shaw wasn't sure he liked Spall's face that way.

"More or less," Spall answered.

Professor Turnbull looked at Spall knowingly before continuing. "Yes, loosely translated. Though most people would say 'Lower Kingdom.' Mr. Spall grew up in Ünterreich." Here Mr. Spall's tattooed left eyelid twitched. Shaw was intrigued; it was the first time he had seen Mr. Spall betray any sign of emotion other than sympathy since meeting him in the hospital.

"You . . . didn't like growing up there, Spall?" Shaw asked, a little worried.

"I was a slave."

Spall's statement made the room feel as though the air, thick as it was, had been sucked out. Nobody spoke for several seconds. Even Professor Turnbull, normally affable and often quite jolly, sat in silence, a heavy expression on his face.

Shaw was dumbstruck. "You were a slave? There's slavery down here?" he finally asked, looking from Spall to Turnbull and back again.

Spall nodded. "Unfortunately so. I am one of the very few who have ever escaped from Ünterreich. Perhaps the only one."

"How did you escape?" Shaw queried.

Spall looked away, as though into his own memories. His expression betrayed a fleeting look that disappeared as quickly as it had formed on his face. Shaw, having learned to read people by their faces and involuntary, almost imperceptible movements, saw the expression and noted it for what it was. *That was rage*, Shaw thought. *Pure rage. He conceals it well, but it's there.* The thought of such a gigantic person having such emotions coiled beneath the thin veneers of civility and gentility like a venomous spider was not an enjoyable one.

"I was thirteen, and strong enough to lift an anvil," Spall replied in a tone that meant no further information would be forthcoming.

Shaw looked at the faded blue line running down the left side of Spall's face.

"The tattoo," he said. "That's how the slaves are marked." It wasn't a question. That told him all he needed to know of Ünterreich. If they tattooed a slave on their face, they were forever marked, forever displayed as "less than," even if they were to gain their freedom. Which meant that slaves were never intended to gain their freedom.

Spall nodded, his face hardening further. Shaw realized that it was not the time to dwell on the subject.

Professor Turnbull, seeing an opening to change the subject, cleared his throat and continued. "At first, everyone lived in harmony and peace. We were all permitted to follow our own consciences as far as religious beliefs, lifestyle preferences, and political views. Women were treated as full equals for the first time in any modern society, with the right to vote and pursue any employment they wished. No distinction was given to gender, race, color, or creed. Every person was to be equal to every other. Our founders wanted things to be so, in order to avoid the causes of all the conflicts that have afflicted the human race on the surface throughout history. The first twenty years or so were a utopia. Sadly, human nature is seldom able to maintain the status quo for long, at least as far as peace is concerned. Our ancestors had believed they had successfully eliminated all the causes of human discord and aggression. How wrong they were.

"You see, one of our founders had developed a full-spectrum light bulb that would last for many, many years of continuous use. Without this development, the settlement of the caverns would have been impossible. We could not grow crops, the cattle would have no grass to eat, and even the bacteria in the soil would have died. We needed these light bulbs and a constant flow of electricity in order to maintain life down here. That is where the divisions in our society began.

"Everyone in our society is a member of one or more guilds. The guilds ensure that every member performs their chosen trade or profession with the utmost care and attention to proper procedures and regulations. This benefits our society by maintaining an extraordinarily high level of craftsmanship and professionalism. I myself am a leading member of the Guild of Educators, as well as president of the Guild of Historians. My wife and I are also members of the Show Animals Guild, as we breed champion English sheepdogs. There are guilds governing everything. All of them maintain our high standards and keep the citizenry productive and happy. Unfortunately, the guilds caused the small divisions forming in our society to increase."

Shaw's brow furrowed. "So instead of religion or politics, people started to divide themselves based on their guilds?"

"Precisely. The most powerful guild always had been the Electricians Guild, more commonly known these days as the 'Tricians.' They were immensely powerful throughout Inner Earth, as you might imagine. They controlled all electricity production in the underground, and therefore all light and food production everywhere. At first they were good members of our society, but as their power grew, so did their arrogance and ambition for more power. They began to feel that they should control the government and that all other guilds should serve them, which was in opposition to the founders' original ideals of equality. A great deal of unrest began to form, which eventually led to fighting in the streets and even an attempted coup against the elected government. This incident finally forced the government to pass a bill, dissolving the Electricians Guild permanently. Their members were to be disbanded and absorbed into other guilds as appropriate to their main duties."

Shaw smirked. "That probably worked as well as a lead balloon."

"A lead balloon? Not a bad phrase." Professor Turnbull chuckled to himself. "I've never heard that one before. You are correct, of course. The Tricians retaliated by cutting power to Echo City and seizing control of the cavern and city of Ünterreich in year 64. By the time our people were able to restore power and resume crop production, the Tricians were firmly entrenched in Ünterreich and had begun to produce weapons to fortify the cavern."

"So is that why I see so many gaslights around here?" Shaw asked, pointing out the window. "Your ancestors didn't want to be so reliant on electricity?"

"Precisely. Of course there are many electrical devices we cannot do without, but the gaslights are very effective, and our steam vehicles are extraordinarily efficient these days. Many farmers still have to use the full-spectrum light bulbs, so much food is still produced using electricity. We will never be free of electricity; however, we are free of the Tricians. Which brings me back to my story. The Tricians were arming themselves and fortifying the cavern and city of Ünterreich. It was easy for them, since Ünterreich had always been a highly industrialized city before it was seized, and there was a great amount of skilled labor to be taken advantage of. For the next few years, we and the now sovereign state of Ünterreich were locked in an 'arms race' of sorts—"

"That's the term we used on the surface," Shaw interrupted.

"I suppose it is the best description, isn't it?" Turnbull replied before continuing. "We desperately tried diplomacy for years with minimal success. Once it became clear that diplomacy was not working and that war was inevitable, all the families and supporters of the Tricians who had been left behind here in Echo City were gathered together and sent to live in Ünterreich. The government certainly didn't want to have them staying here to sabotage us. In all, more than 47,000 people were sent to Ünterreich during those early years. A significant number, considering that the population of Echo was only 350,000 or so. Despite our best efforts, all we were able to accomplish was to forestall the eventual war for several years. In the end, Ünterreich attacked in the year 68, and the Great War of Inner Earth began; it lasted seven years and consumed nearly four million lives."

Turnbull paused to sip some more water and looked out the window of the hospital room at the glow of the city. At this distance from the city center, the greenish light from the quake shield on top of the palace was somewhat overpowered by the streetlights from below, giving Turnbull a sickly yellow-green pallor.

"At first, Ünterreich gained the upper hand quickly; we hadn't anticipated such an onslaught. As you might imagine, with the entirety of our founders being pacifists and scientists, we had a dearth of people with military experience and tactical thinking. There had been no need for such skills when the caverns were founded, since it was thought that all 'traditional' origins of conflict had been eliminated. As a result of all this, the first few years of fighting gained very little for either side, and we had a terrible time pushing the Ünterreich forces back to where they currently sit. We had no proper soldiers and certainly no proper leaders. We had police officers, of course, but nobody who understood how to fight in a war."

"Not the sort of thing you want to learn on the fly," Shaw said.

"Indeed. The Tricians took many caverns before we were able to counterattack. They had developed and built many new weapons that we were unprepared for. Shard guns, Black Hands, fire throwers, scythe mines—the list of horrible weapons of war goes on."

"Shard guns? Scythe mines? I don't recognize any of those names. Except maybe the fire thrower. It must squirt a jet of burning fuel, right?"

Spall nodded, speaking for the first time in several minutes. "Correct."

"And the shard guns? How do those work?" Shaw asked, intrigued. He had always been interested in unusual weapons.

Turnbull was a little out of his element talking about how weapons worked, so Spall went on. "Shard guns use an electromagnetic charge to launch hardened wolfram projectiles at more than one thousand meters per second. The pistol versions are much slower; however, they are still extraordinarily deadly. Scythe mines are devices that are placed in or on the ground. When stepped on, they launch themselves upward and then detonate at waist level, showering fragments in a circle outward. They tend to cut people completely in two, hence the name."

"We called them 'bounding fragmentation mines' on the surface," Shaw interjected. "What about the Black Hands?"

"The Black Hands are perhaps their most horrible weapons, based on their effects. They consist of a pair of metal gauntlets connected to a large battery on the operator. The gloves are capable of discharging massive amounts of electricity directed wherever the operator wishes, up to a range of perhaps seventy meters. They can be adjusted for intensity, from a mild painful shock to the equivalent of a bolt of lightning. Naturally, lightning is difficult to come by down here, so that last is conjecture. Fortunately the Black Hands are not usually seen anymore, except on the Tricians' leadership. They are a sign of status these days."

"Not sure I'd want to get hit with a bolt of lightning, no matter where I was," Shaw noted. "Did they have all of these weapons developed before the war started?"

"Not right away," Turnbull replied. "The shard guns had been developed for police officers before the war, so were used in battle immediately; however, the other devices appeared later, as the Tricians perfected them. Faced with these new and terrible weapons, we were forced to retaliate with new advancements of our own. Armored steam-powered vehicles armed with heavy guns, automatic firing rifles, even rockets with explosive tips."

"Tanks, machine guns, and missiles." Shaw nodded. He was amazed at how much the history of the underground had paralleled the surface, even down to some of the weapons used.

"So the surface had all too much in common with us, at least as far as warfare goes. The effect of many of those weapons on soldiers was monstrous. No doubt your wars were as horrifying as ours."

"Pretty horrifying. So what happened once the war started?" Shaw asked.

"After the first year or so, both sides were locked in a stalemate of sorts, with battles involving tens of thousands of soldiers gaining minimal ground, and often gaining nothing at all. Every time a new weapon was introduced, another would be quickly developed to counter it. Neither side could gain a true advantage over the other. Finally, diplomacy was able to resume, and the war was over—or, at least, stalled. The battleground is still there, with the fortifications built and the soldiers still manning their posts. It is less a peace and more of a stalemate, and it came at a terrible cost."

Turnbull paused, remembering the events he learned about in his youth. "Near the end of the war, the Tricians developed a poison gas weapon that was able to kill thousands of troops in minutes. Fortunately we had a working filter mask that was able to reduce the weapon's effectiveness, but that weapon was the catalyst for our development of an even more horrible weapon."

"Biological or nuclear?" Watching Turnbull intently, Shaw noticed a flinch when he mentioned biological weapons. "I'm thinking biological. It doesn't look like you guys have split the atom yet."

"Split the atom? I wouldn't have thought it possible until you said it," Turnbull continued. "No, the government convinced our finest medical researchers to construct a bacterial weapon that was easily spread through a gas of our own design. We were able to infect a large portion of the Trician army with a form of anthrax in just a few days. The war would have been won had some of our own soldiers not become infected with the same disease. The airflow through Winterswijk, the cavern where the main battles were being fought, was predominantly from the enemy side to ours."

"Slight miscalculation there," Shaw added sarcastically. It wasn't the first catastrophic military blunder he'd heard of. The exact same thing had happened in World War I, if he remembered correctly.

"Indeed so," Turnbull agreed. "Indeed so. Of course both battle-grounds were quarantined, which turned out to be the driving force behind peace talks resuming. Many of the soldiers died from the disease, and even now the battlegrounds are considered contaminated. The soldiers at the fortifications in Winterswijk have to wear special suits and breathing apparatus to man their stations."

"They hadn't developed a cure? Antibiotics?" Shaw looked worried. "They released a biological weapon they couldn't control…" he trailed off. The magnitude of how many discoveries not available in Inner Earth that were commonplace on the surface was frightening. That meant that nearly eradicated diseases like polio, measles, and smallpox could still cause massive disasters in the caverns. He was suddenly worried that he might carry diseases from the surface that could cause problems underground. He decided to ask Doctor Chan about it next time he came in.

Turnbull sighed. "You are right, of course. It was an act of desperation to stop the Trician army from overrunning our defenses. Winterswijk is a massive cavern, a little smaller than the one we are currently in, and each end has a large area of dry land with an ocean in between. The Trician army occupied one end, and the Echoans the other—"

"Echoans?" Shaw asked, confused.

Turnbull smiled. "The people of the Republic. We call ourselves Echoans because we live in Echo City. Anyway, the Tricians had

**64**

managed to land their forces on our beach and were taking ground quickly. That was when our generals released the biological weapon, as you called it. We were very fortunate that the disease didn't make its way into either capital city. The entire underground would have been contaminated. It would have been another disaster like Lille Danmark."

"Lille Danmark?" Shaw thought for a moment. "Little Denmark. . . .What happened there?"

"I will have to tell you that story another time. Suffice to say, nothing grows in that cavern anymore; it's been sealed off for years now. That brings us to the current situation between us and Ünterreich, which has existed for the last fifty years. An uneasy peace, with neither side able to gain an advantage or do anything to effect change in the other's actions. Occasionally we will have some sort of attack here in the city or in another of our caverns, but those events are generally found to be the work of anarchists here. We had one a few weeks ago, just before your arrival down here. A large energy production facility was bombed in the town of Thaw, built right next to the Hawthorne Sea, where you were found."

"It has been supposed that the shock from that explosion may have been the cause of your fall from the surface," Spall pointed out.

Shaw nodded then looked back over to Turnbull. "So you have terrorists here as well. Feels like I'm back home already," he added sarcastically.

"'Terrorist.' A very good name for them." Turnbull smiled wryly. "They claim to want change, but it's clear that all they want is to be feared and to spread terror and mayhem. Though I, and many others, think they may just be working for the Tricians. We have been trying to get the Tricians to abolish slavery in their territories for more than sixty years but have never had any success. During those sixty years, the Tricians have conquered numerous smaller caverns in their region, enslaving all the people who aren't killed. They have become ruthless, bloodthirsty empire builders. Some of the inhabitants of Ünterreich who were still loyal to the Republic were either killed or enslaved, as were the peoples of Lägre Hem, Mpya Africa, and one of the Chinese caverns, whose name I cannot adequately pronounce."

"Lägre Hem? Mpya Africa?" Shaw wasn't sure he had heard the names right.

"My apologies. We try to pronounce everything as closely as possible in the native languages. 'Lägre Hem' is Swedish for 'Lower Home,' and 'Mpya Africa' is Swahili for 'New Africa.' The Tricians have enslaved almost every person of Swedish descent, and many Chinese and Africans as well. The only people left from those caverns are the ones who were in the Republic when the Tricians took Ünterreich. And our Mr. Spall, here."

Shaw looked over at Spall, realizing that due to his size and physical traits, he was clearly one of those who had been enslaved from the Swedish cavern. Spall's face was a mask of inexpression, but Shaw could tell that Spall was hiding some very strong feelings toward the Tricians. Shaw looked back to Turnbull.

"I still can't believe slavery is practiced down here. It's all but eradicated on the surface, except for some criminal organizations. You're right; things have deteriorated. Not exactly the utopia your ancestors hoped to build."

"Certainly not. We came down here to avoid war and bloodshed, and we seem to have brought it with us. Rather unfortunate."

Shaw nodded silently.

"Indeed so. Well, shall we take a short break? I confess that I seem to have consumed too much water, and I can't hold things in quite so well as I used to. If you gentlemen will excuse me?"

Professor Turnbull left to find a restroom, leaving Shaw with Spall.

Spall stepped forward. "With you working for our government, though, things may change for the better. If you would be willing, of course."

Shaw looked at Spall, surprised. "The government wants me to work for them?"

"Well, with your military and police background on the surface, you will have knowledge and training that is far more advanced than our own and that will greatly benefit us in solving crimes and reducing casualties on the battlefield, should hostilities resume. You may even be able to assist us in developing weapons and defenses to counter some of the Trician equipment that has been plaguing us in recent years."

"Uh, I don't know how much help I can be. You may be better off without me."

"I doubt that. At the very least, you would be able to identify some of the artifacts that have fallen down here from the surface."

"Well, that I should be able to do. You said earlier that everyone is part of a guild. Which guild are you?"

Mr. Spall held out his right hand, displaying a large steel ring on the middle finger. The ring was stainless steel, set with numerous small gears between two outer toothed rings that followed the circumference of the inner ring. When the outer rings were rotated around the inner ring, the small gears would spin individually. The ring was very intricate and beautifully made, despite being steel rather than a more precious metal.

"This ring is a symbol of the Artificers Guild. We are the designers, engineers, tinkerers, inventors. We imagine everything and then build it. I also built this."

With that, Spall opened the left side of his coat, revealing a holster containing a huge revolver. The workmanship was extremely beautiful. The frame displayed old-fashioned color case-hardening, and many of the other visible parts were a deep blue-black over a high polish. What struck Shaw as most impressive was that the revolver itself had two cylinders side by side, with two barrels in the same arrangement.

"Is that a double revolver? You built that? I don't think I've ever seen anything like that before. Does it fire one shot at a time or two?"

"It can do both. I built the pistol so that if one pulls back on the single hammer spur, both hammers are cocked. I can then press the front trigger to fire one barrel, then the second trigger to fire the second barrel. If I were to pull the second trigger first, both barrels would fire simultaneously."

"How many rounds does it take?"

"Fourteen total. Seven in each cylinder."

"What's the caliber? It looks pretty big."

"11.5 by 33 millimeter."

"What? I've never heard of it," Shaw added, confused. Growing up on a farm as he did, followed by military and police work, he felt more than adequately knowledgeable about firearms.

"It is actually a very old cartridge, originally brought down from the surface."

"Can I see one of the cartridges?"

Spall opened the revolver by pressing a lever on the back of the frame behind the left cylinder and breaking the frame open via a large hinge on the front under the barrels. All fourteen bullets began to automatically extract from the cylinders, but Spall stopped opening the pistol before they could fall out. He retrieved one of the cartridges and handed it to Shaw.

"Oh, we have tons of these on the surface—.45 Colt. Lots of cowboy-style guns are chambered in these. I've just never heard of it in a metric caliber."

"Forty-five? Forty-five of what?" Spall looked genuinely confused.

"Forty-five hundredths of an inch. The diameter of the bullet."

"An inch? Ah, the imperial system of measurements. We have always used metric here. Does the surface still use the imperial system?"

"No, most of the world uses the metric system for most things. The United States still uses the imperial system exclusively, but just about everyone else uses metric."

"Interesting," Spall said as Shaw handed back the cartridge. Spall reinserted the cartridge into its chamber and snapped the pistol shut with a metallic click before holstering the heavy weapon.

Shaw watched the huge pistol disappear beneath Spall's suit coat. "You're allowed to carry weapons of your own design in the Secret Service?" he asked.

"Normally just government agents and police carry firearms; however, with the recent increase in anarchist attacks, many citizens have started to carry weapons as well. Many members of the Artificers Guild may carry a weapon of their own design if they are to achieve the rank of Master Artificer. There have been some . . . unusual designs in the past."

"No doubt. Just from what I've seen here in the hospital, it'll take some getting used to. So everyone in the Artificers Guild is armed?"

"Not everyone, but many are these days. Normally there is very little crime here."

Shaw nodded. "What other types of weapons are there down here?" He was normally fascinated by complex machines and mechanisms, which explained why he found firearms so interesting. He couldn't help but betray his curiosity.

Spall thought for a moment before replying. "The police and other members of the Public Workers Guild all use the standard-issue police pistol, what we call a 'steam gun.' It doesn't actually use steam; it uses compressed air. Much quieter than mine." Spall betrayed the slightest look of pride when referring to his own creation. "The Miners Guild creature control officers use a variation of the steam gun that operates using highly compressed air and a flammable liquid propellant. Several other guilds use various ordinary revolvers, automatics, and air-powered firearms. The different weapons have come to be seen as status symbols at this point."

"Weird. So you can tell who belongs to what guild by what weapon they carry." Shaw displayed a look of confusion. "Hang on. Miners Guild 'creature control officers'? What creatures do the miners have to worry about?"

"We have a vast assortment of animals brought from the surface," Spall answered, "some of which have escaped over the years and

BENEATH A SKY OF STONE

turned feral. There are many other species in the caverns that have evolved independently of anything on the surface. Some are quite dangerous, but we can educate you about those some other time. You will have enough to occupy your time just learning our history and teaching us yours."

Shaw looked worried momentarily before carrying on. "What about the Tricians? What weapons do they carry?"

"They mostly carry their shard guns, which I described earlier. Though their agents here will carry anything else to avoid detection."

"They have spies in Echo City?"

"Yes. We have our own spies in Ünterreich. Another task I feel you would be well suited for, as it happens. You may be able to assist us in catching Trician spies."

Shaw lay back in his bed and sighed deeply. There had been a lot to take in in such a short time, and now Spall was asking him to help with his government's military research, weapons development, and even their spy hunting activities.

"Of course I would expect you to consider this proposal for some time before accepting," Spall added, seeing the tension in Shaw's face. "I understand that I have given you a lot to think about without giving you much incentive for accepting." Spall paused as Professor Turnbull reentered, a look of satisfaction on his jolly bearded face. "You are, of course, free to choose your own path down here, and there is no rush for you to choose what path you take. I shall leave you in the hands of the professor here so that you may learn more of our history. Good day, Mr. Shaw. I shall visit periodically throughout the coming weeks."

With that, Spall left the room as silently as ever, never making a sound.

Professor Turnbull chuckled. "Well, shall we continue with your history lessons?"

# 8

## Healing

"I'm quite pleased with how well you're healing, Ryan," Doctor Chan said the next morning while on his rounds. He had just checked Shaw's reflexes and other basic physical examinations, and there seemed to be little to no permanent damage—an even bigger miracle than Shaw's survival in the first place.

Shaw smiled. "Thanks, I guess. I still feel really weak, and the pain is still really bad sometimes."

"The pain will lessen as your injuries finish healing, but the weakness will take some time to go away, I'm afraid," Chan noted. "And it will depend greatly on your willingness to work hard at strengthening your limbs after you're fully healed. It will take some months before you're able to do most things that you could do before."

"Yeah, I know I have a lot of physiotherapy ahead of me. I'm worried about some of my injuries, though. My leg especially. Do you think I'll be able to walk properly again, or will I have a limp?"

Chan shrugged. "Honestly, Ryan, it's far too early to tell. The bones are healing very well and surprisingly quickly, but we won't know what the long-term effects of your injuries will be until you're up and moving about. Before you ask," Chan added, seeing the question on Shaw's face, "it will be a couple of weeks yet before we will be getting you out of this bed on a regular basis. With the trauma you've suffered, we can't risk rushing your treatment. Will you walk again? I have no doubt. Will you have a permanent limp? Perhaps . . . perhaps not."

Shaw nodded. He couldn't argue with anything Chan said; he had to focus on healing first and then recovery. Patience was the key.

"My eye still bugs me though," he confessed. The blown pupil always struck him when he saw it in the mirror.

Chan nodded. He'd had a conversation with Shaw already about the damaged pupil, and they both knew nothing could be done about it. Shaw would have it for the rest of his life. It was perhaps fortunate that he now resided in a place where there was little bright light.

"Yes, like many other things, it will take some getting used to," Chan admitted, smiling. He wasn't normally a smiles and sunshine sort of doctor, rather leaning toward the cold, clinical, and high-strung. In spite of his nature, though, he had come to like Shaw.

Having witnessed the process of grief in countless patients and their loved ones through his career in medicine, Chan had plenty of experience in assisting those who had been forced to deal with traumatic events, serious illnesses, and sudden deaths. Shaw had amazed him with his ability to look at his situation rationally. There had been moments of sorrow, anger, and depression, it was true, but Shaw seemed to be able to even himself out rather well.

*He still needs to engage with one of the psych doctors, though*, thought Chan. Shaw might just be very adept at burying the trauma, which never went well for the patient in the long term.

"I had a thought yesterday while Professor Turnbull was in here," Shaw said. "I'm worried about possible contagion."

Chan nodded. The thought had occurred to him almost immediately after Shaw had arrived and it was confirmed that he was from the surface.

"Indeed, Ryan, we had the same concerns when you were first brought in. You were put under quarantine immediately after we stabilized your condition. We have been running blood cultures on you since you first arrived, just to ensure that you aren't carrying anything we aren't prepared for. The same is true in reverse, of course. We also had to be certain there wasn't some illness down here that could seriously harm you."

Shaw grimaced. "I hadn't thought of that angle," he confessed.

Chan nodded. "Fortunately, we haven't found anything that suggests you're a carrier of any diseases we haven't seen before. In fact, we have isolated several antibodies in your blood serum that are showing promise in treating several diseases we currently have no cure for. I have been meaning to ask you about some of the vaccines you've been given on the surface."

Shaw had to think for a minute. There had been so many things he had taken for granted that now seemed so important. How many people, aside from doctors and nurses, could list all the diseases they've been immunized against? Shaw had no idea.

"Uh . . . I know there's MMR. Measles, mumps, and . . . rubella? I think that's what the "R" stands for. I don't even know what that disease is, to tell the truth. Polio. Hepatitis. Tetanus. Those are the ones I can remember right now. Maybe once I'm off these painkillers, my memory will be better. Everything's still a little fuzzy."

Chan scratched a few notes onto a metal notepad. "Thank you, Ryan. This will help our lab a lot." He checked his watch. "I need to go and complete my rounds, but I'll be back later to check on you again. Nurse Diaz will be in soon to check your medication."

"Thanks, Doc," Shaw said, smiling as the physician left the room.

There was still so much to absorb. It would likely take months or even years to fully adjust, Shaw knew. So many things were the same, yet so many things were different.

Shaw remained in the hospital for an additional eight weeks, during which time he was visited nearly every day by Professor Turnbull. As Shaw's strength returned and his injuries healed, he enjoyed his history lessons more and more. Professor Turnbull also enjoyed himself as he scoured Shaw's memories of the surface for historical significance. Shaw felt bad that Turnbull could only get so much from him. Shaw was never a scholar, nor did he care much for history in school as a child. Despite his excellent memory for facts, he felt that most of the information he gave Turnbull was conjecture. Nevertheless, Turnbull was ecstatic about everything that was told to him, regardless of its veracity.

Spall visited on occasion as well, and was his usual quiet, brooding self. He would tell Shaw about the war with the Tricians and the ensuing cold war. He would also tell Shaw what he could of the Trician spy agency, AEGIS. Shaw could tell that Spall was anxious to have him work for the government, but Shaw wasn't ready to make that kind of commitment yet. His body was healing, but his mind was taking longer to get itself sorted out.

Shaw would wake every night from dreams of falling forever through endless blackness; he felt intense fear and vertigo even when thinking of long drops. The dreams were horrible, but upon waking and finding himself safe, he would remember where he was and the reality of his situation would collide with his mind like so many tons of rock falling from the cavern ceiling.

**74**

He was still coming to terms with the fact that he would never see his family or friends again, that everything he knew and loved was lost to him forever. He was well and truly trapped in the underground, and it was taking a long time for him to accept it. He tried not to dwell on what he had lost and be thankful that he was alive, but he would still receive flashes of memory from the surface and realize that so much of that life was now lost forever. Seeing the sun, the moon, the stars. The clouds in the sky, reflected in the ocean. The feeling of being outside and not hemmed in all around by the crushing pressure and the incalculable psychological weight of the immensity of solid rock overhead.

The worst part, after the feelings of loss and regret and loneliness, was the dark. Shaw had not felt afraid of the dark since his childhood. Apprehensive, perhaps, but most people are when faced with the unknown. Unseen dangers that lurk in the dark plague the imagination of most people, but Shaw would look out his window and see the cavern disappearing into blackness beyond the glow of the city and feel an overwhelming dread, as though the blackness itself was alive and was biding its time, waiting to devour the light and all that existed in it.

The dark, he realized, was the embodiment of all the fear and uncertainty he felt at his future here in Inner Earth. He was gradually sliding toward accepting his fate and the fact that he would likely never again see his home or his loved ones, but being confined to the hospital as his injuries healed and he regained his ability to walk and perform physical tasks meant that he was not experiencing the outside (*inside?*) world enough. Many things were similar, he had discovered, but many things were completely different.

On one occasion he spent his entire meeting with Professor Turnbull talking about his loved ones. It was the first time Shaw had talked about them to anyone since arriving in Inner Earth, and Turnbull, understanding that Shaw needed to share his deepest thoughts and feelings, stayed quiet throughout their interview and listened. Shaw spoke of his parents, his sisters, and even his girlfriend, who he had asked to marry him just a short time before he had left on his trip. Much of the grief he felt arose as he realized that none of them would ever know that he was alive and well, that they would never get their chance to say goodbye. Shaw expressed anger at the underground for not enabling him to leave; he even felt resentment toward Spall, but he later realized that he felt that way because Spall had been the one to break the bad news to him.

Turnbull just sat uncharacteristically silent throughout and nodded in agreement. He had been told by Doctor Chan to expect some of these things from Shaw during their time together. Shaw had continually refused to speak with the hospital's representative from the Psychotherapists Guild, which included doctors, counselors, therapists, clergy, and even funeral directors. He still didn't feel ready to face everything.

Turnbull ended up being the first sounding board for Shaw's grief, which turned out to be exactly what Shaw needed during his recovery. He felt so much better after that session that he was able to start talking more about his surface life, not just the hard facts of history and technological advancement.

One day, Nurse Diaz came in and, finding Shaw sitting in his bed crying quietly, held his hand and sat with him.

"Thanks," he said, wiping the tears from his eyes once they had stopped flowing. His face flushed a little with embarrassment, even though he knew that tears were nothing to be ashamed of. He had cried plenty of them during his recovery and physical therapy—some from pain, some from frustration, and some from the grief that still constricted his emotions like the heavy atmosphere constricted his chest.

"Of course," Diaz said, smiling. "What are you missing today?" she asked. He had confided in her many times since that first grief session with Turnbull, and now it was a question she asked Shaw regularly.

"I saw a bird fly past the window," he said, looking out at the glow beyond the glass. "I didn't even know your ancestors had brought them down here. I suddenly realized that every creature I've ever seen, every plant, every insect, will forever be out of reach. The only things I'll ever see for the rest of my life are the things that were brought down here more than a hundred years ago."

Diaz nodded in sympathy. "Mm-hm."

"Then that made me think of my family again," he went on. "My parents. My sisters. My fiancée."

"I didn't know you were engaged to be married," Diaz said. "I'm so sorry."

"Yeah, I had just asked her. We've been together a couple years now." He stopped talking abruptly, lost in thought.

"How many sisters do you have?" Diaz asked.

"Four. I'm second oldest. There's Kyra, myself, Emma, Corinne, and Allison. Cori and Allie are quite a lot younger than us older three, so they're still both in school. I'll never see them graduate."

Shaw teared up again, but he was able to calm himself down as he looked back out the window.

"Where were you from on the surface?" Diaz asked. "Where was home?"

"I'm Canadian," Shaw answered.

"Where is Canadia? I've never heard of it," Diaz said. There were quite a few caverns that had accents similar to Shaw's, but their residents had all descended from ancestors who had come from the United States of America.

Shaw chuckled. "It's Canada, actually. It's the northern half of North America. The United States is south of us, then Mexico." He looked at Diaz, with her white skin and blonde hair and thought she must have married into the name. "Where are your ancestors from?" he asked.

"Spain," she replied. "Apparently I'm the twin of my great-grandmother, down to my hair and eyes," she boasted.

"Huh. I didn't know they had much blonde hair and blue eyes in Spain," he noted. "I always thought of Spanish people to be like the ones in Mexico."

"Well, I don't know anything about Mexico, but you should visit España Caverna. I think there're more blondes there than any other cavern."

"But you sound British," Shaw observed.

"Oh, I grew up in Echo City. Everyone has this accent here."

Shaw nodded. He still had a lot to learn.

Finally, Shaw was healed enough for the nervous Doctor Chan to release him from the secure wing of the hospital. Shaw was moved into a different wing for the last week of his stay, which meant that he was permitted visitors. Almost immediately, he was bombarded with requests for interviews by different reporters, most of whom were very polite and professional—and one who was anything but.

"So tell me, Mr. Shaw," began the latest reporter, who introduced himself with a surprisingly rumpled metal business card identifying him as Edwin Schmidt-Hess, the lead editor, and (Shaw thought) perhaps only employee, of the *Echo City Gossippeer*. He reminded Shaw of a large trout, complete with thick, protruding lips, goggly eyes, and a greasy, almost slimy appearance. "How long have you been working for the Tricians?"

"What?" Shaw was completely blindsided by the question. All the other reporters had asked him about the surface and how he had been adjusting to life in the underground.

"Well, you don't expect me to believe that you survived a fall all the way from the surface, do you? I think it's much more likely that you are a Trician spy, cleverly sent here to pry information from us, isn't that right?"

"That is probably the stupidest thing I've ever heard," Shaw said, suddenly realizing that the underground, like the surface, had its share of tabloid journalists.

"That's not a denial," the slimy reporter leered with his distressingly uneven yellow teeth. Even his breath smelled like he had just been reeled in and dropped in the bottom of the boat. Shaw found himself wishing for a fish bat to hit him over the head with.

"Of course I'm not a Trician spy! Why would anyone think that?" Shaw decided immediately that he didn't like Schmidt-Hess.

"That's just the sort of thing a Trician spy would say, Mr. Shaw."

"And it's also the sort of thing an innocent person would say, you idiot. Don't you think there'd be easier ways to get a spy down here? It's a miracle I survived!"

"Was it a miracle, or was it by design? My readers are most curious about your motivations now that you're here. Naturally, the readers of the *Gossippeer* are the only ones to have the full facts about anything, and I don't intend to disappoint them! Who is your superior?"

"Mr. Schmidt-House—" Shaw started.

"Schmidt-Hess," the slimy reporter corrected him.

Shaw gave him a sardonic smile. "I prefer my pronunciation. Anyway, it seems like this interview has gone on for two minutes, and that's two minutes I'll never have back. You're going to have to leave." Shaw pressed the brass button on the wall to signal the nurse's station. He hoped Nurse Diaz was back on shift. He had never met a healthcare worker who was so intimidating to people who bothered her patients.

Schmidt-Hess continued to display his smile, making Shaw think of a collection of crooked tombstones in a forgotten cemetery. "Ah, so you won't even deny the accusations! My readers will be very interested to read this!"

"I'm surprised your *readers* can read at all," Shaw said sarcastically as Nurse Diaz entered.

"How did you get in here?" the fearsome Nurse Diaz demanded angrily, shooing Schmidt-Hess toward the door. "I told you not to bother him! The last thing he needs is for some lunatic like you to upset him! Out of here this instant!"

Schmidt-Hess continued to smile as though being forcibly ejected from an interview was something he was quite accustomed to. He looked as though he enjoyed that part of his job. "Very well, madam. I shall return when he is more well rested, then."

"Please don't," Shaw said as Schmidt-Hess's unsettlingly aquatic features disappeared through the doorway with the now furious nurse close behind. The conversation had upset Shaw more than he had expected, and he sat still for a while to calm himself. It wasn't surprising that there were crackpots like Schmidt-Hess working for tabloids in the underground; people seemed to be the same everywhere one went. At least as far as conspiracy theorists and troublemakers were concerned. *The biggest problem with the printing press,* Shaw thought, *is that crazy people can communicate with other crazy people. It's a good thing they don't have the Internet.*

"I'm sorry that you had to deal with him, Mr. Shaw," Nurse Diaz said as she returned. "He's been trying to get into the hospital since you first arrived. He's the worst kind of journalist. My mother reads his garbage every day and believes every word."

"That's too bad," Shaw remarked. "We have a lot of people like him on the surface as well, and millions who read their stuff. He threatened to come back too."

"Not if I can help it. Unless you *want* to talk to him again?"

"I'd rather have you sew my head to my pillowcase while I sleep."

"Good. He's been barred from the hospital, but he is clever. Anytime a celebrity or a politician is admitted to the emergency room, Schmidt is there trying to dig up something. He's ruined quite a few careers with his scribblings."

"Ah. That's a comfort, now that I seem to be a celebrity."

"I shall make sure you don't see him in here again."

"Thanks, but I'm thinking of when I leave the hospital next week. Unless you plan to follow me around and keep him at bay."

Diaz laughed as she left the room, leaving Shaw to consider Schmidt-Hess's accusations. If such outlandish ideas had struck the hastily ejected reporter, there had to be some members of the government who were asking the same questions. There were paranoid people who were, in fact, *paid* to be paranoid, after all. Shaw wondered if Spall was one of those people.

"How is your assessment of Mr. Shaw coming along?" Prime Minister Whitley asked his seemingly empty office.

"Thus far, he appears to be genuinely from the surface, Prime Minister," Spall replied from the shadows. "How did you know I was here, sir?"

"I didn't. I just randomly ask questions to the corners of the room in the expectation that you are there. Bunsen thinks I'm losing my mind, poor fellow. He's come into the office quite a few times with paperwork for me to sign, only to find me speaking to the shadows by myself."

"Given the choice, sir, I would prefer the unsound mind currently in my possession. The world is much more interesting that way."

"Yes, I have often thought of your mind as 'unsound,' Spall. So you feel that Shaw is as he appears?"

"It would seem so, sir. He has been able to describe several inventions and advancements from the surface in sufficient detail that the Artificers Guild has been able to build functioning prototypes. Once he is out of the hospital, I plan to introduce him to Doctor Schlenker. Between the two of us, we will be able to detect any flaws in his story.

In listening to his conversations with Professor Turnbull, however, he has shown a significant knowledge of weapons and warfare that are far beyond our own capabilities and development. If he is genuine as he appears to be, he will be of great assistance to us, sir."

"Indeed he will. Do you think he'd be willing to work for us?"

Spall considered. It was a question he had been asking himself ever since he first met Shaw.

"I think so, sir. He is a former soldier and police officer, which speaks to his sense of duty and honor. He has made great strides in his physical recovery, and his mental recovery is progressing as well, though it may take years for him to fully adjust. He may, however, choose to embrace his celebrity and enjoy the financial rewards he will no doubt amass with his knowledge rather than face the uncertainty of work in the Secret Service. I will continue to work with him and do my best to convince him to aid us. He has learned a large amount of our history, and that of Ünterreich. I would think that anyone who would uphold the law would choose to aid us against a regime that practices slavery."

"I certainly hope so," Whitley said. "When is he to be released?"

"Next week, Prime Minister."

"Excellent. Bring him here after his release so that we may meet. I am becoming weary of answering questions about him, so it will be nice to finally meet the man. It's time he entered the social scene and embraced his celebrity." Whitley stopped, pondering. "Should we perhaps arrange a ticket for him to attend the Artificers Guild Ball?"

Spall considered for a moment and then shook his head. "No, sir, the ball is in less than two weeks. He is still quite weak and tires easily; I would suggest allowing more time for him to regain his strength before plunging him into society. The Policeman's Ball is in two months; perhaps that will work better."

Whitley nodded. "Excellent thinking. I'm sure you can arrange everything. Continue with your efforts, and keep me informed of your final assessment."

"Of course, sir."

With that, Spall once again melted into the shadows of the room and was gone.

# 9

## Echo City

Shaw's final week in the hospital was uneventful, at least as far as crackpot journalists went. Nurse Diaz managed to keep her promise, and Shaw didn't see anything of Schmidt-Hess for the remainder of his stay. He did get the occasional visit from Professor Turnbull, as well as a few more reporters and journalists. Much of his days were spent in the convalescence wing of the hospital, where the nurses and caregivers worked with Shaw to ensure he would be able to walk properly. His legs were still very weak from the time spent allowing them to heal, and he required a cane to get anywhere quickly. Finally, Doctor Chan signed Shaw's hospital chart, proclaiming him well enough to be released.

Shaw felt some anxiety about leaving the hospital. Outside was an entirely new world, under an impenetrable sky of stone. What he could see of it from his hospital window was strange enough, as was Professor Turnbull's description of things.

The city seemed to be a place that truly never slept. The lights were always on, the people came and went at all hours, and even the vehicle traffic never stopped.

*The complete lack of daylight will be the hardest to get used to*, Shaw thought. Now he had to face the new world as best he could. Professor Turnbull had prepared him admirably, but there were still so many questions that were unanswered, and that he had to answer for himself. As he ambled along the corridor on his last walk through the halls, the rubber tip of his cane squeaking on the stone floor, he felt his heart racing faster the closer his release time came.

"Mr. Shaw," Spall greeted him with a crooked, nearly undetectable smile as he returned to his room in the convalescence wing. "I trust you are ready to leave?"

"More or less. The paperwork's all done, so they can get rid of me."

"Well, I have brought you some clothes; they should fit rather nicely, unless you have grown fond of your hospital gown."

Shaw looked at the metal suitcase Spall was holding and smiled. "Thanks. I was a little worried about what I was going to wear when I left. The nurse told me they had to cut off all my surface clothes when they brought me in."

They walked slowly down the hallway to Shaw's room, where Shaw opened the suitcase to reveal a brown pinstripe suit with a short bowler-style hat. He tried everything on and was amazed to find that Spall had been correct; the suit fit better than anything he had bought off the rack on the surface.

"You don't miss a trick, do you Spall?" Shaw asked, indicating the tailoring.

"I anticipated that you would require clothing once your stay was finished," Spall answered. "I had the nurses measure you several weeks ago, while you were still unconscious."

"Well, I'm glad you did, and I'm not even slightly surprised. How do I look?" he asked, feeling a little silly wearing something that looked, to him, like it came from a tailor's shop in about 1910. The hat was what struck Shaw as the strangest item. It was a bowler hat, but it was made of thin, polished stainless steel. It was then that Shaw looked at Spall's hat and realized it too was made of metal, but painted black.

"You look very smart. Try the hat."

Shaw put the strange hat on his head and looked in the mirror. He felt like he had been transported back in time a hundred years rather than seventeen kilometers straight down. He removed the hat and tapped it with a knuckle.

"Why's the hat made of steel?"

"I understand that the originals were made of beaver hide or silk. Those materials are hard to come by down here, of course. Polished stainless steel is a much more available material. You may see others wearing hats made from aluminum, silver, and even gold. The hat is a symbol of status and fashion here, as it was on the surface when our ancestors left it."

"Interesting. I figured you'd have concealed weapons inside yours."

"Ammunition mostly," Spall said humorlessly. He turned toward the door. "Shall we? I am here to escort you to your lodgings and to introduce you to your new . . . landlord. There will be more clothing for you at your lodgings as well; we have taken care of everything for you."

Shaw picked up his aluminum cane, and they both left the hospital room and headed for the front entry. Shaw once again noticed how quietly Spall was able to walk on the stone floors. He never made a sound, and compared to Spall, Shaw felt like a herd of elephants. As they walked the halls, Shaw shook hands of nurses, doctors, and orderlies who had all come to know him over the weeks. They were just about the only people Shaw knew in the underground, and he felt a pang of sadness to be leaving them.

They reached the front door and exited the hospital itself into what felt to Shaw like a tunnel of light. The front walkway of the hospital was lined with tall lampposts that cast a bright glow onto the ground. The lampposts weren't unexpected, but Shaw had to stop and close his mouth after looking at the ground under the lamps.

He had been expecting a barren expanse of rock, but what he saw was a small field of luminescent grass. When he had looked out the window of the hospital, he had assumed the bluish-green glow on the ground was just reflected light from the quake shield, but now he could see that was not the case. Everywhere he could see on the hospital grounds was the faint glow cast by the bioluminescent flora.

For a few moments, he was speechless. He ambled closer to the grass and slowly, painfully knelt to touch it. He almost expected the grass to feel warm, but it felt just like regular grass. "Incredible," he almost whispered. "Is everywhere in Inner Earth covered with this glowing grass?"

Spall looked at the grounds and replied, "No. This particular breed of *Festuca aurora* is planted exclusively here in Echo Cavern."

"*Festuca* what?"

"*Aurora*. More commonly called glowing fescue. You don't have it on the surface?"

"Nope. We have a few glowing bugs and such, but I can't think of any glowing plants. Maybe some mushrooms. I don't know for sure."

"Hm. Perhaps it was developed down here after the caverns were settled. These grasses have been around since before I was born. We also have glowing trees that line the boulevards throughout the city. At this time of year the bioluminescent plants are at their dimmest; in another six months they will be bright enough to cast a shadow."

"This time of year," Shaw was puzzled. "I thought you don't have seasons here."

"Not real seasons as such; however, the plants still follow periods of growth and dormancy, though not as pronounced as on the surface, apparently. The trees shed their leaves once a year and then regrow them several weeks later."

"Strange. How do the trees and grass live? Don't they need sunlight?'

"Not these. I confess that I am ignorant of how these particular plants function. Perhaps the botanists who developed them managed to cross their pangens with those of fungi? We shall have to ask a friend of mine; he has forgotten more than either of us shall ever know."

"Pangens?" Shaw asked as he struggled back to his feet. Spall grasped his arm and lifted him up as though he weighed no more than a small cat.

"The smallest unit of hereditary characteristic. I believe the term was first used by Hugo de Vries in the late 1800s on the surface. His book *Intracellular Pangenesis* was a very important work in its day."

"I think we call pangens 'genes' on the surface. It's part of the study of genetics."

"Ah. We call it 'pangenesis' here. How interesting. Come this way."

Spall began to walk down the path again, but Shaw had turned back to look at the hospital that had been his home for two months. He had expected a large, stately stone building, but what he saw made him feel dizzy, and he nearly fell over. The hospital had been carved out of the foot of a huge column of rock, hundreds of meters in diameter, extending up to the ceiling of the cavern almost out of sight. Behind the column could be seen the near end of the cavern wall, a mere ten kilometers away. Looking again at the stone column, Shaw could make out hundreds of tiny lights spiraling up the exterior, floor after floor of them. The column itself was wider at the top and bottom than in the middle, and Shaw realized that it had likely started out as a stalactite and stalagmite that had joined together into a column millions of years in the past. He turned away from the awesome sight and followed Spall.

Spall looked askance at Shaw. "You have never seen a speleothem of such size, I imagine?"

"If you mean the stone column, then yeah. It must have taken millions of years to form like that."

"Oh, yes. Tens of millions. They serve as very sturdy structures for our settlements."

"No doubt. Why can I feel wind on my face? Aren't we sealed in down here?"

"Certainly not. All our caverns require an air exchange system; otherwise we would use all the oxygen in the caverns and then suffocate. The fresh air in Echo Cavern comes from an extinct volcanic lava tube called The Well at the far end of the cavern. It doesn't lead completely to the surface, but it is connected to a series of fissures and crevasses through which enough air is drawn to provide sufficient oxygen for the population. We also have a great number of plants, grown for food crops and gardens, that purify the air."

Spall had led Shaw down the main path toward a cobbled street on which was waiting a strange vehicle. It resembled a car of about 1940s vintage, with the classic large, rounded fenders. The body was a combination of curves and angles that reminded Shaw of what science fiction cars looked like in old black-and-white movies. The front grille was polished chrome with narrow vertical slits down both sides that reminded him of a cowcatcher on a train. The cluster of eight headlights surrounding the grille gave the front a spiderlike look, but the rest of the vehicle was quite sleek and appeared to be built for speed. The windshield was narrow and composed of two separate panes of rounded glass separated by a central pillar. The vehicle was painted a bright candy-apple red with a series of white stripes running along the body front to back. He wondered why it had such a conspicuous paint job when he looked at the top and saw a lit "Taxi" sign. Shaw smirked to himself when he saw what seemed to be a smokestack sticking out from the top of the roof at the rear of the vehicle behind the sign. A nearly invisible vapor coming from the tube indicated that the vehicle was running; however, there was no discernable sound.

"That thing's engine runs really quietly," Shaw remarked as they approached.

"It should. It runs on steam," Spall said as a sudden (and well-timed) hiss of steam escaped from beneath the vehicle, followed by a cloud of vapor that rose to envelop the car for a few seconds.

Shaw gaped at Spall as he opened the door and beckoned Shaw to enter. Shaw got into the vehicle and sat on what seemed to be regular cloth. A quick glance showed him that all the upholstery in the vehicle was fashioned from the same sturdy material. It was fabric made of thin wires woven together into cloth. He couldn't make out the metal, but it was well polished where people had been sitting and slightly darker in the corners and along the back edges where there was little wear. There was no leather or traditional cloth that he could see anywhere on the inside.

"Government Spire," Spall said to the heavyset man in the driver's seat.

The man nodded, pressed several buttons, and pulled a large lever that started a small clockwork mechanism mounted in the dashboard. Shaw could see numbers beginning to count up through the mechanism as the vehicle started to move along the roadway. They picked up speed surprisingly quickly, and Shaw felt somewhat strange at being in a vehicle that still made no discernible sound aside from a quiet *chuff, chuff* as they traveled. The loudest noise came from the rubber tires on the roadway.

Their trip into Echo City was completely uneventful for Spall, but for Shaw it was simply incredible. He had to keep reminding himself to shut his mouth as they passed innumerable wonders to Shaw's eyes. Every vehicle they passed was unusual, but they all shared the same smokestack protruding from a high point of the exterior. Some of the vehicles were shaped similarly to surface vehicles, and Shaw saw trucks and cars with the occasional motorbike, all running on steam. The most unusual ones were what Spall described as "monocycles," which consisted of a large single tire with the operator's cabin in the center. These seemed to go very fast, with the operators wearing caps and goggles that were hilariously similar to the ones worn by World

War I aviators. There were buses and taxis, all painted bright colors to show up well in the brightly lit streets. Every vehicle had a large cluster of lights on the front rather than the usual two. It made sense when Shaw thought of it; should the power go out, or should the driver leave the city, they would have no other light sources.

Shaw marveled at the streets themselves. The streetlights were large and looked like they were all powered by gas, but they were interspersed with bioluminescent trees that cast a variety of colors on the streets. Most of the light was emitted by the leaves, but Shaw could see a faint glow coming from fissures in the bark itself. Some trees were orange, some red, yellow, blue, and there were even a few with glowing purple leaves. The effect made Shaw think of Christmas on the surface, with all the trees lit.

In the more dimly lit spaces, the glow cast from the quake shield lit everything in a bluish-green hue. Shaw was surprised to see traffic lights that looked like ordinary surface ones, minus the sunshades. He supposed they must have been invented before the first settlers came to the caverns, just like steam power and vulcanized rubber.

Most of the buildings were made from solid stone or concrete faced with stone. Shaw was enthralled by the beauty of even the simplest buildings; everything was carved and decorated with detail and craftsmanship that could only be found in older cities and cultures on the surface. Much of the architecture resembled a modernized version of ancient Greek and Roman buildings, with large columns and open, airy archways. Many of the doors he could see were built from copper, steel, or bronze and were likewise beautifully wrought. It made sense to Shaw that most of the building materials would be stone and metal. Wood would be extremely scarce and, from what he could see of the trees, would probably glow in the dark.

Their trip took them onto a long, circular roadway that seemed to be skirting the city near the outer edge. Eventually they reached an intersection with a large avenue that took them straight toward the city center and Government Spire.

"Do all the roads lead to Government Spire, or just this one?" Shaw asked, turning to see that Spall had been watching him closely.

"Echo City is built along a series of radial roadways, intersected at regular intervals by avenues, which circumnavigate the entire city. Government Spire sits in the center of the city with several other government buildings. All the main radial roadways lead to it."

"So from above, the city would look like a giant dartboard?"

"I suppose it would," Spall admitted after brief consideration.

Shaw grew silent again as they continued along the road toward the brightly lit tower at the city center. They passed shops, homes, office buildings, parking garages, schools, and even police stations. It felt to Shaw that he was on vacation in a foreign land, where everything was the same but different enough to feel . . . well . . . different. The buildings, though beautifully built, were constructed in much the same way as any building on the surface. The roads looked like something similar to asphalt or tarmac, with some cobblestone streets and avenues thrown in, and the sidewalks looked like any concrete sidewalk he had ever walked on.

Government Spire was a tall tower that looked as if it had erupted out of the dark stone of the ground around it. The tower was built from white marble, with green stone to accent the exterior, though the glow cast on it from the quake shield made the whole tower look greenish. Shaw couldn't help but think of the Emerald City in the Wizard of Oz stories.

*Too bad I can't just click my heels together and wish myself home,* he thought.

The traffic grew slightly heavier as they neared the government district, which, Spall explained, occupied the entire center of the city. The number of pedestrians increased as well, Shaw noted. He could see that the clothing fashions of Echo had stayed in the early 1900s, but things had still evolved to be different from what he could remember of photos on the surface. It was true that many people still wore hats, but he could see that women's clothing wasn't nearly as restrictive as it had been when the caverns had first been settled. Many women were wearing trousers, and he could see quite a few skirts that were above the knee (if only just). He wondered where all the cloth came from, then concluded that they must have many farms producing wool, flax, and cotton, just like the surface; the difference being that these farms must be well lit by artificial lights.

It seemed that everywhere he looked, Shaw saw something else that amazed him. They passed a large van parked along the opposite curb that didn't immediately draw his attention, but then he noticed a score of mechanical spiders, perhaps half his arm span across, scuttling out of the back of the van and picking up what little litter they could find. He watched one find a small drift of leaves and crouch down to scoop them up with a small rotating brush in its belly. Another used its thin steel legs to stab at a crumpled bit of thin metal that looked like a newspaper.

He saw one lady walk past with a brightly polished chrome leg, attached just below the knee using leather straps. The leg had been engraved over its whole surface with beautiful filigree work like an intricate tattoo. A gentleman zipped past on the sidewalk in a wheelchair that was clearly powered by a small steam engine. The gentleman looked quite content as he sped along nearly as fast as the vehicles on the roadway.

They passed several city parks during their trip, and Shaw was delighted to see that the parks were well lit by the vegetation. The grass and trees combined to provide amazingly bright illumination, to the point that streetlights were seldom needed in these areas. Some of the parks had sports fields and playgrounds, with children playing games and running around freely in the multicolored light. Other parks appeared to be variations of rock gardens, with only limited vegetation and quiet pathways illuminated by the warm glow of the gas lamps. Everywhere Shaw looked he could see people out enjoying the variegated lights cast by the lampposts and trees. Shaw smiled as he thought that, despite the knowledge that he was far underground, there were very few shadows in Echo City. He wondered how bright things would be in six months, when Spall had said the plants would be at their brightest.

They suddenly passed a block of the city that had no lights or bio-luminescent plants at all. It was as though an artist had just painted a black square in the middle of an otherwise bright painting. Shaw could still make out a very large cathedral-like building in the center, build of black stone and finished in a rough texture to reflect as little of the light from the quake shield as possible.

"What is that place?" he asked, feeling strangely drawn to the forbidding darkness.

Spall glanced out the window. "Mmm. That is the Temple of The Brotherhood. There are still many religions down here, though they are not permitted to exert influence in government matters. Have you never heard of The Brotherhood of The Dark?"

"No, I don't think they exist where I'm from," Shaw said, raising an eyebrow. "They must be an underground religion."

Spall nodded. "That would make sense. They worship the darkness, believing that mankind should shun the light and embrace blindness. Most of their followers wear thick blindfolds or hoods to cover their eyes."

Shaw was even more incredulous. "Seriously? People actually *want* to be blind? Do they . . ." He trailed off, afraid of the answer to his next question.

"A very few of their more stalwart followers allow themselves to be blinded, yes," Spall said. "Though I understand it's not a requirement of the religion."

Shaw didn't know what to say, so he returned to his observation of the city as they continued on toward the city center.

They drove past a large coliseum-looking building, from which they could hear a deafening cheering through the windows of their taxi. It sounded as though tens of thousands of people were within.

"What's going on in there? Football?" Shaw asked.

"Not today. We do play traditional football, of course; however, the current stone-ball season is underway, and it is much more popular. Football and rugby are played much more in schools."

"Hmm. What about other games, like soccer, baseball, basketball, and hockey?"

"Hockey is only played in the caverns close to the great glaciers, near where you were found. Basketball is played only very little, as is baseball. Soccer, I confess, I have never heard of. How is it played?"

Shaw considered for a moment before answering. "Actually soccer is probably what you call 'football.' I was thinking of American Football. It's actually a lot like rugby. I really don't know why the Americans call it football. They almost never touch it with their feet."

"How very odd."

"I've never understood it, but it is a lot of fun to watch, and I played a bit of it when I was a teenager. I was terrible at it. What about stone ball? How does that game work?"

"It would be easier to show you; we shall have to attend a game in the next few weeks."

"Is the ball actually made from stone?"

"Of course. That's why it is called stone ball."

"Is the ball heavy?"

"Ten kilograms, if memory serves."

"That's like . . . over twenty pounds! They don't kick it, do they?"

Spall scoffed. "Certainly not. The ball must be carried. If the ball is dropped, the opposing team obtains possession of it. I shall get some tickets for the next game, if you wish. I have never been a fan of professional sports; however, stone ball *is* entertaining. Schlenker is

**95**

a rabid fan; he drags me out to games whenever I can't find a decent excuse to avoid them."

"I'd like that," Shaw admitted excitedly. "What about other kinds of entertainment? You must have theaters and such?"

"Oh, yes. Echo has many fine theaters. We enjoy plays, orchestras, and the occasional opera. We even have motion pictures, though they are not as popular."

"Really? Movies aren't that popular? On the surface, movies are probably the biggest form of entertainment, aside from getting into arguments on the Internet."

"Ah, yes; you'd mentioned the Internet before. I would like to hear more about it," Spall said.

"I'll explain later. Looks like we're here."

Their steam-powered taxi had pulled up to a large set of gates in a massive stone wall surrounding the Government Spire. Three well-armed uniformed guards immediately surrounded the taxi and peered inside. One of the guards requested their documents. Upon seeing that it was Spall, the guards gave a nod and opened the gates immediately. Their driver continued on to a side entrance, where they were again challenged by uniformed guards. A second time, Spall's presence quickly persuaded the security detail that there was no threat. Shaw noticed that none of the guards would make eye contact with the giant.

*They're all intimidated by him. I guess that makes sense,* he thought. Spall was intimidating, perhaps even menacing, but he wasn't scary, at least not to Shaw. Perhaps he had become so familiar with Spall that he felt comfortable in his presence.

They left their taxi after Spall paid their fare in some unusual coins, and they ascended the steps of the marble tower. Most of the exterior, as far as Shaw could see, was polished to a high sheen. The steps, however, had been finished in a very rough texture to improve grip. Shaw nodded appreciatively. It was difficult enough getting around with his cane; he could only imagine how hard it would be if the steps had been as smooth as the rest of the structure.

Passing through a massive set of heavily engraved copper doors, they entered a series of opulently carved hallways that would not have looked out of place in the palace at Versailles, Shaw thought. The stonework was some of the most beautiful he had ever seen, with many accents of various precious metals. There were also paintings adorning the walls, though they all appeared to have been painted on sheets of metal rather than canvas or wood. The frames for the paintings were works of art in themselves, many of them carved and wrought from metals and stone. The floors and walls, much like the exterior, were highly polished marble that gleamed in the bright gaslight.

Spall led Shaw up several flights of stairs, passing many government workers who stopped and stared at Shaw. He could hear whisperings as he limped past small groups of them. It seemed that he was indeed famous, as Spall had told him. Never having thought of himself as extraordinary in any way, the thought unsettled him a little.

Eventually they came to a large hall with an elevator door at one end. Shaw was glad the palace was lit with warm gaslight. Had the hall they were in been lit with surface fluorescents, the room would have been blinding with all the white marble. Spall led Shaw into the elevator and signaled the uniformed operator to proceed.

The operator pulled a large lever that shut the doors and then a second lever, which caused the elevator to begin its ascent.

"Which floor are we headed to?" Shaw asked, seeing the indicator above the doors going from 3 to 120.

"The top," Spall replied simply.

Shaw gulped, feeling uneasy in the knowledge that he would be traveling to the top of the tallest building in the city. His newly discovered fear of heights was going to take some getting used to. He instead concentrated on something else that had occurred to him when he thought about lights.

"Spall, I've noticed that everyone looks . . . well . . . not as pale as I'd expected," he mentioned to the bulky form next to him. "Do you have tanning lights or something?"

Spall nodded. "Indeed. From my understanding, physiological deficiencies caused by lack of sunlight were identified quite early on. Tanning lamps are perhaps the most common household appliance, at least in Echo City. Most citizens have a daily routine that includes some time in front of a lamp."

Shaw nodded in agreement; it made perfect sense. Another question he had been meaning to ask popped into his mind, and he queried Spall further. "I've also noticed the names of a lot of caverns are in different languages. If they wanted no conflicts down here, why separate the different nationalities into their own caverns?"

Spall thought for a moment before answering. "I'm not certain, I'm afraid. I suppose that most early settlers thought their surface cultures would become extinct in the coming war; I imagine that each group wanted to preserve as much of their surface culture and heritage as possible. It follows that they would settle into communities with their fellow countrymen. Most cultures are represented in the underground, in some form or another."

The ride was fairly quick, and as Spall finished speaking, the doors opened onto a beautiful foyer. Spall and Shaw exited the elevator and approached a long stone desk, behind which was a small, stern-looking gentleman with thick glasses and a stuffy three-piece suit. Shaw couldn't help but stare at his horrific comb-over. Vanity was just as common in the caverns, it seemed.

"And h-wat can I do for you, gentlemen?" The little man appeared to take great pains in pronouncing the "h" before the "w." He also didn't seem to care for Spall.

"Prime Minister Whitley has requested that I bring Mr. Shaw here to meet with him, as you are well aware, Mr. Bunsen."

Bunsen's eyes narrowed, comically magnified behind his thick glasses. He looked at Shaw, his eyes studying him from top to bottom as the stuffy secretary pursed his lips. He appeared to come to a decision about Shaw but then turned back to Spall and addressed the giant. "I don't much care about this whole 'surfacer' business, and I don't seem to have either of you in the prime minister's ledger for today, Mr. Spall. Not that you ever pay any attention to the ledger."

"I answer directly to the prime minister. If that is a significant problem for you, that is unfortunate," Spall stated matter-of-factly.

Mr. Bunsen stood up from his chair, which succeeded in adding only a couple of centimeters to his height. He was truly a tiny man. Shaw could look right over Bunsen, and Spall could look right over Shaw. The effect of Bunsen attempting to enforce his will on the gigantic Spall was comical to say the least, like a small irritating rabbit standing in front of an irritable *Tyrannosaurus rex*. One of them was about to be eaten, and it was not difficult to determine which would be the eater and which would be the appetizer.

"How dare you disrespect me inside my own office! If it weren't for me, the prime minister couldn't cope! I manage everything around here, and it's stone-headed people like you who come in and mess with schedules and meetings, causing all sorts of problems for me to deal with! You feel like you can just sneak in h-wenever it suits you. Don't think I haven't noticed you sneaking in! If I ever find out how you do it, there will be repercussions! Do you know how much pressure I am under to keep things running smoothly?" The tiny bureaucrat's face had turned a bright shade of crimson as he leaned forward on the desk. Shaw involuntarily leaned back, afraid that Bunsen might actually explode.

Spall, clearly accustomed to such outbursts from the officious administrator, didn't move a millimeter.

"I am sure you are under a great deal of pressure; however, if you don't let us in, as the prime minister has specifically requested, I shall see to it that you burst." Spall's expression was such that Shaw believed he would love nothing more than to make it happen.

Bunsen's color deepened to a frightening shade of purple as Spall pulled Shaw along past the stone desk and through a set of double doors made from vertical polished gold and tarnished brass panels riveted together. This resulted in attractive wide green and gold stripes running the height of the doors.

"Is he going to have an aneurysm?" Shaw asked, looking back over his shoulder at the fuming Bunsen.

"Certainly not. I have been trying to give him one for years without success."

They entered a spacious office dominated by a large carved walnut desk, behind which sat the prime minister of the Republic of Inner Earth. A pale woman of about fifty sat opposite the prime minister, a small metal folder in her lap. They stopped talking as Spall and Shaw entered the room.

Prime Minister Whitley stood as Spall and Shaw entered, a large smile on his face. "Ah, Director Spall; excellent timing! We just finished our meeting. This may be the first time I have witnessed you actually using my door. I knew it was you as soon as I heard my assistant's blood pressure rising." He looked over at Shaw, beaming a wide smile of perfectly straight white teeth. He extended his large hand. "You must be the famous Mr. Shaw. I am Bartholomew Whitley."

Prime Minister Whitley took Shaw's hand in a firm handshake as Spall gravitated toward his customary shadow in the corner.

"That's me, Mr. Prime Minister. I don't know about the famous part, though," Shaw answered.

Whitley gestured toward the lady, who had also stood to receive them.

"This is Deputy Prime Minister Brinkmann," he said, still smiling.

Brinkmann stepped forward and shook Shaw's hand, a thin smile on her face. She was quite attractive, and Shaw had a hard time determining how old she might be, as she had very few wrinkles. If it hadn't been for the gray in her dark hair, he would have guessed she was in her thirties. Her light brown eyes reflected the glow from the lights in the room, making her seem even more youthful.

"A pleasure, Mr. Shaw. Please forgive me for meeting you and leaving so quickly, but I was just finishing my conference with the prime minister, and I have other meetings that I must rush to."

Brinkmann smiled again at Shaw and turned to leave; Shaw noticed that her smile disappeared instantly as she glanced over at Spall. She was clearly as much of a fan of Spall as Bunsen. She closed the doors behind her as she left the room.

Whitley gestured for him to take a seat. Shaw sat in an exquisitely soft Victorian-style leather chair with wood arms and legs. A quick glance around the room affirmed the lofty station to which Whitley had been elected. There was almost no visible stone in the entire room. Like Shaw's armchair, many of the furnishings and decorations were beautifully carved from various types of wood.

*Everything in this room must have cost a fortune*, he thought. *There's probably more wood here than the rest of the city combined.*

The prime minister returned to his chair behind the desk and sat. "Oh, I think you'd be very surprised how famous you truly are down here, Mr. Shaw. You're already in the *Gossippeer*, which is usually a good indicator of someone's prominence."

"The *Gossippeer*? Oh, I remember that guy. Schmidt-House."

"Schmidt-Hess, I believe."

"That's the guy."

"Yes, he is rather an unpleasant fellow, isn't he? He's been a thorn in my side for my entire career. No matter. May I offer you anything? Brandy? Tea?"

"Nothing for me, sir. I had some coffee before the hospital discharged me."

"Of course, of course. How have you been keeping? I trust you have made a full recovery?"

"Mostly, sir. The bones are all healed up. Just a few more weeks of rest and I can start getting myself back into some kind of shape."

"Excellent. I was very glad to hear that you had survived your fall from the surface, and that you would make a full recovery."

"I had some good doctors."

"Indeed. The finest we could offer. Has Mr. Spall here been of some help to you?"

"Absolutely. He's been a lot of help explaining things down here. There are a lot of differences between my world and yours. It's going to take me some time to adjust."

"Yes, I have no doubt about that. I trust Professor Turnbull provided you with an adequate history lesson to begin your acclimatization?"

"The professor was really helpful, yes. I think he might have gotten more information from me than I did from him, though."

Whitley smiled. "He is a very curious historian. He was one of my professors at Echo University during my college years. Good man. I'm glad he was able to be of some assistance. Now, have you given any thought to your future down here with us?"

Shaw smiled nervously. "Well, Spall said he has a place for me to stay, and that he wants me to help with a few projects he's working on, but I admit that everything is so new to me down here that I really don't know what I would be suited for. Or what's suited to me."

"Of course. Best not to be too hasty with these decisions. Well, you are in excellent company with Mr. Spall here. He is the finest man I've got; he'll take good care of you. I understand that you will be staying at Doctor Schlenker's house. That should prove very interesting for you, and I am certain you will be able to help the good doctor with some of his own projects. He is the one who has been analyzing some of the artifacts we have recovered from the surface over the years."

"Yeah, Spall's mentioned that before. You must have quite a collection by now."

"Well, many things have been shattered beyond repair, but some have been found miraculously intact. As you were."

"I don't feel very intact. Spall mentioned that I'm the first to survive. How many others have fallen down here before me?"

"I'm afraid I don't know. In my fifteen years as prime minister, I know of only two. I'm sure there have been many throughout the years. Schlenker will be able to tell you more." The prime minister finished speaking and glanced at the shadow where he knew Spall was standing before looking back to Shaw. "Well, Mr. Shaw. It has been a pleasure to meet you in person. I look forward to getting to know you better in the future. Before you go, I need to extend an invitation to attend the upcoming Policeman's Ball in a few weeks' time. It will be the perfect opportunity for you to enter society, as it were. And I understand that you yourself were a policeman on the surface."

Shaw nodded. "Yes, sir, I was. I suppose there's no way for me to refuse an invitation from the prime minister himself, so I'll be delighted to attend the ball. As long as I don't have to do much dancing."

"Oh, you won't have to dance at all, unless you wish to. Please try to make the most of your stay down here with us. I understand that there will be some adjustment, and that it will be difficult for you, not being able to return to where you came from. Mr. Spall is perhaps the best person to help you through your adjustment period, as he has gone through a similar scenario in his past. Now you must be tired. Spall will convey you to your new lodgings. Do take care of yourself."

With that, Prime Minister Whitley stood and shook Shaw's hand. Spall had silently emerged from the shadows and appeared at Shaw's side with Shaw's cane. They turned and began to leave through the gold-and-brass doors when the prime minister added some final advice.

"Spall. Kindly refrain from antagonizing Bunsen on your way out. I know that he brings it on himself, but one day he really will give himself a stroke or heart attack, and it will be very difficult to replace him. Thank you."

Spall and Shaw left quickly past the diminutive Bunsen, who shot Spall a narrow-eyed look of pure hatred and muttered curses under his breath. His face was still the alarming shade of crimson, tending toward purple. Shaw was reminded of an old Donald Duck cartoon, half expecting steam to start shooting from Bunsen's ears.

The elevator ride to the bottom was quick, as was their walk back through the administrative floors to the waiting taxi outside. Spall helped Shaw into the vehicle, and Shaw didn't resist the offer of help. He had traveled farther on foot in one day than he had since before his fracture-inducing arrival. Shaw collapsed into the back seat and let out an exhausted sigh as he rubbed the more painful areas of his bad leg.

*Gotta avoid overdoing things*, he told himself. He knew it would be a difficult road to recovery, both physically and mentally, but he was finding the hardest part was adjusting to taking things slowly. He had always been active, and now having to fight against his own body's frailties and weaknesses was challenging both his character and his patience. Shaw had to keep telling himself that he would eventually be able to do the things he had done before, but he had to pace himself for a while. Without warning, these thoughts gave way to thoughts of his family back home, and the woman he loved and had hoped to marry one day. These thoughts deepened his melancholy, and he sat in silence as the vehicle began to chuff along out of the courtyard and onto the bustling streets of Echo.

Shaw wasn't sure what time it was, but he suddenly felt hungry. This was aggravated by the sight of many people sitting in cafés and restaurants along the main road they traveled, illuminated by the variegated lights of the streetlamps and the luminescent trees. It looked as though fine dining was alive and well in the caverns, as well as not-so-fine dining in the form of what looked like many diners along the way. Shaw felt himself wishing for a nice, greasy burger and fries, or a slice of pizza. He wasn't even sure if they had those sorts of foods in the caverns. He had found the hospital food to be fairly typical. Steamed vegetables, mashed potatoes, mystery meat, eggs, oatmeal; he wondered if there was a universal hospital cookbook that had been passed down through the generations.

"Spall, what kinds of food do those restaurants serve? Do you have hamburgers, fries, pizza, soft drinks?"

Spall looked thoughtful. "We have hot hamburger sandwiches, and I have had a pizza pie before. Not my particular cup of tea, but we may stop for one if you like. What are fries?"

"French fries. Fried potatoes."

"Ah. We call them 'chips' here."

Shaw breathed a loud sigh of relief. "Good. What about soft drinks? Please tell me you have those."

By way of answering, Spall pointed out Shaw's window at a brightly lit billboard in a vibrant style urging people to drink the "Fabulous Brain Tonic, Dr Pepper!" Shaw almost began to cry.

"Thank whatever gods you all believe in down here," Shaw said at seeing the billboard. "I didn't know when it was invented. Looks like your ancestors brought down quite a few things from the surface that're still around. Can we stop for lunch?" He stopped, a thought occurring. "Oh, wait; I don't have any money. Never mind."

"Do not concern yourself with such things yet, Shaw," Spall said. "I have more than enough for my own requirements."

They stopped at a small restaurant and paid their driver, who sped off into the little clouds of steam left by passing traffic, looking for his next fare. Shaw watched the taxi pass a similar vehicle stopped at the curb, but this vehicle was white with black stripes and had "Police" painted on the sides. A single rotating red light sat atop the roof, and Shaw could see two police officers standing on the sidewalk, scratching out a ticket on metal foil to the gentleman in the wheelchair he had seen earlier. Clearly it was against the law to go screaming down the sidewalk in a powered vehicle at breakneck speeds, even if that vehicle was a wheelchair.

Spall turned away from where their driver had so recently been and his expression changed.

"Oh, no," he said.

"Sausage? Sausage in a bun?" A skinny little man had approached and hailed the two of them as Spall had been paying the taxi driver. Around the man's neck was looped a thick belt that helped support a tray that carried numerous food items. Shaw could see meat pies, sandwiches, and even, yes, sausages in a bun.

"Wow. I didn't expect hot dogs down here," he said.

The little man looked perplexed. "Hot dogs?"

"The sausages," Shaw pointed.

"Nah, these are top-quality meats in here! Nothing but the finest for me customers! No dog at all!" The man was smiling his biggest smile for what he hoped would be an actual customer, occasionally giving nervous sidelong glances at Spall. "Very little dog! Okay, some dog. A lot, actually, to tell the truth. Mostly dog . . ." He was starting to sound agitated as he withered under Spall's silent gaze. "Not to worry, though. They won't be missed! I'm not a dog-napper! That's all rumors started by me competitors! Here, you gentlemen can both have one for only a dollar each, and that's cutting me own throat!"

Shaw's eyes narrowed as he studied the strange little man. "Have we met before? You seem familiar . . . ," Shaw asked, feeling a sense of déjà vu.

Spall spoke up. "Shaw, meet Mr. Withers. He was just about to leave in fear for his life." Spall had clearly had the misfortune of tasting one of Withers's sausages in the past.

"Of course, Mr. Spall! How silly of me to forget! I do apologize for the last time! A very rare incident, I assure you! I have no idea how that bone managed to find its way into that particular sausage."

"Yes, an entire fish skeleton carefully packed into a sausage casing is certainly a rare and unforgettable experience," Spall said, his expression making Withers visibly . . . wither. "Begone, Mr. Withers, before I feed you your own wares."

Withers, in a rare display of self-preservation overcoming the urge to make a sale, scuttled away quickly, his abysmally skinny legs moving like they had more than the usual complement of knees. Shaw watched him go.

"Weird. I really felt like I'd met him before."

"It wouldn't surprise me if there is someone like Withers in every city in, or on, the Earth," Spall remarked. "Possibly the entire universe."

"Hmm. You may be right. Are his sausages really that bad?"

Spall, uncharacteristically open, made an expression of utter disgust and visibly shivered. "Words fail me," he said. "Shall we?"

They turned to look at the restaurant their taxi had dropped them in front of. The place looked like a small diner, though built using much fancier materials than a surface one. In front of the establishment, a long row of monocycles were parked in a neat row at an angle to the curb. Shaw smiled to himself.

"Hah. You have biker bars here." He saw the raised eyebrow on Spall's face and continued. "No worries, I've been to plenty; I'm not bothered."

They entered, and Shaw was forced to stop to take in the atmosphere. He had been expecting, well, a biker bar—premises not generally known for their high manners and exquisite food. Which is why he was so surprised to see that the monocycle enthusiasts were not exactly like stereotypical motorcycle riders on the surface. The entire place was filled with gentlemen and ladies in well-tailored riding outfits, all of them enjoying music from a small string quartet in the far corner of the room. Many of the patrons had their comical riding caps and goggles nearby and were engaged in conversation over tea and what looked like fairly high-class food.

The interior of the restaurant resembled a surface diner as much as the outside had; it was long and narrow, with a single counter and stools running the entire length of the place and booths along the outside windows. The decor looked a bit higher class, though, since of course everything was made of solid stone, wrought iron, and lots of polished brass and copper. Spall and Shaw took a booth near the back of the establishment, and Shaw noticed that Spall took care to sit with his back to the wall. They sat on cast-iron benches that were upholstered in the same sturdy metal fiber cloth that covered the seats in the taxi. Shaw was still surprised that it was so comfortable to sit on woven metal. Glancing closer at some of the monocyclists, Shaw could see that many of their outfits were woven of the same material.

The female server approached, and Shaw immediately ordered a Dr Pepper. The menu had some familiar diner dishes, such as liver and onions, steak, and fried chicken, but many things had to be translated somewhat by Spall. The Joliette Potato, for example, turned out to be a baked potato covered in cheese curds and hearty beef gravy. Shaw had laughed, and then had had to explain the French-Canadian dish called poutine to Spall. The only difference, of course, was that the underground used a baked potato and not french fries. Other things were familiar, but called older names. Shaw could have ordered a frankfurter, for example; he wasn't sure if he had ever seen a hot dog called a frankfurter on a surface menu. The server looked at him strangely when he referred to a "hot dog," forcing him to explain that it was just the name and not a reflection of its contents.

They both ordered a hot hamburger sandwich with chips, and Shaw downed several tall glasses of his soda as though it was the first time he had tasted such a thing.

"You seem to rather enjoy your drink," Spall noted after Shaw had finished his third glass.

Shaw pushed his empty glass away to join his similarly empty plate and sighed contentedly. "Dr Pepper was my favorite soft drink on the surface. I'd assumed you wouldn't have it down here. The food was good too. Sorry I can't pay for it myself."

"Don't mention it. I am well paid in my current position, and Doctor Schlenker is independently wealthy. I am also certain that you will become wealthy yourself if you are able to recreate some of the innovations from your life on the surface. You will also be paid for your services to Special Branch by assisting us in identifying and cataloging the surface artifacts."

"That shouldn't take me too long. I'm interested to see what you have down here."

"Well, you shall see soon enough. Let us settle our bill and be off."

Spall paid their bill with more coins, some of which looked to be solid gold, and they walked out to the street to hail another steam-belching taxi. A few people regarded Spall strangely, and it seemed they were all looking at the dark blue stripe tattooed down his face. Spall acted as though he didn't notice, but Shaw knew the giant noticed everything. Other people were looking at Shaw and whispering excitedly among themselves. He had to remind himself that he had appeared in the newspapers several times. His fame was growing.

They entered their taxi, which began to take them away from the center of Echo and into a much quieter area of the city, with large houses.

# 10

## Doctor Schlenker

"I must say that I appreciate the job, especially since it looks like I'll be down here forever," Shaw said to Spall as their taxi traveled down one of the main thoroughfares. "I imagine there'll be a lot for me to learn about how things work down here."

Spall nodded. "There will be many things to learn, no doubt, but you will catch on quickly, I suspect. I feel you will be well suited to the job as well," Spall said matter-of-factly as he reached into a vest pocket and retrieved an intricate pocket watch with a crystal casing; the gears and inner workings were all fully visible and showed beautiful craftsmanship.

"That looks like a very nice watch, if that's what it is." Shaw remarked. He had already learned that he couldn't assume anything was the same in the caverns as it was on the surface. For all he knew, the device could have been for warding off stray dogs or keeping the taxi from exploding.

"Thank you. It was a gift. There is only one other like it."

Shaw felt some surprise that Spall would have received a gift from someone. It didn't seem to Shaw that Spall had many friends; most people appeared to be afraid of him. He glanced over at the giant, folded up just enough into the taxi seat as to look uncomfortable. Spall, at first glance, had come across to Shaw as being quite rigid and inflexible. On closer acquaintance, that initial impression hadn't changed, though he had noticed some . . . humanity, if that was the best way to describe it. Spall didn't suffer fools lightly, if his reaction to both Mr. Bunsen in Government Spire and Mr. Withers outside the restaurant was any indication, but he was gentility and politeness itself with their server and most of the other people they had interacted with.

Spall closed his watch and replaced it in his vest pocket before looking at Shaw. "We are almost to your lodgings. It is just up another block."

Shaw could see a massive Victorian-looking mansion rising out of the greenish-yellow gloom from the quake shield and gas streetlights. It was a full three stories, with a large turret to one side rising the entire height. The facade of the mansion was made from slabs of white marble with green marble trim, similar to the Government Spire. Shaw noticed that every detail of a surface house was reconstructed here out of stone and metals, down to the shingles on the roof and even the gingerbread accessories. The mansion was truly beautiful, and Shaw couldn't help but wonder what a mansion like this would cost on the surface if it were made from wood. A solid stone mansion would cost as much as a castle.

The taxi came to a hissing stop and Shaw exited with Spall in front of the mansion.

"This is the residence and workplace of the person who gave me my watch," Spall began, "and he has expressed an overwhelming interest in meeting you. Don't be alarmed," he began, seeing an exasperated expression cross Shaw's face at the thought of another curious observer; "he has an overwhelming interest in everything. It was he who offered to lodge you, as long as you wish to stay. He is quite eccentric, and I find him best in small doses; though to be fair, I find most people best in small doses. He is called Doctor Schlenker. You may want to prepare yourself. His home is . . . unique, even by the standards of Inner Earth."

At this, they had finished climbing the stone steps to the enormous polished bronze front door, which appeared to be over three meters high. Shaw stood, leaning on his cane and catching his breath as best he could. He had come a long way since the hospital just a short time before, and the heavy atmosphere still felt as though he was trying to breathe through a pillow. His previously shattered leg was also taking its time to return to normal and had started to ache after the day's heavy use. Spall pulled a long chain, which rang a chime that could be heard within the stately house.

It was only seconds before Shaw could hear (and feel) loud, slow footsteps approaching the door from within. It sounded like an elephant wearing a heavy suit of armor. There was the scrape of a large metal bolt being withdrawn, and then the heavy door opened on well-oiled hinges to reveal a truly unexpected sight.

A butler, dressed in full coat and tails, had opened the door to admit them entry. This in and of itself was not unusual, with the exception being that the butler was human only in shape. What stood before the two men, dwarfing them both, was a monstrous three-meter-tall steel construct with a featureless spherical, polished copper head the size of a beach ball. The few parts visible protruding from the gigantic outfit looked to be made more for digging and heavy labor than butlering. The feet were immense steel castings with reinforcing bands riveted across them widthwise, giving the impression of a medieval armored overshoe. The hands had two wide, curved, spade-like fingers that looked like they belonged on some form of digging apparatus, with a smaller spade arranged as a thumb. They looked capable of clawing their way through solid rock, which

112

was, unsurprisingly, what they had originally been designed for. The massive bulk stood framed in the doorway like a walking steam shovel adorned in a costume straight out of a Jane Austen story.

The creature regarded them (or as close as it was possible for something that didn't appear to have any eyes) for a second or two before a loud steam whistle sounded from somewhere within the massive coat of tails, causing gouts of steam to issue from various places in the outfit.

*Whistle!*

Spall looked up at the mechanical monster. "Copperhead. How nice to see you again. You are keeping well?"

*Whistle!*

Spall's expression hardened. "Please refrain from your usual foul language, if you can. I have brought the doctor's guest, and you don't want to make a bad impression, do you?"

Shaw got the eerie feeling that the automaton's full attention was directed at him without the creature moving at all. It was more of an intuition that he was being studied, like when one feels that someone is watching them.

*Whistle!*

"Yes, I know you don't care about what anyone thinks, especially not me, as you've made very clear," Spall said in response to whatever it was the whistle had conveyed. "We would like to see the doctor. This is the gentleman from the surface, as you've no doubt heard."

The giant beast's eyes narrowed—quite the feat since it had no eyes to narrow.

*Whistle!*

Shaw's expression had gone from amazed, to confused, to worried as Spall had carried on his conversation. From what he could hear, every whistle coming from the steaming contraption sounded like every other. He was beginning to wonder about Spall's sanity or, more worrisome, his own.

*Whistle!*

Spall looked back at Shaw with a raised eyebrow and noticed his confused expression before turning back and replying to the beast. "Don't take that tone with me. He's not simple; as I said, he's from the surface, and he has never met an ill-tempered contraption such as yourself before. On a different note, I still haven't forgiven you for what you said about my mother. Now take us to Mr. Shaw's room so that he can get settled, and then you may take us to see the doctor before I put a bullet through your head again."

Spall gave the creature an expression that clearly showed he was in no mood for further banter, prompting the steel butler to turn and walk deeper into the house, releasing tiny jets of steam from random places as he thumped through the hall.

Shaw was glad that the house was made of stone. Among other things, gravity seemed to be working perfectly well within Inner Earth, and he suspected that Copperhead would travel right through the floor of a conventional wood-framed house.

They had walked only a few paces from the front door when they were approached by a middle-aged lady dressed head to toe in blue lacy frills; she looked like a birthday cake from a Mad Hatter's convention. She looked at Shaw and immediately dropped into a polite curtsey before speaking in a thick accent that sounded Irish at first, but Shaw wasn't quite sure.

"Ah! Yoo moost be the fellow from the sairface! I be Missus Clary, the doctor's cook and 'ousekeeper, and I believe yoo are Mr. Shaw. 'Tis a pleasure to meet yoo, and no mistake."

She took Shaw by the hand and gave him a good, solid handshake. She smiled, revealing deep laugh lines and a mouthful of distressingly yellowed teeth. Shaw knew that toothbrushes were common in Inner Earth, but apparently Mrs. Clary hadn't heard the same news.

"It's a pleasure to meet you too, Mrs. Clary," Shaw said, shaking her hand. "I'm glad to be staying here. It's a beautiful house, and well kept."

114

"Ach, yoo're too kind, lad. I 'ave plenty o' work, cleanin' oop the messes left behind by this great heap!" Here she gestured at Copperhead, who stood and steamed. "Noo, if there's ever anything yoo need, doon't hesitate to ask. And yoo're always welcome to help yoorself to anythin' in the kitchen if ye be feelin' peckish!"

With that, she bustled off, waving her hands at the clouds of steam being emitted from Copperhead and muttering under her breath at the steel beast.

"A word of caution, Mr. Shaw," Spall began as soon as Mrs. Clary was out of earshot. "She is an excellent housekeeper, but I would be wary of anything she describes as 'food.' Doctor Schlenker enjoys her cooking; however, most normal people require an iron stomach to digest what she creates in the kitchen."

"Really? Her cooking is that bad?"

"I do not consider myself picky, but the last meal I ate here would have provided enough oil to lubricate a locomotive. I suspect it may have been *cooked* inside a locomotive."

"Ugh. Say no more. I'll be careful," Shaw said.

*Whistle!*

Spall turned to look at Copperhead. "Yes, lead on."

Copperhead turned and once again began to lead them deeper into the house. Spall and Shaw followed at a quick pace, as even Spall's long strides were unable to match those of their guide. The mechanical butler led them through the main hall and up a long, curving flight of stone steps to the second floor. Here there was a long hallway with more polished bronze doors leading off both sides at regular intervals. At strategic locations down the hallway, stone and metal pedestals held many unique and beautiful objects. Some could be identified as unusual weapons, while others appeared to be mechanical versions of what would be electronic devices on the surface. Shaw even thought he saw a mechanical calculator, complete with gears. Still other objects couldn't be identified at all, which made

Shaw wonder at the genius that could build such unusual machines. He suspected that not every household in Echo had the benefit of a steam-powered mechanical butler, and wondered how long it had taken the doctor to build it.

Copperhead led them down the hall, passing open doors leading to what looked like a library, a games room with a pool table, and even a music room complete with a grand piano that looked as though it was made of black slate. The hallway had a long runner down the middle that dampened the sounds of their footfalls, though it understandably did very little with Copperhead's massive feet hammering the floor.

They reached a second hallway that led to the bedrooms, and Shaw's was the first on the right. The room was nicely furnished, though of course everything was either metal or stone. He wondered how difficult it was to heat such a house. Stone and metal were never known for their outstanding insulating qualities, though Shaw didn't even know if there was any need for heat or air-conditioning in Inner Earth. There didn't seem to be seasons in the classic sense. He was pleased to see that the bedclothes and mattress were similar to those in the hospital, though much nicer.

*At least they can make fabric down here*, thought Shaw. He shuddered to think what he would have had to sleep on (or wear) if they hadn't been able to produce textiles.

Shaw examined his room, which had an adjoining bathroom, complete with a copper claw-foot tub, and indicated that he was more than satisfied with his lodgings. Copperhead, who had been standing immobile in the doorway, gave a short blast from his steam whistle and began to walk back down the hall in the direction they had come from. Shaw and Spall followed as the massive butler led them back down the staircase, through the house, and out into the back garden.

The garden was just as breathtaking to Shaw as the house had been, but in an entirely different way. Since his arrival in Inner Earth, he hadn't been able to approach any of the luminescent plants, and here were many beautiful varieties. There were numerous glowing trees, grasses, and even a glowing purple moss that covered several rocks next to a small pond. Interspersed among the plants was a Japanese-style rock garden that contained more large rocks covered in glowing mosses and lichens of varying colors. They were following a path of large gray flagstones set into the turf, contrasting the glowing plants with their dark, almost hole-like appearance. At occasional points along the path, they passed cast-iron benches that would have been at home in any surface garden or park.

Through the garden and down a short slope, they came upon a massive shop, clad in metal siding. The building was almost the size of an aircraft hangar, with large sliding doors at one end and several Copperhead-sized doors at intervals.

The steel monster opened one of the smaller doors and entered what looked like a combination of Leonardo da Vinci's workshop, the Smithsonian Institution, and a foundry. There was a labyrinth of workbenches, shelves, and various myriad machines, all covered in inexplicable piles of gears, cogs, levers, springs, nuts, bolts, and other bits and pieces. Near one end was what looked to be the chassis of a freight train sitting on a pair of rails set into the floor. One entire wall was dedicated to a rack holding weapons of all shapes and sizes and various stages of completion, from strange revolvers and automatics to large belt-fed machine guns. There was even an artillery cannon and what for all the world looked like a massive blunderbuss at one end of the room. Shaw was able to identify an old-fashioned forge, a lathe, a milling machine, a portable crane, and countless hand tools.

Of course the identifiable items were clearly outnumbered by the unidentifiable ones. There were large wires and cables strung throughout the steel rafters, and many other unusual items hung from these. There didn't appear to be room for anything else in the massive jumble; however, there did seem to be a certain crazy order

**117**

about it all, as though the mind that worked here was brilliant and able to work on many projects at once.

Shaw watched the steel butler wander effortlessly through the mess, and wondered how it was able to see. He still couldn't find any method by which the mechanical man could navigate. After a minute or so of wandering through the disaster, the group arrived at a huge, antique-style rolltop desk made of aluminum. A thin gentleman sat in front, assembling a collection of very tiny gears and springs. Next to the man's current project were three pistols in several stages of disassembly, two large piles of paper-thin metal, and a contraption that seemed to be some kind of typewriter—if a normal typewriter and a rotary aircraft engine had loved each other very much and had a child. Shaw was once again reminded that there was very little paper in Inner Earth, since he hadn't seen much wood in the caverns aside from the glowing trees, which would be far more useful as light sources.

The man noticed their approach and turned around to face them, which almost made Shaw break out into laughter. The man was wearing an apparatus on his head with numerous large and small lenses on multiple arms. The lenses in front of his face magnified his eyes to several times their normal size, giving the impression of an anime character. The man smiled broadly and extricated himself from the bizarre helmet, revealing the rest of his face as he replaced the strange contraption with a pair of ordinary glasses. He had a warm expression on his clean-shaven features, and it seemed to Shaw that the gentleman was only a few years older than himself. He didn't seem to be much older than forty, though it was difficult to tell. Shaw still hadn't figured out Spall's age; it could have been anywhere from thirty-five to fifty.

The man stood to welcome them, and Shaw noticed that he was much shorter than Spall. Of course it didn't take much effort to be shorter than Spall. Shaw himself only came up to Spall's shoulder.

The gentleman smiled and introduced himself in a German accent. "Ah, Spall; I have been waiting patiently for you to arrive with our guest! I am so very pleased to finally meet you, Mr. Shaw. I am Doctor Jürgen Schlenker. Welcome to my humble home."

Shaw returned the smile and shook Doctor Schlenker's hand, which had a surprisingly strong grip. The doctor looked like more of an intellectual, but Shaw could tell there was much more to the doctor than his appearance suggested. His thin frame seemed to hum with a nervous energy as though he was just a human skin being piloted by a colony of bees. Schlenker's eyes scanned Shaw repeatedly, taking in every detail of his new guest.

"I'm pleased to meet you as well, Doctor," Shaw said, returning the handshake and the smile. It felt very easy to smile at the doctor. "Thank you so much for your generosity in allowing me to stay in your home. It's beautiful. Spall's already told me a few things about you, so it's nice to meet you in person"

"Ah, Spall can't have said much about me. He never says much of anything if he can avoid it, especially since I seem to talk far too much for both of us. Isn't that so, Spall?"

"Hmm." Spall grunted.

*Whistle!*

"Yes, Copperhead, I know that *you* think he talks too much, but I also think you might talk a bit too much yourself. I've had to start wearing earplugs around the house," he said in a very loud whisper to Shaw. He turned back to Copperhead and shook a thin finger at the bulky creature. "I know you still haven't apologized for what you said about his mother. That was very rude."

*Whistle!*

"Well, you had better apologize, before I turn you into a tractor and set you to work in the Grand Cavern," he said sternly to the mechanical butler before turning back to Shaw. "So, Mr. Shaw—"

"Oh, you can dispense with the 'Mister,' and my parents are the only ones who ever called me by my first name; everyone else just calls me Shaw," he said, a small wave of melancholy passing through him at mentioning his parents. *Still a lot to deal with*, he thought, not for the first and certainly not the last time.

"Delightful! As I was about to say, I have a goodly amount of questions for you about the surface, especially regarding its history and technologies. I have been practically salivating since Spall first informed me that you had arrived down here. I wanted to come to the hospital to visit you so many times before now, but I have been away in another cavern for the past couple of months on a project and have just concluded my trip. I hope your trip down from the surface wasn't too painful?"

Shaw chuckled. "The trip was quick, but I could have done with a softer arrival."

The doctor chortled a genuine, good-natured laugh. Shaw liked him already. He could tell that the doctor had little to no deceit in him, and that he was the sort who spoke whatever was on his mind. He also had a sense of humor, which was more than Shaw could say about Spall. He regarded the thin doctor, who was a little shorter than himself, but not by much. His dark blond hair was thin and fine, almost wispy, and looked neatly trimmed recently. The doctor wore a brown wool suit, though at the moment he was wearing only the trousers and a white linen shirt with the sleeves rolled up past his elbows, the suit jacket hung out of the way on a nearby coat-tree. Schlenker's overall demeanor displayed a sense of great care for his personal appearance, but not in a vain way. It seemed at odds with the state of the workshop, Shaw thought.

"What is it you're working on, if I might ask?" Shaw queried, looking at the jumble of parts on the desk.

"Oh, I am in the final stages of developing a device by which a person may transmit a signal over long distances to activate an electronic device using radio waves. I intend to make it work for switching electric lights on and off, perhaps even vehicles. I shall call it Schlenker's Incredible Wireless Signal Transmitter for Long-Distance Electronic Device Activation. I think the name will catch on, don't you?"

Shaw smiled. "Uh, sure. On the surface, we call those things a remote control. Or just a remote."

Doctor Schlenker showed an almost comical interest, like an excited puppy. "Is that so? How interesting! Have you had these devices on the surface for long?"

"Oh, a few years," Shaw replied.

"Fascinating! The name doesn't have the same effect, though. I prefer mine."

"Yeah, I guess it has more . . . personality. It might take a while for me to get it right. I'll probably call it a remote control for a long time," he admitted, smiling at Schlenker's almost childlike delight when discussing mechanical inventions.

Schlenker continued to smile. "Yes, well, we can hardly expect you to change overnight. No doubt you will continue to do and say things like you would on the surface for a long while. No matter. I would like to learn as much about the surface as you are willing to teach me. No doubt you have many questions about our little world here in the underground, eh? I am just the man to ask! Spall manages to roll his eyes and make discreet escapes whenever I get going on one of my lengthy lectures (Shaw forced himself to keep from laughing, as Spall had rolled his eyes and quietly walked to another area of the workshop only seconds before), but I have the impression that you might be able to tolerate my company."

"Oh, I look forward to learning as much as I can here. I have a lot to learn. I've also realized that I should have paid more attention in history class. I do have one question, though. Did you build the giant robot?"

"Robot?" Schlenker looked confused. "What an interesting word! I like the sound of it, though it's unfamiliar to me. To what do you refer?"

"Oh, sorry. I guess there're a lot of words that came about after your city was first settled. 'Robot' means an artificial person, I guess. I don't know how best to define it."

"Ah, you mean Copperhead! He has been my butler for more than ten years. I did build him, but not completely, you understand. He started as a simple mining behemoth, which is why he is so large and made of tempered steel. I found him in a junkyard, and I rebuilt him."

"Should have left him there—" they both heard Spall mutter from his corner.

Schlenker chuckled and went on. "The mining behemoths are very simple steam-powered creatures; they have no head and cannot see or hear. I gave him that beautiful head, with which he can do both. In use, they are instructed to dig in one direction, and they won't stop until they are told to do so via controls on their backs. I built Copperhead in such a way that he no longer requires a human operator, and he is able to perform many functions of a regular human servant. The only problem is that he can be very hard on good china."

Shaw looked at Copperhead's huge steel hands. It wasn't difficult to imagine those hands clawing their way through solid rock, or inadvertently crushing a nice china teapot. Or an entire crate of nice china teapots. The effect created by the massive coat and tails was such that, after a while, one managed to forget that the steel behemoth was originally made for boring tunnels underground and not for turning down beds and serving tea. Copperhead must have noticed Shaw looking at him.

*Whistle!*

Schlenker's eyebrows narrowed. "Copperhead! That was rude. Apologize at once!"

*Whistle.*

"Thank you. Now go and see if Mrs. Clary needs any help with dinner. And mind your manners with our guests in the future."

Copperhead clomped out of the huge shop and shut the door behind him. Shaw turned back to Schlenker.

"What did he say?"

Schlenker looked taken aback. "Oh, you don't understand him? I guess you wouldn't, would you? Not to worry, it's fairly easy; you'll get it soon enough. He just insulted you, and then apologized. It's a habit with him, I'm afraid. He and Spall are constantly trading insults."

"I'll have to take your word for it."

Spall glanced once again at his crystal pocket watch before interrupting. "Well, gentlemen, I must return to the office, as I have duties elsewhere. Shaw, I leave you in very good hands. If he starts talking too much, just wander off; he won't notice for some time." This last was said in a very sarcastic tone, which caused Schlenker to laugh loudly.

"Oh, Spall. I always notice when you try to escape. I'm just too much of a gentleman to mention it for fear of hurting your delicate constitution." He smiled his wide grin at the giant, who didn't return it. Schlenker turned back to Shaw. "We're actually very good friends, though you wouldn't think so at first. Spall is less capable of feelings than Copperhead."

Shaw nodded in agreement and chuckled along with Schlenker as Spall shrugged and headed for the door.

*I'm not so sure of that*, Shaw thought. He still recalled the flash of rage on Spall's face when he had been talking about the Tricians and Ünterreich with Turnbull.

# 11

## An Honest Assessment

Shaw learned a lot more about Echo City in the next few days, and his condition continued to improve, despite Mrs. Clary's cooking, which could be described using such terms as carbonaceous, viscous, and, in one case, belligerent—though, according to her, the incident with the albino octopus was a rare event. Doctor Schlenker was able to fill in many details about the history of the underground; he was also full of questions about the surface and the happenings since the great exodus. Shaw, being of a similar mind to Schlenker, was able to describe much of the machines of the surface, which delighted Schlenker immensely. He would pause occasionally to make notes or to allow Shaw to draw rough sketches of what he was describing. Schlenker was nearly giddy at the knowledge he was able to obtain from Shaw, and within a week they were paid a visit by Mr. Spall.

"Ah, Spall," Doctor Schlenker exclaimed as Spall was led into the workshop by a somewhat sulky Copperhead. Copperhead's ability to appear disgruntled whenever Spall was around was truly amazing considering he lacked a face.

"Shaw, it is good to see you are doing well. I do not wish to interrupt, but Schlenker, may I have a word in private?" Spall asked, ignoring as best he could the cloud of steam that Copperhead had released onto him at a suspiciously opportune moment.

"Of course! Let us go into my office. Shaw has been drawing a rough schematic of an amazing machine called an 'airplane.' It is positively fantastic!"

"Yes. I am likewise ecstatic," Spall remarked without showing the slightest emotion or interest. "I require your opinion on an important matter, Doctor."

"Certainly. Shaw, I will return directly. Please don't leave anything out of your sketch."

Spall and Schlenker left the workshop, leaving Shaw with Copperhead, who just stood there, staring (*staring?*) at Shaw and sounding like a boiling kettle. Shaw was still a touch uncomfortable around Copperhead, mostly because he didn't know what he should do. Copperhead would just stand there, percolating until given something to do. The faceless "staring" was the worst part. It was like being watched by a hissing basketball.

Shaw decided to ignore the giant copper ball and return to his elementary school art class–level drawing of the inside of a passenger jet. He was simultaneously pleased and humiliated at how much better it was turning out than he had hoped, and how poorly it still looked.

Schlenker sat in his office chair behind a surprisingly tidy desk. The effect was strange for anyone who was used to seeing the doctor in his workshop. Mrs. Clary evidently kept things neat inside the house and left Schlenker to his own devices out in the shop. Schlenker looked uncomfortable. Spall, in his usual abrupt manner, broke the silence.

"Schlenker, I need your assessment."

"Yes, I thought you would. I have no doubt whatsoever that he is from the surface. He has knowledge of mechanical objects and advances that are nearly unfathomable to us, and he is able to explain how many of these objects function despite never having been schooled properly in them. I have probed him on various weapons from the surface, which he has much knowledge of, and he has been able to explain them all. I am particularly interested and somewhat horrified in his explanation of what he calls 'nuclear weapons.' If the Tricians had developed any of these weapons, the war would be over already, and they would not have had to send a spy with such knowledge here to trick us. I have no doubts as to his truthfulness. He is from the surface, and he is willing to help us."

Spall considered this for a moment, then seemed to come to a decision. "Very well. I trust your judgment above anyone's, and I have also come to the same conclusion. If you agree that he will be an asset to our team, I shall inform the prime minister."

"I think he will be more beneficial to this team than a hundred artificers. Shall I ask him to join our project?" Schlenker peered at Spall over his small glasses, his intelligent eyes dancing with delight.

"Absolutely," Spall replied, and they left the office and headed back out through the luminescent garden to the workshop. They found Shaw sitting on his stool, staring up at Copperhead, who was leaning over Shaw and staring back. It looked like a child staring up at a schoolteacher, if the schoolteacher was the same size and temperament as a locomotive.

"Have we interrupted something?" Spall asked, glaring up at Copperhead, who did not move but let out one of his intermittent steamy hisses from somewhere inside his damp butler's uniform. Shaw broke his gaze and looked at Spall and Schlenker.

"Um, no, not exactly. I was just testing something. How exactly does he see me? And why does he keep staring at me like that?"

"Well," Schlenker began, the glee at explaining one of his inventions obvious on his face, "his entire head houses a sophisticated device that transmits a non-audible sound wave in all directions. This sound wave is reflected by objects nearby and is received and translated by his Committee to form a visual map of sorts, which he may use to navigate, much like a bat. I call it 'Schlenker's Incredible Auditory Wave Receiver and Interpreting Mechanism.' I am quite proud of it."

"Why not call it something simple, like . . . an echolocator? That sounds better," Shaw suggested.

"Well, I suppose you are right, if you are short on time and dramatic flair," Schlenker conceded. "I prefer mine. He may also receive sound waves from any other source and interpret them as well. In fact, the more noise around him, the better he can 'see.' He can even hear a human heartbeat, so sitting as quietly as you can will have little effect on his ability to see you. As to why he stares at you, it's because I gave him instructions to watch you closely when I am out of the room. I do apologize. He does tend to take instructions too literally."

Shaw nodded. "Okay, so what's a Committee? Some kind of computer?" He thought for a moment then added, "and why did you tell him to watch me?"

"It's a CMMTE. It stands for 'Cobblepot's Miraculous Mechanical Thinking Engine.' Cobblepot was the inventor who accidentally discovered it."

"So a computer. Wait, how did he *accidentally* discover a computer?"

"He was working on a cure for the common cold," Schlenker explained in a tone that suggested this sort of thing was a totally reasonable thing to have happened.

"Which makes perfect sense," Shaw said sarcastically. He had discovered why Spall was always so sarcastic around Schlenker; the genius didn't seem to notice it or, if he did, didn't seem to care.

Schlenker smiled. "It's quite elementary, I assure you. In any case, as to why I instructed Copperhead to watch you, it was because we had to determine if you were truly from the surface and not a Trician spy."

Shaw sat in silence for several seconds before replying. "You thought I might be a spy?" He looked from Schlenker to Spall and then back again. "Why on Earth—ugh, sorry—why *in Earth* would you think that?" The crushing air pressure was becoming less of a bother for Shaw lately, but the euphemisms and expressions were still something he had to get used to.

Spall answered this time. "We are at war; that is why. The Tricians are clever, and we couldn't rule anything out. But Doctor Schlenker here has determined that you are a genuine surfacer, and we are in agreement. If our roles were reversed, I assure you that you would have done the same."

Shaw stared at Spall, then at Doctor Schlenker. Neither showed any shame in their expressions; they looked as though they were telling him a simple fact.

"Okay, I can see where you're coming from. You both had a job to do. And now that your job is done, and you're satisfied, does that mean you no longer have any use for me?"

Schlenker looked horrified. "Of course not! We wish for you to stay with us and join our little team. I am certain you will be invaluable to us on our quest, and I daresay that we are growing fond of you. I know that Copperhead likes you. Tell him, Copperhead."

Copperhead took an uncomfortably long time to reply.

*Whistle.*

"There, you see? He wants you to stay."

Shaw looked back up at Copperhead, still looming overhead like an angry god, occasionally releasing steam from around where his neck should have been. If the automaton could have had an expression, it probably wouldn't have included a friendly smile.

Shaw smiled a dubious smile. "I'll take your word for it. What quest are you referring to?"

Spall looked at Schlenker before replying. "It might be better if we showed him first, Doctor."

Schlenker nodded in agreement. "Yes, I was thinking the same. Well, Mr. Shaw, do you fancy a trip through Inner Earth?"

"I suppose. Where to?"

"Oh, it will be much more enjoyable if it's a surprise," Schlenker said. Of course we will have to wait until the end of the Policeman's Ball. It's in only two days, and then we will be able to take our trip."

"Oh, right. The ball. I'd forgotten. What should I wear?"

"I took the liberty of having Copperhead make some alterations to one of my party outfits. It should fit you perfectly. Copperhead is an excellent tailor."

Shaw looked up at Copperhead again, who hadn't moved a centimeter and seemed to be glaring intently at him with what was essentially both a massive copper eyeball and ear. As hard as it was to believe that Copperhead, with his shovel-sized hands, was a good tailor, it wasn't the most difficult thing to believe that he had encountered since his arrival from the surface.

"Fantastic. Do I need a date for the ball? I don't know any women down here yet."

"Ah, neither of us will have a date, but I believe Spall has asked his secretary to be your company for the evening, if that will be acceptable to you. If nothing else, she will provide you with an easy escape should the need arise. A lot of people will want to talk to you."

"Sounds terrific. What's her name?"

"Miss Muir," Spall answered. "Before you ask, she is quite attractive. She has red hair."

"Well, that's good news. Is that all you've noticed about her?" Shaw's observations of Spall had indicated that Spall was frightfully inept when it came to interactions with people. He was willing to bet the giant had probably never had a girlfriend.

Schlenker stepped in. "I think Miss Muir is very attractive as well. What's her first name, Spall?"

Spall looked lost. "I haven't the foggiest. It's never come up."

*Ah, one more mark against Spall's observations of people,* Shaw thought. It wasn't surprising. If you needed a weapon built from a pile of metal shavings or a collapsing bridge held up, Spall would be the man to call. If you wanted an honest assessment of the physical characteristics of a female coworker, one would be better off asking an office chair. At least the office chair could give an honest and thorough opinion of the person's backside.

# 12

## An Actual Stone Ball

The next two days were spent in Schlenker's lab, tinkering away at various 'artifacts,' as the good doctor called them. Shaw had successfully identified ice picks and other climbing equipment from the last hundred years that had fallen to Inner Earth. There was some tattered clothing with modern zippers, which Schlenker called 'clasp lockers,' but the doctor explained that those had been invented long before the founding of the Republic and weren't particularly interesting.

Surprisingly, after examining the zippers, Schlenker had quickly set aside the clothing that had come to him over the years and hadn't noticed some other points of interest. Shaw pulled a waterproof jacket out of a pile and held out one of the sleeves.

"This," Shaw began, "is called Velcro."

Shaw ripped apart the Velcro holding the jacket cuff closed with a flourish. Schlenker's eyes widened when he realized that Shaw hadn't just torn the fabric apart.

"Astounding!" He exclaimed, examining the fastener closely with the magnifying glasses he had worn when Shaw first met him. "And it can detach and reattach as many times as you like?"

"Sure. Well, eventually it wears out, but usually by then the whole jacket would be worn out too."

"Incredible. You sound as though this is an everyday sort of thing in your world."

Shaw shrugged. "Yeah, we have Velcro everywhere. It's like me and Copperhead. We've been working on self-aware machines for decades with no success, as far as I know. Down here it was discovered by accident."

"Like your penicillin," Schlenker added. "My colleagues in the medical sciences were very interested to hear of that particular discovery. It may take years, but they're confident that this new direction will prove fruitful. It's a pity you don't know how it's produced and refined on the surface."

Shaw shrugged. He had been telling Schlenker everything he could about nearly every aspect of surface life for what seemed like forever, but he suspected that he could keep telling the doctor about seemingly trivial things for years without running short of things that simply did not exist in Inner Earth.

The same was true in reverse, of course. Though many things at first appeared to be quite similar to things on the surface, Shaw discovered every day that when he examined something, it proved to be unlike anything he had experienced before. There were many things in the caverns that still ran on electricity, but many technologies had strayed away from the perceived influence of the Tricians.

Returning to the stacks of surface artifacts, Shaw kept going through every item with Schlenker to ensure that nothing was missed.

Many items had been previously identified by the doctor or someone prior to him, such as ballpoint pens and felt-tip markers, both of which had been found on several occasions and had been reverse-engineered for production and sale in the caverns. Likewise, many battery-powered items such as flashlights had found their way down to the underground, which had led to improvements in light-emitting and electrical storage technology. Items of clothing and lengths of climbing rope had been examined and had resulted in new artificial fabric developments (though everyone seemed to have missed the Velcro). Metallurgical analysis of climbing equipment had borne fruit in improved alloys for industrial uses.

Even the autopsy examinations of many of the unfortunate surfacers who had fallen to their deaths over the years had provided unexpected benefits to the underground. Though many of the victims' bodies had been badly damaged in their falls, items such as artificial joints and surgical plates used to repair broken bones had been located and studied. Surgical scars on internal organs led doctors in new directions for treating various conditions; in one case, the discovery of a transplanted kidney in one victim had simultaneously mystified and encouraged a score of surgeons. Dental work, reconstructive and plastic surgeries, analysis of medications, and even an EpiPen had demonstrated many of the advancements of the surface over the years.

Many of these discoveries remained mysteries, but there were many others that had benefited Inner Earth.

Some items had been shattered beyond recognition or repair, including what looked like an old transistor radio. What it had been doing underground falling into holes was anybody's guess. Schlenker had been nearly beside himself with pants-wetting glee when he helped Shaw get his smartphone working again. Like Shaw, it was a miracle that the phone had survived, though Shaw had sealed it inside a hard-shell waterproof case in his pocket when he had gone caving. He didn't remember doing so, but the case had been found on him when he was discovered, and the phone was intact.

The battery was run down, but Schlenker and Spall agreed that they would be able to cobble together some kind of charging device over the next few weeks. As it was, they had been forced to analyze the phone's electrical requirements and cobble together a small transformer to power up the device without causing damage.

Shaw was dismayed that so few functions on his phone were still usable in the caverns. Naturally, he couldn't get any kind of signal through seventeen kilometers of solid rock, so there was no way to access the Internet, the possibility of which had Schlenker practically salivating.

Shaw was overjoyed to find that he could use his phone to listen to his music list. More than two months of hearing nothing but the music of the underground had made him wistful for some of his old favorites. Inner Earth had a large variety of musical styles, ranging from classical to ragtime and even a form of jazz. Unfortunately, the underground hadn't discovered rock and roll, despite the prevalence of a type of music that Spall had termed "that dreadful noise where they pound on everything, especially the inside of one's head." Schlenker had taken Shaw to one of these concerts; it was true that they did pound on everything, but Shaw had found the music to be very enjoyable, though heavy on the percussion.

Shaw had made the mistake of agreeing to go to another concert with Schlenker without asking what the music would be. Spall had quickly found something else to do when asked to join them, which should have given Shaw a clue to what he was in for. As it turned out, the Ukrainian Kazoo Orchestra had a surprisingly varied repertoire, but Shaw spent the entire time stifling laughter at the sight of thirty men and women in full evening dress playing such instruments with straight faces.

When first introduced to the music from the surface, Schlenker was simply amazed at the variety. He listened intently to every song and seemed to enjoy every one. Perhaps the most unusual aspect of the entire surface music experience was when Spall asked how one would dance to such music. Shaw, describing himself as a "decent dancer," had obliged by demonstrating various dances as he could remember them, only to find Copperhead behind him mimicking the dance moves. It was comical to watch a three-ton steel behemoth in a coat and tails belching steam from arm and leg joints as he followed along with a country music line dance.

"Well, Copperhead, your mother would be proud," Shaw said after the monster had finished his metallic gyrations. "You'll have a girlfriend in no time with moves like that."

Copperhead nodded in agreement (or bobbed his torso up and down, since he had no neck) and stalked toward the house to help Mrs. Clary with her dinner preparations.

Other artifacts they were able to get working were flashlights, or torches, as Spall and Schlenker called them, as well as small radios, headlamps, and even a GPS unit, despite a shattered screen and the inability for it to actually do anything aside from sit on the table using up battery power. Occasionally they would take a break from their in-depth analysis of surface debris to work on one of Schlenker's projects.

Schlenker seemed to be interested in absolutely everything, as evidenced by his lab. He had projects going all the time, from a botanical experiment involving glowing plants to a large blunderbuss-shaped mini-cannon. He told Shaw that he had planned to develop the weapon as a small infantry support cannon to be carried by a single soldier; however, the completed firearm was over two meters long and weighed in excess of one hundred kilograms. Schlenker was still optimistic about having the cannon mounted on a vehicle, so they tinkered with it and got it to fire reliably. The eighty-millimeter shell it fired was impressive, though. They managed to blast some very large holes in the rocks at an abandoned mine that Schlenker used as a testing range outside the city. The hardest part was testing it, and they had been forced to adapt it so that Copperhead could hold and fire it. After that, they had returned to the lab and continued their work on what Shaw began referring to as "that pile of surface crap."

At one point, Schlenker observed that Shaw was looking bored and must be in need of some entertainment. Schlenker called Spall over using a beautiful old-fashioned telephone, and the three of them took a taxi to the stadium Shaw and Spall had driven past on their way to the prime minister's office. They paid their fare and joined the jumble of people filing into the establishment. They bought tickets at one of many booths and eventually found their seats. The stadium was impressive, and it looked to Shaw that it was full nearly to capacity. What that meant as far as numbers, Shaw could only guess, but he supposed there must have been close to fifty thousand people for whatever game they were there to see.

"So what are we here to see, anyway?" he asked when they had sat and Schlenker had purchased refreshments.

"This is stone-ball," Spall answered simply.

"Okay. I've been looking forward to this. What's with the hexagonal field?" he asked. The entire center of the circular stadium was grass, which was marked with two hexagons, one smaller one inside the other, much larger one.

Schlenker spoke up after hastily swallowing a mouthful of popcorn. "The field shape is traditional, as is the non-glowing grass turf. Terribly expensive to maintain, of course."

"Of course," Shaw agreed. Anything that grew in the underground was terribly expensive, it seemed. "So how is it played?"

Schlenker beamed. Aside from building (or dissecting) unusual mechanical and electronic devices, Schlenker loved nothing better than to explain something to someone. It wasn't vanity, a trait shared by so many knowledgeable people in demonstrating their knowledge; it was simply that Schlenker was incredibly generous and loved to pass his knowledge to others. The fact that most people didn't desire many aspects of his knowledge hadn't entered his mind.

"Well. The field is hexagonal, with two scoring zones. One is outside the outer hex, and one is inside the center hex. The hexagon in the very center is ten meters across the flats, and the outer hexagon is one hundred ten across the flats, meaning there will be a minimum of fifty meters from the inside hex to the outside hex in any direction. There are two teams of twelve players each. One team faces inward from the outer edge of the field, while the other team faces out from the middle. The middle team begins in the very center with possession of the ball, which of course is made of stone and weighs exactly ten kilograms—"

"So what is that, like twenty-two pounds or so?" Shaw interrupted.

"Yes, I suppose, if you still use the old system. Anyway, the team with possession of the ball starts in the center of the field and must carry the ball in any direction to any point outside the outer edge to score a point. Should the opposing team manage to take possession of the ball, they must return the ball to the center of the field to score a point for themselves. Once a point is scored, the teams switch from outside to in and vice versa; then the team with possession must carry the ball in the opposite direction to score another point."

"So they have to carry the ball all the time?"

"Well, they certainly wouldn't want to kick it."

"I guess not. So can they pass it?"

"They may pass the ball, but only backward or to the side. Never forward."

"Okay, like in rugby. Now say the team with the ball makes it to the outside of the field and scores a point. Then they turn around and head back toward the center?"

"Yes. They will still have possession of the ball, and must now carry it inward to the center to score another point. If the opposing team cannot gain control of the ball, then the first team would simply continue carrying and passing the ball to the outside, then the inside, then back to the outside. The opposing team may use tackles and other means to stop the ball and gain possession of it. It's a very physically demanding game, and it can be quite fast-paced."

"I bet. There aren't any time-out or anything like that?"

"A coach may call for a four-minute time-out twice during the game. Overall, the game itself is played in two forty-minute periods, with a single ten-minute break at the half point of the game."

"This sounds like it'll be a fun game to watch. Are there fouls and illegal plays as well?"

"Of course. Things like tripping, kicking, and punching are disallowed, and will result in the offending player being removed from the game if the infraction happens more than once. My favorite rule is the handicap. If a team is leading the other by several points, they lose a player for every two points they have over the other team."

"What? So the better they play, the fewer people they have to play with?"

"Of course. I've been to games where the winning team has half as many players as the losing team, and they continued to score more points. Of course if the losing team scores more points, the winning team gets players back. It makes things very interesting very quickly."

"I bet. What about penalties? Is there a penalty for something like kicking the ball?"

"No, kicking the ball usually comes with its own penalty. There is very little need to give a player an infraction for being an idiot and breaking his own toes."

Shaw laughed. "Point taken. Say a player is removed from the game for infractions. Is there a substitution?"

"Not for an infraction. If a player is removed due to poor sportsmanship, their team is penalized for the duration of the game. If a player is removed due to injury, a new player is allowed to take their place without any issues. If the coach wishes to make a substitution for any reason, it is allowed, but only three times during the entire game."

"Wow. Looks like I have a lot to learn about this game. What kind of stone is the ball made from?"

"Granite. Oh, look! It's starting. Let's stand for the National Anthem."

They stood as they watched a young man walk out into the center hex, followed by a large marching band and soldiers bearing the national flag of the Republic of Inner Earth. A large device on a stand was carried out by several people and placed in front of the young man, and Shaw realized that the device was a microphone. The band formed a large ring around the center and began to play what sounded almost like a marching tune, and the young man began to sing in a beautiful tenor. Most of the spectators could be heard singing along, and a few uniformed soldiers in the crowd were saluting their flag with an almost religious fervor and a few teary eyes.

The National Anthem of the Republic concluded, and the band, flag party, and singer all departed for the outskirts of the field as the spectators sat down. Suddenly the stadium erupted in cheers and applause as two teams ran out onto the field, one team in alternating light blue and dark blue jerseys, the other in orange and black.

"I cheer for Echo University. Much better than Polska Cavern College," Schlenker shouted to Shaw over the roar of the crowd.

"Which one is which?" Shaw shouted back.

"Our team wears the orange and black jerseys."

"Oh. Are all the teams college level?"

"Just this game. The professional teams play tomorrow. In my opinion, though, the college and university teams are better to watch. Ah, we've won the coin toss, so our team begins with possession of the ball in the center."

"How many teams are there?"

"Every college and university in the Republic has a team; twenty-eight teams altogether. Too bad we're at war with Ünterreich. They would likely have an incredible team."

"How many professional teams are there?"

"Twenty-two. Many of the smaller caverns can't afford a team, and many places don't have the space for a stone-ball field. A standard stone-ball field covers 10,478.9 square meters, which everyone knows."

"Of course. How could that not be common knowledge?" Shaw agreed sarcastically.

"Ooh! They're starting!"

At that, Schlenker stood and began to cheer wildly, spilling a bit of popcorn on Spall. Spall, naturally, was scanning the field and the crowd with his eyes and only displayed minor annoyance at Schlenker's unexpected popcorn shower.

The game was very fast-paced, as Schlenker had promised. Shaw found it very easy to get into the game, and the rules seemed easy to pick up quickly. By the end of the first period, he felt that he had a good grasp of the rules and many of the finer points. Schlenker was quite energetic, and almost as entertaining to watch as the game itself. He would erupt from his seat whenever Echo University scored a point, usually spilling more of his popcorn on Spall, who pretended not to notice. Even more entertaining was when Polska Cavern College would obtain possession of the ball or, worse yet, score a point. Schlenker would stand and yell his outrage, as would many of the other fans in the crowd, many of them wearing their team colors and even a few shirtless and painted in their team colors. These last would not have looked out of place in any large stadium on the surface.

Before long, Shaw felt himself being swept up in the roar of the crowd, and he was soon cheering for the Echo team as well. In the end, there were many disappointed fans in the stadium, as the Polska Cavern team defeated the Echo team seven to four. All in all, Shaw enjoyed himself immensely, and even Spall seemed content, if not happy. Schlenker, despite his favorite team losing to what he described as "those Polish upstarts," was smiling merrily as they walked through the crowd and out to catch a taxi in the throng.

As they waited for a taxi, Shaw looked down the street and saw a small group of shabbily-dressed men walking along, bumping into one another as they shambled. Several of them seemed intoxicated, while others seemed not altogether right in the head. Two of them were muttering to themselves as they stumbled along, bouncing off walls, signs, parked vehicles, and one another. Occasionally a passerby would stop to give one of them some money, and they eventually made their way up the street, where they passed quite close to Shaw and his companions. Shaw could see one of them hauling a large rat on a leash, while another seemed to be glowing slightly. They were all clearly homeless and jobless, but the crowds looked as though nobody was particularly afraid of them.

"I know the kings of England, and I quote the fights historical from Marathon to Waterloo, in order categorical. Gods bless you, ma'am." One of them was locked in what sounded like a comic opera with himself as a sweet old lady handed him a shiny gold dollar. He then continued with his personal performance as though nothing had happened. "I'm very well acquainted, too, with matters mathematical; I understand equations both the simple and quadratical. About binomial theorem I'm teeming with a lot o' news, with many cheerful facts about the square of the hypotenuse—"

Another was talking to himself as well, but his monologue seemed more incoherent. "Toast on Tuesdays! You shovel the gravel and I'll bring the cats out. Always wear a hat in the bath! Toast! Toast is the best! Jelly and toast in the bath! Where's my cat? Down the well! People down the well. Metal people down the well. People eating toast with cats in the well!"

A third looked like a skinny young man, but his head was almost entirely wrapped in a reddish scarf, concealing most of his face. He shivered constantly as though freezing to death. He occasionally spoke to one or another of his companions, but he was so well wrapped that nothing could be understood.

As the strange group shambled away, Shaw looked over at Spall, who was shaking his head slowly.

"Well they seem pretty...colorful," Shaw said. "Who are those guys?"

"The Astronomers Guild." Spall replied.

Shaw smiled, a quizzical expression on his face. "The Astronomers Guild? Do you realize how crazy that sounds...oh. Okay, I get it. The Astronomers Guild." Shaw chuckled. "That's actually a pretty good name for them. They're clearly all nuts. They just live on the streets?"

"Oh, yes. Everyone knows the Astronomers Guild," Schlenker answered. "They're all mad, but perfectly harmless. Efforts have been made to admit them into a sanitarium, but they all prefer this life, and they cause no harm to anyone. Of course they were all too insane to be allowed admission into the Guild of Vagabonds, Ruffians, and Layabouts."

"There's no such thing," Shaw said, disbelieving.

"Of course there is," Spall said. "What other guild would there be for the beggars, tramps, and scroungers?"

"They have a guild for bums?" Shaw asked, still disbelieving. "Do they pay dues? That seems like a really strange section of society to have a guild for keeping things professional."

"Of course there are rules and regulations for beggars. They have a place in our society, just as anyone else," Schlenker said.

"I think my head is about to explode," Shaw said, still trying to wrap his consciousness around what he had just heard.

Eventually they hailed a taxi and returned to Schlenker's, where Mrs. Clary had prepared what Spall described as "food of some type." Spall happily avoided the meal prepared by Mrs. Clary by munching on the large amount of popcorn he was able to extract from nearly every point in his suit, helpfully placed there at high velocity by Schlenker during the game.

The game over with, they returned to their routine of identifying and fixing, where possible, the surface artifacts that had accumulated over the years. Shaw felt invigorated after watching the game and was able to focus a bit better on the task at hand.

# 13

## The Policeman's Ball

The day of the Policeman's Ball arrived, and that evening the three of them dressed in their best suits and hats for the occasion. Spall, of course, had his usual gigantic pistol concealed (mostly) under his coat, but he still looked forbidding even without it. Shaw wasn't afraid of Spall, but he could see why many people that didn't know him would be.

The three of them went outside to find Copperhead waiting with a large stainless steel limousine, belching steam from underneath in a similar fashion to the behemoth. The driver's compartment had no roof, and the driver's controls looked enormous. Shaw realized that Copperhead, in addition to being the world's largest (and probably dampest) butler, was also the world's largest (and probably dampest) chauffeur. Copperhead opened the door and the three finely dressed gentlemen entered.

The seats were upholstered in luxurious leather rather than the utilitarian metal upholstery that Shaw had seen in most other vehicles.

Despite the size and decor of his house, Schlenker very seldom betrayed that he had a lot of money; however, his mode of transportation was a clear indicator of what could be bought in Echo with sufficient funds. He wondered how long it had taken to convert the vehicle for use by a mechanical driver with a copper ball for a head. For Schlenker, probably an entire weekend.

Copperhead drove them through the city to another area populated with elegant town houses, all built from a light gray granite, tastefully carved in a Tudor style reminiscent of sixteenth-century England. They stopped at one of the houses, and Spall took Shaw out of their vehicle to the front door. Spall turned a small key that resembled an old-fashioned windup key mounted in the doorframe, which rewarded them with the sound of chimes from within. The key continued to turn and play the chimes until an attractive young lady opened the door.

Shaw had been a little flustered at having been set up with a blind date for the Policeman's Ball, but upon seeing the woman who opened the door, he quickly changed his thinking. She was dressed in a long, form-fitting green dress that looked right out of the 1920s. Her long red hair was curled tightly and pinned back, leaving two long tendrils to frame her face. She had piercing blue eyes, made even more noticeable in contrast with her pale skin and bright red lipstick. She blushed and smiled as she looked at Shaw.

Spall cleared his throat. "Miss Muir, this is Mr. Shaw. Shaw, this is . . . Miss Muir."

"I can't believe you still can't remember my name, Mr. Spall. It's Saoirse. And it's very nice to meet you, Mr. Shaw. I've heard a lot about you," she said in an Irish accent as she shook Shaw's hand.

"Saoirse. It's nice to meet you as well. Please call me Ryan."

"Of course, Ryan. And it's pronounced 'Sir-sha.' It rhymes with 'inertia.' The way you said it, it sounded like you'd sneezed," she said, smiling again.

"Saoirse! Who is it?" asked a raspy woman's voice in a much thicker Irish accent from within the house.

She turned and looked back through the doorway of the house before shouting, "It's my date for the Policeman's Ball, Mother. Don't wait up; I'll be late!"

"How late? Is it that awful Mr. Crendler come 'round again? He's not fit to date a privy, let alone me daughter!"

"No, Mother! He tried to get fresh with me, and I kicked him in the unmentionables! I told you that last month!"

With that, Saoirse closed the door quickly, blushing more brightly than before.

Shaw quickly continued their previous conversation. "Sorry. I've never met anyone with that name before. Let me know if I mispronounce it again, or if I get fresh with you."

"Oh, there'll be no doubt about that," she said with a smile.

Spall, in a rare moment of social awareness, realized that he was suddenly superfluous to the conversation and cleared his throat. "Ahem. Shall we move along? I have an aversion to being late and watching the two of you blush at each other."

Shaw took Miss Saoirse Muir's arm as they walked down to the waiting silver limousine. He noticed that she had a slight limp in her left leg, but it didn't seem to bother her. Copperhead had miraculously extricated himself from the driver's compartment to open the door for them, and they piled inside. Saoirse sat next to Shaw and continued to smile in her enchanting way.

Shaw, in what turned out to be a mistake, asked after her mother. Saoirse rolled her eyes.

"One half's dead and the other's as senile as an old goat. Though I love her to bits, the old bat. She moved in with me a few years ago so I could keep an eye on her. She wanders. Last time my neighbor found her in his laundry pile, curled up like a wee babe and naked as the day she was born."

"Oh." Shaw didn't know what to say. Fortunately, Schlenker was ready with a quick change of subject.

"How is your leg healing, Miss Muir? Your limp is almost completely gone."

"Oh, I'm nearly fit as a fiddle, Doctor, thank you for asking. Just a few more days and I'll be able to return to active service."

"Active service?" Shaw asked. "What do you usually do?"

"Oh, I haven't always sat behind a desk," Saoirse replied. "I've been an agent with the Secret Service for the last three years. I broke my left femur while following a Trician agent three months ago. I left a goodly dent in the blasted steamer that hit me though."

"Steamer?"

"Oh, right. A steam-powered vehicle. I ran across a road to keep my target in sight, and a bloody taxi hit me."

"Oh, I'm sorry to hear that."

"The driver was sorry too. I was in a marked pedestrian crossing and he didn't even slow down. I broke his jaw and gave him a concussion. Idiot made me lose my target."

Shaw looked again at Saoirse's hair color and freckled face and wasn't surprised in the least. She would probably have punched the taxi if the driver hadn't presented a more convenient target.

They traveled further into the center of Echo City, approaching the government district. Next to the Government Spire was a long, low building surrounded by pillars called the Hall of Assembly. This building was constructed from much darker stone than the Spire, though it was difficult to tell exactly what color it was. The entire building looked like a Greek temple, and it was even lit from the outside by large braziers with open flames at regular intervals. Their limousine pulled up to the front of the building, which was thronged by a large crowd of journalists and photographers. Shaw smiled at the old-fashioned-looking cameras. He was so used to digital camera equipment that seeing cameras with the old accordion-style front and large flashbulbs almost made him laugh.

Copperhead pulled to a stop in front of the crowd, and a waiting footman opened the door for the occupants. A small amount of lights flashed as Doctor Schlenker, Mr. Spall, and Saoirse exited, but as soon as Shaw left the vehicle, he was literally blinded and deafened by the almost continuous camera flashes and the roar from the journalists hoping to get an exclusive with the now-famous "Man From the Surface." The group bunched together and hurried up the steps through the main doors. Shaw began to take in a deep breath, thinking he had successfully avoided answering millions of random and annoying questions; but when he entered the main ballroom of the Hall of Assembly, he was faced with what looked like a million pairs of eyes, all turned toward him.

"Ah, crap," he said.

They moved their way slowly into the room, and once fully inside the view was spectacular.

The ballroom was immense. Shaw hadn't realized it from the exterior, but the Hall of Assembly had been carved completely out of a formation of flowstone that must have accumulated over millions of years.

What struck Shaw most was the variegated color through the stone in every visible surface. To call the colors a rainbow would not have done the stone justice, since a rainbow has never boasted the seams of gold and silver that Shaw could see casting their sparkle in the polished surfaces. There were even ribbons of brown and jet black twisting their way through the other colors in a sinuous visual dance. He felt as though he had stepped into a giant room of polished agate.

The interior of the oblong hall boasted a vaulted ceiling that must have been a hundred meters or more overhead, arching gently down to meet the walls. Romanesque pillars, also carved out of the stone and blending seamlessly with the rest of the excavation, skirted the entire room every few meters, separating the main expanse from a narrow hallway forming the circumference of the building. Gaslights burned in iron sconces mounted around each pillar, and gigantic gas chandeliers threw warm light across every surface, causing the colors in the stone to come alive across the dance floor.

The next hour was a whirlwind of activity. Shaw was introduced to the who's who of Echo City, all of them dressed in their finest. He was vaguely aware of Saoirse on his left arm, watching the crowd in the same way that Spall was. Spall was a full head taller than everyone else in the room, but it was uncanny how everyone just seemed to not notice him, flowing around him like an invisible barrier in an ocean of people. He didn't seem to mind. Doctor Schlenker was nowhere to be found, though it wouldn't be difficult to disappear in such a gathering.

After having been introduced to what felt like nearly everyone in the entire world, including the prime minister again and the chief of police, Shaw was pulled toward a large buffet table by Saoirse. At this point, much of the novelty had worn off, and most of the crowd had discovered that people from the surface were boringly similar to people underground. Many had gone off to dance and mingle with other important persons. Shaw managed to take a deep breath.

"Thanks, Saoirse. I was starting to want to make a run for it. I'm usually more of an introvert. Large crowds make me nervous after a while."

"Don't mention it. I always get nervous in large groups of people, especially when I'm protecting someone important."

"Is that why you're here? To protect me?"

"Not the main reason. I wanted to come to the ball, and I wanted to meet you as well. Director Spall merely suggested that I also keep an eye out for anything unusual in case someone wished to harm you for any reason."

"Well, I *am* a celebrity after all," Shaw joked.

"Are you? I hadn't noticed," Saoirse joked back.

Saoirse Muir was surprised how easy it was to talk to Shaw. Her love life the past few years could be described as "rocky." Her schedule in the Secret Service made it difficult to meet eligible young men, unless they also worked as an agent. And she had already dated a few of those and decided she was better off not bothering. Most were too focused on their careers to pay much attention to anything else. Shaw felt different, though. Despite having gone through an unimaginable trauma not long ago, he had a relaxed, easygoing manner that she found endearing. *He was also very good at concealing his anxiety about the crowd,* she thought. *He puts people at ease almost effortlessly. He must have been a very good police officer.*

"Tell me about yourself," Shaw said, taking a drink from a polished gold tray borne by a server who was meandering through the crowd.

"Well, I was born in Éire Íochtarach—"

"Sorry, you'll have to translate that for me; I don't speak Irish," Shaw laughed.

Saoirse smiled. "My apologies. It's 'Lower Ireland' in English."

"Ah, that makes sense. Go on."

"I'm a spoiled only child. My parents wanted to have more, but I must have been a handful," she said, pointing at her hair color and smirking.

Shaw laughed. "One of my sisters is a redhead. But she never had the temper that everyone thinks redheads are famous for." His smile faded a little. "Sorry, I keep interrupting you."

"It's fine. My father is . . . best not mentioned for a number of reasons. My mother took me away and we settled here in Echo City when I was seventeen. I finished school and then studied engineering at Echo University."

"You've got an engineering degree? Why'd you end up as a government agent?"

Saoirse thought for a moment and shrugged. "I've never had to put it into words, but I suppose I'd have to say that I didn't fancy sitting at a drafting table designing things all day. I'd much rather be out making a difference and staying active. I'm a . . . what did you call it?"

"Introvert."

"'Introvert.' I've never heard the term before, but from the sound of the word and the context, I think it means someone who prefers peace and quiet?"

"Pretty much. Someone who . . . recharges, I guess . . . in solitude."

"That's me, but I still like to be out and interacting with people sometimes. I was drawn to the Secret Service because I find weapons fascinating and the work sounded appealing to me."

"Well, you seem well suited to the job," Shaw observed. He had known multitudes of soldiers and police officers of every description and background, and he had developed a good eye for what made a person suited for the life. Saoirse was fit, brilliantly intelligent, well-spoken, and had a self-confidence that hadn't devolved into arrogance. Shaw found it immensely attractive.

"Thank you, Ryan. How about yourself? I only know what I've read in the news, which is mostly speculation and a tiny bit of what you've told the press. Director Spall isn't much for sharing either."

Shaw laughed. "No he isn't, is he? I couldn't even get your first name out of him."

Saoirse laughed as well. "He's a fearsome agent until you get to know him. Once you get past his intimidating size, you realize he's quite a gentleman, just socially closed off."

"I've started to realize that too," Shaw said. "Anyways, I grew up on a small farm in Canada—"

"That's North America, right?"

"Yeah. The whole northern half. The summers were really nice, but the winters could be long and cold. My parents raised cattle for the most part, aside from myself and my four sisters. After school I went to university, but I hated it, so I left and joined the army instead. After eight years in the army, I joined the police, and I've been doing that ever since."

"Summer and winter are two of the seasons, right?" Saoirse asked.

"Right," Shaw said, a little taken aback. It still surprised him whenever someone asked about things he had barely paid attention to. To him, the seasons, despite each having appeal for various reasons, were quite mundane. Everyone on Earth experienced the seasons to some degree or another. Even places along the equator had changes of weather to mark the passage through the year, though the temperatures barely changed at all.

People *in* the Earth, though, had no idea. The seasons of the year were as intangible to them as the sun or the moon. They may have heard of them, but there was no way to experience them.

Shaw looked around, as he could hear hushed whispers traveling through the crowd. The orchestra stopped playing, and the people on the dance floor ceased their movements and stared.

Shaw followed the crowd's gaze across the room to where a group of people had entered, surrounding an older gentleman dressed in a black suit with an electric blue robe over top. At a respectful distance from the lead gentleman and his entourage, several other people followed, each of them bearing the same dark blue stripe down the left sides of their faces as Spall.

"Ugh. The Ünterreich delegation," Saoirse spat. "Flaunting their slaves. And every one of those bodyguards around the prefect is a trained agent."

"The prefect? That guy in the robe?"

"Yes. He's like an ambassador, but more of a prat. Trician piece of garbage. I've cleaned up higher life-forms that my mother's cat sicked up on the carpet."

The prefect approached Prime Minister Whitley and they shook hands, though the air between them looked like it would turn to ice any second. The Trician agents were watching the crowd with the same intensity as Spall generally watched everything, but Shaw was certain they had much more to fear in this room than Spall.

Glancing over at the giant, he could see Spall regarding the Trician delegation with the same expression he always had, though Shaw could see that Spall's jaw was clenched tightly shut. Several of the Trician slaves looked over in Spall's direction and quickly looked away as though afraid. Shaw got the impression that even looking at a freed slave was frowned upon in Ünterreich, not that he imagined there were many. He still couldn't believe that slavery was so brazenly practiced.

The mood in the room had cooled significantly, but Prime Minister Whitley, an astonishing diplomat, had been able to greet the Tricians with grace and dignity, causing many in the room to relax. Conversation, after flagging noticeably, began to pick up again and the dancing continued. The Tricians moved off to a corner of the room, where the prefect would be approached by the occasional businessman or diplomat trying to be polite.

"I can't believe the prime minister would extend an invitation to those creatures," Saoirse said, a look of disgust marring her otherwise beautiful features.

"Stranger things have been done in the name of diplomacy," Shaw said, the Cuban Missile Crisis popping into his mind. "With the stalemate on the battlefield, I doubt the prime minister wants to antagonize the Tricians."

"You're right, of course," Schlenker said, appearing at Shaw's shoulder and causing Shaw to spill his drink in surprise.

"Where did you come from?" Shaw asked, wiping the remains of his drink from his pants.

"I've been through the room several times and emptying the buffet table while everyone was occupying themselves with the curiosity from the surface," Schlenker replied. "Who do you think ate all the pickled onions?" he asked, the unmistakable odor of pickled onions wafting through the regrettably small space between them.

"I can only guess," Shaw answered, holding his breath. "Why do you think the Tricians brought their slaves with them tonight? They must be aware of how slavery is viewed here."

"Which is why they brought them," Schlenker said. "They are trying to show us that they may do whatever they like, even within our own borders. Take that attractive black-haired agent guarding the prefect. Her name is Cyla Etheridge, and she is known to us as one of their top agents. She is even suspected of carrying out several assassinations of prominent citizens here. They bring her here to try and humiliate us because she is protected by diplomatic immunity."

"Of course. We have the same thing on the surface. I've never had to deal with it myself, but I understand it can be very frustrating."

Saoirse nodded. "Certainly. You see the shortest male agent over there? Ivan Bondarenko. We've twice caught him conducting illegal activities, but we've had to let him go in the interests of diplomacy. They send him home to Ünterreich, and a few short months later, he's back here. Disgraceful."

Shaw noticed that Spall was making his way toward them, and as far from the Tricians as possible.

"Schlenker. I require something to occupy my mind," Spall stated as he arrived in their group.

"I thought you were working. Does that not occupy your mind?" Schlenker asked.

"Of course I'm working; however, I am also entertaining myself with thoughts of slowly twisting that prefect's head off—and really enjoying myself while doing it. I am not certain that such thoughts would be construed as normal."

"You're not normal, Spall," Schlenker noted.

"Yes, I've heard it mentioned before."

"You mention it yourself all the time, Spall."

"I know."

"In this instance, my friend, I think you are perfectly normal. I have given a thought to how enjoyable it would be to see those poor slaves freeing themselves through various violent means," Schlenker said.

"Excellent; I am not the only one. Now, tell me of your attempts to design an underwater locomotive."

"Truly? You wish to hear about that project now? It will take some time," Schlenker warned.

"Humor me."

"Very well."

Spall continued to scan the room as Schlenker began to explain in nauseating detail his latest attempts to design and build a submersible locomotive. Shaw, having already gained a sense of self-preservation when it came to Schlenker's lectures on his projects, ideas, and everything else in the entire universe, began to move away quickly with Saoirse. Saoirse continually scanned the room as she limped slightly through the crowd. Shaw felt somewhat saddened by the fact that his date had also decided to work during their evening together. He didn't have much experience with blind dates, but he had hoped the young lady would pay more attention to him. Saoirse must have realized what Shaw was thinking, because she turned to him and smiled.

"I must seem a terrible companion this evening," she said. "You probably think I'm ignoring you."

"Oh, don't worry about it. I understand that you're working too. Would you like to dance?"

"Certainly."

They began to dance among all the others on the dance floor. Even while twirling slowly to the music, they both continued to keep their eyes on the Trician delegation as much as possible. Shaw had decided that if his hosts didn't feel comfortable with their backs to the Tricians, there was a good reason why. Saoirse continued their conversation.

"I am working, but I'm also supposed to be your date. I really was very keen to meet you."

"And are you glad you did?"

"Of course! I wouldn't mind another date after this one, as long as there are fewer people around."

"I would like that too. What sorts of things do men and women do for dates down here?"

"Well, probably the same things they do in your world. Dinner, dancing, the symphony, the ballet, music concerts, even a motion picture."

"I wouldn't mind seeing what the movies are like down here."

"Oh, they're dreadful. They don't seem to attract the best writers or actors. Is it the same on the surface?"

"It depends. There are many amazing actors and movies, and there are just as many, if not more, terrible ones. Sometimes I like to go to a terrible movie just to sit and make fun of it."

"I think I would enjoy that."

"Terrific. Who is she looking at?"

"Who?"

"That black-haired Trician spy Schlenker told me about. She scans the room, but her eyes keep returning to the same place."

"I'm not sure. She is very pretty, though, don't you think?"

"I guess. She's not my type; I'm more of a redhead guy myself."

Saoirse blushed to the roots of her hair, which was almost the same color. "I should warn you that flattery might get you very far indeed, Mr. Shaw. Of course it might also get you too far."

"I suppose that would be when I receive a kick in my unmentionables?"

Saoirse laughed as they continued to dance their way around the room. Shaw occasionally looked back at the Tricians, who seemed to a man (or woman) to be purposefully not enjoying themselves. The orchestra concluded their song and began another. Suddenly Shaw witnessed something that made him stop dancing, causing Saoirse to stop as well.

The black-haired Trician spy, Etheridge, had left her camp in the corner and was crossing the dance floor in the direction she had been looking repeatedly. She wore a form-fitting ankle-length sleeveless dress that was such a dark shade of blue it was almost purple. Her black curls were pinned back, revealing diamond earrings that sparkled in the brilliant gaslights, matching the impressive necklace dangling from her throat. Most of the men in the room followed her with their eyes; more than a few women did the same.

Shaw suddenly realized to whom her eyes had been returning. Etheridge walked up to Spall, who towered over her, and began to speak to him.

"Mr. Spall."

Spall looked down at her for a moment, clearly considering his options before replying, "Miss Etheridge. How nice to meet you."

Etheridge smiled. "You are a talented liar. May I have the pleasure of this dance?"

Spall looked momentarily surprised, which, if one was to ask anyone that knew him, was a difficult thing to accomplish. He recovered himself after a second and favored her with his near-undetectable smile. "Certainly."

With all the laughter and chatter on the dance floor, Shaw couldn't hear what was being said, but he could only anticipate what might happen if she were to provoke Spall. Visions of Spall tearing Etheridge's head from her shoulders using only his two hands flashed across his mind's eye, when the most unexpected thing that could happen happened. Spall offered her his arm and they left Schlenker where he was, still talking to himself about underwater locomotives, and walked to the dance floor, where they began to dance together. Shaw and Saoirse could only stand and stare open-mouthed as the two twirled slowly around the room. It appeared that the female spy was enjoying herself (or trying to appear to enjoy herself), but Spall, owing to his usual expressionless self, didn't look like he shared the feeling. Though to be fair, he didn't look like he *wasn't* enjoying himself, either. A few people had stopped dancing when they noticed the couple dance past, but they all continued after the shock had worn off.

Etheridge continued to smile in her most charming way. "Now, Mr. Spall. I have heard so much about you that I just had to finally meet you. I can tell that you were surprised that I asked you to dance. Why did you say yes?"

Spall fixed Etheridge with his usual stony expression. "Curiosity."

"Indeed? How charming. May I ask what you were curious about?"

"Why you asked me to dance. I don't often receive an invitation to dance from a member of the enemy camp."

"Is that what I am?"

"A fact of which you are no doubt aware."

Etheridge laughed. "Perhaps I am your enemy. But that doesn't mean we cannot be civil to each other, does it?"

"I will take your word for it. In the interests of civility, perhaps you could answer my question."

"Oh, did you ask me a question?" Etheridge was still smiling sweetly, playing innocent as she and Spall continued to twirl about the room.

"You know I did. Why did you ask me to dance?"

It was Etheridge's turn to fix Spall with a stony expression. "Curiosity," she said.

"And what were you curious about?"

"Everything. You are something of a legend back in Ünterreich. Surely you were aware of that fact?"

"I couldn't care less what the Tricians think of me."

"Of course you couldn't. But I am curious about how you managed to escape all those years ago. A young lad of only fourteen."

"Thirteen."

"Thirteen. It is still a great mystery. None of our agents have been able to find anyone that knows how it was accomplished."

"Because I have never told anyone."

"Never?"

"Never. I confess that it surprises me that you are trying to glean such trivial information from me. The Tricians' top agent in Echo dancing with me, and *that* is what you want to hear?"

"Yes. We don't think of it as trivial information of course. You are the only one to have escaped. I think that is as far from trivial as it is possible to get."

"I am sorry to disappoint you, Miss Etheridge."

Etheridge laughed. Oh, I am far from disappointed, Mr. Spall. The simple fact that you've agreed to dance with me has told me volumes."

Spall raised an eyebrow. "Indeed?"

"Oh, yes. If nothing else, I've gotten a better look at your weapon," she said with a wink. "I didn't realize how big it was. It suits you."

"I like to keep things proportionate. Your sidearm could be bigger, though it would be more difficult to hide in that dress."

"Oh? I didn't realize you'd figured out where I keep it."

"You aren't the only top agent in the room, Miss Etheridge."

"I'm glad you agree. Are you always this observant?"

"I make it a habit to thoroughly examine everyone."

She laughed again. "Well, don't you just make a lady feel special."

Spall looked Etheridge in the eyes. "Just so we understand each other, I see you as an enemy, nothing more. I can only speculate at your motives for dancing with me, but I am certain they are all professional, despite your attempts to make it seem otherwise. Other men may be easily swayed by your beauty and charms; however, you will find that I am more difficult to influence."

"Oh, I have never doubted that, Mr. Spall. In fact, I would have been extremely disappointed if you had turned out to be other than you are. I shall look forward to our encounters in the future, and there will be many, you may depend upon it."

"Indeed? Planning some upcoming illegal actions, are you?"

Etheridge smiled coyly. "Always. I feel that things are going to get extraordinarily interesting for you in the very near future." She winked at Spall, which still generated no reaction from the giant.

"I will take your word for it," he said. "Please let me know when they occur; I would hate to miss them."

"Oh, you won't need me to tell you. Sadly, it seems our song is coming to an end. Hopefully we shall meet again soon. I hope to discover your great secret one day."

"I hate to disappoint you again, madam, but that is as likely to happen as a rabbit biting a man's head off."

Shaw, once he had gotten over his initial shock and closed his mouth, decided that he should continue dancing with Saoirse so the entire event wouldn't seem so strange. He had begun to dance with Saoirse when he noticed the Trician group once again. The slaves appeared to be just as cowed and miserable as they had when they first arrived. The rest of the Tricians, however, had been watching Spall's movements through the room with an unnerving level of attention. Several of them had clear expressions of shock and varying amounts of anger. Only the prefect, standing in his bright blue robe, appeared to have been unmoved by the entire incident.

Saoirse and Shaw had danced through the room, repeatedly trying to dance their way closer to Spall and his companion. Unfortunately, they weren't able to get close enough to hear what was being said before the song ended. Spall and Etheridge parted from each other, after which Spall bowed courteously and Etheridge curtseyed. They returned to their opposing sides of the room, and both stood as though nothing had happened. Shaw and Saoirse left the dance floor themselves and approached Spall, who was once again listening (or pretending to listen) to Schlenker's mind-numbing account of how he had been attempting to solve the problem of submersible venting of exhaust gases from steam-powered engines as used in a self-contained locomotive suitable for use at one thousand atmospheres of pressure.

"Sorry, Doctor, but we have more pressing things to discuss at the moment," Saoirse interrupted Schlenker. "Spall, what in Earth was that about?"

Spall turned and appeared to notice them for the first time. "Ah, you saw that. She asked me to dance."

"Yes, we could see that. What did the two of you talk about?" Shaw asked.

"Eh? What's happened?" Schlenker looked bewildered.

"We'll fill you in later," Shaw said. "So? What's going on?"

Spall looked at Shaw. "Nothing whatever is going on. Etheridge asked me to dance, and I obliged. As far as what we discussed during our dance, it was the usual trivial things men and women usually discuss. I assure you that she did not pry any secrets from me, nor I from her."

Schlenker's expression changed as he realized what everyone was talking about. He looked over at the Tricians, who were beginning to depart as quickly as they had arrived. Neither Spall nor Etheridge so much as glanced in each other's direction. Shaw wondered how much trouble she would get into for the stunt she had just pulled. Or was it all part of a careful plan? To what end? He turned back to Spall.

"What made her decide to ask you to dance? Looking like she does, she could have danced with anyone here, Trician or not. Why you?"

Spall sighed. "No doubt it was part of a carefully laid plan. For what purpose, I have no idea at this time. Rest assured, I chose my words carefully throughout our dance; I likewise carefully concealed my revulsion. Dancing with that woman was quite unenjoyable."

The remainder of the evening passed uneventfully, more or less. Shaw still had to contend with his celebrity, as people would occasionally approach him to have their picture taken or to ask about the surface and what life was like in the sunlight. Finally, the Policeman's Ball began to wind down and the crowd thinned out. The prime minister left with his entourage, after which Spall and Saoirse were both able to relax a bit.

161

"Mister Shaw," said a thickset man with a Russian accent in a well-polished army uniform, "I am general Verbitsky; I just wanted to introduce myself."

Shaw had seen the general approaching and suddenly knew exactly what was going to be discussed.

"General, it's nice to meet you, Sir." He said, shaking the soldier's hand firmly.

"Balderdash! I can tell you've met far too many people this evening to still be enjoying such things. I shan't keep you too long," the general said with a smile. "I understand you served in your military, up on the surface, and I wanted to express my interest in your knowledge and...expertise, so to speak."

Shaw nodded. This was going exactly as he'd thought it would.

"Well, Sir, I'm not sure what use I could be to the army."

"Oh, I think you could be our most valuable asset, young man," the general winked. "The implementation of a single advanced weapon or military tactic down here could mean the difference between the current stalemate and total victory for the Republic. Just think of the possibilities!"

"Oh, I've been thinking about them; I'll just need some more time to...figure out my footing down here," Shaw said noncommittally.

"Well, don't take too long. Lives may depend on it," the general said. He shook Shaw's hand again and joined members of the crowd that were moving toward the exits.

"He's practically salivating," Saoirse noted. "I'm sure he'd love to hear all about your military service."

"He'd love to hear about anything he can use to break the stalemate, you mean," Shaw said.

"Oh, definitely. But would that be such a bad thing? Being instrumental in freeing the slaves from the grip of the Tricians would feel pretty nice, I'd think."

Shaw nodded. It would feel good.

"You're right," he admitted. "I'm not sure why, but I just feel that it's not the right time for all that. Not yet. Maybe once I'm feeling 100 percent again."

Saoirse and Shaw danced a last couple of dances, and then they joined Spall and Schlenker before extricating themselves from the festivities to find Copperhead waiting outside with Schlenker's shiny limousine. They piled in and began their drive through the city to drop Saoirse off. Their conversation focused around Spall's dance with Etheridge, and what purpose it must have served. None of them could come up with a possible scenario that made any sense, especially when one took into account the facts that Etheridge was a Trician spy in very high standing (likely their top spy in Echo) and that Spall was an escaped Trician slave. No doubt there would be some unpleasant repercussions for Etheridge if her actions weren't part of a larger purpose. After recounting his conversation with Etheridge in detail, Spall sat quietly thinking throughout their trip, occasionally answering questions.

Shaw dropped Saoirse off at her front door and ran into a few nervous seconds where he wasn't sure if it was appropriate to kiss a woman good night on the first date in the underground. He settled for kissing her hand instead, which made her blush again. He wished her good night and left as she closed her front door.

They all returned to Schlenker's house, where they bid one another good night. Spall left to return to his own home, while Shaw and Schlenker retired for the evening. They agreed to begin preparations for their mystery trip the following morning, the destination still completely unknown to Shaw.

# 14

## Ripples

Prefect Fromm was not normally an overly patient man, but as he sat in his spacious office staring at Agent Bondarenko, he delighted in delaying the coming interview and watching him squirm. Bondarenko was his top agent, it was true, but Bondarenko knew the price of failure. He was in Echo City to keep things running smoothly, and Etheridge's stunt had caused some unpleasant ripples. Ripples that had traveled upward, all the way to Ünterreich.

"I'm not pleased, Bondarenko," he stated coldly.

Bondarenko, normally a pale man, had become even paler under Fromm's gaze. He wasn't easily rattled, but he could tell when his life hung by a thread. The metaphorical thread currently dangling him above an unpleasant death was as thin as it had ever been. It wouldn't do to make excuses, either.

"Of course, my lord," he offered, trying his best to keep the tension out of his voice. "I can make no excuses for Agent Etheridge's

**164**

behavior. I failed to anticipate such initiative in her. I will not make the same mistake again."

Prefect Fromm scrutinized Bondarenko. It would be a waste to dispose of such a skilled agent for something that, technically, wasn't his fault and couldn't have been foreseen. Unfortunately, because of Etheridge's connections to the upper ruling class back in Ünterreich, she was untouchable. Fromm was quite adept at smoothing over delicate situations, and he felt he could find a way to get through this without having to offer his superiors a scapegoat; but if it came down to it, Bondarenko would be the one to take the blame.

"I have dispatched Agent Etheridge back to Ünterreich for the time being," Fromm said at last. "She was quite . . . cavalier about the whole matter. She told me she wanted to *rattle* the Echoan agents, especially that dog, Spall."

"I issued no order for her to interact with the Echoans at all tonight, my lord," Bondarenko offered. "She was instructed to remain with your delegation throughout the evening."

"A fact of which I am aware," Fromm stated coldly. "Which is, incidentally, the only reason I haven't ordered you shipped back to Ünterreich in multiple small packages."

Bondarenko gulped. The thread felt thinner by the second. It would be better to stay silent, he decided.

"Consider this interview as a choice between future rewards and glory or an ignominious end, Bondarenko. If any of our agents step out of line in the future, rest assured that anything I could do to you will pale when compared with what the Lord Galvanus could, and likely would, do to you. Do not let me detain you further."

Bondarenko bowed and left the room as quickly as possible. He didn't have to be told twice.

Prefect Fromm turned to the shadows in one corner, and there appeared an agent who had been standing perfectly still and silent throughout, watching and listening.

"Raker."

"My lord," the agent replied emotionlessly.

I will do what I can to keep Bondarenko from the inevitable wrath of the Galvanus, but should that fail, I trust you will be capable of dealing with him?"

Agent Raker nodded silently.

"Excellent. Now I require a report on your other activities. I suspect you may have to move up the timeline."

# 15

## An Unusual Train Ride

Spall, Schlenker, and Shaw prepared for their trip the following day but did not depart until two days after the ball for their mystery destination, which Doctor Schlenker would only hint was "another cavern nearby."

By this time Shaw had become fully accustomed to the atmosphere and didn't notice the extra effort that breathing required. His injuries had fully healed, though his one blown pupil still made him shudder whenever he looked in the mirror. There were a few scars here and there, but most of them weren't too bad, he thought, and in any case most were covered up by the suits he wore. He was starting to feel more at home, though he still had frequent flashes of melancholy when he remembered something from his former life.

Saoirse Muir visited the evening after the ball, ostensibly to drop something off for Schlenker, but she couldn't stop thinking about Shaw and wanted to see him again. She arrived at Schlenker's and was shown into the back garden by Copperhead, who was wearing a tiny apron and had clearly been scrubbing pots for Mrs. Clary. His shovel fingers were already starting to rust.

Saoirse found Shaw sitting in the garden on a bench, staring up at the cavern ceiling with a wistful expression.

"Ryan?" Saoirse asked, uncertain if she should disturb his reverie.

Shaw looked over at her and suddenly smiled broadly. He quickly wiped at his eyes, and Saoirse realized he had been crying quietly by himself. She was about to leave, not wanting him to feel embarrassed, when he stood and gestured for her to join him.

"Don't go; please join me," he said, his wet eyes sparkling in the iridescent glow of the garden plants.

"Are you sure? I don't want to intrude—"

"Absolutely. I know it looks like I was sitting here feeling sorry for myself. Maybe I was. I don't know. But everything's better now that you're here. I hadn't expected to see you quite so soon," he said as brightly as he could.

"Alright. But please let me know if you need me to go; I'd hate to intrude," she said. She wasn't used to men showing their emotions. Her father had always been a stoic man; perhaps that was why she had never been intimidated by Spall. The two were remarkably similar in personality, if nothing else.

She sat on the bench; Shaw sat next to her and again looked up at the cavern ceiling.

They sat quietly for a few seconds before Shaw broke the silence.

"It's funny how you can miss things you took for granted your whole life," he said. "I was heading in to relax and read for a bit before bed, and I sat down to look at the garden. Then I looked up."

Shaw paused, the same wistful expression crossing his features. Saoirse sat quietly, understanding that, whatever Shaw's situation, he was still healing inside as well as out. Finally Shaw spoke again.

"I'll never see them again. I used to look up at the sky at night and see the stars and the moon. I'll never see them again."

**168**

Saoirse could see the pain in Shaw's face, but she didn't know what she could do apart from just listening.

"I was engaged, you know. Before. I loved her. Her name was Tricia." Here he laughed—a short, humorless laugh. "Tricia. Probably not a common name down here, is it? At least not in Echo City. Maybe in Ünterreich."

"I don't know about Ünterreich, but definitely not here," Saoirse agreed.

"Yeah," Shaw went on. "She thinks I'm dead. They all do. My family. My parents and my sisters and my nieces and nephews. I'm dead to them. Just like the stars and the moon are dead to me."

Saoirse reached over and took Shaw's hand, squeezing it tightly.

"I'm so sorry, Ryan. I know you've probably heard that a lot lately, but it's the truth. I wish I could understand everything you're going through, but what I *can* do is be here for you if you need to talk."

Shaw looked over at Saoirse, and at that moment he knew he could easily fall for those blue eyes and crimson hair. He smiled as his second thoughts chased the notion out of his head.

"Thanks. It really means a lot." He took a deep breath. "I have to tell you that I really like you. I'd like to ask you out sometime, but I'm not there yet. I know I'm not in a great place right now, and the last thing I need is to drag someone else in there with me."

Saoirse could feel the tingling in her skin as she blushed. "I understand that completely, Ryan. I really like you as well, and I can't wait to get to know you better, but I agree that this sort of thing should probably wait for a while. At least until you're ready. Don't worry; I'm a patient woman."

They sat in silence, holding hands for a few minutes more. Saoirse looked up at the only sky she had ever known, made of impenetrable rock, and wondered.

"Could you tell me about the moon sometime? And the stars too. I learned about them in school, of course, but I've never seen them myself."

Shaw smiled. "Sure. Not tonight, though. I'm pretty worn out. I think I'll head to bed."

Saoirse stood as Shaw got off the bench. She reached out and embraced him tightly, feeling his warm breath on her hair and neck. It sent goose bumps down her spine. She could feel the tension in his body and wondered how long it would take him to finally come to terms with everything and how she could help him. *It doesn't matter right now; just be there for him and let it happen as it's supposed to,* she told herself. She was a patient woman. Shaw seemed like he was worth waiting for.

Shaw held her back, fighting the tears that were trying to come. They stood like that for a few moments until Saoirse released her grip and gently pushed Shaw to arm's length.

"I need to be going. I meant what I said, though, about being here for you. I may not understand everything, but lots of things can be made better just by talking about them with someone. The doctor has my number if you need to call."

"Thanks. I probably will when I get the chance," Shaw said. "See you later?"

"Definitely."

They went into the house and parted at the stairs. Shaw went up to his room while Saoirse let herself out the front door and headed for her car. As she walked, she glanced around herself, taking in the entire street and the buildings. No people to be seen, no shadows around corners, no suspicious activity. The house was always under surveillance by Secret Service agents, but they wouldn't be visible unless they wanted to be. Of course the same was likely true of Trician agents too. Saoirse got into her vehicle and drove home, thinking about Shaw.

The next day was the day of their departure, and Shaw was feeling much better after a good night's rest. Over the preceding weeks he would occasionally awaken at night in a cold sweat, nightmares of falling forever fresh in his mind. Worse were the nightmares of being in the hospital, featuring masked doctors with frightening instruments, chopping and hacking away at parts of his body. These dreams were thankfully quite blurry and difficult to remember, and Shaw assumed that part of his brain must have been somewhat aware of what was happening to him in the emergency room after his fall and rescue.

Last night had been blessedly free from those dreams, and he awakened well rested and looking forward to their journey. Schlenker and Spall were in the dining room, Schlenker having just finished a Mrs. Clary breakfast, when Shaw came down the stairs.

"Shaw! Ready to go?" Schlenker asked. "Mrs. Clary has some breakfast here for you, and then we can grab our things and get going."

They took a taxi from Schlenker's residence to the train station across the city, skirting the Government Spire at one point. The train station was an open, almost airy structure, built from curved steel beams and buttresses with brightly polished copper plates riveted together into the walls and ceilings. It was shaped like a long half-cylinder, with the beams forming ribs overhead. The place was lit entirely by gas lamps, which threw their warm glow across the copper of the arched walls. Shaw felt like he had stepped inside a gigantic copper whale (though the effect was lessened somewhat by the fact that the whale contained a number of steaming, smoking locomotives and hundreds of people).

Shaw looked at one of the locomotives closely, since he hadn't been near an actual steam-powered locomotive since he was a child visiting a historic Old West town with his parents. This one looked very similar to the ones Shaw remembered from the surface. It was made of steel, with all manner of pipes and mechanisms, but this engine was quite streamlined and looked as though it could go very fast. Perhaps dangerously fast. The outer surface reminded him of the stylized retro-futuristic look of the 1930s and 1940s. The only detail that struck him as odd was that the engine had two sets of drive wheels; one smooth set rested on the tracks, and the other set, overtop of and slightly raised above the smooth set, was toothed, like gigantic gears or cogwheels.

While looking closely at these giant gear wheels, he noticed that all the wheels on the train cars had outrigger wheels that ran along the sides of the track, under the top flange that formed the wearing surface of the rail. It reminded Shaw of roller-coaster wheels, but he assumed they were just to prevent derailment in the event of an earthquake or something like that.

They purchased two tickets from the booth (Spall merely showed his Secret Service badge and was permitted to go wherever he wished as a government agent) and stepped into the beautifully decorated first-class carriage. As with most things in the underground, Shaw noted that there was almost nothing made from wood or paper. One gentleman had a beautiful walnut walking stick, and a nurse with a well-to-do baby was feeding said baby with a carved wooden spoon. The reversal of things between the surface and the underground was amusing; a wooden spoon was a sure sign of wealth in the underground, whereas a silver spoon was as common as rock.

The interior of the train car was laid out just as any on the surface Shaw had seen. A narrow hallway ran the length of the coach along the left side, with a number of private compartments occupying the remainder of the space. Each compartment had a door with a window to either side looking out into the hallway, with thin metal venetian blinds for privacy. Strangely, Shaw noted, there were not the usual bench seats facing each other inside each compartment. Instead, the compartments had four individual seats, all separate from one another and all facing the same direction toward the front of the train. Behind the seats were large cabinets for luggage that looked extremely sturdy and could be secured with heavy latches. Everything was made of metal, mostly darkened steel or polished aluminum, with beautiful flowery engraving and gold inlay work adorning the compartment doors. Shaw did a double take when he realized that the wallpaper in the compartments was actually made of thin metal with this same engraving work. There were some plastic items here and there, but still no wood or paper.

They took their seats, which, Shaw noted, were upholstered with leather rather than the usual finely spun metal wire cloth. They were amazingly comfortable. Shaw had noted many differences inside the train cars; however, he was curious about the locomotive itself.

"Schlenker, I noticed that the engine has two sets of drive wheels. There's the usual track wheels, but what are the big gear wheels for? It doesn't look like they're even touching anything."

Schlenker looked amused. "Ah, those are for another part of the journey. They engage a special track further on when the grade gets too steep."

They waited several more minutes for the train to depart as the last few travelers rushed into their respective cars and found their seats. Soon the platform conductor blew his brightly polished silver whistle and shouted out the last call for their train. Shaw could feel a slight vibration as the engine began to build up a head of steam. After a few seconds, a loud steam whistle blew on the engine, and they began to move down the track, building up speed quickly. Shaw smiled.

"So, what did the locomotive just say?" He asked.

Spall gave Shaw a look with one eyebrow raised in concern. "Do locomotives talk on the surface? They don't seem to have picked that up down here." Spall then returned his attention to the daily news, which, like everything else, was printed on thin sheets of metal.

**173**

The first part of the journey went smoothly uphill, meandering between giant stalagmites and occasionally going through a tunnel in the jumbled, craggy cavern floor. Shaw glanced out the window of their compartment from time to time and could see they were steadily approaching the wall of the cavern. The green glow from Echo City's quake shield was growing fainter, showing fewer and fewer buildings the closer they got to the wall. After a half hour or so, the train began to slow as it neared the side of the cavern, eventually stopping at a small way station with a hamlet of stone houses nearby. A few people disembarked from the train, and a few more stepped aboard while myriad strange sounds came from the locomotive. Shaw looked out the window ahead and was bewildered to discover that there didn't seem to be any tunnel in the cavern wall. Instead he could see what looked like a well-lit bridge in the distance, but it was difficult to tell what was odd about it without a closer look. His questions died on his lips as a female voice with a German accent sounded hollowly through the train compartment, emanating from polished brass gramophone horns at both ends of the car.

*Attention, please, all passengers. We will shortly be starting the vertical portion of the rail line. Please conclude any visits to the lavatories and secure your belongings immediately, and do not forget to fasten your safety belts. A rail officer will be along in ten minutes to ensure that all passengers and property are secured. Thank you very much for choosing Inter-Cavern Rail.*

The message was then repeated in German, French, Swahili, and Mandarin Chinese as other passengers could be heard hurrying back to their seats.

Shaw looked over at Spall and Schlenker, the agitation showing clearly on his face. "She said vertical. We're going up the side of the cavern?" he asked, feeling his breathing and heart rate speeding up.

Spall reached into the seat cushions and extracted a braided-steel safety belt, which he fastened around his waist as Doctor Schlenker did the same. Schlenker looked back at Shaw and smiled again.

"Yes, we will be climbing more than eleven hundred meters on the cliff face before we enter the tunnel to our destination. It is rather thrilling."

"Is that what those big gear wheels on the engine are for?"

"Absolutely. The track wheels are retracted up into the locomotive, and the gear wheels are lowered onto toothed tracks set in the stone wall. The steam boiler is even built to pivot through ninety degrees so it can continue to run properly while in the vertical. The entire process of switching the locomotive over takes only a few seconds; the reason we have stopped here is for passengers. The entire locomotive design is quite fascinating."

Shaw wasn't sure if it was fascinating or terrifying. Since his fall into the underground, he had experienced momentary flashbacks of the incident, which gave him vertigo and an intense fear of heights. He managed to locate his safety belt in the seat and hastily secured the buckle. He had gone quite pale and a cold sweat had broken out on his forehead. Schlenker noticed and patted Shaw on the arm.

"You needn't be afraid of anything. The rail line is perfectly safe. It's not even truly vertical, to be honest."

"Yes, it's only seventy-seven degrees, a full thirteen degrees off true vertical," Spall piped up, still reading his metal newspaper as though unconcerned with the thought of traveling vertically (or nearly so) up a cliff for more than a kilometer.

"Oh good, seventy-seven degrees. That's a lot better than ninety. Glad I checked. I was wondering why all the seats in the train were facing forward." Shaw was already gripping his armrests, his knuckles turning white. He then realized why the train cars had the outrigger wheels. It would be an eventful (though short) trip if one or more of the cars came off the tracks at such an angle.

In the narrow corridor outside their compartment, several stewards were seen hustling their tea trolley back to the galley in preparation for the trip up the wall. A rail official entered the compartment; checked their tickets, safety belts, and belongings; and left to complete his duties. Another minute went by, then the locomotive whistle sounded before the train began to lumber forward toward the cavern wall. Shaw was not inclined to joke about the whistle this time.

The ride was noticeably less smooth on the toothed rails. There was a vibration running through the train that increased in frequency as they built up speed. After a short distance the locomotive reached the structure Shaw had seen from the window, which turned out to be a gently curving transition between the two portions of the track. The rail company had built a large curved ramp, which acted as the bridge between the horizontal and the vertical.

Within seconds, the first-class car had joined the locomotive on its upward voyage, and Shaw felt as though he was gradually rolling onto his back as gravity changed directions. He closed his eyes and tried to pretend he was not in a nineteenth-century-era steam locomotive that was propelling him almost straight upward at forty kilometers an hour, leaving the lighted areas of the cavern behind.

After a minute, Shaw opened his eyes and looked at his companions. Spall was still reading his newspaper. *Or is it a news-metal? No, news-metal sounds stupid,* thought Shaw. Doctor Schlenker had taken out his pocket watch and seemed to have partially disassembled it with tiny screwdrivers and other instruments from a small pouch. There was already a pile of watch pieces and tools arrayed on a pocket handkerchief spread across Schlenker's chest. Neither of them appeared to be in any state of distress, as though they had made this trip hundreds of times before. Shaw couldn't wait for it to be over. The thought of the cavern floor accelerating away hundreds of meters beneath them made Shaw sick to his stomach.

"At least there's no turbulence in this thing—," Shaw began to say, but he was cut off as the entire train lurched sickeningly forward and then slowed down suddenly.

"Uh-oh," Schlenker said, his brows knit together.

Shaw gulped and looked over to see that Spall had put down his news-whatever and was trying to look out the window, but all they could see was blackness.

After what seemed an eternity to Shaw, but was actually only a few seconds, the train sped back up to its usual pace, chugging along merrily in a direction that no train had any business going to Shaw's way of thinking.

Fortunately for Shaw, the trip was blessedly short, and the train suddenly changed back from vertical to horizontal on another curved section of track. Gravity was once again acting in the proper direction as the train left Echo Cavern and entered a series of tunnels that bridged many smaller interconnecting caverns.

"What happened back there?" Shaw asked, still sweating from the dizzying ordeal.

"Uncertain," Spall answered.

"I suspect it was something wrong with the main gearbox," Schlenker offered. "I'll go ask the engineer."

Schlenker began to fold up the handkerchief still containing his disassembled watch when Spall spoke up.

"You will do no such thing. The last thing the engineer needs is to be cornered by you in the control cabin. You'll no doubt talk the poor man's or woman's ears off while you try to tinker with the controls to make the train go faster."

Schlenker smiled brightly. "I actually *do* have some terrific ideas that would make this train more efficient—"

"Which will be kept to yourself," Spall said sternly, like a parent approaching the end of their patience. "I'd rather not have you monkeying with the controls of a passenger train while it's hurtling along at speeds that could kill us."

Schlenker sat back in his chair, a little crestfallen. He opened up his handkerchief and again began to tinker with his watch as Spall started reading the news again.

Being outside of Echo Cavern for the first time made Shaw realize just how much light there was in Echo City. With the bioluminescent trees and grasses, the gas and electric lights, and the massive energy beam atop Government Spire, there were few places in the city where shadows could loom. In the tunnels and small caverns outside, though, things were different. The train passed occasional towns that emanated light and life, but the majority of the journey was lit only by the train itself.

Shaw had experienced true darkness only a few times in his life, most of those times while exploring caves much nearer the surface. The darkness outside the windows of their compartment felt so overwhelmingly black that Shaw felt like he could reach out and touch it, like it might be made of a physical substance.

*It doesn't feel like it's just the absence of light anymore*, he thought, mesmerized by the sight. *It feels like the presence of something else instead of light.* He didn't like the idea very much and buried it quickly.

The vibration of the toothed wheels lessened until Shaw could feel they were once again running on smooth rails and the gears had been retracted. Shaw released his death grip on the unfortunate armrests (the leather now sporting well-defined finger grooves) and visibly relaxed. Schlenker had somehow managed to reassemble his watch without losing any pieces or tools, and Spall was still reading through his... whatever it was called. Schlenker looked over at Shaw as he unbuckled his safety belt.

"Ah, you look much better now. I apologize for not telling you about that portion of the journey. I keep forgetting that you arrived with us via gravity."

Shaw let out a breath he thought he might have been holding the entire time. "That's okay. I'm just dreading the thought of the return trip. Will we be taking the train back down the cliff, or will there be a giant catapult?"

"Catapult!" Schlenker replied, laughing to himself.

"Cannon, actually," Spall interjected, setting aside his reading material and looking out the window at the little village they were passing.

Shaw looked at Spall with widening eyes until he saw the faintest sign of a smile creeping into the corners of Spall's mouth.

"Spall, did you . . . just make a joke?" Shaw and Schlenker shared a look and then began to laugh at the unexpected bit of humor from their companion.

The rest of the journey passed quickly, with occasional tea service (coffee for Shaw) and some conversation between Shaw and Doctor Schlenker. Shaw was getting more details of the history of the underground civilization, and Schlenker was likewise obtaining the history of the surface during the twentieth and early twenty-first centuries. Schlenker was particularly fascinated by Shaw's account of the wars and weapons of the surface world, but he was also interested in architecture, space exploration, and politics, among other things. Shaw found it easy to talk to Schlenker, with his open face and intent style of listening to every word. Spall was entirely different, but Shaw sensed that Spall was also listening closely despite the detached air he projected.

The train continued on its way through the tunnel system for several hours, occasionally passing more small settlements with bright lights and train stations. Shaw glanced out the window as they were approaching the end of their trip and noticed that he could see the walls of the tunnel.

"Are we coming into another big cavern? There's a lot of light up ahead," Shaw noted to the others.

"Yes, we are approaching our destination, called the Grand Cavern. You may want to shield your eyes."

Shaw was about to ask why when the train compartment was suddenly filled with almost blinding light. Shaw gasped as his hands involuntarily shot up to cover his face. The light was searingly bright, perhaps more so because of the unexpectedness of it. Despite its brightness, Shaw hadn't realized how dark Echo Cavern had been until he had emerged into this new cavern. Whatever the cause, this particular cavern was as bright as day. After a minute, Shaw's eyes had adjusted enough that he could look out the window of the rail car. Shaw gasped again, this time at the sight that met his eyes.

# 16

## The Grand Cavern

They had emerged at one end of a breathtakingly massive cavern, filled with trees and farmland stretching out of sight into the distance. The cavern ceiling could be seen through clouds towering more than four thousand meters overhead, and the walls stretched away into the hazy distance on either side. The far end of the cavern could not be seen; it must have been hundreds of kilometers away. A river ran the length of the cavern, meandering its way through forests and crop-covered hills. Cows could be seen grazing in some pastures along with sheep, goats, chickens, and other farm animals. Shaw realized that this cavern was where the majority of food production for Echo City happened.

Shaw opened the window of the coach, stuck his head out to see further forward, and was met with a warm, moist breeze as the train continued on its way through the farmlands, occasionally following the course of the river or crossing it on a bridge. Shaw looked upward at the source of the light and could not look directly at it due to the brightness. If he hadn't been able to see the cavern ceiling above them, he would have thought they had traveled to the surface.

"What is that thing? It's as bright as the sun!"

Doctor Schlenker chuckled. "Yes, it should be. It *is* a sun, of sorts. It was created by seven of our greatest scientists as a source of light and energy for our food production. Isn't it magnificent? A self-contained fusion reaction. You are looking at Wolf's Star."

Shaw was awestruck. He stared at Schlenker for several seconds before he could speak again. "You people haven't even got proper television, but you have an artificial star? How is that even possible? And don't tell me it was accidentally discovered when these scientists were trying to make a better mustache wax or something."

Schlenker laughed again. "No, they were working on the project for many years with little success. Then one day they solved some crucial problem and—voila! A self-contained reaction. The star has been burning for almost fifty years now."

The train finally reached its destination at a large town with a train station where the three travelers disembarked and stood on the platform. This station, in stark contrast to the station of their departure, and indeed everything else Shaw had seen in the underground, was built entirely out of solid logs in a grand log-cabin style. Some distance behind the station could be seen an enormous hotel built in a similar style to the train station on the edge of a huge lake that was being filled from one end by the river and from above by an enormous waterfall flowing through a crack in the cavern ceiling. The resulting perpetual mistbow was a sight in itself. The town between the train station and hotel was clearly a large tourist destination.

Shaw walked over to the edge of the platform and stared into the hazy distance beneath the star.

"Incredible. I wouldn't have believed it if I hadn't seen it first. Is that why there are so many huge trees here? Fifty years of perpetual daylight?" he asked, looking closer at several of the logs. They didn't have rings. The trees just grew and grew.

"Yes, the plants do grow rather quickly. We do have to shelter many of the smaller plants from the constant sunlight. They burn quickly if left in the direct light for too long, as do we."

Shaw looked around at the incredible sights and turned to feel the artificial star's rays on his face. It had been months since he had felt the sun on his face, and he hadn't realized how much he had missed it. Suddenly he felt an ache for home that was so strong it was almost unbearable. He felt alone and empty, and once again realized that he would never see his home, family, friends, or true sunlight ever again. He was forever trapped in a world with artificial sunlight under a sky of stone.

Incredibly, it was Spall who sensed the situation. He approached Shaw and placed a hand on his shoulder.

"I understand how difficult it still is for you down here. Remember that you are not alone. Take whatever time you require; we shall wait for you over there." Spall pointed over to a wooden bench. Shaw smiled at him as Spall and Doctor Schlenker walked to the bench and sat down.

Unbeknownst to them, a man had observed them leave the station. The observer, confused and worried, hurried away with his thoughts in turmoil. *How could they be here? Why? We need to accelerate the plan; we can't afford to wait another three months.*

The man, once away from view of the train station, broke into a run.

Shaw took a few moments to collect his thoughts of home, and then joined his companions.

"Thank you for that. It just . . . hit me. Really hard. The homesickness, I mean. I thought I'd almost worked through it, but I guess not. I suppose it'll take longer than I figured to get used to everything. The sun feels nice, though."

Doctor Schlenker stood and took Shaw by the shoulders. "Well, my friend, should you ever need to talk about anything, I also have much knowledge in psychotherapy."

Spall raised an eyebrow. "I'm not sure how much comfort *that* will be for him, Schlenker. You could benefit from some psychotherapy yourself."

Schlenker and Shaw both laughed as the three walked through the enormous log-cabin train station toward a line of steam taxis waiting to take the numerous travelers through the town.

Once in their taxi, Spall instructed the driver to take them to the hotel, and they set off through the charming town, passing a stone sign welcoming them to Silver City. Most of the buildings in this town, Shaw noted, were built of stone like the buildings in Echo City; however, a few could be seen that used wood. These were invariably the wealthier looking houses and buildings, which didn't surprise Shaw. Despite the abundance of wood in the cavern, it would still be quite rare and valuable when compared to metal or stone.

They arrived at the massive log hotel and walked around to the back, near the lakefront. Here, tourists could be seen in boats and frolicking on the beach in swimwear that would have gone out of style on the surface when Shaw's grandmother was a girl. Shaw found himself wishing for a glimpse of a bikini but was certain he wouldn't see one in this place.

He wasn't surprised to see how white everyone's skin was; even those of African descent seemed pale. The sunlamps in Echo City didn't seem to do much aside from producing vitamin D. The hotel workers and residents of the town could be easily picked out due to their suntans. Shaw, being the outdoorsman that he was, felt like he was almost home, though his own tan had faded completely.

Schlenker walked over to a large brass telescope mounted on a heavy pedestal fixed to the porch. Shaw and Spall joined him, and Schlenker turned the telescope to point directly at the star in the distance, peering through the eyepiece. Once he was satisfied, he turned to Shaw and motioned for him to have a look for himself. Shaw approached the lens and looked through, surprised to see that the telescope was filtered to look directly at the star, much like an eclipse viewer.

The view of the star was interesting, and Shaw admitted that he hadn't known what to expect. He could see the star itself, with a nearly invisible bubble around it some distance from the star's surface. The bubble appeared to be coming from a cone-shaped structure set into the ceiling of the cavern like a metallic stalactite with myriad cables and structures running from the cone across the ceiling to the ground. Whatever the bubble was, it seemed to be holding the star in place.

"Is that held there by some electromagnetic field? Is that what I'm seeing? Why do you call it Wolf's Star?" Shaw asked, once he had finally looked away from the telescope.

Doctor Schlenker smiled his usual smile when it seemed someone else was speaking his language. "We call it Wolf's Star because that was the name of the scientist who dreamed it was possible and then coordinated the other geniuses to help him build it. As for the electromagnetic field, that is exactly what you are seeing. The facility in the cavern ceiling generates a massive magnetic field that holds the star in place. The brilliance in the design is that the machinery is solar powered, like much of the electrical implements in this cavern, so the star is essentially holding itself in place. As long as the star burns, the magnetic field will not fail. At least, that is what was intended. Unfortunately, some developments in the past eighteen months have caused us great deal of concern, which is why we have brought you here to see it."

Shaw looked worried. "Concern. Something bad is happening, isn't it?"

Schlenker nodded. "For reasons unknown to us, the star you see is failing. At first it was imperceptible, but the solar radiation output has been reduced by almost 1 percent, and the reduction is accelerating. We have therefore been given a task by the prime minister himself."

Shaw looked at Schlenker, then at Spall. "You mean—?"

Spall interjected. "We have to find a way to either replenish the star or create a new one. We need your help to do it, Mr. Shaw."

# 17

## The Quest

Shaw scoffed. "My help? The only reason I know anything about scientific stuff is because I watched movies! I'm not a scientist, and there's no way I could be any help to you on a project like this. I wouldn't even know where to start!"

Doctor Schlenker continued to smile at Shaw. "You needn't worry about such things, Shaw. As far as deciphering what to do, I can manage that. I am, as Spall has described me, distressingly intelligent. What we need you for is your superior knowledge of police and military skills from the surface. You see, we have to track four scientists down to obtain information from them, and I daresay it will be quite dangerous. That comment by Etheridge to Spall about things getting interesting has made me nervous, and I'm wondering if the Tricians may start to interfere as well."

"I agree," Spall added. "Thus far we have had only minor difficulties; however, things have gotten much more troublesome than we had anticipated."

"You see," Schlenker went on, "seven respected scientists, each the top in their field, worked on the original project together. It took them years to develop the machinery and knowledge to build such a scientific miracle. Once they had finished their work, however, they realized that it could be perverted to become a weapon, as many discoveries have been before. Where their creation had the potential to help create and sustain life, it also had the ability to destroy life in astronomical numbers, perhaps even the entire world, if it fell into the wrong hands. So the scientists decided to hide their research; they split up their plans and calculations into what we call the Seven Fragments. And that, my friend, is where you find us. We have retrieved three of the Fragments so far from the three scientists still residing in Echo City or, in one case, from his descendants. Unfortunately, we are having trouble with the other four pieces."

"Why? Are all the scientists dead? They must all be in their eighties or nineties if they made the star fifty years ago," Shaw observed.

Schlenker looked hard at Shaw. "Of course they are all into their nineties, but that doesn't mean they should all be dead now. We live very long lives down here in the dark. How old do you think I am?"

Shaw looked hard at Schlenker before deciding to avoid the question by asking another. "So if they're not dead, why are you having trouble? Haven't you explained what's happening to the star and what you want to do? This can only benefit everyone." Shaw reasoned.

"We can't find them. Understand that they worked on the star almost fifty years ago. Once they had their success and split up their work, they went their separate ways. Three of them, Professor Wolf included, remained in Echo City, but the other four left. We have been trying to track them all down with varied success. We know that one of them, Professor Milton Chan, took a post as headmaster of the University of Panthalassa. Another, Professor Alberta Rasmussen, left for another cavern; we suspect she died there during some unusual troubles in that cavern a few decades ago.

**187**

"I'm guessing that must have been that cavern . . . what was it? Little Denmark?"

"Lille Danmark, and you are correct. She died there during the troubles; many people did. Many good people . . ." Here Schlenker trailed off for a moment, lost in what must have been a memory of long ago. He came back to himself a moment later and went on. "The third person, Doctor Wolfgang Bergstrom, we have no idea; he simply disappeared with no records that we can find. The fourth, Professor Ivan Turgeneyev, returned to his birthplace, which will cause some significant problems for us."

"Why is that?"

Schlenker paused. "He was born in Ünterreich."

Shaw took a deep breath. "Ünterreich," he said at last.

Schlenker nodded. "Naturally, we intend to save that Fragment for last. Finding Chan in Panthalassa will be difficult enough."

"What is Panthalassa? Another war-torn city?" The name sounded distantly familiar to Shaw, but he couldn't figure out why.

"No. Panthalassa is within our dominion; however, we have had no contact with it for nearly thirty years. It is, or was, an underwater city; however, the tunnels connecting it to us flooded unexpectedly in year 97, and it was assumed by all that the city was lost due to some cataclysm."

Shaw's eyebrows went up as he exhaled a big sigh. "Great. You're saying that we'll have to go there and search for this Fragment underwater. How deep is it?"

"Approximately six thousand meters from the ocean surface, but it is also underground, you see. It's a massive ocean within a cave."

Shaw's heart had begun to flutter at the thought of possibly returning to the surface by using a submersible, but he then realized that this lost city was itself cut off from the surface. "Super. I hope you've built a submarine capable of thousands of atmospheres of pressure."

"I'm halfway finished," Schlenker replied with a smile. Shaw had to quickly change the subject before Schlenker got a full head of steam and began talking about his latest ideas for hours on end.

"Great! Well, I guess we'll cross that bridge when we get to it. What happened in Lille Danmark? You've mentioned it a few times."

Schlenker looked grave. "Lille Danmark was originally settled by a large number of Danes. It was a very prosperous city-cavern, with more than forty thousand inhabitants at its peak. Many of our finest scientists and soldiers came from Lille Danmark. It was a place where they could preserve their native language and heritage, much like other caverns scattered about."

"You should visit Shenzhen. The Chinese make excellent food," Spall added.

"Oh, yes indeed," Schlenker agreed. "Anyway, two or three years after Professor Rasmussen retired to Lille Danmark, people began to show symptoms of a mysterious illness. The doctors were baffled. No signs of an airborne pathogen could be found, and it did not seem to be passed through skin contact or bodily fluids. No pattern could be found for the contagion. Things began to grow worse, and people began to die. Doctors and nurses took every precaution possible, and still people continued to die. Soon all the medical facilities were contaminated as well, with the medical staff dying of the same disease. The cavern was quarantined, with nobody allowed to leave."

Schlenker took a deep breath and continued. "The government at the time sent in extra medical personnel and scientists to try to discover the cause of the disease, but they all began to show symptoms. Eventually, the government decided that their only option was to seal off the entire cavern to prevent the spread of the disease. The military blasted all entrances shut and sealed in the remaining infected citizens."

"They just sealed them all in? That's horrible," Shaw said.

"There were very few left alive at the time. Every inhabitant had either died or exhibited late stages of the disease. All the extra personnel who had entered Lille Danmark had also either died or had late stages of the disease. Even the animals and food crops had died. What was worse, the bodies stopped decaying. Even the bacteria and other microorganisms had died. The government was terrified. They felt that there was no other option. The cavern was sealed, and the disease was stopped. No other signs of the disease were seen outside of the cavern after it was sealed. It caused such trauma to the Republic that few people even speak of it anymore. I don't think anyone is even still researching the cause of it all."

Shaw looked pensive. "Hmm. Do you remember what the symptoms were? We might have run into something similar on the surface."

"I don't recall what the physiological effects were. I will have to look it up."

"Okay. That one will be a challenge, but it sounds like radiation poisoning to me, especially if the bodies stopped decaying. Radiation will kill just about everything, including the bacteria that cause decomposition."

Schlenker considered for a moment before speaking. "Radiation . . . you may be correct. There hasn't been much research with radioactivity down here, I'm afraid. Certainly not enough to confirm symptoms of radiation poisoning."

Shaw nodded, deciding to explore that line of thinking later. "How about our disappearing act? Bergstrom. What avenues have you followed?"

Spall spoke up. "We have exhausted all his former colleagues and coworkers. He has no living relatives. The last word is that he was working at Echo University but was having issues. He was close to being terminated when he disappeared four years ago."

Schlenker nodded. "Yes, his colleagues didn't know what happened to him. He was simply gone. His office and rooms were packed into storage."

"And you've looked for the Fragment in this storage, I imagine?" Shaw asked, switching effortlessly back into the investigator he had been for so many years.

"Yes, we have seized and gone through everything many times, with no success. The other scientists we've retrieved Fragments from had cleverly concealed their information using various means and cyphers, but we could find nothing. Bergstrom either hid it or had it with him when he disappeared. If he has fallen down a crevasse or even the well, we might never find him. It happens down here from time to time, sadly. People go exploring or just wander off, and they're never seen again."

Shaw thought for a moment. "You said he had been having issues," he said, addressing Spall. "What sort of issues?"

"'Issues' was all they would tell us," Spall replied. "We had to assume they meant issues with the university's board of governors."

Shaw once again though for a moment. "What if," he began, "they really meant 'other' issues? Such as an addiction, or mental problems?"

Schlenker's expression brightened once again. "Ah, you think he may have been collapsing mentally?

"Why not? Someone that brilliant might have been having all sorts of troubles. Mental illness is more common than most people realize. Is there an asylum that we can check into?"

Spall looked strangely at Shaw. "Don't you mean 'check out'?"

Schlenker laughed. "You've told me to check into an asylum many times, Spall."

Spall's brow furrowed and he continued, purposefully ignoring Schlenker's joke. "I had checked the prison, but I confess that I hadn't thought of checking the asylum separately. I will telegram them immediately."

With that, Spall left in the direction of the front desk.

Schlenker continued, "I hadn't considered that possibility either. We have been searching for Professor Bergstrom for many months now with no success. I hope this may be the direction we required. You see? You are already proving to be a great asset to our team."

"I don't know about that," Shaw said. "Let's wait to see if my theory proves true before you pass judgment on how useful I am."

"Oh, I know you will be very useful to us if you wish to stay and work with me at my home. You will always be welcome there."

"Thanks. It's nice to have someplace I can call home for now. I will need a job to pay for my room and board, though."

"Oh, don't worry about that. Spall intends to have you sworn in as an agent with the Secret Service, if you wish. I think you are better qualified for that position than any other person in the entire underground, and it will be much more stimulating than mundane police work. For one thing, you will be working with both Spall and myself."

Shaw thought for a moment and was at once thrilled and terrified of working with Spall and Doctor Schlenker. He had seriously considered joining the Echo City Police Service over the past few weeks. Police work had always appealed to Shaw, and he knew he'd be able to do a lot of good work there with his unusual experience and knowledge.

He had also considered just setting up a shop and "inventing" things from the surface. He was already a celebrity, and he knew how a lot of things worked, or could figure them out fairly easily. He could even just sit down with one of those typewriters that looked like they could be used in warfare to smash bunkers and write out some movie plots into books. These last options didn't feel very honest to him, plagiarizing others' work as they would be, but there were some things from the surface that could benefit the underground, he told himself.

Knowing what he knew about the Tricians and the looming threats faced by the Republic, though, he just couldn't bring himself to bury his head in the sand and ignore it all, not when he could help. His honor and sense of duty wouldn't allow it. *Couldn't* allow it.

Spall was intimidating and difficult to read, but Schlenker was like Leonardo da Vinci, if da Vinci had been born a wiry German. Shaw had a strong sense that the quest to which he had been invited would be very dangerous indeed, and that Schlenker saw the danger as a triviality that could be disregarded if he ignored it hard enough. Unfortunately, Shaw's adventurous side was too strong, and he suddenly heard himself say, "Alright, I'm in. I'll help you track down the other Fragments."

"Delightful! I am so happy you have made this decision! And of course, there are many projects I am working on that you might be able to help me with in the interim. I would also like to have a closer look at some of your surface technology as well. That 'smartphone' of yours looks very mysterious indeed."

"Well, since I didn't fall down here with my phone charger, we still have some work to get it to charge up. I'm still astounded that it wasn't smashed when I fell down here. But I look forward to helping out. I'll be wanting a weapon, though. More than ten years as a cop, and I feel naked without a sidearm."

"Ah, Spall has a very nice pistol that he built himself. We could make you one like it."

Shaw thought of the massive double revolver that looked like a normal-sized pistol in Spall's giant hand. "Um, no, I don't think so. Too big and heavy; it must weigh a couple of pounds. Sorry, kilograms. I'm still not used to metric everything. The surface still uses imperial for a lot of things."

"Not to worry; I think Spall will have a suitable weapon for you, as well as a badge. Shall we go collect him and see if he has gotten an answering telegram?"

With that, they stood up and walked into the hotel. They found Spall at the front desk, standing with his usual arrow-straight posture which, when combined with his temperament suggested, to Shaw anyway, that Spall had the proverbial stick stuck up the proverbial place where one would usually be told to put a stick. Shaw smiled at the thought.

Spall was given a small sheet of metal by the concierge as Shaw and Doctor Schlenker approached. The concierge moved to the other end of the front desk as Spall began to read the telegram. Looking up and seeing Shaw and Schlenker, Spall betrayed a fleeting smile on one side of his face as he handed over the sheet. The message was a single sentence of text stamped into the thin metal:

*W. Bergstrom a patient at this facility; any further inquiries must go through head of Psychiatry, Dr. H. Slattispoone.*

All three looked at one another and smiled (or as close as Spall came to smiling).

Schlenker clapped Shaw on the back. "Well done, my friend! You see? You've brought us good fortune already! We've been looking for Bergstrom for months! We now know where to find him!"

Shaw looked at Spall. "And where is that, exactly?"

Spall, displaying none of Schlenker's enthusiasm, answered, "We are going to the darkest prison in the darkest hole in all the world, my friend."

Shaw grimaced at the thought of returning to the darkness of the rest of the underground. "What's the prison called?"

"Isolation."

# 18

## Wolf Station

"Isolation?" Shaw asked, not liking the sound of it.

"Quite so. It was aptly named, I assure you. It takes nearly a full day to get there. We will have to plan several days for the entire visit," Spall said. "But that can wait awhile. Doctor Schlenker must visit Wolf Station, the star generating facility. He has to take readings every few weeks. Care to join us, Shaw?"

Schlenker clapped Shaw on the back. "Shaw has agreed to join us on our project, Spall. I told you that bringing a pistol and badge was a good idea!"

"Yeah, I think I might be able to help you guys a little." Shaw was excited to see the star closer up, and to feel the warmth and light of the sun again. "I think I'll have to live here in this cavern from now on, though," he said, closing his eyes and turning his face to the light.

"You definitely seem happier here," Schlenker noted. "Spall has arranged our visit to Wolf Station, and the car should be here shortly."

Shaw smiled. "I'd love to see the star. How do we get there? Some big elevator?"

"Something like that," Spall answered. "Here is your Secret Service badge, and I have brought a steam pistol as well, though you may wish to select a different weapon when we return to Schlenker's. We have developed many superior firearms in the disaster."

"Disaster?"

"Schlenker's lab," Spall explained, handing over the badge and steam pistol.

Shaw took the proffered badge and gun. The badge was made of solid silver, polished brightly, and held within a brown leather badge holder. Shaw had seen many different official badges and insignia during his career, and the majority of them followed similar design features and arrangements. This one was truly unique, though. Most of the badge was circular, with thick semicircles radiating out to either side of the center, like a caricature of a sound wave. *Or an echo*, Shaw realized. The center was a flaming torch over a shield. At the top were the words "Secret Service," and at the bottom were the words "Special Branch Agent."

The pistol was shaped similarly to others Shaw had seen and used in the past, but the top of the pistol, above the grip and trigger mechanism, was occupied by three cylinders in tandem containing the bullets, like a revolver. Looking at the cylinders, though, Shaw could see that it contained only projectiles; there was no cartridge casing that would have held propellant. In the center of the cylinder was a long tube that reminded Shaw of a $CO_2$ cartridge for air pistols, which is essentially what it was. The cylinder held eighteen projectiles in three rows of six. After firing the sixth shot from the first cylinder, the pistol would switch to the second cylinder, then the third, until the entire assembly was empty. The cylinder tube assembly could be ejected completely and a fresh one inserted, reloading the pistol as fast as any Shaw had used before. He felt the weight and metallic texture of the weapon and nodded in approval. Being a soldier and then a police officer, he felt incomplete without one of the essential tools of his chosen profession.

"Thanks. I feel almost normal again. Do we have to have a ceremony now that I have a badge?"

"Not unless you wish to have one. We gave Schlenker a badge, and he promptly lost it, though I suspect he turned it into a flying machine or used it to build a device for talking to animals."

They left the lodge and found an official government vehicle waiting for them, which drove them out of Silver City and into the huge forest on the outskirts. Shaw was amazed that such large trees could have grown in so few decades. He reminded himself that there was no night in this cavern, and that most of the plants would grow very quickly with constant sunlight and no change of seasons. He wondered if they'd had to adjust the genetic code of many plants to handle the lack of seasons or darkness.

The roadway wound through the forest, and they seemed to be going downhill. Suddenly the forest ended on their left, and Shaw saw that the road was following the shore of the lake. Their route passed almost beneath the waterfall, which was deafening at close range, even from inside their vehicle. They traveled more than two hours, passing occasional farming communities and slowly growing closer to the star ahead. The vegetation began to thin out as they neared the star, and Shaw could feel the heat from outside. They left the tall pines and other temperate plants behind and were soon surrounded by palms and other tropical plants. These brought with them more festive-looking vacation communities built along the small lakes they encountered on their meandering drive toward the center of the cavern. The ranchlands of tall grasses and the fields of grain began to give way to fruit orchards and vineyards, which in turn gave way to sugarcane, banana palms, and other tropical flora. These eventually stopped altogether, and Shaw could see little vegetation other than cacti and sparse desert growth. Shaw couldn't think of anywhere in the upper world that someone could see so much diversity in such a short span. They couldn't have traveled more than three hundred kilometers, but in that distance they had gone from a temperate climate to the hottest desert.

Finally, after they had left all traces of civilization and vegetation behind and were surrounded by what looked like endless dark gray, almost-scorched rock on all sides, they came to a large walled compound nestled into a cleft in the rock at the base of the cavern wall. They drove up to a heavy steel gate, and their driver opened his window to speak into a large talking bell like an old ship's intercom. They were met with a blast of dry, very hot air from the open window, which almost took Shaw's breath away. Their driver had a blessedly short conversation with whomever was inside the compound, and the heavy gate began to swing inward. They drove into the compound and then down a short ramp into a cool underground parking area. The temperature was a good fifteen degrees cooler inside, which made all three visitors feel much better.

They followed their driver through a secure door and into a large guardroom with several guards watching them closely.

"Identification," one of the guards requested. His attitude was such that Shaw felt that even Spall wouldn't bother to argue. These guards meant business.

They handed over their identification cards, and the guard inspected them against a roster on his desk. Shaw realized that his name wasn't on the list; however, the guards seemed to know Spall sufficiently well that they took his word that Shaw was a Secret Service agent. Shaw felt almost like a criminal in the surroundings. The three of them stood in a small caged-off area surrounded by steel bars. The guards stood on the other side of the bars, watching them all closely. After a minute, the guard inspecting their identification finished checking them in on his metal sheet and nodded to the others. Their identification was returned, and they were permitted entry into the rest of the guardroom.

"You'll find your transport through those doors, sir. It's ready to go," one of the guards spoke to Spall. "You just missed the shift change, so you'll have an entire spider to yourselves. If you'd gotten here twenty minutes ago, you would have had to share it with a bunch of sweaty technicians."

"Spider? What's he talking about, Spall?" Shaw asked, starting to grow worried. "Aren't we taking an elevator?"

"This is an elevator, of sorts. It just doesn't have any cables," Schlenker said with a smile. Shaw had come to distrust the doctor's smile.

They left the guardroom and entered a much larger parking garage containing the strangest vehicles Shaw had seen yet. As they approached the nearest one, Shaw was able to take in the unusual machine.

The center of the vehicle was a large glass-and-steel sphere, held together with extremely thick riveted steel bands. Inside the sphere could be seen six seats in two rows, so three people could sit side by side in each row. The front-center seat was surrounded by myriad control levers, switches, buttons, and toggles. The seats themselves were held in a hemispherical frame that sat on numerous rubber wheels inside the glass ball. It looked as though the entire crew compartment was able to spin around inside the ball in any direction. From the ball radiated four large articulated steel legs at regular intervals. Each leg was jointed and contained numerous gears and pistons, suggesting that they could be operated to move and bend in almost any direction. The legs themselves were coiled up in a large cage-like fashion with a good space between them and the glass, completely surrounding the spherical crew compartment like a protective enclosure. At the end of each leg was a large flat steel foot with huge coils of copper wire fastened on top. A short way up from each foot was a giant set of retracted steel pincers that looked quite aggressive. The entire effect, with the legs extended, was of a monstrous metal spider with four legs and a single body fragment. Shaw didn't like the thought of where they would be taking it.

"That would be a spider, Shaw," said Schlenker. "Though it is something of a misnomer, as it scarcely resembles an actual member of the class Arachnida, order Araneae. It would require two more pairs of legs and a second component to the crew cabin to resemble the opisthosoma, or abdomen. The current crew cabin only resembles the cephalothorax—"

"Yes, I am certain Shaw can clearly see it does not resemble an actual spider, Doctor," Spall interrupted. "I am also certain that had he wished for a lecture on the anatomy of spiders and how they do not resemble a vehicle of the same name, he would have asked a question along the lines of 'May I please have a lecture on the anatomy of spiders and how they do not resemble a vehicle of the same name.' Not that I would expect any rational person to do so. Shall we proceed?"

Schlenker, seeming to either not notice or not care about Spall's brusque manner, began pointing out how the spider machine's legs had too many joints in them when compared to a true spider, while Shaw and Spall opened one of the glass-and-steel panels and entered the sphere. Schlenker got into the vehicle after them, still rattling off random facts about various spider species and how they differed from one another and, of course, the vehicle in which they sat.

"He really doesn't give up, does he?" Shaw asked Spall.

"Not usually. The trick is to get him to talk to someone else while you take a nap."

"I'll keep it in mind. So we're going to ride this thing all the way up to the star?"

"Absolutely. Many of our caverns and cave systems were initially discovered and explored via spiders. They were developed by several of the first engineers to settle in the caverns. They enable us to explore walls and ceilings and any other rough terrain."

"How do they work?"

"Well, simple motion in one direction is controlled by the two main levers here. To turn, pull back on one and push with the other; the legs will slow on the pull side and quicken on the push side. Most leg functions are automatic, and they move in diagonal pairs."

"No, I mean how do they cling to the wall? Those big claws?"

"Yes, the claws may be activated and the legs operated independently for climbing when there is no spiderway."

"Spiderway?"

"Like a roadway, but made of steel for the spiders to travel on. When the claws are not engaged, the large feet you can see are electromagnets. They cling to the steel surface of the spiderway and allow us to travel quickly up cavern walls and ceilings. The electromagnetic feet are also automatic, and the power engages as the foot is coming down. Once the foot is coming up, the power disengages and releases the foot from the spiderway surface. The cabin is on rollers and will adjust itself so that we will always be sitting level with the ground, regardless of the position of the rest of the vehicle."

"Sounds terrific. So we'll be clinging to a sheet of steel that's been bolted to the cavern wall and ceiling with nothing else to keep us there but four electromagnets?"

"Quite so."

"I don't really like heights."

"You had mentioned that. Incidentally, much of the time while moving, the spider is clinging to the wall with only two electromagnets. In my experience, the best way to get over your fears is to meet them head-on."

"I'd rather not meet a three-kilometer drop if I can avoid it."

"There is nothing to fear. Every system in the spider is tripled. If one circuit fails, another takes over. And should all three redundant systems fail, the spiders are designed to withstand a catastrophic crash."

Shaw's eyes widened the longer Spall talked, and he swallowed hard. "How is that?"

Schlenker, finally realizing that nobody was listening to his riveting lecture on spider anatomy and their presence in the fossil record, joined the conversation. "Ah, the legs are built under extreme tension. If the power fails, the legs will automatically snap into the protective cage around the crew compartment, as you see here. They have dropped spider vehicles from over five thousand meters, and there was no damage to the crew compartment."

Shaw still looked horrified. "Was there damage to the crew?"

Schlenker thought for a second. "Well, all the parts were there. Perhaps not exactly as their owners had started out with them—"

"Oh, good. That makes me feel better. These things are electrical? No steam?" he asked, noticing the lack of bulky boilers and generator.

"Totally electric," Spall continued. "Fuel tanks and boilers are too heavy to make a steam-powered spider. Batteries and motors are much lighter and require less maintenance."

"How long can they go on a full charge?"

"Long enough. Buckle your safety belt; we're moving."

With that, the spider began walking forward in a surprisingly smooth and graceful motion with Spall at the controls. The crew compartment was subjected to a calm rocking motion as they built up speed, a fact that calmed Shaw somewhat. They drove the spider up a long ramp and out a large overhead door that shut silently behind them, sealing the heat of the scorched desert out of the parking garage. Spall turned a large knob on the steel dashboard, and they were met with a gentle flow of cool air from vents under their seats.

"Air-conditioning? Am I ever grateful you've discovered that!" Shaw said.

"Yes, artificial cooling is a modern convenience we enjoy," Spall explained. "Much of the time in the caverns, it is unnecessary; however, here under the heat of Wolf's Star it is essential. Otherwise we would slowly roast to death inside this four-legged fishbowl."

They traveled a short distance away from the compound and approached the tumbled rocks that marked the transition from the cavern floor to the cavern wall. Shaw could see that a wide swath had been cut through the rocks ahead, forming a smooth transition over which massive steel plates had been bolted. The plates made a straight roadway, which curved smoothly upward along the cavern wall and disappeared into the hazy distance above as it approached Wolf Station, three kilometers overhead. Shaw's stomach turned.

The spider continued forward and quickly began to scramble up the cavern wall. Their progress slowed only minutely, and Shaw was impressed (and a little terrified) at how quickly the ground was falling away below them. The crew compartment had noiselessly adjusted itself so that they were still sitting comfortably horizontally, while the spider was clambering nearly vertically.

"So how long will it take us to get to the top?" Shaw asked, curiosity and terror both fighting for dominance.

"We will usually be traveling for only ten minutes or so," Schlenker answered. "The top speed of this particular spider is nearly forty kilometers an hour, but it is much less in a full vertical climb, and there is no rush. The faster we go, the more energy we drain from the battery. There is no need to waste power."

Shaw swallowed and focused on the view directly ahead, which consisted of sheets of polished steel traveling quickly downward. After a few minutes, he could feel the spider slowly transitioning from vertical travel back to horizontal. The only problem Shaw could see was that their horizontal travel was using steel plates *above* them. He would have much preferred to have stayed on the bottom of the cavern rather than the top. Not for the first time since his fall, Shaw was feeling that there were some very good reasons for humans to remain on the ground, not the least of which was the fact that once away from the ground, humans tended to return to it with a somewhat terminal finality.

Their steel path along the ceiling was mainly straight, with occasional meanders around stalactites and other rough formations. After what seemed like an eternity to Shaw, Spall slowed their progress. Looking ahead, Shaw could see another spider crawling along the ceiling toward them. They seemed to be coming at top speed.

"Blasted station workers," Spall said. "They have been told to stop racing these vehicles several times. They used to have contests to see which driver could make it to the top or bottom in the shortest time."

"Are they going to hit us?" Shaw asked, his anxiety getting the better of him.

"No, there is enough room on this section of the spiderway for us to pass. I will have to say something to their superiors when we get back to the bottom."

Shaw watched the oncoming spider as it neared them. It had three workers in gray coveralls inside, and they seemed unconcerned with the approach of the agents' vehicle. They didn't slow at all, and made no attempt to swerve out of the way. Spall slowed their progress and pulled as far to the side as he could without having to engage the claws and grab the rocks protruding on the side of the spiderway. The other spider continued onward, and Shaw held his breath as it became clear that they were going to collide head-on. Suddenly the oncoming spider clambered over their own vehicle, using its electromagnetic feet to grab their spider rather than the spiderway. Spall uttered a few choice words under his breath as the offending spider continued unimpeded along the spiderway, now diminishing behind them toward the ground.

"What in the world do those half-wits think they're doing?" Schlenker asked to nobody in particular. "They could have killed us!"

"Most certainly," replied Spall. "I shall definitely say something to their superiors. They will be fortunate to still have their jobs when I'm finished."

Shaw finally let his breath go when he realized he had forgotten to start breathing again after their near-collision. He looked back behind them to see the other spider still rambling its way at top speed toward the ground. It was a tiny speck at this distance. Shaw felt a sense of unease when he thought of the spider that had climbed over theirs. He had expected to see expressions of delight on the faces of the workers inside the capsule; instead, he had seen only a look of pure concentration and determination on the face of the other driver. It was as though he was just doing his job. *Strange. They didn't have the expressions of thrill-seekers*, he thought. Turning around, Shaw could see that they were nearly at their destination. Wolf Station was a large facility clinging to the cavern ceiling like a gigantic barnacle, which shape it resembled. It was circular, tapering outward as it approached the ceiling like a broken-off stalactite. Three stories of the facility protruded from the ceiling, with the Wolf's Star field generator on the bottom. At this distance, Shaw could feel the heat from the star and wondered how hot it really was outside. Schlenker must have been reading his mind, because he suddenly spoke up.

"You may find this interesting, Shaw. Outside right now, the air temperature will be roughly four hundred degrees Celsius. If we were to come much closer, parts of the spider would begin to melt."

"Is that why we're heading for that tunnel?" Shaw asked, indicating a long metal tube attached to the ceiling, the entrance of which they were now approaching.

"Indeed so. The tunnel you see runs for five hundred meters into the station. It protects the spiders from the worst of the heat as they get near the station. The entire station had to be made from the same heat-resistant alloy, and then covered in a ceramic fiber coating. The area immediately above the Star itself withstands more than five thousand degrees on a constant basis."

As Schlenker continued with his lecture, they entered the spider tunnel, which caused a sudden decrease in the temperature inside their cabin and simultaneously made them all blind. The tunnel itself was a simple semicircular tube fastened to the cavern ceiling. There were no windows or openings, and Spall had to turn on the spider's lights so they wouldn't hit the side of the tube. Shaw had gotten used to the intense heat and light of the artificial star as they had approached it, and now that they were shielded from both, Shaw felt disoriented, blind, and cold.

Their trip took another minute, and then they reached the outer wall of the station. A set of large automatic doors slid open noisily on huge gears as they approached. Once the doors were fully open, Spall guided their vehicle into the large circular opening. Spall activated a few buttons and flipped several levers, and their spider began to spin around inside the tube, finally finishing with the entire spider moving along the floor of the tube rather than the ceiling. The tube ended inside a big garage area with two other spider vehicles resting in their curious coiled-up fashion in parking stalls along the far wall. They were inside the top floor of the station itself, evidenced by the stone ceiling of the cavern forming the roof of the garage.

"Hmm. I was expecting a larger welcoming committee," Spall mused.

"How large were you expecting?" Schlenker asked.

"Well, larger than the one we have."

"Anything is larger than zero," Shaw noted. "Should we be concerned?"

"Yes. This is most unusual."

"Perhaps they're having some technical difficulties? They just had a change in shifts," Schlenker added helpfully.

"We shall see," Spall said, his eyes narrowing in suspicion.

Spall parked their spider and folded the legs up in their strange manner that reminded Shaw of a pad of coarse steel wool. Once the spider was powered down, Spall opened the hatch to exit and immediately reached down to his holster, drawing out his enormous double revolver.

"What is it, Spall?" Shaw asked, following suit and drawing his own pistol.

"I smell gunfire."

"Well then I was correct. They are having technical difficulties," Schlenker said as they exited their spider. To Shaw's surprise, Schlenker had also produced a pistol from somewhere.

"I suspect their difficulties may have ended rather abruptly, Doctor. Quickly, now."

Spall led the trio away from the spider. Shaw could hear the metal on the legs clicking as it cooled; they must have been hot enough to fry eggs on at least. He made sure not to touch any part of the vehicle's exterior as he began to scan the large room for danger. They made their way to a stairwell that led downward into the next level of the facility. The second level seemed to consist mainly of crew quarters and common areas. Shaw wondered how long a shift lasted here. It wasn't exactly an easy place to get to.

They turned a corner and found the crew dining area, which was littered with debris. Broken dishes and cutlery were strewn about the floor, but Shaw's eyes were immediately drawn to the two bodies on the floor. They had been shot several times, with a final shot into each victim's head. They were dressed in the same gray coveralls the workers in the other spider had been wearing.

Everything suddenly made sense to Shaw.

"That's why they were in such a hurry. Those in the other spider. They did this."

Spall looked at Shaw. "The control room. Now!"

The trio exited the dining area with their guns still drawn and made their way through the crew quarters to the next stairwell. Following the stairs downward, they came to a room that covered the entire bottom floor of the station. It was notably smaller than the top floor, owing to the station's tapered upside-down cone shape. Here they found four more bodies lying on the floor. Each one had been shot several times, with the same final shot to the head at close range.

"Doctor, is the star in any danger?"

"Not that I can see, Spall. Everything is as it should be."

"You mean, aside from the dead bodies?" Shaw asked. "Or is that normal?"

Spall gave Shaw a look, then began to search around the room and among the bodies, checking for signs of a pulse in any of the victims.

Shaw looked around the room, and was surprised to see that nothing looked damaged. The circumference of the room was taken up by slanted consoles with numerous switches, dials, and lights, which would have looked at home in a nuclear power plant. Above the consoles were thick, darkly-tinted panes of what must have been extremely heat-resistant glass. The center of the room had a few more consoles surrounding a central pillar made up of massive cables and pipes leading down into the floor toward the star generator beneath their feet.

"Mr. Shaw," Spall called urgently to him from the other side of the pillar. "What does this look like to you?" he asked, indicating the pillar. There was a large device strapped to it that had clearly been put there in a hurry. The device was strange to Shaw, but there was no mistaking its purpose when he could hear the sound coming from inside it.

"I think, Mr. Spall, that this would be a very large bomb. And it's ticking."

# 19

## The Attack on Wolf Station

"Can you disarm it?" Spall asked.

"Uh, I don't know. I don't even know what kind of explosives you people use down here. If you hadn't pointed this thing out to me, I wouldn't have guessed that it wasn't supposed to be here!"

"Well, we need to try. Let me know what you need."

Shaw took a breath and holstered his weapon. The bomb was housed inside a large metal case that had been strapped to the central pillar with aluminum bands. To look at the workings of the device, he would have to remove the bands so he could open it.

"I need something to cut the bands. I have to get inside it."

Spall wordlessly left the room and headed up the stairs. Shaw spent the intervening minutes examining the exterior of the device. The housing was nothing more than a heavy aluminum toolbox with regular metal clasps. There didn't seem to be any external wires or booby traps that Shaw could see, leading him to think that the people who had set the device hadn't intended for anyone to get there in time to try disabling it. He wondered how long they had left on the timing device he could hear inside, ticking away what could be the last few minutes, perhaps seconds, of their lives. Spall returned a short time later with a large cutting tool from the garage. It resembled a heavy angle grinder, but much larger and sporting a thick metal cutting disc. Shaw had seen one in Schlenker's workshop, but this one displayed heavy use and wasn't on a bench covered in half-finished projects.

"Hold the device, Shaw. I will have it free in moments," Spall said as he powered up the cutting tool.

Shaw held the device as Spall used the tool to slice through the thick bands. Suddenly the device was free, and Shaw was amazed at the weight of it. He gently lowered it to the ground, avoiding setting it in a pool of blood from one of the unfortunate workers. Spall set aside the cutting tool and approached the device slowly as Shaw began to open the case.

Shaw could feel himself perspiring and the old-familiar rise in his pulse from his army days. There was always that bit of uncertainty when dealing with anything that was supposed to explode and, for whatever reason, hadn't. As he unlatched each clasp, he examined the crack of the case with minute precision, searching for wires or trip-switches that might release if the case were opened fully. Finally, all the clasps were open; Shaw slowly opened the case, still checking for any sign of a booby trap. Finding none, he was able to open the case all the way and examine the bomb inside. There was a large clockwork mechanism on top, with gears and wires protruding from it at all angles. Underneath the clockwork mechanism were several canisters of what Shaw assumed to be high explosives. Seeing the canisters, Spall and Schlenker both drew in breath.

"From your reactions I assume this is bad," Shaw noted aloud, looking through the wires and gears.

Schlenker leaned in closer. "I looks like they used Antex explosives. Extraordinarily powerful. That bomb could destroy this entire facility, and more."

"Well, it looks like we might be in luck. The timer says we have just over eight minutes left. I might be able to figure it out quickly, if the timer is showing the right amount of time."

"Why would they set it for such a long time?" Schlenker asked.

"They needed time to get away," Spall explained. "If it went off too early, they would have had to contend with the guards at the bottom. And there's no telling how powerful the explosion would be."

"They must not have been expecting anyone else to come up here today. It's sure lucky we came when we did. What do you think the chances are that we would get here the same time there was a terrorist plot to blow up the station?" Shaw asked, tracing the wires from the clockwork to each canister.

"About one in ten billion, four hundred eighty million, nine hundred and seventy three thousand, six hundred and twelve," Schlenker answered.

"Really?" Shaw asked, stopping his work to look at Schlenker, an incredulous look on his face.

"No. I actually have no idea."

Spall rolled his eyes theatrically as Shaw did the same and returned to his work. The clockwork mechanism was intricate and much more sophisticated than Shaw had first thought. The wires were clearly a source of electrical ignition, but the detonators were concealed inside the individual canisters, and it was impossible to tell if cutting a wire could detonate the device. The canisters were sealed in such a way as to prevent opening them without cutting through to remove the detonators, and he couldn't find the source of electricity in any case. Shaw decided that he would have to risk tampering with the timer mechanism itself, which was always the most dangerous route.

"Have you much experience with this sort of device?" Schlenker asked.

"Nope. We had a lot of complex devices like this in Bosnia, but we would always just BIP them."

"Bip?"

"Blow in Place. We'd just set a charge next to them and set everything off from a safe distance. That doesn't seem to be an option here."

"Yes, I would prefer to avoid setting the device off intentionally, if possible." Spall explained. "Accidentally would be just as bad, if it comes to it."

"I'll keep that in mind."

Shaw examined the bomb for another few minutes, watching as the timer clicked its way down. Seven minutes. Six. Five. At four minutes, Shaw realized that his hands were shaking and forced himself to calm his breathing and control his heart rate. At three minutes, he stopped and stood to face his companions.

"Guys, I can't figure it out. If I had an hour or two, it wouldn't be a problem. But we're down past three minutes. I can't disarm it in time."

Spall nodded. He drew his pistol and aimed it at one of the black windows through which could be seen the glare from the star below them.

"Shield your eyes and faces."

With that, Spall pressed his trigger, firing two bullets simultaneously. They struck the window and caused a huge hole to form in the center, with large cracks radiating outward toward the edge. From the hole, blinding sunlight shot through and illuminated a portion of the ceiling. Shaw could feel the heat from across the room as superheated air began to pour through the opening. The sound of the magnetic bubble holding the star in place was an almost deafening buzz. Shaw was amazed that such an assault on his senses had been held at bay by what appeared to be a single pane of tinted glass. He had to hand it to the Inner Earthers. They seemed to know how to make glass at least as well as the surfacers. This glass had withstood thousands of degrees. For decades.

"Shaw, help me with that bomb!" Spall yelled over the sound of the magnetic field.

They closed the bomb case and picked it up before carrying it over to the damaged window. The heat from the opening was searing, and Shaw could see the metal framework surrounding the inside of the window beginning to glow. Shaw hoped that the bomb would not detonate as soon as it hit the heat. They carried it as close to the window as they dared, and then swung it forward and back a few times to gauge the distance and effort required to throw it through the remainder of the window. Spall nodded at Shaw, and they heaved the bomb as hard as they could at the damaged window. The metal case struck the hole and shattered the rest of the window as the momentum carried it through the now open window frame and out into the inferno generated by Wolf's Star. The three of them ran across the room to an intact window as far from the broken one as possible to watch the bomb as it sailed downward past the star. Even through the heavily tinted glass, the light from the star was intense, and they could see a small fireball arcing down from their position toward the ground. The bomb continued downward outside of the magnetic bubble and the star's corona before the heat got to the internal workings of the device, detonating it. It was sufficiently far from the three companions that they could barely hear the explosion over the metallic buzzing of the magnetic field below.

"Well, that was interesting. Let's fix the opening before everything burns in here, including us," Schlenker suggested.

Fortunately, they discovered that the facility was prepared for such contingencies as a broken pane of glass, and they quickly found emergency heat shields in a large cabinet close to the stairs. The shields were sized exactly for the window openings and were made of the same metal alloy as the rest of the station, with a coating of the ceramic fibers that Schlenker mentioned to Shaw. They were able to quickly take out a shield and maneuver it into position with long, heat-resistant gloves and face shields from the same cabinet. Once in place, they secured the shield with two long bars, which ratcheted open across the window frame.

The air inside the control room was still very hot, and the three were sweating heavily in their clothing. They could smell hot metal, and they all had afterimages in their retinas from the bright sunlight that had so recently been banished from the room.

"Well, I hadn't expected this sort of thing when you said we were coming up here," Shaw admitted.

"Naturally," Spall replied with his usual sarcasm. "Unfortunately, we cannot call the guard station at the bottom. Those men destroyed the communications equipment upstairs. I discovered everything smashed while you were working on that device."

"Why would they have smashed the comms equipment and left the rest of the controls?" Shaw asked.

"They must have been worried that smashing the controls would have caused a catastrophic event. They wanted to be well away before destroying the star in case there was a larger reaction. Smashing the communications equipment was just insurance, in case they might have missed a member of the crew here, I suspect."

Shaw had a thought. "Or if they knew *we* were coming here. You said the Tricians have spies everywhere. Maybe they saw us and decided to try and take us out along with the star?"

Spall nodded, considering the thought.

"Well, we must notify the guards at the bottom as soon as possible," Schlenker said. "I know that we have no method of catching those men, but we must try to get the information out quickly. I saw two of the perpetrators quite well, and I could sketch their faces fairly accurately, I think."

"Excellent. Shaw, I will need you to remain here and examine these bodies for any evidence you feel will be useful." Schlenker and I shall return to the guard station at once. We shall come back when we are finished there."

"Wait, you want me to investigate these murders?"

"I feel that you are the best qualified person here to do so, and likely the best qualified in the entire Inner Earth. You stated that you had spent time as a homicide detective in your police agency, and I have no doubt that your investigative skills and knowledge are far superior to our own."

"Okay, I see your point. I'll do what I can here. When you get down there, though, make sure nobody touches the suspects' spider."

"Finger marks?"

"Yes. Theirs will be all over that spider. I don't remember if they had gloves on. I could fingerprint this entire place, which might take days because I have no idea what they might have touched. There will be a lot fewer prints to eliminate from staff members and guards in the spider."

"Very well. Anything else?"

"No. I'll have to make myself a forensic kit if you plan to have me investigating these sorts of things in the future. I'm just glad that bomb didn't go off. This whole cavern might have been destroyed."

"The entire cavern?" Schlenker asked. "Why do you think that?"

"Well, from my limited knowledge of astrophysics, which was gained from years of watching *Star Wars*, *Star Trek*, and every other sci-fi show and movie, I can think of three possibilities had that bomb gone off. First, the star would have just destabilized and 'fizzled out.' Second, the reaction could have run away with itself; and without the containment field, it might have exploded all the fuel in the star in a massive nuclear fireball. And don't ask me how big the explosion would have been; I don't have a clue," he added upon seeing Spall open his mouth and knowing what the question would be. "The third option is that the star would have collapsed into itself like stars do at the end of their lives. It might have become a superdense. . . I forget the word. Singularity; that's it. Basically it becomes a massive gravitational point and sucks everything into it. Even light can't escape."

"You know these things from watching your 'movies,' as you call them?" Schlenker asked.

**215**

"Hey, it's just guessing. I'm basing this from TV and reading *National Geographic*. You guys had better go."

"Yes, we should be away. Come, Doctor. Unless you prefer to remain here with Shaw and help with his investigations."

Doctor Schlenker looked at Shaw and then at Spall. "I think I shall remain here with Shaw. I may be of some assistance with my knowledge of anatomy and other subjects."

"Very well. I shall return as soon as I am able."

Spall left the slowly cooling control room, heading for the spider garage. He passed the two bodies in the dining area, and made certain to quickly search the remainder of the facility as he went, just to ensure that there was nobody left, friend or foe. Satisfied, he got back into the spider and began the journey back down the long steel road.

Shaw and Schlenker, meanwhile, began to examine the bodies one by one. All of them had received multiple wounds from what appeared to have been ordinary firearms, which made sense to Shaw, as Spall had first suspected something was wrong when he smelled burnt gunpowder. It didn't look like the workers at the facility had access to weapons themselves, relying solely on the guard station below. *Going to have to talk to them about their security measures here,* Shaw thought. The guards at the bottom had seemed like they knew their business, but the three men they saw coming down from Wolf Station had clearly gotten through the security measures somehow. *They got through security and then came up here and murdered everyone.*

"Why didn't they just kill all the guards below before coming up here?" He thought aloud.

"Hmm? Oh, there are a lot of guards at the station below. Many of them would be able to mount a defense quickly, and there are a lot of alarms that could be activated to lock the guard station and this facility down to prevent attacks. Their best method of attack would have been the method they have just used: infiltrate and destroy from within."

"Who do you think these guys are?"

"They may be anarchists. We have had many problems with them over the years. Though I have no doubt they were Tricians, or at least working for them."

"Why do you think they would try this?"

"It makes sense from a strategic view. Destroying the star would be catastrophic to our food production. This cavern produces over 80 percent of our food. Our population and army would starve. And this attack was completed by highly trained people and was very well planned, even though it feels . . . almost rushed in a way. To get through security at the bottom they would have needed false identifications, shift schedules; they may even have had to work here for some time. The guards would have been very suspicious if three unknown workers had shown up at once."

"You're right. I would have been suspicious too," Shaw agreed.

"Indeed. The more I think about this attack, the more I feel that the Tricians have to be responsible."

"That would be an act of war, wouldn't it?"

"Yes, though we have technically been at war with the Tricians for several decades. This would start the fighting up again, if we could prove they were responsible."

"Well, let's see what we can find," Shaw said, rolling up his sleeves. "Once we get home, I'll need sit down with you so I can get the descriptions of the guys in the other spider committed to paper."

They continued their examination of the bodies, and Shaw began a sketch of the crime scene along with measurements using a long tape measure that Schlenker found in the garage. Schlenker assisted with some of the investigation, and whenever he wasn't needed he would sit at one of the monitoring stations and sketch the men he had seen in the escaping spider. Shaw, using his very limited knowledge of blood spatter analysis, was able to determine that most of the men had been murdered where they stood, indicating that they had either known one or more of the attackers or had not seen the attack until it was too late. One of the workers had attempted to run for the stairs but had been cut down with multiple shots, falling several meters from his escape route. Shaw was able to find a couple of bullets lodged in the heavy insulation on the wall along this worker's route of escape. He pried them out of the insulation with a small knife.

"Hmm. Jacketed lead. Looks like a nine millimeter or so."

"Yes, the most common caliber for pistols is the 9.5 millimeter," Schlenker said. "It is a very effective cartridge. I wonder why we haven't found any spent cartridge cases?"

"Tradecraft. These guys are obviously professionals. They either had equipment to catch their cartridges or just walked around and collected them afterward."

"But why collect them at all?"

"Because the spent casings can be used to trace the weapon. If we were to find a suspect and his weapon, we could fire a cartridge from that weapon and determine if it came from the same gun. The casings tell us even more about the weapon than the projectile. The casings can sometimes be fingerprinted too."

"Ah, I hadn't thought of that."

"Forensics has come a long way on the surface in 125 years."

"Clearly. Is there anything else you can determine from everything here?"

"Not really. Aside from the fact that these guys were very professional, and very cold-blooded. They just walked in and started shooting. I think one must have stayed upstairs while the other two came down here. All three started shooting at the same time. That's why those two upstairs in the dining room didn't try to make a run for it."

"Yes, I suspected that as well."

Shaw and Schlenker were finishing up their respective efforts when they heard the automatic garage doors above them opening and the unmistakable sounds of arriving spiders. They ran up the stairs to see three spiders had arrived with multiple guards from below in each. Spall was in the last spider with the guard captain, who looked incensed.

"Captain Dittrich," Spall began, "these are my companions. Doctor Schlenker you know. Shaw, this is Captain Dittrich, the head of Wolf Station security. Captain, this is Agent Shaw."

"The man from the surface, yes. Charmed, I'm sure. I wish our first meeting had been under better circumstances."

"Me too," Shaw replied as he shook the captain's hand. "Have you found out how our suspects managed to breach security?"

"Not yet," replied Dittrich, "but we will. They must have been planning this for years. We have identified our three suspects, though undoubtedly they all had crafted false identities. One of our suspects has been working here for thirteen months; the second has been here eight. The third just started last week, but we have had no warning that this might happen. They were very well connected to have falsified all of the documentation we have on record."

"That doesn't surprise me," Shaw said. "Any idea where they might have gone from here?"

"None. As soon as Mr. Spall here arrived back at the guard station, I knew something was wrong. When he informed us of what had happened, we immediately contacted the Silver City Police Service to watch for them at the train station. We also had police go to their lodgings in Silver City; if they return there, we will have them."

"They won't. Like you said, they've planned this for years. As soon as they left your compound, they will have disappeared. They've got it all planned out, I'm sure. How many exits are there from this cavern?"

"Two by rail, and seventeen by either steam car or foot," Dittrich replied. "The road here is seldom patrolled, since we're the only ones that come out here. The local police don't bother. These murderers could have taken any number of alternate roads off the main roadway and vanished."

"Well, I've been working on sketches of two of them," Schlenker interjected. "These may be of some use."

"Yes, they may," said Spall, looking at the two sketches. They were quite good. "This one with the full beard was driving, I believe."

"Yes. I got the best look at him."

"Well, gentlemen, I have an investigation to complete and a manhunt to conduct," Dittrich said. "Is there anything else you require from me?"

"No, Captain, we should be fine for now, thank you," Spall answered. "Is there anything else you require from us?"

"Nothing, aside from a detailed report from Agent Shaw here, once he's finished. If you three hadn't come here to take readings, I can't imagine what might have happened."

With that, Captain Dittrich left the garage for the lower levels. Spall turned to Shaw.

"Shaw, have you found anything useful that might help us in tracking these Trician spies?"

"You're sure they're Tricians too?" Shaw asked.

"I have no doubt. This was very well planned and executed. It was only through sheer luck that we happened to visit when we did. Anarchists would not have taken the time to plan and execute such a scheme. They generally go for easier targets with less risk."

"If you say so. No, I didn't find much that would be of use. I dug a couple of slugs out of the wall in the control room, but they're a really common caliber. Looks like all three shooters used the same pistols. No casings, though. Shows they're well trained and professional."

"I agree. I have never heard of shooters gathering their spent cartridge casings. Why bother?"

"Well, I explained it to Schlenker earlier. The casings can give us a lot of forensic evidence, sometimes fingerprints."

"Ah. Clever."

"Yeah. But policing one's brass is a very professional move on the surface, and I think it's even rarer down here. These guys are very, very good."

Spall nodded in agreement and gestured toward the waiting spider. They climbed in and secured the hatch in the glass bubble before turning around and clambering out of Wolf Station. Twenty minutes later, they were back on the ground in the guard station, Shaw practicing his deep breathing to calm his accelerated heart rate. The journey down was just as nerve-wracking for him as the journey upward had been, and he was thankful that he was once again on solid ground. This thought was tempered by the sure knowledge that he would have to ride the vertical train back down when they returned to Echo Cavern. He shuddered.

The three agents were ushered into a waiting steam car and driven back the way they had come. The journey to Silver City was long and uneventful, so Shaw decided to enjoy what he could of it without spending too much time worrying about their near disaster in Wolf Station. As they traveled from the desert terrain and into the tropical foliage, Shaw imagined that he was back on the surface, on his way to some fantastic destination. He enjoyed the heat and light of the artificial star, and the look of the farms and cropland as they slowly began to take over from the tropical scenery. Eventually they arrived back in the huge forest, which meant they were drawing near to Silver City.

Finally they arrived back at the huge log-cabin hotel, where they checked into three adjoining rooms due to the late hour. They enjoyed a meal in the hotel dining room before retiring for the night. Shaw slept more peacefully than he had in weeks, despite the stress and fear of the day.

# 20

## Isolation

The next morning, the three special agents of the Echo City Secret Service returned to the train station and boarded the train to Echo Cavern. This train appeared to be the same train, or nearly so, as the one that had brought them out of the city. The train faced the same direction as it had before, except the engine had been turned around to push the cars instead of pull. The seats were still facing the engine, meaning they would once again be facing up when they descended the vertical track. This made sense to Shaw, as he suddenly remembered their outward journey with a clenching stomach. This time they would be falling backward down the vertical track instead of being pulled forward. Shaw was visibly queasy about the upcoming journey, and looking over, he could see that Doctor Schlenker had once again pulled something complicated from his pocket and begun to disassemble it into his handkerchief. Spall had removed his massive double-barreled revolver from its holster on his left side and had broken it open to eject the fourteen large cartridges from the two cylinders into his lap. Spall meticulously inspected the steel monster, testing the hammer, both triggers, both cylinders, and both barrels before inspecting each cartridge and inserting them all back into their chambers.

Spall grabbed the barrels of his pistol and closed the case-hardened frame with a firm metallic snap. Satisfied that the pistol was in perfect working order, Spall placed it back into the holster and leaned back in his seat with a sigh of contentment, closing his eyes.

The return journey was every bit as hair-raising for Shaw as the outward journey. Spall napped for much of the trip (or pretended to, thought Shaw), and Shaw and Doctor Schlenker continued to share stories of their respective worlds.

Once they reached the top of the dizzying vertical track, the train stopped for a few minutes.

"Why are we stopping here?" asked Shaw.

Schlenker looked out the window. "Ah, we are at your favorite part of the journey, I'm afraid. They have to connect the deceleration cables."

Shaw closed his eyes and took a deep breath of the thick air.

"Deceleration. Cables." He said humorlessly.

"Oh, yes. Just imagine how fast a train this size would go if gravity's acceleration weren't countered," Schlenker said with his usual smile. "There are gigantic steel cables being attached to the back of the locomotive as we speak so the train doesn't run away on itself. The cables are connected through boreholes to impellers in an underground lake not far from here. The resistance from the impellers is enough to slow the train down, and the whole process pumps a lot of water into reservoirs for the villages we passed along the line. Quite ingenious. If the train weren't slowed down, it would go so fast the wheels and bearings would all melt."

"Plus everyone would probably die," Shaw added with the same humor he had used before.

"Very likely, yes," Schlenker admitted. He always seemed to consider life-threatening risks only after they had been pointed out by other people.

The trip back down the cavern wall was slower than their upward journey had been, but it still only took a few minutes. It was a few minutes too long for Shaw's taste, and he was relieved when it was over. He was pretty certain the leather armrests would have the indentations from his fingers forever.

Soon they had returned to the gas-lit interior of the copper whale-esque Echo City train station and were on their way back to Doctor Schlenker's mansion in his stainless steel steam-belching limousine with Copperhead at the controls.

Once they had arrived at their destination, Spall left in a steam taxi to make preparations for visiting the prison and asylum at Isolation the following day. Copperhead opened the door and ushered them into the dining room, where a late lunch had been prepared for them by Mrs. Clary. Shaw was so hungry that his mouth was watering in spite of his knowledge of Mrs. Clary's cooking, or rather his knowledge of her lack of knowledge regarding cooking for humans.

The meal was surprisingly tasty, though universally fried in oil, and once it was over, Shaw immediately felt bone-tired from the trip. Despite the fatigue, he accompanied Schlenker out to the lab, where the two of them sat and sketched out more details of the Trician attackers at Wolf Station. Hours passed, during which Shaw vaguely remembered Mrs. Clary bringing a dinner tray. He glanced at the clock and discovered it was nearly midnight; no wonder he felt so droopy. He had had a long day of unpleasant traveling and had absorbed a lot of new information in a very short time, not the least of which was the prospect of following his two new companions on a crazy quest to reignite an artificial star. Shaw left the lab and staggered into the house and up the stairs to his room, where he lay down on the bed and was asleep as soon as his head touched the pillow.

The next day seemed almost as busy as the previous one had. Spall arrived before breakfast and joined Doctor Schlenker and Shaw on their culinary adventure through Mrs. Clary's gastronomic delights. Following their breakfast, the three agents adjourned to Schlenker's lab to discuss their requirements and expectations for the trip to the asylum. Shaw, after glancing at numerous unusual weapons (and even a metal water pistol, which Schlenker inexplicably had lying around), selected his steam pistol, as it more closely resembled a surface-designed semiautomatic pistol, though the large cylinder made it feel somewhat muzzle-heavy in comparison. With the accompanying holster and extra reload cylinders, Shaw felt the familiar, comforting weight on his belt that meant he was armed and ready for action. Spall had even brought a shiny new identification card (thin metal, of course), identifying Shaw as a special agent in addition to the badge he had already received. Shaw was feeling more like himself with each piece of equipment that was given to him. For many people, once they have put on a uniform, it becomes an integral part of them, a piece of their identity.

"Well, now you are truly part of the team!" Schlenker remarked.

"A dubious honor, to be sure," added Spall.

"I'm honored to be a part of your team, and thank you for asking me to help with your project. I'm excited and a bit scared, as well. I really have no idea what to expect. Wolf Station was a definite surprise."

"Well, the first three Fragments were quite simple for us to obtain, so I am optimistic that the rest will be fairly straightforward." Schlenker's relentless optimism was infectious, except for Spall, who interjected.

"As straightforward as visiting insane scientists, diving six thousand meters underwater, entering a poisoned cavern, and infiltrating an enemy city can be. Did I miss anything, Doctor?"

Doctor Schlenker favored Spall with an exasperated sidelong glance before continuing. "Well, what equipment shall we pack? We will be staying in somewhat civilized areas this time, though

I know how you like to be fully prepared for absolutely anything, Spall. Your thoughts?"

"I always have extra ammunition of course," Spall stated. "A light source, ropes, and extra provisions are always well worth the weight. Just in case."

Schlenker rolled his eyes theatrically in a humorous impression of Spall and handed the giant a leather satchel. "Here you are, then. I packed it before breakfast, especially for you, Spall. You are quite predictable."

Spall opened the satchel, grunted with apparent satisfaction, and closed the leather straps again. Shaw grabbed a smaller satchel lying open on a nearby shelf and packed a length of rope, some of Schlenker's dubious emergency rations (Schlenker wouldn't tell anybody what was in them, but Shaw could swear he smelled fish when he opened one), and his LED headlamp that had miraculously survived both the fall from the surface world and Schlenker's dissection to find out how it worked.

"Oh, we will need another couple of satchels," Schlenker noted aloud.

"What for?" asked Shaw.

In answer, Agent Muir entered the disaster area, dressed much less exquisitely than she had been at the ball. Instead she wore a dark blue suit and flat shoes, looking very capable, and her red hair was tied back in a neat bun. She was still limping slightly, but so was Shaw, and she looked as though her injury wasn't going to slow her down anymore.

"Saoirse! I didn't know you'd be coming on this trip with us," Shaw exclaimed, happily surprised. It was strange, but he thought she looked just a pretty as she had at the ball.

"Agent Muir will be joining us on a permanent basis," Spall noted. "With the recent attempt on Wolf's Star by the Tricians, I felt it prudent to have more agents on the team. Special Agent Adebe will also be joining us; I expect her any minute.

Shaw helped Saoirse pack a few items into the satchel she had brought with her, and then an extra satchel for Adebe, who arrived a few minutes later.

Ama Adebe was dressed similarly to Saoirse, though her suit was gray and cut differently for her broad shoulders. Adebe was more stockily built compared to Saoirse, but a little shorter. The two women both had an air of professionalism and capability about them, much like Spall. Shaw suspected that every agent in Echo City had the same demeanor. It made him feel more confident in their mission.

Adebe shook Shaw's hand as they were introduced, and she inspected the satchel the others had packed for her.

"Thank you for joining this team, Adebe," Spall said, looking approvingly at the assembled group. "I trust you left the anarchist investigation in good hands?"

"Yes, sir," Adebe replied. "My second-in-command, Agent Cardinal, should have no trouble keeping that investigation on track."

"Excellent." Spall checked his crystal watch. "We have a few minutes before we should leave. Finish whatever preparations you need to."

Once they were all satisfied with their provisions, they made their way to the train station again. Shaw found himself always looking at his watch to find the time. It was difficult to accurately determine the passage of time when the light was always the same everywhere they went. The gaslight in the streets and buildings was charming and warm in contrast to the stark light from modern fluorescents, which Shaw didn't miss at all, but the light always made him feel as though it was early evening, even when it was seven in the morning. Shaw actually felt surprised that nobody in the underground had developed a new method of telling time that was removed from the surface method.

They arrived at the station and boarded a train that was traveling in the opposite direction as the one they had taken the day before. The train wasn't leaving for another forty-five minutes, so they sat in

227

their first-class compartment. Shaw and Schlenker continued their usual conversation about the history of the surface world versus the history of the underground, this time with many questions from both Adebe and Saoirse.

Eventually, their train departed and the agents settled into a relaxed discourse. Shaw and Schlenker were really beginning to enjoy talking to each other; Spall just sat and listened, occasionally asking a question or two of Shaw. Saoirse and Adebe both listened intently to Shaw's tales of traveling to different countries on the surface and how it was accomplished.

Powered flight, despite the underground having all the necessary components, had never been explored, no doubt due to the fact that there wasn't much sky in Inner Earth. True, should some inventor in the underground build an aircraft and fly it, it could get a person from one end of a massive cavern in short order, but that would be it. Travel between caverns would still be by rail or, much less common, via steam vehicle in a traffic tunnel. Piloting an aircraft through nearly any tunnel would be suicidal at best.

The trip out to Isolation was much, much longer than the trip to Silver City in the Grand Cavern, with many more stops along the way. The agents took lunch and then dinner in the dining car before returning to their compartment each time and continuing their discussions. After nearly eleven hours in the train, the entirety of which was blissfully horizontal, Shaw noted, their train eventually slowed to a stop at a long, unremarkable stone train platform situated in a wide spot in the tunnel. There was no welcome sign or mass of people awaiting the train; there weren't even any benches to sit on. There was just the platform and several armed guards with the usual extremely pale skin of the working classes who didn't get enough full-spectrum light. Once the agents had disembarked from the train, the conductor blew the steam whistle and the locomotive began to move almost immediately, as though the train itself was anxious to get away from the place. Shaw didn't blame it. He hadn't seen a less cheery place yet in the underground. The light here was coming from stark incandescents very much like the ones in the hospital when Shaw woke up. They were too far apart and cast too little light for the area, making all the shadows very long and harsh. The few guards on the platform seemed to be expecting the agents, but none of them seemed pleased about it.

A clean-cut guard wearing captain's stripes approached them and addressed Spall.

"Good evening, sir. I am Captain Blake; we have been sent to escort you to the prison to see the warden. But first I need to see your credentials."

They all withdrew their badges and identification cards from their pockets and displayed them for Captain Blake. Blake peered closely at every badge and card, checking them meticulously against a brightly polished brass clipboard with a stamped sheet of metal paper. Finally, appearing satisfied, Blake tucked the clipboard under his arm and said, "Please follow me."

With that, Blake led the agents through the platform and into a large rectangular tunnel running at an angle away from the main tunnel. They passed a small, sparsely furnished guardroom chiseled from the side of the tunnel wall. Several other guards could be seen inside the room, playing cards at a small table and telling jokes.

They followed the tunnel for some distance, occasionally walking down steps carved from the floor. The tunnel was just as sparsely lit as the train platform had been and was just as bare. It was simply a large rectangular hole cut through the solid rock, tall enough for Spall to walk unimpeded, and wide enough for three or four people to walk abreast. Eventually they exited the tunnel into a large room, also carved from the rock. This room was much better lit, and it housed a large powerplant that was attached to two huge flywheels hauling a series of massive cables.

Upon entering the room, Shaw immediately stopped dead, causing Doctor Schlenker to bump into him from behind. Shaw could feel a cold sweat breaking out all over as his heart rate increased. The entire far end of the room had no wall; it opened onto sheer impenetrable blackness where the floor, walls, and ceiling stopped. There was a partial guardrail, but most of the empty wall was completely open to whatever cavern lay beyond. The cables stretched from the flywheels on either side of the room out into the void beyond, disappearing into the blackness after a disturbingly short distance. The darkness was almost solid. Shaw immediately knew why Isolation had been chosen as a prison.

After several minutes, a large brightly lit cable car could be seen approaching on one side. There were a few more guards on board, peering out at the rectangle of light that was the endpoint of their journey. The cable car arrived, and one of the guards pulled a large lever that stopped the mechanism, halting the car. Captain Blake opened the steel door of the car, which was built of sheets of steel riveted together, and ushered the five agents on board. Once the door was secured, Blake nodded to the guard operating the mechanism, who pulled another lever, sending the cable car shuddering back the way it had come. Shaw didn't dare look out the barred window openings because he knew full well that he couldn't see the dizzying drop below them. His imagination was doing plenty on that score as it was.

Doctor Schlenker looked at Shaw, who was sitting on one of the prisoner benches with his feet on either side of a shackle ring, making an effort to appear calm.

"Don't worry about the height, Shaw. These cables are unbreakable; we are in less danger here than we were on the train."

Shaw gave Schlenker a sickly combination of a grimace and a smile. "They said the *Titanic* was unsinkable, right up until it sank."

Schlenker looked perplexed. "The *Titanic*? It must have been a large ship, yes?"

Shaw nodded. "Yes, it was the largest passenger liner of its time, and it hit an iceberg on its maiden voyage in 1912 and sank. Over fifteen hundred people died. I'll have to tell you about it another time. The thought of sinking isn't very pleasant to me right now."

The cable car continued along its route, occasionally shuddering as it was pulled over a track on a tower that held the cable. Shaw could see the towers as they went past, disappearing to one side, which suggested that they were attached to the wall of the cavern rather than solid ground below. The thought was not a happy one.

Schlenker, not to be dissuaded from what he thought of as his good deed for the day, sat down next to Shaw and continued his attempts to ease Shaw's fear of heights.

"Did you know that this is the longest cable car system in the entire underground? Over twenty kilometers. It takes nearly one hour to traverse the distance one way. Interestingly, if we were to fall, we would fall almost the same distance."

Shaw groaned and looked over at Spall. "Spall, do you know how to make him stop talking? I'm close to throwing up on his shoes."

Spall looked over at Shaw. "If you figure it out, be sure to tell me the secret. I have spent many years in search of that knowledge."

"Oh, Spall, you speak so little that someone needs to fill the silence. Now where was I? Ah! Yes, at its deepest point, the Isolation Crevasse is more than thirty kilometers from top to bottom, and it is nearly fifty kilometers long. Perhaps the most interesting fact is that the crevasse itself runs perfectly north–south through Earth's crust. Isn't that fascinating?"

Doctor Schlenker continued on with his Isolation Crevasse lecture for the majority of their trip through the blackness. He described how the pulley systems worked, how the cavern was first discovered, even how the prison was constructed. Shaw found himself surprisingly diverted by this last bit of fact. Schlenker explained that the outer walls of the prison consisted of two separate walls with a hollow space between, which carried on down into the deepest foundations. This space was filled with water, providing both a deterrent from tunneling through the walls as well as an indicator if the walls were ever breached. There was nothing, Schlenker explained, like the force of millions of liters of water to show someone there was a hole in the wall. Add the fact that none of the prisoners were overly eager to drown in their cells during an escape attempt.

Spall, meanwhile, had spoken with Captain Blake about their approaching meeting with the warden of the prison. Blake assured Spall that the warden was awaiting their arrival regardless of the hour, and that the warden would be fully supportive of their interviewing Doctor Bergstrom. The problem, Blake explained, would be the head of the asylum, Doctor Slattispoone. Slattispoone and Warden Reichert did not see eye to eye on most subjects, and they certainly did not care for each other. The warden oversaw the entire prison, including the asylum, which was under the jurisdiction of the penal system. Doctor Slattispoone had always felt that he should have full autonomy and shouldn't have to answer to the warden in asylum matters. Blake warned Spall that even though Warden Reichert might allow them to conduct their inquiries, they would still have to go through Slattispoone.

"We all call him 'slotted spoon' behind his back. Even most of his staff in the asylum. He hates it, so we do it constantly. He is a pompous, arrogant creature."

Spall grunted, which Blake took to be a laugh of sorts. They arrived at the prison a short time later, and the sight of it was quite forbidding to the five visitors. The outside was brightly lit with both electric spotlights and gas lamps along the walkways, so the entire facility could be seen from some distance. It was built on a gigantic outcropping of rock, jutting out into the blackness from the east wall like an accusing finger. The prison itself had been built from the same dark stone that composed the walls of the crevasse. It was an uninteresting cube shape, with similarly uninteresting walls surrounding the cube. Guard towers adorned all four corners of the center structure, as well as the corners of the walls. Guards could be seen walking their rounds along the ramparts with large, aggressive-looking dogs. The only other feature of note was a tall tower perched on top of the center cube, nearly as tall as the cube itself. Shaw could see that one wall of the prison was formed by the cavern wall, since the prison had been built right where the finger of rock was attached to the wall. A large amount of space surrounding the prison on the other three sides was taken up by a number of smaller buildings and what looked like residences.

Shaw spoke as he looked out the windows at the prison. "Looks like a nice place. No wonder you said it was the darkest hole in the underground, Spall. No offense," Shaw said, glancing over at Blake and the other guards.

Captain Blake smiled. "We don't regard it any higher than that either. We try to rehabilitate as many prisoners as we can; however, most of our inmates cannot be safely reintroduced to society. The original founders of the underground never intended to have prisons, but it became clear after only a few years that there will be criminals who prey on the law-abiding in any society. This particular prison is considered the worst, unless you take into account the prisons in Ünterreich. I've heard some unpleasant stories about those."

"They are not much worse than just living there." Spall added.

Captain Blake glanced at Spall's facial tattoo with a knowing look, then turned his attention to their impending arrival in an opening of the prison wall where the cables could be seen disappearing. As they approached the wall of the prison, Shaw realized exactly how huge the place was. The wall alone was ten stories high at least, and the center structure must have been able to house thousands of people. The cable car arrived in a large rectangular cutout in the outer wall, and they stopped abruptly when a guard in the arrival room pulled a lever in the floor.

Immediately, the car was surrounded by armed guards, all with large, effective-looking rifles held tightly into their shoulders at the low ready. Captain Blake was the first to exit, followed by the three agents and then the remainder of the guards. The armed guards relaxed visibly when the captain addressed them.

"Goldenrod, ladies and gentlemen."

The guards lowered their rifles and began to exit the arrival platform for various destinations within the prison. Captain Blake looked over and laughed at the confused expressions on the agents' faces.

"Goldenrod is the all-clear signal for today. They were on high alert due to our unscheduled cable car transport, so all precautions were followed."

"I assume there would have been a different word if you were under duress?" Spall asked.

Blake smiled. "Of course. And they would have shot everyone here they didn't recognize. That was why I and the other guards in the car removed our hats before arrival. It is best to be well recognized by the arrival company."

Doctor Schlenker asked, "Have you had many problems with people trying to sneak *into* the prison?"

"No, never. But I prefer to have security tight enough that we never have to worry about it. We have some very well-organized criminal elements in the underground, and it wouldn't do to allow them to break one another out of prison."

"No doubt if this position doesn't suit you, Shaw, you could probably make a name for yourself in the Echo City Police," Adebe noted. "The surface probably has a lot of advancements in fighting crime."

Shaw nodded. "There've been a few, though I never worked in the Organized Crime unit in my agency. Maybe if we have a lot of time between this Fragment and the next one I could lend myself out to the police and see if they can use me."

Blake beckoned for the agents to follow him through several security gates in the outer wall and then the prison itself, where they and their credentials were scrutinized many times. The entire building was the same dark stone, and Shaw felt slightly claustrophobic navigating his way through the maze of narrow back corridors. After some thought, it made sense that the guard corridors should be so difficult to comprehend. Should a prisoner somehow find their way into them, they would soon become lost and would be easier to catch. The agents eventually found themselves in an elevator of sorts and were transported upward into the central tower they had seen before their arrival.

Following their trip to the top of the tower, they were escorted into a spacious office, paneled in white oak that contrasted with the dark stone of the rest of the prison. Shaw was surprised to see so much wood in one place outside of Silver City. The office must have cost a fortune.

A well-dressed stocky gentleman arose from the leather chair behind an ornate iron desk at the far end of the room. He was middle-aged, with graying temples and beard. He had a stern expression, but he smiled warmly as he addressed the agents.

"Ah, you must be Agents Spall, Shaw, Adebe, Muir, and Doctor Schlenker. Very pleased to meet you. I'm Warden Reichert. I trust my second-in-command Blake here has treated you kindly?"

Spall shook the warden's proffered hand. "Yes, our trip here was quite satisfactory. I apologize for the hour of our arrival."

Warden Reichert continued to smile as he shook Shaw's and Schlenker's hands. He gave Shaw an extra hard look. "You are the man from the surface, are you not? The survivor of the great fall?"

Blake's eyes widened as he looked at Shaw, whose face reddened. He still wasn't comfortable with the fame of basically being an alien visitor.

"Yes, that's me, I'm afraid. And there's really not much that's special about me. I'm just like everyone else down here."

"I'm sure that isn't true. I imagine you must have many entertaining stories to tell of life on the surface. But that can wait for another day. I am sure you must be tired from your long trip from Echo City. Captain Blake has prepared rooms for you in the officers' barracks to make you as comfortable as possible. As the hour is quite late, I think it will be best for everyone to have a restful sleep before tackling the doctor. Slattispoone can be a formidable opponent, and not one to lock horns with when tired—much like myself, my wife has informed me on many occasions."

Doctor Schlenker thanked the warden, and the five agents were led from the office and back into the elevator by Captain Blake. They then spent a good twenty minutes weaving their way through the labyrinthine maze of the guard corridors before coming to a door marked "Officers Quarters." Through the door, they entered a large room with round tables, many of which were occupied by senior guards in various states of uniform. There were several card games going on, others were reading metal newspapers and books, and there was a gramophone playing what sounded like an old ragtime melody while one of the officers sat nearby polishing her nails. Some of the officers looked up as the strangers entered, but most of them continued with their activities. They were used to strange comings and goings at all hours; prisoners required twenty-four-hour guarding, after all, and there were always government inspectors and overseers touring the place.

They walked through the common room and down an adjoining hallway with small bedrooms on both sides. The agents were given five small vacant rooms as close to one another as possible, and after a short conference they turned in for the night.

# 21

## Slattispoone

The following morning, they met in the officers' common room, which was nearly deserted, as they had missed the early-morning shift change. They were fed breakfast, after which they were collected by Captain Blake.

"Good morning, ladies and gentlemen. I hope you had a good rest?"

"Absolutely! Your officers sleep in very comfortable surroundings," Doctor Schlenker pointed out.

"They are somewhat better than the guards' quarters one floor down, but still not as nice as the married officers' quarters. Those are outside the prison on the crevasse side of the precipice. Actual houses."

The five agents were once again led through the labyrinth to the elevator, which took them up to the warden's office. Warden Reichert was sitting at his ornate iron desk as he had been the night before, and he was having a somewhat heated discussion with a visitor when the agents were brought in.

"I understand your misgivings, Doctor, but I have a policy of full cooperation with all government agencies. These agents simply need to interview one of your patients, and I see no harm in allowing them to do so."

Doctor Slattispoone was as well dressed as his opponent on the other side of the desk but was taller and more slender. He was better looking than Warden Reichert as well, with long flowing dark hair that barely betrayed a few gray hairs. He had the same pale complexion as everyone else Shaw had seen in the underground, but his cheeks and forehead were flushed with anger.

"You clearly don't understand my misgivings at all, Reichert. If you did, you would have refused this request immediately. And the fact that you agreed to this course without asking for my approval is quite unacceptable. I'm well aware that you are in charge of this prison, and my asylum, a fact you have reminded me of many times, but when it comes to the mental health of my patients, I must have the final word. To do otherwise would be irresponsible at the least."

Warden Reichert glanced over at the five agents standing with Captain Blake, causing Doctor Slattispoone to turn and see them as well. Shaw could see Slattispoone's piercing blue eyes narrow with suspicion once he had sized up the newcomers.

Warden Reichert stood. "Doctor Slattispoone, may I present the Secret Service agents I was telling you about. This is Agent Spall, Agent Shaw, Agent Muir, Agent Adebe, and Doctor Schlenker."

Slattispoone stood and shook their hands; he was clearly not happy about it but did not wish to appear impolite. Not at the moment, anyway. He betrayed an even more disapproving look when he reached Saoirse and Adebe. He clearly had strong opinions about women in positions of power.

"Yes, we have just been discussing this state of affairs. I am afraid this entire debacle has been orchestrated behind my back, and I must insist that you leave my patients and asylum unmolested."

Spall spoke first. "I am that we cannot, Doctor. Your patient, Doctor Wolfgang Bergstrom, has information that is absolutely vital to an ongoing investigation by the Secret Service. I assure you, if there were any other method to obtain this information, we would have taken it already. Our only option is to interview Bergstrom. We would prefer to do so with your permission, but if need be, we will do so without it."

Slattispoone glared at Spall, who was nearly a head taller than he, and could see that Spall would not be easily dissuaded. "I see. And who shall be conducting the interview? Bergstrom has several serious mental conditions which I cannot discuss with you, and which prevent him from speaking in a rational manner for extended periods. He seldom speaks with anyone but my medical staff."

Doctor Schlenker beamed at Slattispoone. "Ah, that is one of the reasons I am here. I am a fully qualified mental health professional, among many other things. I think I will be able to make some sense of his condition."

Slattispoone regarded Schlenker with even more suspicion. "You are a trained psychiatrist? I find that hard to believe. In any case, as his doctor, I cannot allow this to continue. He is too mentally fragile to undergo an interrogation."

"This will not be an interrogation, Doctor. As I stated, I am a fully qualified mental health doctor, and I am perfectly equipped to ask your patient a few questions."

"If you would be so kind as to tell me what information you are after, perhaps I can be of some help. He has shared much of his past with me in our sessions; it is likely that I have the information you require. We might be able to avoid any distress to my patient."

"I am sorry, but we cannot share any aspects of our investigation," Spall interjected. "I am afraid that I must insist that we be permitted to interview Doctor Bergstrom as soon as he may be made available. If the proper authority is an issue, you may be assured that we have the full support of the prime minister himself to conduct this investigation."

Mentioning the prime minister had the desired effect. Slattispoone visibly deflated and lost a lot of his defiance. "Very well, I can see that my own *superiors* (here he shot a look of contempt at Warden Reichert) and the rest of the government are arrayed against me, to the detriment of my patient. I shall comply; however, I will be making a full report to the board of physicians as soon as I am able, and I will note every issue that arises with Bergstrom. I will ensure that everyone knows that any relapses he suffers will be your fault!"

Schlenker smiled his best getting-to-know-you smile. "Excellent! I would expect nothing less from such a professional doctor. You are a credit to our profession, sir."

Slattispoone looked like he didn't know what to say. After a few seconds he turned and muttered "follow me, *gentlemen*."

With that, he walked from the room and into the elevator, followed by the agents and Captain Blake. The elevator dropped quickly through the tower floors, then through all the prison floors, stopping in the sub-basement level. The doors opened onto a hallway of more dark stone with intermittent electric lighting casting its harsh glow. The walls looked wet, and there were several puddles on the floor along the hallway. The smell of damp was thick and unpleasant in this part of the prison. The dark walls, ceilings, and floors with water dripping everywhere created an atmosphere of a horror movie to Shaw. He almost expected a blood-spattered maniac to come around the nearest corner.

Slattispoone began talking as they followed him down the damp, dark hallways. "Here you can see one of the reasons I'm so angry with the penal system. The asylum seems to be just an afterthought to everyone, a place where they put people to forget that they exist."

"Like an oubliette," Shaw added.

Slattispoone appeared to notice Shaw for the first time. "Yes, exactly like a medieval oubliette. I'm surprised you know the word. Few people here would have known what it was."

Doctor Schlenker, as cheerful as ever, had to put his two cents in. "Ah, well, Shaw here has a lot of knowledge that others don't. He is from the surface, you see."

241

Slattispoone stopped and looked more closely at Shaw. "Of course. I thought I recognized you, but I couldn't remember from where. I saw your photograph in the news. How did you end up working for these people?" He gestured at the other agents.

"Just lucky, I guess," Shaw said, smiling in spite of the unpleasant feeling he was getting from the doctor.

Slattispoone began walking down the slimy hallway again. "If it weren't for that dratted water in the walls, we wouldn't have the leakage problems here. But of course the prison directors don't care."

Slattispoone continued his tirade as they passed through several more depressingly damp corridors and finally through a large set of steel doors. Beyond the doors was a large room, guarded by a pair of prison guards who looked as though they would rather have been guarding a bathroom at an Irritable Bowel Sufferer's conference. Inside the room was what looked like another cable car, but the cables disappeared into the ceiling. Shaw stopped dead as he realized that there were no other exits to the room other than through the massive hole in the floor underneath the cable car and a small back hallway. He was certain they weren't taking the hallway.

"That isn't an elevator, is it? Please tell me it isn't," Shaw almost gasped, his heart rate increasing as his stomach lurched.

It certainly looks like one," Schlenker helpfully pointed out. "It seems that the way to go is down."

Shaw groaned as his stomach turned over a few more times. He hadn't fully forgotten that the entire place had been built over a dizzying twenty-kilometer drop with just a finger of rock to hold it all up. And it seemed they had managed to drill down through the bottom to whatever horrifying result. The thought made him nauseous.

Slattispoone entered the cable car and turned to give the five agents a look of impatience. "This is the only way to the asylum, so if you are coming with me, you better get in. The asylum is a full four hundred meters below us, and this is the only way down."

Schlenker boarded the steel and bronze elevator car, with Spall partially dragging Shaw behind him. Once they were aboard, Captain Blake touched the brim of his uniform hat and bid them farewell.

"You're not coming, Captain?" Schlenker asked.

"The warden and Doctor Slattispoone have an understanding of sorts. The only time that prison guards are permitted to enter the asylum is during our monthly inspections. This is to prevent the guards from aggravating any of the asylum inmates. I also have a large number of duties that must be performed today, so I cannot accompany you. I will be back to escort you when you have finished."

"Which cannot be soon enough, Captain. I also have many duties to perform today, so we cannot stand here talking to you. Good day!" Slattispoone snapped as he shut the door and pulled a lever resembling a ship's telegraph on the wall of the car.

The car began to descend through the hole in the floor, and they must have passed fifty meters or more of solid rock before coming out the bottom of the foundation into the chasm below. Shaw stood as close to the center of the elevator car as possible, preventing him from looking out the windows to see the light coming from the asylum below. He thought about their terrifying trip on the cable car the day before and realized he hadn't even noticed any lights from the asylum beneath the prison at the time. Not that he had been looking really hard out the windows. Avoiding looking out the windows was a better description. The only thing visible to him was the nearby cavern wall, with a thick bundle of cables and pipes harnessed to the wall with steel bands. It looked like some kind of conduit for the asylum, carrying electricity, water, and other necessary utilities down from the prison above.

Their descent took only a minute and was satisfyingly smooth compared to the previous day's ride on cables. Suddenly their elevator car was surrounded by light emanating from electric lamps set on tall posts around the platform where their car came to a sudden stop. Slattispoone opened the door and stepped out, beckoning impatiently for the agents to follow. Shaw exited, followed by Spall and Schlenker, and they all walked to a door set into the cavern wall. The platform they had arrived on was an elevated section of the roof of the asylum building, which appeared to have been built attached to the wall of the cavern. There was very little to see on the roof, and as Shaw glanced upward he could just make out the opening far above through which they had come, as well as the outline of the rock promontory holding up the prison. Everything else was black. It felt as though they were perched on a tiny island of light in a never-ending sea of darkness.

Shaw had seen true darkness many times already in his short life underground, but this seemed . . . darker. Perhaps it was the thought that there was truly nothing else around them for thousands of meters in any direction, except the cavern wall. To Shaw the surrounding dark felt simultaneously pressing in upon him and gulping wide to swallow him into its seemingly infinite depths.

Doctor Slattispoone produced a set of iron keys, all of which sprouted very strange-looking heads, and selected one which opened the door and allowed them to enter. Once inside, they followed a narrow staircase that had been chiseled out of the stone as it spiraled down several flights to another door. This one opened onto what looked like a hospital wing, which ran along the wall of the cavern. Shaw groaned again as he realized that the entire asylum had indeed been built against the wall of the cavern, clinging to it like a gigantic steel bat. Underneath the floors was nothing but more of that horrible blackness and the dizzying twenty-kilometer fall. Slattispoone looked over at Shaw with a quizzical expression.

"Do you not like hospitals? I keep this one as clean as any you're apt to find, Agent Shaw."

Schlenker replied, "He just has little fondness for heights. I think he has just realized that the building itself is attached to the cavern wall."

"Ah. Yes, the asylum was built much later than the prison—as an afterthought, of course. Naturally, there was not enough room on the 'island,' as the finger of stone above us is usually called. So they built the entire facility down here. I suppose it is much better than nothing, and we could always be packed into the cellars of the prison, which you have just seen."

"Why was it built so far down from the island?" Saoirse asked. "I should think they could have just as easily built it directly beneath."

Slattispoone turned to Saoirse as if noticing her for the first time.

"How should I know? I'm not an engineer. I'm sure they had their reasons. Or perhaps not. Who knows with engineers and architects?"

Shaw looked down the wing of the asylum and could see many doorways leading straight into the cavern wall, which formed the inside wall of the hallway. The outside wall consisted of massive sheets of glass, which struck Shaw as funny because there was no view to be had, and the glass walls must have cost a fortune compared to stone or steel. The windows might as well have been painted black.

"How many levels are there like this one, Doctor?" Spall asked.

"We have seven complete levels; however, only six are for patients. This first level houses some administration offices, storage, and some minimum-security cells. The further downward one travels, the higher the security. Of course we run this facility more like a hospital and less like a prison. The bottom level is made up of staff offices and rooms, as well as the infirmary, where I am able to perform medical procedures when necessary. We usually house between 90 and 120 patients. Come this way. Doctor Bergstrom is on level three."

With that, they followed the hallway along the cavern wall toward a large staircase at the far end. They took the staircase down two identical levels and then followed Slattispoone to one of the doors along the corridor. This door looked like all of the others, with the exception of the stamped metal nameplate attached to the door bearing the name.

## W. BERGSTROM 34127

Slattispoone removed his ring of keys and selected a key with which he opened the door. Once the door was opened, Slattispoone's expression betrayed some confusion and anger as he looked inside.

Spall glanced inside the small room before turning to Slattispoone and asking, "Do your patients always disappear from their locked rooms, Doctor?"

# 22

# The Curious Case of Doctor Bergstrom

Doctor Slattispoone stormed into the small cell, which was furnished with nothing more than a bed slab, a sink, and a metal chair bolted to the floor. After satisfying himself that there were in fact no occupants in the room that just happened to escape his notice, Slattispoone stormed out again and down the hall toward the nurse's station. An orderly could be seen walking quickly toward them, a worried look on his face.

Slattispoone stopped, a look of fury on his face. "Henry! Where is Bergstrom, may I ask?" The unfortunate Henry had stopped just outside of physical striking distance, but close enough to receive the full brunt of Slattispoone's verbal assault. "Must I constantly remind everyone of who is in charge of this facility? Nothing happens here without my approval, especially the movement of patients! Where is he?"

"I . . . I . . . just moved him into an interview room, Doctor." The orderly stammered. "I knew you were on your way with these agents, and I thought—"

"Don't give me that! You aren't paid to think! If I had wanted him in an interview room, I would have instructed you to put him there! Now get out of my way!"

With that, Slattispoone swept past the cowed Henry, fuming. The five agents followed at a short distance as they approached a door just beyond the nurse's station. Slattispoone used another key to open this door, beyond which was a room much larger than the cell they had just observed. The room was bare except for a desk with a lamp and a comfortable looking chair behind it, and a metal chair bolted to the floor in the center of the room, with a single bulb providing light overhead. Shackled to the metal chair was an elderly man with scruffy, greasy hair and wild eyes. His skin was as pale as milk, and the hair on his head and his chin was yellowed, much like his remaining teeth, of which there were few. His skin sagged from his bones, showing that he had lost considerable weight in recent years. He was naked from the waist up, and his bare feet displayed long, cracked yellow toenails and purplish veins.

"Gentlemen, here is Doctor Bergstrom. As you can plainly see, he is not well," Slattispoone snapped, still furious over the orderly taking initiative where it was not wanted.

Doctor Schlenker looked closely at Bergstrom then turned to Slattispoone. "Yes, he is a picture of good health, Doctor. When was this man last fed?"

Slattispoone sneered at Schlenker. "He has to be force-fed these days. He cannot feed himself. As I have said several times, he has many mental disorders that make his life very difficult, and treatment impossible. You likely won't get any useful information from him. In all likelihood, you will just aggravate his condition, which means more work for me after you've gone. Now, I must leave you. I am very busy, and I must attend to other more important matters. I had several surgical procedures booked for this morning that cannot wait any longer. I trust you can find your way out when you've finished. There will be an orderly outside the room to let you out."

With that, Slattispoone turned on his heel and stalked out, closing and locking the door behind him. Bergstrom sat in his chair, staring wide-eyed at (or, more accurately, through) the far wall with bloodshot eyes. He had not moved since the agents had entered and had made no sign that he noticed anything around him. Schlenker moved in front of Bergstrom and began to perform a thorough physical examination, jotting notes in a black notebook he had produced from his pocket, scratching on the thin metal sheets with a sharpened scriber. Much like when he was working on his projects and experiments in his lab, Schlenker muttered quietly to himself as though there wasn't enough room inside his head for all his thoughts.

"Hmm. General malnutrition over at least two years. Hygiene very poor. Signs of high blood pressure and some jaundice . . . appears catatonic. Minimal response to visual and auditory stimuli. Hmm. Reflexes are good."

The others stood, watching Schlenker in silence as he made his notes. They had learned to stay out of his way when he was working. He would be all too happy to share his findings when he was finished. The real trick was getting him to stop sharing. After a few minutes, Doctor Schlenker finished his physical exam and stood up.

"Well, I've seen people in worse physical states, but not many. For his advanced age, I'm surprised he is still alive, considering the state he's in."

"What of his mental condition, Doctor? Will you be able to get anything from him like this?" Spall asked quietly.

"I'm not sure. I will begin my psychological examination in a moment. I am optimistic; however, his catatonic state is not a good sign. 'Slotted Spoon' (here he chuckled a bit) was kind enough to leave Bergstrom's file here for us, though I suspect it was the unfortunate orderly that did that for us. It gives a diagnosis, among other things, of dementia praecox, which would suggest that this poor man may have been suffering with this for most of his life."

"What's dementia praecox, Doctor?" Adebe asked. "I've never heard of it."

"Well, it's characterized by a deteriorating psychotic disorder, usually developing in early adulthood. It often manifests with abnormal social behavior, confusion, hallucinations, and a failure to recognize what is real."

"Sounds like the schizophrenics I used to deal with on the street as a cop," Shaw noted.

"Schizophrenics?" Schlenker asked with the almost delighted expression he reserved for whenever Shaw used a word or expression he was unfamiliar with. New words meant he was about to learn something new.

"It comes from 'schizophrenia.' I think it must be what they call your dementia whatever on the surface nowadays," Shaw explained.

"Praecox. Yes, I suspect you are right. It is one of the more common mental disorders. In this case, however, he appears to be fairly far gone into full dementia. Although he may be medicated as well. We need to ask."

Spall turned and knocked on the door, which unlocked and opened, revealing the harried Henry from earlier.

"Yes, sir? Are you finished already?"

"Unfortunately not," Schlenker said. "We just need some information. Hopefully you can answer some questions we have about this patient. Is he currently medicated?"

Henry looked worried. "I'm not certain I should be talking to you. The doctor is in a very bad mood today. He didn't want you talking to this patient at all."

"Yes, he has made that perfectly clear to us. Nevertheless, we must continue our examination. Has he been medicated today?"

"No, this patient usually remains unmedicated. Nothing much seems to work for his condition. He's catatonic most of the time, and the rest of the time he's completely insensible. I've been here three years, and I've never heard a coherent word from him."

Spall grunted. "That does not bode well. Do you think you might be able to get something from him, Doctor?"

Schlenker paused. "I haven't spoken to him yet, so I'm still hopeful. Please leave us for a while so that I may continue my examination."

The others left with Henry, who found them seats at the nurse's station. Spall, as was his usual habit, did not stay seated for long, opting instead to walk the length of the hall inspecting everything. He found the entire structure very curious. The framework of the asylum, exposed from within, consisted of large steel girders whose ends were bolted directly to the cavern wall like gigantic shelf brackets. The floors and walls were then hung from the girders. All the cells and most of the offices and storage rooms had been carved into the cavern wall, with the nurse's stations and assorted offices and rooms arrayed along the outside walls on each floor.

Spall was always fascinated by the different approaches to architecture in solving difficulties of construction. The only drawback that Spall could see to the construction was that it was vulnerable to corrosion. Should the anchoring ends of the girders or the fastening bolts become sufficiently weakened, the entire structure would collapse into the chasm below. As the head of security for the prime minister, Spall was always looking for weak points in everything; he simply could not turn the habit off. Spall thought it best not to mention the structural vulnerability to Shaw. He was jittery enough.

Shaw, meanwhile, had started a conversation with Henry and several nurses, after he had been recognized as the "miraculous man from the surface," as one nurse put it. He was still not comfortable with his semi-celebrity in the underground, though the pretty nurses hanging on his every word made it a little easier to bear. They kept asking him about the different places he had been, what the real sun was like, what it felt like to have actual day and night as well as the seasons of the year.

Saoirse, in spite of herself, was surprised to realize she was feeling a touch of jealousy when Shaw talked to the nurses. She was quite confident in her own good looks, but the one Asian nurse was absolutely stunning, and a couple of the others weren't too far behind her in attractiveness. She started pacing around like Spall, feeling restless and surprisingly uneasy. She wasn't as used to competition as she had thought.

Spall wandered his way back to the nurse's station after a while, and rolled his eyes when he could hear what Shaw was talking about. Rather than sit and listen to Shaw talk about his life aboveground, Spall decided to explore the remainder of the asylum. Seeing Spall wandering off, Adebe decided to join him and have a look around.

Spall and Adebe headed for the stairwell and followed it back up to the top floor, passing the occasional nurse or orderly. As Slattispoone had said, they found only some unremarkable offices and storage rooms on the top floor. One large room puzzled them both, however. This room was marked on the door as another storage room; however, the room itself was mostly empty. At the far end of the room, Adebe found a long crack in the stone, forming a sort of hallway leading down at a gentle slope further into the cavern wall. The floor had been hewn roughly to make passage easier, but the walls and ceiling had been left in their natural state. After taking out flashlights and walking for a minute or so, they found the rough hallway blocked by a large steel door, solidly locked. Both agents were intrigued and made a mental note to ask the helpful orderly about it.

Spall and Adebe returned the way they had come and finished inspecting the first floor before descending through the other floors. The remaining patient floors were pretty much identical, though it seemed that the patients (or prisoners) became more and more restless and aggressive the further down one went in the facility. Security grew stronger further down as well, with locked doors blocking each floor from the stairs. By the last occupied floor, they could see three orderlies wrestling with one patient at the far end of the hallway, and it looked like at least one cell had what appeared to be urine leaking under the door. Several incoherent voices could be heard echoing out of the cells. Spall and Adebe continued down into the bottom level.

Here, it felt much quieter than the previous levels, almost as though the sound from above was unwilling to travel down the stairs. The door was unlocked, and the hall was very dimly lit, with no nurse's station at the midpoint of the corridor. Spall felt an inexplicable sense of unease as they came to the bottom of the stairs, prompting him to draw his pistol and walk as softly as possible.

Adebe drew her pistol silently and whispered up to her superior. "What is it, sir? Do you see something?"

"Something is very wrong," he replied.

There were no more nurses or orderlies to be seen.

As he proceeded down the hall, Spall glanced into all the rooms through the open doors, Adebe instinctively crossing the hallway to provide cover. There were no cells on this level, and Spall found several offices, a staff common room, and the kitchen, but no staff members. They all seemed to be up on the other levels performing their duties. Near the far end of the hall, however, they found a set of doors marked:

HOSPITAL

# 23

## An Unexpected Attack

Spall felt a sense of dread as he approached the doors, though he couldn't explain why. Adebe could sense it as well, feeling a surprising tingling that signified a rush of adrenaline was imminent. She just knew that something was terribly wrong behind those doors.

Never one to turn away from a mystery, Spall discreetly held his pistol behind his right leg as he pushed the doors open and entered another hallway leading straight into the cavern wall. This hallway was better lit, with several gurneys parked on both sides and multiple doors leading off at right angles to the hall. Spall glanced into the first one he came to, Adebe close behind.

The room was filled with much of the furniture and accoutrements one would normally find in a doctor's office in the underground. There was the metal examination table, a steel chair nearby, a sink and counter filled with various glass jars containing assorted doctor's tools. There were stainless steel tongue depressors in disinfectant, different sized syringes, even terribly expensive cotton swabs. Seeing nothing interesting, they moved on. Several other rooms produced the same results. More examination rooms and a few operating rooms, all spotlessly clean. Near the end of the hall, however, Spall heard what sounded like muffled screaming. Turning his head, he could see that Adebe had heard it as well.

They followed the sounds and quickly realized that it was a man's scream, and that it sounded like the screamer's mouth had been covered with something. Spall approached one of the doors and could tell that the screamer was behind it. Adebe took up a position across the door from him, and he pushed open the door and peered inside.

The room was dark except for the bright lights surrounding the operating table in the center. There were several nurses flanking the table, handing implements to Doctor Slattispoone at the head of the operating table. Slattispoone was dressed for surgery and had a good amount of blood splattered down the front of his operating tunic. Spall could see why when he realized what was happening. Adebe gasped quietly.

The patient that was being operated on was still conscious.

He was covered with a sheet from the waist down, and his arms, legs, chest, and head were fastened to the operating table with solid steel bands. The patient's mouth had been sewn shut, and there was a long metal tube up one nostril of the patient's nose. The top of the patient's skull had been removed, exposing the brain, which Doctor Slattispoone was working on. Spall could see him inserting long metal probes attached to wires deep into the brain tissue. There were already several dozen probes packed into the small space in front of him, and every time a probe was inserted, the patient would convulse and scream his muffled scream.

Spall was about to enter the operating room to confront Slattispoone when he sensed a presence behind him. He pulled his head out of the doorway and saw a large man dressed in an orderly's uniform standing close with a steam pistol raised. Adebe spun around and immediately raised her left hand to knock the pistol away and heard the gun fall to the ground.

Spall raised his own pistol, but his attacker was too quick, knocking Spall's pistol out of his hand and sending it sliding across the floor. The attacker kicked out at Adebe, knocking her backward against the wall and hitting her head hard enough to completely daze her. She slid limply to the floor, doing her best not to pass out.

Spall grappled with the orderly, who was extremely strong and had clearly learned to fight people at close quarters from years in the asylum. The orderly held Spall extremely close, preventing Spall from using punches and kicks against him. The assailant began to use a free hand to deliver swift, ferocious punches to Spall's midsection that forced the air out of his lungs. Spall struck out at the orderly with his elbows, feeling a rewarding crack as his left elbow found its mark below his assailant's right eye, knowing he had shattered the bone there. The orderly groaned and his grip loosened, allowing Spall to spin out of his grasp and attack from a safer distance. The orderly's right cheek had a soft, slightly indented look, and the eye above it was already swelling shut. Spall did not hesitate. He aimed a swift kick into the assailant's sternum, knocking the wind out of his opponent. The orderly doubled over and fell backward into a vacant operating room, but as Spall moved closer to knock him unconscious, the orderly lunged at him, grabbing his waist and pulling him to the ground. Spall could tell that his opponent was much more experienced at close grappling than he was. He would have to finish the fight quickly if he was to survive, injured though the orderly was.

Spall landed heavily on his back with the orderly on top of him, trying to squeeze his lower rib cage. Spall had his wind knocked out again, and he began to strike at the orderly's temples with his hands and elbows, feeling another crack as his right elbow caused a fracture near his assailant's left ear. Spall rolled over, gasping for air and taking the orderly underneath him. Spall was no stranger to hand-to-hand combat; however, he still had to fight the panic caused by being unable to breathe properly. His diaphragm was spasming painfully from his attacker's initial assault, made worse by the sudden impact of his back on the stone floor.

The orderly's grip on his waist was starting to slacken, but Spall continued his assault, striking the assailant in the face with his fists and breaking the orderly's nose and jaw. The orderly, blood now pouring from his mouth and nose, released Spall's waist and grabbed his throat, trying to get a sufficient grip to choke him. Spall responded by reaching up and violently smashing the orderly's arms to one side, turning his opponent almost right over. Spall then wrapped a long arm around the orderly's neck from behind and squeezed as hard as he could. The orderly began to gasp and kick madly, blood spraying as he thrashed about to break free from Spall's arm. Spall held the orderly by the neck as his opponent continued to fight, reaching for anything to use as a weapon. Spall finally twisted sharply to one side, feeling and hearing a sickening crack as the orderly's neck broke. The body went limp immediately.

Spall released his hold on the orderly and eventually caught his breath. The entire fight had lasted less than two minutes, but fighting for one's life can take a lot of energy, and Spall felt like the ordeal had taken hours. He ran back to Adebe, who was still sitting against the wall where she had collapsed.

"Adebe, are you alright?" he asked as quietly as he could, feeling the back of her head. There was some blood there, but it didn't feel like she had any serious injuries. She shook her head groggily and her eyes slowly focused on Spall.

"I . . . I think so . . . sir," she said, still quite dazed from the blow to the head. "My ears are ringing pretty badly though."

"Alright, let's get you up."

Spall lifted Adebe as though she weighed nothing at all and set her on her feet. She wobbled for a bit, but she leaned against the wall and was able to get her balance after a few seconds.

Spall retrieved both pistols, since he always subscribed to the notion that one could never have too many bullets, except perhaps when swimming. He dragged the body of the orderly through a set of doors into a vacant storage room and wiped the blood from the floor with a towel from a nearby shelf. Spall was surprised that nobody had come to investigate the noise, but back in the hallway, he could once again hear the muffled screams of the unfortunate patient in the operating room. Slattispoone and the nurses wouldn't have heard a thing.

Spall quickly realized that confronting Slattispoone on his own would be inadvisable, considering that the entire staff was on Slattispoone's payroll and might react in a similar manner as the orderly whose body was now cooling slowly in the next room. This incident was clearly an ambush, and Spall and Adebe had to get back to their comrades quickly before something similar was sprung on them.

They crept out of the hospital hallway and immediately found themselves face-to-face with another orderly. The orderly's eyes widened when he took in Spall's disheveled appearance, which included blood from the asylum's most recently departed employee. The surprised orderly quickly reached into his uniform smock and began to draw a pistol. Spall was quicker. He kicked the unfortunate man in the sternum, similar to the first orderly; however, this orderly was much smaller and was sent flying backward into the wall as the gun flew from his hand. The orderly fell to the floor as though all of his bones had been removed, the fight clearly gone from him.

Spall quickly left the groaning man and headed back to the stairs, towing Adebe. As they passed the sixth level, Spall saw two orderlies escorting a prisoner to a cell nearby. This prisoner had several lobotomy scars clearly visible on his scalp and seemed to be as docile as a newborn calf. This alone wouldn't have raised any concern in Spall's mind, but Spall could also see that the prisoner's eyes had been sewn shut long ago. Clearly this was another of Slattispoone's experiments.

The orderlies were chatting about stone-ball and were not paying any attention to their prisoner or their surroundings, allowing Spall and Adebe to continue up the stairs unimpeded. Eventually they were able to make their way back to the third level, where Shaw was still entertaining the nurses and orderlies with his tales of the surface. Shaw stopped talking when he saw Spall's expression, as well as his disheveled state and Adebe's condition. The blood on Spall's shirt certainly commanded attention.

"Muir, get Schlenker," Spall said.

Henry gave Spall a puzzled expression. "Where did you two just come from? Weren't you here the entire time?"

Spall fixed the orderly with a piercing gaze. "No, we took a trip to the hospital. We're leaving. Now." Here he directed his gaze at Shaw, who stood and moved for the interview room door. "I suspect your boss will have a few words for you when he learns that you failed to stop us from looking around."

Henry turned even paler than he already was and moved a discreet distance away as Spall took Henry's key ring and eventually opened the door to the interview room. Spall watched the small group of nurses, while Saoirse looked in to see Schlenker sitting in the chair opposite Doctor Bergstrom.

"Ah, Miss Muir. I was just about to get all of you. I've made a perplexing discovery with our friend here."

Shaw entered the room, looking even more confused than he felt. "I think Spall has made a discovery as well, and we have to leave. Now. I hope you got what you needed from Bergstrom here."

"I wish that were so. You see, this is not Doctor Bergstrom. I believe Doctor Bergstrom is dead."

# 24

## Tricians Revealed

"Dead? How?" Saoirse asked.

"I will have to explain later. If Spall says we must go, it would be wise to go at once."

With that, Schlenker grabbed his coat and notebook and they left the interview room. Spall grabbed Schlenker by the arm as they hurried toward the stairs.

"Well, Doctor. What did you find out?"

"Unfortunately, not a thing. The man I was attempting to interview was not in fact Doctor Bergstrom."

Spall grunted. "I cannot say I'm surprised. How did you discover that?"

"Well, certainly not from speaking with him. The man, whoever he was, was as aware of his surroundings as a side of beef. It was my physical examination that showed me who, or rather what, he was."

They had reached the stairs and were now hurrying toward the top level. Both Spall and Shaw were checking behind them at intervals, and they could see Henry and a couple of nurses following at a distance.

"And what was he?" Spall asked Schlenker.

"He was a miner for most of his life. He had a drill callus on his left hand. And I know that Doctor Bergstrom, the *real* Doctor Bergstrom, would never have held a mining implement in his life."

Spall nodded in agreement. Miners and all members of the Miners Guild were well respected in the underground, but it was still heavy, dirty work. And most miners used a heavy pneumatic drill for a lot of their work, the design of which caused a noticeable callus on the left hand at the base of the pinky finger. Schlenker was right. A respected scientist, a genius like Bergstrom would never have had to work as a driller.

"Well, that explains your discovery. Now I shall tell you mine. Slattispoone is experimenting on his patients. I watched him inserting metal probes into a man's brain down in the 'hospital' on the bottom level. The patient's mouth had been sewn shut, and he was trying to scream."

"The patient was still conscious?" Shaw asked.

"Unfortunately so. Adebe and I were about to confront Slattispoone when we were attacked by an orderly with a pistol. Fortunately I was able to convince him that attacking us was a bad idea."

"You killed an orderly?" Schlenker asked.

"He was trying to kill us," Spall noted. "He knocked Adebe into the wall; she's not badly injured, just quite dazed."

"Point taken," Schlenker admitted.

They had reached the top level and were approaching the exit door when shots began to buzz past them, striking the far wall. The four agents dove for cover in an alcove beside a cell door. Fortunately the cell doors were set into the wall a short distance, providing some cover. Spall drew his own pistol and took a quick glance around the corner. He could see three orderlies standing near the exit door with pistols drawn. One of them took aim and fired as Spall looked around the alcove, narrowly missing him. Spall turned to Shaw and Saoirse.

"Three of them. All armed. The tallest one on the right is a decent shot, but the other two seem unsure of what to do. Shaw, take the one on the left. I will take the one on the right. Muir, you have the middle."

Shaw and Saoirse nodded, then the three of them swung outward from the doorway into the hall. Spall's massive double revolver roared through the asylum as he fired a single shot, taking the top off the tall orderly's head, killing him instantly. The orderly flopped bonelessly to the floor as Saoirse took aim and fired two shots into the middle orderly, dropping him almost as quickly. Shaw fired three shots at the leftmost orderly, hitting him squarely in the chest with two shots and shattering his target's arm with the third. The orderly dropped his pistol and doubled over before falling to the floor, coughing blood. The three agents moved forward with pistols ready, but no more orderlies showed themselves. They made their way to the stairwell door as Schlenker took the orderly's key ring from Spall and started trying keys in the lock. The keys were a difficulty, as they all had the same-shape heads with only minor differences. All of them fit into the locks, but only one would turn the lock to open the door. Schlenker had to try every one. Shaw looked around and was surprised to see that Henry the orderly was still hanging around with his group of nurses at a distance, all of them looking scared and ready to run.

Saoirse, Spall, and Shaw, meanwhile, began to collect pistols and ammunition from the dead orderlies. Adebe still had her pistol out; she looked a lot steadier than she had, but she was still in no condition to fight.

Before Schlenker could find the proper key, however, more shots rang out from the direction of the stairwell. Spall and Shaw were on guard and were able to provide some returning fire at the orderlies who had shot at them. Henry and the few nurses that were with him quickly ran past the agents and ducked into one of the doorways. It looked like one of the nurses had been injured.

"It looks like Slotted Spoon is with them!" Saoirse yelled over the loud boom of Spall's pistol. There was a sizable group of orderlies with Slattispoone at the end of the hall, all of them armed.

"Yes, that was who I was aiming at. He's quick," Spall replied, aggravated at missing the doctor. After seeing what the doctor was doing with his time in the asylum, Spall would have been only too happy to take his head off with a well-placed shot. He wondered how many patients had been experimented on, and what it was that Slattispoone had been trying to accomplish. His thoughts turned to how many bodies had been dumped into the abyss below. Perhaps only Slattispoone knew.

Suddenly the orderlies ran up the last few stairs from their place of cover and sent a barrage of bullets at the agents. The incoming fire was too intense—Spall took a bullet in the upper left arm and Shaw was hit in the shoulder. Saoirse was struck in the upper-left thigh and fell to the ground. Adebe grabbed her and began to drag her along the floor.

The hail of bullets drove the agents back from the exit door and into the nearest alcove, which turned out to be one of the storage rooms, and where Henry and the nurses had taken refuge after the first firefight. Spall and Shaw attempted to return fire; however, Slattispoone and his minions had taken too much ground and would open fire the instant either of them showed their face around the corner. Doctor Schlenker used the set of keys to open the door to the storage room, which happened to be the one Spall had investigated earlier, the one with the unusual fissure leading out the back. The agents pushed Henry and the nurses into the room and stood to either side of the doorway.

Spall and Adebe posted themselves at the door while Schlenker looked at Shaw's and Saoirse's wounds. Fortunately, the bullet had passed right through Shaw's trapezoid muscle without hitting any bone—extremely painful, but not completely debilitating. Schlenker tore Shaw's shirt and used some of it as a bandage, fashioning the rest into a sling for his left arm. Saoirse's wound was little more than a scratch; the bullet had just grazed her. Her intense pain had been caused by the bullet hitting nearly perfectly where her leg had been broken only weeks before.

"Shaw, how bad is it?" Spall asked from the doorway.

"I'll live. It's my first bullet wound, though, so I think I'm going into shock," Shaw replied.

"Muir?" Spall asked.

"I'm okay. Just grazed me. Bastards hit me right where that damned taxi did, though. Just a lot of pain, but I can still walk," Saoirse replied as she pulled a long cloth bandage from her satchel and began to tie it around her bleeding leg.

Schlenker could see that Shaw was turning pale.

"Shaw, sit down on the floor and take nice, deep breaths. Calm your heart rate. The shock will pass," Schlenker said, helping Shaw to the floor and taking two of the pistols Shaw had collected from the dead orderlies. He moved to take a position behind Spall.

"Spall, you are bleeding as well. Can you tell how bad it is?"

"Not bad," Spall grunted. "The bullet struck the bone, but I don't think my arm is broken. The pain is considerable."

Doctor Schlenker grabbed Henry. "You can treat wounds, can't you? Bandage his arm while I keep watch with Adebe."

Henry looked stunned by the events of the last few minutes, but he nodded and began to work. He tore strips off his orderly's smock and began to bandage Spall's wounded arm. Spall looked down at Henry.

"Why are you in here with us rather than out there with the rest of your comrades?"

Henry looked up at Spall with dazed eyes. "I've wanted to leave ever since I learned what he does here. But he won't let anyone leave. If anyone tries, he uses the other orderlies to capture them and then perform experiments on them. Why do you think he's the only doctor down here? There used to be six! They're all dead now. All of them! I've had to watch him eviscerate some of my friends while they were still alive and conscious. He's a murderer, and most of the orderlies are here to help him. I think some of them are from Ünterreich and—"

Here Henry was cut off by several orderlies who tried to come around the doorway and fire into the room. Adebe and Schlenker opened fire, killing all but one. Adebe was regarded as one of the best shots in the Secret Service, and even when dazed she could still easily out-shoot Schlenker. The floor outside the room was now littered with the bodies of dead and dying orderlies. Suddenly the agents could hear Doctor Slattispoone's voice from around the corner.

"Why don't you come out, gentlemen? Ladies? You can't stay in there forever, you know."

"How could you, a doctor, do such horrible things? What in Earth could have possessed you to perform such unnecessary and barbaric surgeries on your patients?" Schlenker asked.

"Unnecessary? Who are you to say they were unnecessary? You pathetic people have no concept of what I'm trying to do, do you? I'm close to unlocking many of the mysteries of the human mind. But now I will have to take my research elsewhere. At least there's somewhere in this world who appreciates the work I'm doing. I will be welcomed as a hero!"

"So you're going to defect to Ünterreich?" Spall asked.

"Yes, they were very interested when I told them what I had gotten from Bergstrom. They offered to help me complete my research in exchange for Bergstrom's formulas. So they sent some agents to assist me here. Now it seems I must go. Enjoy what is about to become your tomb!"

With that, they could hear a door closing somewhere out in the hallway. Spall quickly glanced out and saw that with the exception of the bodies lying on the floor, the entire level was empty. After a minute, the agents could hear the sounds of the elevator above them as Slattispoone and his Ünterreich henchmen left the asylum.

"Henry! Is there a telephone to contact the prison above us?" Shaw asked. "We need to stop Slotty!"

"There's a telephone right here at the nurse's station, sir!" Henry seemed relieved to be out of danger and also to be of some help.

They slowly approached the nurse's station, now somewhat the worse for wear and sporting many holes. It seemed that the Ünterreich agents posing as orderlies were not the best shooters in the underground. It looked like they had shot everything in sight. Surprisingly, the telephone box appeared to have survived the hail of bullets. Unfortunately, someone had smashed it to pieces instead. There was no way to warn the guards above.

Spall stopped in his tracks. "Do you hear something?"

"Not since you fired that stupid cannon in here. My hearing will never be the same," Shaw replied. He was still not feeling well, though he no longer felt like throwing up or passing out. Even a flesh wound could cause a lot of trauma and shock, especially a bullet wound.

"Shh! I hear a hissing sound!" Spall cocked his head to listen more carefully. Once everyone had gone completely silent, one by one they could hear what he was talking about. There was a distinct hissing sound coming from somewhere. Spall sniffed the air, looked quickly around, and then his eyes widened.

"Everyone back into the storage room! *Now!*"

They all turned and started to run back into the doorway when they were thrown from their feet by a massive explosion up the hall. The entire floor skewed at an angle away from the wall, causing anything not secured to the floor to start sliding toward the windows. Spall grabbed hold of Schlenker and Henry, Adebe grabbed Saoirse, and they all got to their feet and scrambled for the open doorway. Shaw was closest to the door but had been closer to the explosion. His ears were ringing and his vision seemed to have closed in, only allowing him to see straight ahead. Everything was happening in slow motion. All at once, Shaw could see sheets of metal, likely patient files from the nurse's station, sliding along the floor toward him. He could see one of the orderly's bodies lazily rolling away from the doorway. Shaw somehow got to his feet and began to shakily rush for the opening in the wall that meant safety. He could barely make out muffled shouts from the others, but they seemed like they were underwater, and he couldn't make out what they were saying. His movements felt agonizingly slow, as though he was stuck in tar, trying to fight his way forward against an invisible, viscous mass.

Shaw thought he would never reach the door when he was suddenly pushed from behind by the collected mass of Spall, Schlenker, Henry, Adebe, and Saoirse. Shaw flew through the doorway and landed on his hands, sending a massive, nauseating wave of pain up through his wounded shoulder. Shaw nearly blacked out from the pain and fresh shock as he rolled to his side and saw behind him. Adebe and Saoirse were both sprawled on the floor to either side of the doorway. Spall had hauled Henry and Doctor Schlenker through the open doorway a mere instant before a fresh explosion had rocked the asylum, causing the entire structure to break free from the cavern wall. Shaw could just make out the collapsing building through the doorway, and then the lights turned off and it was simply gone. Though he could no longer see it, there was nothing beyond the storage room doorway but the vast empty void of Isolation Crevasse. Shaw lay back and fell unconscious.

# 25

## Trapped

Shaw awoke a short time later, a vision of maniacal doctors stripping the flesh from his body while he was falling into a bottomless crevasse still fresh in his mind. He was on his back, with a rolled up coat underneath his feet and another coat lying on top of him. He felt a wave of nausea, which passed after a few seconds. Then Doctor Schlenker was above him, a flashlight in his hand.

"Ah, you're awake! Excellent! How do you feel?"

Shaw swallowed. His mouth felt incredibly dry. "Like a skydiver whose chute didn't open. Ugh. Do we have any water?"

"That, we have, though we need to be sparing. There's no telling how long we may be stuck here. What's a skydiver? It sounds very interesting," Schlenker asked, curious in spite of the situation.

Shaw sat up and took a small sip of water out of a metal flask from Schlenker's satchel.

"I'll have to tell you about skydiving later. It's where people jump out of airplanes. It's fun and terrifying at the same time. Where are Spall and Henry?"

"They're investigating the confinement room at the far end of the tunnel. It's fascinating. Henry has been a good helper through this entire ordeal. And the nurses here have been assisting me in caring for you, Saoirse, and Adebe." Shaw turned his head, which sent fresh pain from his shoulder up his neck, causing him to gasp. It turned out that Henry had bustled four nurses into the room ahead of them, and they sat huddled together in various states of shock and disbelief.

"That's great. How long was I out?"

"Only ten minutes or so. Understandable, really. You've just been shot for the first time, and then the entire gunfight and the asylum falling out from beneath our feet. I myself have been shaking this entire time. It will be a while before the adrenaline stops affecting me."

Shaw glanced over at Saoirse, who was sitting on the floor with her freshly injured left leg stretched out before her. She was cradling Adebe's head in her lap, talking to her to keep her conscious.

"Saoirse? Are you okay?" Shaw asked. He didn't know if anyone had been injured further by the explosions.

"I'm fine, Ryan. Still just the flesh wound. Another scar to add to the collection."

"How's Ama?"

"I'll be fine," Adebe answered. "Still just dazed from that blow to the head. The doctor thinks I've got a concussion. All I know is that I've never had a headache like this before. I feel like I'm going to vomit."

Spall and Henry returned from down the irregular hallway that Spall had investigated earlier. Henry explained that the small fissure had always been there, and that the storage room had been excavated from it. At the far end, the fissure ended, and Doctor Slattispoone had ordered a secure door to be installed. The resulting room was used as a sort of solitary confinement for patients who didn't behave themselves.

"So why were you exploring that confinement room, then?" Shaw asked Spall.

"Henry here informed us that after Slotted Spoon had interviewed Bergstrom for some time, Bergstrom had told the rotten bastard about his work on the star. Bergstrom gave him everything—all his formulas, calculations, everything we have been looking for. Slotty had it all. Once he realized what it all meant, he contacted Ünterreich somehow and began spying for them. He helped install an entire network of agents here, and he passed them everything he knew about the star. I suspect they would pay a lot, and probably kill a lot, to get all the Fragments from us. So far, they just have the one Fragment from Bergstrom. But now Slattispoone knows who we are, and it won't take him long to find out where Schlenker lives and possibly try to steal the other Fragments from us, if the Tricians haven't already started planning it. As for why we were looking in the confinement room, Henry told me that Slattispoone put Bergstrom in that room a few days ago, after we had contacted the prison about him. The next day, Bergstrom was gone. They investigated and found a small crevice at the back of the room, leading downward and just large enough to admit a grown man. They assumed Bergstrom had squeezed through and couldn't get back out. Bergstrom never reappeared, and it was assumed that he had either escaped or died somewhere further in."

Shaw waited for Spall to finish before asking his next question. "So why did Slotty try to pass off the old miner as Bergstrom? Why not just have him declared dead and not have to worry about it?"

Henry answered this question. "There would be questions, because of who Bergstrom was. If he had died so soon after your inquiry, everyone would start asking questions about how and why. They might find out about Slotted Spoons' little spying game, and his experiments. He didn't want any extra scrutiny; otherwise his entire enterprise would be at risk. Once he found out that you were on your way to interview Bergstrom, he decided to try and fool you with old

Washburne. He had me put Washburne in the interview room and pretend it was Bergstrom. He even pretended to get angry with me for moving his patient without his approval. It was all a charade to get you to believe it was actually Bergstrom. He never counted on any of you having a look around, especially not all the way down in the hospital. I think that once he discovered you'd seen what was going on, he decided to just kill you and try to make a getaway. I don't think he even knows you discovered the deception with Washburne. Not that it matters now. I wish I had known he had wired the building with explosives."

"Yes, that would have been nice to know beforehand. It might have saved a few lives. It is fortunate that all the cells and rooms are bored into the cavern wall. Hopefully most of the remaining staff were able to get to safety before the place fell away." Schlenker said. "Now we have another mystery."

"You want to look for Bergstrom in the confinement room?" Shaw asked, turning back to Spall.

"I can never make assumptions, so I have to inspect it for myself. We have lights and ropes, and we need to find Bergstrom before we make an attempt to escape from here ourselves. I know that he may be dead, but we must be certain. I cannot continue until I have found him, or at least his remains. If he is still alive down that crack, we need to rescue him. Otherwise the only way for us to retrieve Bergstrom's Fragment is to capture Slattispoone. We cannot forget that Slattispoone is now on the run with a number of Trician agents. These do not seem to be able to shoot accurately; however, I imagine they have many other talents."

"I'll stay right here, if it's all the same to you," Adebe suggested. "I'll only hinder your search in my current condition."

"Well I'm coming," Saoirse announced. She stretched out her injured leg gingerly, testing that her range of motion wasn't too badly impaired.

271

Saoirse handed Adebe over to the infuriatingly attractive nurse she had been jealous of earlier and got to her feet, testing her fresh wound and concluding it wouldn't slow her down.

Shaw got unsteadily to his feet and had to lean against the wall as a wave of nausea and lightheadedness washed over him.

"No, Shaw. I think you will have to stay here with Adebe," Schlenker said.

Shaw looked hard at Schlenker. "Like fun I will. I may not be 100 percent right now—"

"More like 10 percent," Spall added.

Shaw continued, turning his glare toward Spall. "*But*, I came on this mission as part of a team, and I will do what I have to do to help you find Bergstrom. I'm coming with you." With that, Shaw pulled his arm out of the makeshift sling and moved it around to show that he could still use it somewhat.

Spall favored Shaw with his almost imperceptible smile and a nod before turning and walking down the tunnel. They all followed, turning on their lights and pulling out ropes as they approached the now-open door leading into the confinement room. The little cave was just that, barely enough to stand up in, in the case of Spall. It was perhaps ten meters deep and three wide, and it ended in a heap of broken rock. Spall walked to the end of the cave and directed his light at a point just above the floor behind a few large stones. Shaw, Saoirse, and Schlenker looked and saw what he had been talking about. Behind the stones was a small crack leading at an angle downward; it seemed like it would be just wide enough for Spall to squeeze through.

Henry opted to stay behind, as he felt like he had suffered through enough that day. The nurses likewise showed no interest in accompanying the agents. Spall tied a rope around Schlenker's waist and slowly began to lower him down into the small crack, wincing at the pain in his freshly wounded arm. Schlenker had Shaw's LED headlamp attached to his head, so he was able to fend off the sharp rocks as he descended. After a short distance, they could hear Schlenker's voice from below.

**272**

"I'm on the ground; you may tie the rope off and follow me if you wish. This is very strange."

Spall and Shaw tied the rope and gingerly followed Doctor Schlenker down the hole. Shaw had broken out into a cold sweat, and his shoulder was throbbing in agony, sending waves of sharp pain up through his neck and down into his arm. He could hear Spall grunting with effort, and Shaw could see that Spall's injured arm was definitely slowing his progress. Spall was human after all. Saoirse came down the rope surprisingly quickly. She winced a couple of times, but it was clear that she was the least injured of the group after Schlenker.

After a short time, all the agents were at the bottom of the crack, which opened up into a sizable cave. Schlenker gave Shaw his LED headlamp back, and they all turned on their flashlights (or torches, as the others called them) to look around. The cave went on for some distance, twisting and turning, but the most curious thing was that the floor had little drifts, here and there, of black sand. They followed the cave, occasionally stopping to make marks on the walls to prevent them from getting lost. After several hundred meters, they could see the cave ended in what looked like another huge cavern, the floor covered in the same black sand.

The agents came to the end of the cave and stopped. They scanned the area, but their lights couldn't reach any walls or the ceiling of the cavern. Wherever they were, it was another massive cavern. Shaw glanced down at the sand.

"Look at your feet!"

They all looked down at where Shaw was illuminating with his headlamp and saw what he was talking about. A line of footprints led away into the darkness ahead. It was impossible to tell how long they had been there; there was no wind, or rain, or anything else that would wipe the footprints away. It was perhaps the driest desert in the entire world. The footprints could have been there for hundreds or even thousands of years, but the agents all knew that the prints were

Doctor Bergstrom's. They stood before the black desert, wondering what madness could have driven him into the endless expanse of perpetual night.

They looked at one another and came to an agreement without speaking. They silently followed the footprints into the blackness of the desert.

They had wandered for some time when their lights showed a large stone ahead. The stone was strange in that it looked almost pure white in contrast to the black sand that stretched endlessly in all directions. As they approached the stone, they could see that it towered over them, and that it had surprisingly regular sides, as though it had been hewn to shape. Further on, they could just make out more tumbled stones of various sizes and shapes, scattered everywhere. Most were partially buried in the sand, but enough were visible that the four agents were able to see that many were made into fairly uniform shapes or fragments of shapes. There were a lot of squares and rectangles, but a few cylinders could be seen sticking up from the sand like huge broken stone teeth. As they followed the footprints further into the field of debris, they came upon an astonishing sight.

"What in Earth are we looking at?" Spall asked.

Shaw swallowed, not fully comprehending what was before his eyes. It made no sense.

"That, my friends, is an Aztec pyramid."

# 26

## Lost Doctor, Lost City

Schlenker walked closer to examine what did indeed look like a South or Central American native pyramid. It was difficult to see the fine details in the small amount of light cast by their flashlights, but they could all clearly see the stepped shape characteristic of many of the ancient American pyramids.

"Incredible. Are you certain it's Aztec?" Schlenker asked.

Shaw shrugged. "I don't know. Aztec, Mayan, Inca, I don't know. I think they all made pyramids like this. The last time I studied that culture was in grade school. But explorers find ruins just like this all the time in the jungles, and I've seen a lot of pictures."

"How would they have built it this far underground? We must be at least eighteen kilometers down, and most of those civilizations were wiped out hundreds of years ago," Saoirse noted. "What we're seeing is physically impossible."

"I agree. If I hadn't seen it with my own eyes, I would never have believed it," Shaw said. "And I think my eyes are starting to play tricks on me. I see a reddish glow way out in the dark."

"Strange. I thought my eyes were starting to do funny things as well. I'm convinced I saw a large poodle just now," said Schlenker.

"No, our eyes are working properly. There is definitely a light source out there, and it seems to be growing." Spall added, ignoring the poodle comment.

The agents stood and stared out into the darkness, which was growing brighter by the second. Suddenly, a huge ball of fire shot up into the air and lit the cavern for several seconds. They could see that the fireball had come from a small volcanic cone at the far end of the cavern, perhaps a hundred kilometers away.

The cavern they were in was almost round in shape, with a jagged ceiling perhaps three kilometers above. But the biggest surprise for the agents was what was illuminated immediately ahead of them. The stepped pyramid before them was one of dozens of similar structures. Massive temples rose from the black sand; pillars and obelisks jutted like broken bones at a black sky that would forever block out the light of sun and moon. Streets and boulevards stretched off in all directions, filled with tumbled fragments of fallen stones and drifts of black sand. They were looking at an entire subterranean city, built hundreds, perhaps thousands of years before the coming of Europeans to the Americas.

All of this was seen in a flash and was gone. Blackness returned as quickly as it had been banished; however, a red glow could still be seen faintly in the distance, slowly receding.

"Interesting. It seems that the far end of this black desert is dominated by a small volcanic vent. I wonder if it erupts often," Schlenker mused.

"Like Old Faithful Geyser in Yellowstone?" Shaw asked.

"Perhaps. Is it famous?" Schlenker asked in reply.

"About as famous as a geyser can be, I guess. Never mind. I think I've found Bergstrom's trail around the back of the pyramid. This way."

They followed the footprints around the base of the pyramid. The prints were much closer together here, and Shaw realized that Bergstrom must have been bending down to feel his way along the base of the structure, shuffling his feet through the sand. He had forgotten that Bergstrom would have had no light when he had come down, unless there had been one of those short eruptions.

The footprints continued off away from the base of the pyramid after a while. It looked like the imprints in the sand were growing further and further apart, as though Bergstrom had been running. The agents followed the trail onto a roadway paved with broken stones, lined on either side by fallen buildings and tumbled rock. The black sand was still everywhere, drifted into place by unknown forces during the untold centuries in the dark. Shaw felt a shiver run down his spine, once again awakening the horrible pain in his shoulder. He felt as though thousands of eyes were watching him, the ghosts of long-dead inhabitants. Occasionally they would find small patches of what must once have been vegetation and even trees, desiccated almost to dust, but no bodies. Shaw kept expecting to find bones at least.

The trail continued through the subterranean Aztec city, passing intersecting roads built of crazily heaved paving stones with black drifts of sand. They were surrounded by tumbled ruins and somewhat intact stepped pyramids, and Shaw was glad for their trail through the sand. If they hadn't left something for themselves to follow back out, they would surely have become hopelessly lost in the twisting streets and fallen debris. The city must once have been an incredible sight and must have housed tens, perhaps hundreds of thousands of people. Schlenker kept trying to stop to examine carved markings and other artifacts in an attempt to learn as much as possible, but Spall and Shaw kept him moving. They didn't dare separate, even with Bergstrom's footprints leading the way.

"What a great pity I can't stop to examine more," Schlenker lamented loudly as they followed Bergstrom's trail further into the labyrinthine city.

"We shall have to return another day, Doctor," Spall remarked as he grabbed Schlenker by the arm to get him moving for the hundredth time. Spall was clearly in significant pain from his bullet wound to the arm and wasn't in the mood for anything but finding Bergstrom. He looked around as they walked. "I believe we are being followed. I have been hearing strange sounds ever since we entered the city."

"Followed? By whom? There couldn't be anyone else down here but us," Shaw said, suddenly feeling the hairs on the back of his neck rising.

"I do not know, and perhaps it is my fevered imagination," Spall admitted, still scanning their environment. "However, I have spent the majority of my life making as little sound as possible when I move, and that has made me quite sensitive to the sounds made by others. Especially the sounds made by people and creatures that are trying to be silent."

Shaw drew his pistol as they continued onward. "Well, whoever they are, if there *is* anyone out there, I hope they know enough to keep their distance," he said as they continued on through a massive fallen arch and down some steps.

After some time, they could see the reddish glow building at the far end of the cavern once again, and after a few minutes there was another eruption, spreading momentary light through their surroundings, casting shadows through the maze of broken buildings and debris.

"Doctor, how long was that from the last one?" Shaw asked.

"I can't be certain, but I believe it was approximately forty-eight minutes," Schlenker answered. "I may be off by half a minute or so."

"Well, if it happens on a regular basis, then Bergstrom may have been able to navigate down here somewhat. Though what he was navigating toward remains unclear," Spall said.

"More likely he was just navigating *away* from Slattispoone," added Saoirse. "I don't think he cared what he was headed *for*."

Eventually they found themselves in what must have been the center of the city. They were in a huge circular courtyard surrounded by six of the tallest stepped pyramids they had seen. Four were fairly intact; however, the fifth and sixth both had suffered some damage. One was missing the top, and the other looked like it had split in two and partially collapsed. It only took a few seconds, though, for their attention to be drawn away from their surroundings. In the center of the courtyard, on a short raised stone dais, was a strange object. It was a metal disk, perfectly circular and slightly larger than a dinner plate, set into the dais so closely that there was scarcely a sheet of paper's width between metal and stone. The stone had no carvings on it whatsoever, but the metal surface was filled with grooves marking out various geometric shapes and designs.

Schlenker brightened up when he spied the disk. "Ah, this is extraordinary! Let us stop for just a minute, Spall. I know that I've asked this many times, but this is unlike anything we've seen yet. Any idea what this might be, Shaw?"

Shaw shook his head. "Not a clue. Reminds me of an old *Sesame Street* song: 'One of these things is not like the other.'"

"*Sesame Street*?" Saoirse looked at Shaw with a raised eyebrow.

"It's a kids' show on TV. I've told you all about TV. Anyway, they would sing that song and the kids would learn about how things are the same or different. Like this. Whatever this metal disk is, it doesn't look like it belongs here. I've never seen anything like it."

"It is definitely a mystery within a mystery," Schlenker said, reaching his fingers toward the grooves in the metal as he crouched beside the dais.

"Doctor, do not touch that disk!" Spall spoke authoritatively. His tone of voice commanded attention, causing Schlenker to draw his hand back quickly. Shaw was surprised. Spall usually reserved his personal brand of exasperated sarcasm for dealing with the doctor; Shaw had never heard him use such a tone with Schlenker. From Schlenker's reaction, it was clear that he was just as surprised.

"Spall? What do you suspect? It's just a metal disk. I doubt it will hurt me," Schlenker said.

"You may be right," Spall conceded; "however, that disk seems sufficiently unnatural in these surroundings that I would avoid any contact with it for the time being. Notice how even the black sand has not drifted around the stone dais here. We do not know what it is, and it may be dangerous. This may be radioactive."

Shaw nodded. "Yeah, it could be radioactive. "Though that doesn't explain why there isn't any sand drifted over it. For now, let's see if we can find Bergstrom. His tracks start up again in the sand over this way."

They had only followed the tracks for a short distance when Spall spoke up.

"I think we've found him," Spall said. "Over there, Doctor."

Spall's light had followed Bergstrom's footprints as they found their way through the courtyard. A short way further, Spall's light had illuminated what appeared to be a human body. Whether it was alive or dead they couldn't tell. Schlenker quickened his pace and knelt down beside the body, turning it over to expose the face to the light of their electric torches. The person was clearly dead and had been for a short time.

"This appears to be Doctor Bergstrom." Spall said. "He must have stumbled all the way out here and then fallen down. Any clues to how he may have died, Doctor?"

Doctor Schlenker sighed. "Yes, it is Bergstrom. What a sad end to such a brilliant scientist. To lose his mind and then be tortured by Slattispoone is terrible. But then to wander into this place, alone and blind, and then to just die. He can't have been dead for more than a day. As far as the cause of his death, I cannot speculate without performing an autopsy. There don't appear to be any marks indicating an injury."

"Look over here. It looks like there're some weird tracks in the sand. Any idea what made these?" Shaw asked, indicating some strange impressions in the sand near the edge of the courtyard.

Spall examined the marks in the sand, which looked like a cross between human feet and wolf tracks. "'Cores. Nasty creatures. I'd not expected them here; there is nothing to feed on. Aside from the unfortunate Bergstrom of course; however, it does not seem that they got much closer than three meters. I would have expected them to have stripped the body clean by now."

"'Cores? What are they?" Shaw asked.

Schlenker was still examining the body closely, but he couldn't miss an opportunity to pass along knowledge. "'Core is short for manticore. *Puma manticorus*, from the family Felidae, to be more precise."

"Manticores? You mean the mythical creatures?"

Schlenker shook his head. "These creatures certainly aren't mythical. They resemble a cougar without hair; however, their face looks closer to a primate's than a feline's. They are completely blind, of course, since they adapted themselves to life underground thousands of years ago. We still don't know much about them. They are quite cowardly and tend to avoid humans unless they're in large packs. They scavenge whatever they can for food, which also makes me wonder why they're found in this cavern. They must have a food supply somewhere nearby. As to the actual cause of Bergstrom's death and why the manticores haven't touched his body, we can only speculate at this time. It is very strange. Perhaps he touched the disk?"

"At this point, nothing would surprise me," Shaw admitted. "So just more mysteries in the amazing Cavern of Mysteries. I should be keeping a list. Anyway, at least we know for sure that Bergstrom is dead," Shaw said. "So, what do we do now?"

"I would love to explore this cavern; however, we must return to Isolation as soon as possible." Schlenker said. "We will have to catch Slattispoone. He's the only one who possesses what we needed from Bergstrom."

Spall nodded in agreement. "Henry said that Slotty had gotten everything from Bergstrom before he was placed into the confinement chamber. We will have to catch him before he can get to Ünterreich."

"If that is our only option to retrieve Bergstrom's formulas, we must be gone as soon as we can. We'll have to return for the body later, and to study these ruins. Fascinating," Schlenker added, casting his light around and stopping to take a last, longing glance at the metal disk.

The four agents turned and began to follow their trail back the way they had come. They had been somewhat hopeful on the outward journey, but they felt very somber as they left the subterranean city and then entered the cave system which led to the exit. Shaw and Spall had both ignored their injuries as much as they could during their search for Doctor Bergstrom, but now the adrenaline from the gunfight had dissipated and the pain was all too real. Even Saoirse was showing some discomfort as she walked. They also had to determine the best way to escape from the storage room and reach the prison above.

As they walked, they moved somewhat faster than they had during their search for Bergstrom. The memory of their narrow escape from the collapsing asylum and the reality that they were still technically trapped had returned along with the pain from their injuries. They grew more and more anxious as they neared the edge of the ruined city. At first each of the agents assumed this was due to their preoccupation with finding a way out of the storage room back up to the prison above, but Spall suddenly stopped and made an unpleasant observation.

"We are surrounded."

The others stopped dead. Schlenker looked quickly around with his light and seeing nothing unusual, quite a feat considering their surroundings, looked over at Spall with a curious expression.

"What do you mean, Spall? I see nothing."

"Nevertheless, we are surrounded by 'cores. They have been tracking us since we first entered the city, and now I think they realize we are leaving. They are likely readying themselves to attack us rather than lose this opportunity for a meal. Arm yourselves."

They all drew their weapons and stood with their backs to one another, facing outward in a circle. Soon the others could hear what

Spall must have been hearing all along: quiet, almost doglike breathing and the quick padding of footprints on fine sand. It sounded like there were a great many creatures just outside their circle of light. Shaw hoped the creatures, whatever they were, would lose interest and leave, but after a few seconds he began to see his flashlight beam catching tiny glimpses of their enemies. They were getting closer.

"Hold your fire until you have a definite target," Spall advised, cocking the hammers on his massive revolver. "I pray they will scatter once we begin to fire, though we cannot assume anything. These 'cores seem to be far larger and more aggressive than others we have encountered in Inner Earth, and we still do not know what they normally eat down here."

"Well, it doesn't seem to be old, dead scientists," Schlenker added helpfully. "They left Bergstrom's body alone."

"I think his body must have been poisoned for them somehow," Shaw said, the nervousness creeping into his voice. He could see at least ten pairs of dead, blind eyes just inside the reach of his light. There were probably dozens of the things in a circle around them.

Without warning, a large beast ran straight at Schlenker from the darkness in a white blur, screaming as it came. Turning toward the sound of its screeching approach, all Shaw could was a set of teeth that seemed to fill his entire view as the creature leapt at his friend. Shaw turned and fired at the same instant as Schlenker. They must have hit the creature with at least one shot, since the beast fell in the sand between them with a boneless thud.

To Shaw it looked like a large, naked mountain lion with the face of a monkey. Its hairless skin was pure white to the point of translucence; they could see the thing's veins and muscles in some places. The only other color on the beast was the black claws; even its eyes were pure white, and so tiny they were nearly invisible. The teeth and ears were what drew Shaw's attention, though. It had several rows of teeth, rather like a small shark. He didn't fancy getting bitten by one of these things if he could avoid it. The ears were enormous, nearly the size of the creature's head. *They must have unbelievable hearing,* he thought.

He turned from the carcass just as another ran toward him. Shaw aimed and fired twice, striking the creature with one shot and causing it to yelp in a catlike fashion before veering off and limping out of the circle of light. Several shots from behind him told Shaw that Spall and Saoirse were dealing with their own threats, and that the creatures hadn't realized they should leave the humans alone. Another came at him, and he fired three shots at this one before it fell dead nearly at his feet. It coughed black blood on his shoes and then lay still. More shots from behind him, and the sounds of reloading from Schlenker. Shaw turned to cover Schlenker's field of view as the doctor reloaded and fired his remaining shots into two more creatures that had decided to attack at that moment. Realizing that his weapon was empty, Shaw yelled that he was reloading as he ripped the empty cylinder from his steam pistol and rammed a fresh one into place.

Once again with a loaded pistol, Shaw began to scan the area before him as he realized that his companions' firing had stopped. Risking a quick glance, he saw nine bodies of the strange subterranean creatures surrounding them, all of them dead or very nearly so. Spall was quickly reloading his heavy revolver, while Schlenker was actually kneeling down to examine one of the beasts at his feet.

"They seem to have stopped," Spall said, closing his revolver with a loud metallic snap.

"Indeed," Schlenker agreed. "How fascinating. This manticore is nearly twice the size of an average one, and the others are of a similar size. Far more aggressive than others I've seen, with what appears to be an extra row of teeth. I'd say we may have discovered a new subspecies of manticore! Isn't this exciting?"

Spall, Saoirse, and Shaw shared a look before Spall turned back to the doctor. "I am ecstatic, Doctor. However, before you ask whether you might in fact dissect this thing right here, I must remind you that we have about one thousand more important things to accomplish at the moment, not the least of which is that we must return to the storeroom and find a way out of here."

Schlenker looked crestfallen, but he nodded his head and put his pocketknife back into his pocket before his four companions began to walk quickly away from the city and toward what they hoped was relative safety. They were not troubled by the remaining manticores for the rest of their walk, though they continued to search the area around and behind them until they had nearly reached their destination.

"I don't think that we have the luxury of waiting for someone from the prison to send down the elevator to investigate. I would expect Slattispoone to kill a few guards and maybe even destroy the elevator system to prevent us from being rescued. And we don't know if he might have a few of his agents working among the prison guards. We can't trust anything now," Shaw suggested as they reached the rope to the confinement room.

They all slowly clambered their way back up to the confinement room, where Henry the orderly was still waiting patiently with the nurses and Agent Adebe, all of them sitting dejectedly on the floor.

# 27

## Ascent

"Ah, Henry. Glad to see you're still here," Schlenker said as he began to coil the rope, replacing it in his satchel. "You don't have any ideas about how we can reach the prison above, do you?"

Henry shook his head and betrayed a look of despair. Being trapped and alone with his thoughts hadn't been productive for the poor orderly. "No, sir. The only thing I could think of is the conduit, but it's too far to reach."

"The conduit?" asked Spall. "What do you mean?"

"There's a large conduit leading down from the prison; it's where we get all of our power and water supply from. It's bolted to the wall and is still there, but it must be ten meters or more from our doorway. There's no way to reach it."

Spall turned to Schlenker. "If we can get you over to it, do you think you could climb all the way to the prison? Normally I would go myself, but not with this arm, and Shaw is in the same state. Adebe cannot climb in her condition, and Muir's leg—"

"My leg is just fine, sir," Saoirse noted.

"Fine enough to climb more than four hundred meters?" Spall asked.

"Fair enough," she conceded.

"Well," began Schlenker, "my circus days are long behind me, but I think I'll be able to manage it. Let me see the conduit."

"Circus days?" Shaw asked.

Ignoring Shaw, Schlenker leaned out from the doorway into the open blackness of the crevasse, making Shaw's stomach clench. Schlenker looked to the left and then the right before he could see a large bundle of metal pipes and cables several meters above them and, as Henry had pointed out, about ten meters away. The ends of the pipes and cables were a jumbled, twisted mess, with sparks coming from one large cable and water flowing from some of the pipes. It would be very tricky just getting up to the conduit without being electrocuted or having one's grip slip on the wet metal. The conduit itself was strapped to the cavern wall every so often with steel bands. These bands would form a handy hand—or foot—hold, but since the bands were so far apart, the majority of the climbing would have to be on the pipes and cables themselves. Schlenker smiled his usual cheerful smile and leaned back into the room.

"It looks like it should be easy for me to climb. Over four hundred meters, though. It will still take a while. I only ever climbed ropes in my youth and never much more than one hundred meters. It took a lot of effort, and that was when I was in much better shape."

"When were you in the circus?" Shaw asked, not willing to let go of the thought of Schlenker as some kind of clown.

"Oh, a long time ago. I used the money I saved from it to pay for my university degrees. I was an acrobatic tumbler," Schlenker said, beaming with pride.

Shaw raised an eyebrow. "Really?"

Schlenker laughed before replying. "No."

Shaw laughed with his friend. "Well, most of the time down here I don't know what to believe. I can't say that much will surprise me anymore. Not in *this* team, anyway—"

Suddenly a deafening gunshot rang out in the room, making everyone's ears ring. They all turned to Spall, who was replacing his now-smoking revolver back into its cavernous holster. In his other hand Spall was holding a long piece of perforated steel, which had recently been serving as a support bracket to a shelving unit and which had just been violently (and loudly) removed from said shelving unit. The end was still smoking, like Spall's revolver.

"Do not look at me like that. I am working on getting us out of here," Spall said on seeing their expressions.

"Spall, did it occur to you to warn anyone that you were about to fire that damned thing in here?" Shaw asked in a very perturbed voice.

"Yes."

"Oh, good. Why didn't you, then?"

"You were busy obtaining Schlenker's life story, and I know how he likes to talk about himself and everything else. I could either try to get a word in edgewise or get on with things. I chose the latter, and you may thank me later."

With that, Spall grabbed one end of the steel strap and hooked it between two pieces of steel in the shelving unit. Using the strap as a lever, Spall bent it into a long hook shape, grunting with the effort. Either the strap was very strong or Spall was more injured than he let on, preferably the former. Spall and Saoirse began to attach one of their ropes to the end of the hook while Doctor Schlenker used another rope to fashion a climbing harness.

"You know how to make a Swiss seat," Shaw observed.

"Oh, yes. Most people in the underground are very experienced climbers and cave explorers. One can never be too safe." Schlenker finished tying his harness and walked over to Spall, who inspected it.

Spall grunted his approval and handed the makeshift grappling hook to Schlenker. The doctor then moved to the doorway and once again looked over to the conduit end, which was still sparking and spraying water. He turned back to face his companions.

"Shaw, I will need your headlamp, if you don't mind. Thank you. It will be best to have my hands free for this. I will try to get the hook as far above the bottom of the conduit as possible to avoid the water and electricity."

"Good luck," Spall said as Schlenker began to slowly spin the end of the rope.

The grappling hook made a dark circle in the flashlight beams as it began to spin faster and faster. Finally, Schlenker released the hook and it sailed away into the darkness toward the conduit. The hook struck a pipe just above one of the steel bands and bounced away, swinging down as Schlenker began to haul the rope in. Schlenker pulled the hook up and tried again, aiming for one of the steel bands further up this time. Again the hook bounced away, and again Schlenker brought the rope back for another attempt. Their collective heartbeats and breathing seemed to stop every time Schlenker sent the hook out, hoping that this time would be the one. Again and again Schlenker threw the hook, only to be rewarded with a metallic clang as the hook bounced ineffectually off the conduit. Everyone's spirits began to sink further with every missed throw.

Finally, Schlenker threw the hook and managed to catch one of the steel bands a few meters above the damaged end of the conduit. Spall let out a sigh of relief as everyone else cheered. Schlenker gave the rope a few good tugs to ensure that the line was secure before giving the free end to Spall to tie off. Spall took the end and looped it around one of the storage shelves to keep the line taut as he tied it. Schlenker began grabbing some of the pistols they had collected and, ensuring they were fully loaded, secured them in his satchel.

Once he was ready, Schlenker grasped the rope and looked back at his friends. "Well, I'm off. Keep your torch beams on me as long as you can so that I have lots of light for climbing. If there are any unpleasant people up top, I hope they won't be paying attention to the conduit."

With that, Schlenker hooked his climbing harness to the rope with a short length of cord fashioned into a loop and began to climb up the rope, pinching it between his feet and then using his legs to push himself along. He dangled beneath the line, moving hand over hand as he inched further out over the darkness. The rope was at an almost forty-five degree angle, and Schlenker was breathing and perspiring heavily by the time he reached the conduit. Shaw was having a hard time watching the progress. He was still very aware of the long emptiness below them, and the fact that Schlenker was dangling precariously above it. The vast openness made Shaw dizzy and sick, and he was only too aware that he was still suffering from shock.

Schlenker had been able to catch the hook above the damaged end of the conduit, which made things much safer for him, but it was still a bit hair-raising when he reached the end of the rope and began to transition to climbing the conduit. He grasped the steel band he had hooked and disconnected his climbing harness from the rope. Once his lower body was free, Schlenker swung his feet down to one of the pipes and began using his feet to push himself up the pipe. He managed to get his feet up to the band and was able to catch his breath.

"Well, I must say that I am in worse shape than I thought, but I will still be able to make good time," he shouted over to the others. "Spall, I will require the hook as a safety device. Can you untie the rope at your end?"

Spall turned and untied the rope from the shelf, letting it fall out of the doorway.

"There you are!"

"*Danke*!"

Schlenker grabbed the hook from the band and hooked it on his makeshift climbing harness. He coiled up the rope and secured the free end to his harness. In theory, as he reached a steel band, he could attach the hook to the band to act as an anchor point should he lose his grip. He began to climb the pipes.

Doctor Schlenker got into the rhythm of climbing once he realized that it was easier for him to grip the rough insulation on the thinner electrical cable than the thicker, smoother metal of the water pipes. The steel bands seemed to be every ten meters, which made sense to Schlenker. If they had been closer together, a potential escapee could have used them as a ladder. He calculated that a four-hundred-meter distance would have forty bands, assuming that the distance was exactly four hundred meters. He began to count bands as he reached them, which helped take his mind off the fatigue in his arms and legs, as well as the monotony of being out in the darkness without anyone to talk to.

Every few bands, Schlenker would break to catch his breath and allow his sore hands to rest. He hadn't anticipated how tired his muscles would become, or how much strain his hands would have to endure. The insulation on the cable was quite rough, and he already had a few blisters starting. Only 320 meters to go.

He continued to climb, hands and feet, hands and feet, agonizingly slow. When he first started climbing, he had averaged one minute between bands. After the first eighty meters, the time had stretched to four minutes. By the time he reached two hundred meters, he had to rest ten minutes for every ten minutes of climbing, switching off the headlamp as he rested to conserve the battery. His hands were bleeding, and his limbs felt horribly painful. He was sweating profusely, and his heart was racing. Band after band came into view of the bright LED headlamp and was then left behind in the blackness. He could no longer see any effect from his companions' torches . . .

*Why in Earth does Shaw call them flashlights? They don't flash!*

... but a quick glance downward every now and then showed that they were still there, smaller and smaller points of light in the yawning gulf of Isolation Crevasse. He continued on. Twenty bands now. Twenty-five. Twenty-eight. Thirty.

With his body fully occupied in climbing, Schlenker was facing another problem. Boredom. A mind such as his could not stay idle for long, and he needed something to take some of his attention away from the pain, turning to agony, in his arms and legs. His bleeding hands were becoming slick on the conduit, and every time he stopped climbing, he had to wipe the blood off onto his trousers.

Schlenker began to mentally calculate the alloy and construction requirements for a pressure vessel capable of withstanding one thousand atmospheres of pressure. They were not easy calculations to make, and he was thankful for the mental exercise. He continued upward.

While engaged in these calculations, Schlenker also tried to think of how long he had been climbing. Like most people in the underground, he had developed a strong sense of the passage of time without benefit of light. In this case, however, time seemed to have become elastic, stretching out and snapping back. His body felt like he had been climbing for days, but his mind (the rational part, at least) told him it couldn't have been more than three hours. He realized during one of his frequent rest stops that he hadn't eaten since their breakfast that morning in the officers' quarters in the prison. How long ago was that? He had started to lose all sense of time. The entire day had become foreshortened to where it felt like a week or more. Still he continued to climb.

As he got closer to the bottom of the finger of rock that formed the prison's foundation, Schlenker had a series of terrifying thoughts: *What if the conduit just passes through the rock with no extra space? What if there is nowhere else for me to go? Do I go back down? What then? How will we get out if I can't make it to the top?*

Schlenker told himself to stop worrying and to deal with these problems only if they presented themselves. He had passed thirty-seven bands and could just make out the bottom of the rock outcrop ahead. Thirty-eight. Thirty-nine. Forty. Here, he drank the last of his water. He could see only two more bands before he reached the rock. He smirked when he realized that Slattispoone had been wrong about the distance when he told them it was four hundred meters to the asylum.

"I should say 420 meters . . . Slotted Spoon."

He caught his breath and continued. He quickly saw that he needn't have worried about the conduit as it passed through the rock; the cables passed through a circular hole large enough for him to easily get through. He supposed that it made perfect sense: the cables and pipes would have to be inspected on occasion, and a worker would have to be able to inspect them along their entire length. He passed the last steel band and made his way into the hole.

Once in the hole, Schlenker was able to move more quickly since he could brace his back against the side. It wasn't easier for him, though, with his hands bleeding profusely and every muscle in his body either on fire or simply unwilling to respond properly. His arms and legs felt as though they had been torn from his body and then reattached without anesthetic. There were no more bands as he ascended the last fifty meters through the prison's foundation. He turned off the headlamp for this final dash to the top; he couldn't risk the possibility of an enemy agent at the top seeing his light and opening fire. Or an overzealous guard. Finally, Schlenker found the top of the hole, which ended in a large mechanical room filled with furnaces, boilers, and generators. The cables and pipes branched out from the hole and snaked their way through the room to their various points of origin in the belly of the facility.

Schlenker slowly pulled himself out of the hole with what felt like the last molecule of his strength and collapsed to the floor beside the hole, breathing shakily. His entire body began to shake uncontrollably, and the fatigue tried to overtake him as he lay there panting and trying not to retch. He still had his friends to think about, and it would not do to let them down.

He got to his feet, very shakily, and shambled away from the hole that had lately been his path of ascent. The room he was in had a single light over the exit door, though darkened flood lamps in the ceiling meant the room would be very well lit if workers switched them on. Schlenker took advantage of the light to take stock of himself and his equipment. He had left his coat down below since it wasn't necessary for his climb and would have been too heavy anyway. He removed the rope that had served as his safety harness and stowed it back in his satchel. Out of the satchel came the steam pistols he had brought, which he tucked into his belt. Extra reload cylinders were stuffed into his pockets. He tore cloth from his now filthy, sweat-soaked shirt and bandaged his hands to prevent the blood from impeding his ability to operate the pistols, should the need arise. He sat and collected himself for a few minutes as a wave of nausea passed over him. He was well aware that such an ordeal would have physical and psychological consequences that would last for a while. He had never been overly afraid of heights; however, the constant stress and uncertainty of his climb, with the possibility of falling twenty kilometers to his death, had taken its toll.

Doctor Schlenker sat and took deep breaths to calm himself before getting to his feet again, just as shakily. He was heading cautiously for the door when he heard what sounded like gunfire echoing through the hallway outside. There was a battle going on nearby in the prison.

# 28

## Rescue

Doctor Schlenker drew one of the steam pistols and moved toward the door. There was a large window in the door, which to him seemed strange in a prison until he realized that, for this room in particular, it would be a good idea to be able to see a fire inside the room before opening the door from the outside. There was a lot of machinery in the room that could easily explode.

More shots rang out, and this close to the door, Schlenker could hear that they were very close. He knew from his ascent on the conduit that the elevator room was just through the wall to his right, so the hallway outside his door must run straight into it. He held the pistol in his right hand and tested the door handle with his left. He thanked Vulcan that he was in a secure area of the prison; the door was unlocked. He would have lost any element of surprise if he had had to shoot the lock out, and his hands would be utterly useless for trying to pick it. He looked through the window and could see down the hall toward the elevator room. There was no door at the end, and he could see into a small sliver of the room. That meant that as he approached the room, he would have a good view into it, but any occupants of the room would also be able to see him. He would have to move quickly.

Schlenker opened the door quietly and moved through, shutting it behind him as silently as a ghost. He placed his satchel on the ground to prevent it snagging on anything and started to approach the opening ahead. He could see that his hallway entered the elevator room in the far back corner, away from the main doors. He was thankful for the advantage.

As he got closer, he could see the bodies of several prison guards lying on the floor just inside the main doors. They had clearly been shot several times. There was some debris, as well as a lot of bullet holes in the wall surrounding the doors. The doors themselves were partially open, held there by the body of one of Slattispoone's orderlies. Occasionally several bullets could be heard zipping past the open doors and ricocheting through the elevator room. Schlenker crept closer and could see that three orderlies with pistols had barricaded themselves inside the room as best they could. One of them was badly wounded with what sounded like a sucking chest wound, but the other two were firing through the doorway at what Schlenker assumed was a lot of prison guards. The wounded orderly was sitting propped up against the side of the elevator, on top of broken glass from the shattered elevator windows. He looked ready to fall into unconsciousness. The other two were focused on the doors, using the elevator as cover from the guards' incoming fire. Schlenker made the decision to end their standoff.

He moved as quickly as possible into the room and ran at the two orderlies. He opened fire at the nearest one, hitting him with three shots in the torso and a fourth hitting him high in the jaw. The orderly slumped to the floor and never moved again. The second orderly spun at the sound of Schlenker's first shot and fired the last two shots in his pistol. Both went wide as Schlenker was moving;

the orderly got to his feet and started to move and reload his pistol as Schlenker finished with his first target.

Schlenker turned to face the second orderly and opened fire, missing his target as the orderly disappeared in a crouch behind the elevator. Schlenker crouched behind the opposite side of the elevator and began to reload his pistol. He was glad he had the presence of mind to do so; the spent cylinder contained only one last round. Armed with a fresh ten-round cylinder, he began to circle the elevator with the pistol raised. He could just see the top of the orderly's head moving in the opposite direction around the elevator, still using what cover he had. Schlenker wanted to try shooting through the elevator, but from the look of all the dents caused by prior gunshots, the steel was too thick to penetrate.

Suddenly a single shot rang out, and Schlenker could hear the unmistakable sound of a body falling to the floor. Schlenker stood slowly from his crouch (he couldn't have moved any faster if he had wanted to) and could see Captain Blake on the opposite side of the elevator car, a pistol in his hand. Other guards were pouring into the room to ensure the threat was over.

"Doctor!" Blake began. "We thought you must be dead! When I heard the shots inside the room and then saw you circling the elevator, I thought I'd gone mad. Then I realized you would need my help and hurried in."

"Ah, Captain. I'm so glad to see you. I suppose you must have heard about our adventures?" Schlenker asked, as cheerfully as his physical state allowed.

"I have no idea how you appeared here, but I'm glad you did. I truly hope there is an explanation for all of this, but that can wait. We've been occupied with this standoff for several hours, which prevented us from seeing the damage."

"Well, then I have news for you. The damage is total. The entire asylum has fallen into the crevasse below."

"I was afraid of that. When we heard the explosions, we feared the worst. I was on my way down here to investigate when I was informed that Slotted Spoon had left the prison."

Schlenker nodded. "Yes, he left us in a very dramatic fashion. But enough of that for now. Is the elevator in working order? The rest of my team will need rescue, as will most of the staff and patients from the asylum."

Blake looked at the elevator, much the worse for wear after the lengthy firefight.

"My technicians will have a look at it immediately. I hope we can get it down there quickly. May I ask how you got back up here?"

Schlenker sat heavily against the wall and closed his eyes while prison maintenance technicians entered the room and began to clear broken glass and other debris away from the elevator car. Medics and guards were carrying away dead and wounded guards and orderlies, and the one wounded orderly was being loaded onto a stretcher. He didn't look good, but Schlenker thought he might just survive to spend the rest of his life in the prison above.

"I had to climb the electrical and water conduit. I am understandably exhausted."

Blake's eyes widened. "You what? The conduit? You climbed four hundred meters on that?"

"Four hundred and seventy, including the hole through the foundation. That is an approximation, of course. It may have been as many as 473. I don't know how long it took me. Several hours."

"The explosions happened just before noon. It's now eleven-thirty at night. We thought you were all dead. We didn't even know what happened. The elevator came up from the asylum, and then suddenly we heard two explosions below. I came down here to see what was going on and saw that my two guards here had been shot. Then bullets were flying through the doorway. I lost a few good men here."

Schlenker sighed. "Yes, a few more good people were probably lost when the asylum collapsed. Slattispoone destroyed the structural anchors holding the asylum to the wall. We discovered that he had been experimenting on his patients, and he had to make a getaway. He also admitted to being a Trician spy, and that many of his orderlies were Ünterreich agents."

Blake didn't know what to say. The sheer magnitude of the entire revelation was too much to take in all at once. He just sat and listened as Doctor Schlenker explained the events of the past twelve hours. Schlenker left out the part about the Aztec city; he thought that Blake's head might explode as it was. Medics finished with the dead and wounded and then came over to attend to Schlenker. His hands were cleaned and bandaged, as were a few other nicks and cuts from his climbing, cave exploration, ancient mysterious subterranean city exploration, and narrow escape from an exploding asylum. He was able to wolf down a meal that Blake had ordered brought down, and by the time the elevator was ready for use, he was feeling somewhat better, though he couldn't remember a time when he was so tired and sore.

The technicians had been able to repair the elevator to working order fairly quickly, and Blake followed Schlenker and two other guards into the steel car for their first descent.

"You're sure you want to go back down? The last time, you had to climb back up," Blake reminded him.

Schlenker nodded. "I have to be certain my friends are alright, and I am hoping that I won't be getting stuck back down there again. Once was plenty enough for me."

The car was activated, and it descended through the hole in the floor. As they slowly passed the conduit on their way down, Blake informed Schlenker about what he had discovered since the asylum explosion.

"Slattispoone must have taken one of the back hallways to get from the elevator to the cable car. We never saw him or his henchmen. By the time we were dodging bullets in the elevator room, Slattispoone was well away in the cable car. He murdered several guards at both ends of the cable system, and he must have had a private vehicle hidden near the rail line with the ability to use the rails. He seems to have gotten clean away for now."

"Not to worry, Captain. I think my team and I will be able to find him. He may actually come looking for us, since we have a lot more valuable information that he needs."

They reached the end of the conduit, and the elevator slowed as Blake eased off on the operating lever. Blake had instructed the technicians to free up extra cable to allow the car to descend further. They were able to descend until they were even with the storage room door, though the elevator car was still a good six meters away from the wall at that point. Their lights were able to illuminate Spall, Shaw, and Henry, all safe and sound and looking in need of rescue.

"Doctor Schlenker! I cannot tell you how glad I am to see you. And Captain Blake. Thank you so much for coming to our rescue," Spall yelled over to the elevator.

"Here, Spall. Catch the line!" Schlenker yelled back as he threw one end of a rope over to the stranded agents. Spall caught the line and began to tie it around Henry's waist. Shaw immediately grew concerned.

"I suppose they're just going to reel us into the elevator now, like a fish?"

"It's either that or tie the rope off and you pull yourself across. This way, we don't have to worry as much about anyone falling, since it's tied to the elevator car and the person's waist. Off you go, Henry."

With that, Henry swallowed hard and walked off the edge of the doorway and into the abyss. He swung like a human pendulum beneath the elevator car several times as Blake began to haul on the rope with the other guards. Schlenker's hands were so painful that he couldn't help. Soon, Henry was safely inside the car and the rope had been thrown across again. Spall caught the end and began to tie it around Shaw's waist.

"I'll have you know that I would rather not jump out there," Shaw said to Spall. "If we live through this, I'm never leaving Schlenker's house ever again."

Spall finished tying the knot. "To tell the truth, I am not anxious to go myself."

Shaw looked at Spall. "I find that surprising. You don't come across as someone who is afraid of much."

"Fears are best hidden," Spall proclaimed.

"Okay," Shaw began, "just give me a second to collect myself—"

Spall, never one for ceremony, interrupted Shaw by pushing him backward into the void of the crevasse. Shaw screamed and yelled a surprising amount of foul language at Spall as he swung beneath the elevator car. After a few seconds, Shaw was inside the elevator car, shaking from another adrenaline rush. Spall was thrown the rope again, and he secured it around one of the nurses, who was pulled up when it was her turn to jump. One by one, all the other nurses were rescued, followed by Adebe and Saoirse, before Spall tied the rope around his own waist and stepped off. It was a good thing he had gone last. Spall's sheer size and bulk meant that he weighed significantly more than anyone else, and they needed everyone on the elevator to help pull him up. Soon he was inside the elevator and the five agents had been reunited. The elevator was brought back up, with four relieved agents and one incredibly annoyed agent on board.

"Well, Schlenker, it seems you took some abuse on your climb. I must say that you have once again impressed me," Spall congratulated him. "Once you had left the range of our torches, we had to content ourselves with watching the headlamp. Our hearts stopped beating every time you switched it off."

"I confess that my heart stopped beating several times as well. It was no easy feat, and one I never intend to duplicate," Schlenker admitted.

They arrived back in the damp prison foundations and were escorted from the scene by Captain Blake, while Henry and the nurses were taken to another area to be questioned regarding their knowledge of Slattispoone's activities. Blake had left a subordinate in charge of the cleanup and rescue, since a report had to be given to Warden Reichert.

"Will you be able to rescue everyone still down there, do you think?" Schlenker asked Blake.

"I think so. We were not fully prepared for this sort of thing. Especially not the director of the asylum turning traitor and destroying the facility. It's fortunate that most of the asylum rooms were bored into the cavern wall. All the patients who were in their cells will be safe but hungry, and I hope that once all your shooting started, the staff were able to seek shelter in their rooms and offices. It may take us a few days to get everyone out with the elevator, especially the dangerous ones and the ones you told me about, Doctor. Some of them may have been better off if they had fallen with the building."

"I agree," Spall said. "I am not normally shocked; however, what Slotted Spoon was doing down there gave me chills. It reminded me far too much of Ünterreich."

Shaw looked at Spall, who had a faraway look in his eyes, as though he were seeing scenes from the past best forgotten. He hoped to one day hear the tale of Spall's escape from the dreaded city and cavern of Ünterreich, but there were many other things he hoped to never hear. If witnessing experimentation on live subjects reminded Spall of his former home, there must have been many horrors there indeed.

Blake led them all through the prison to the main elevator, which they rode all the way to the prison hospital. Shaw couldn't help thinking about how much they had been through in less than sixteen hours, since they first met Slattispoone in the warden's office.

The warden was sitting at the main nurse's station in the hospital, and he rose to his feet as they entered.

"Agents! I am so relieved to see you alive! When everything started to happen all at once, we didn't know what to make of it. And Slattispoone. I hope he's caught and then sentenced to time here. I would make it my personal duty to make the rest of his life very interesting indeed."

"We will be pursuing him as soon as we can be away from here," Spall stated. "Is the cable car functional, or did Slattispoone damage it as well?"

"It is functional, and standing by as we speak. Blake will escort you as soon as we get you patched up and you provide me with what you know of this event."

# 29

## Back to Echo City

The five agents related their story as quickly as possible to Warden Reichert, leaving out the Aztec ruins to save time. Reichert was well aware of the agents' need to leave; however, he also needed to be satisfied with their explanation of what had happened. So many events that day had been so bizarre. After a few minutes, Warden Reichert thanked the agents and instructed Blake to see them out when the medical staff had finished. They had their wounds examined and stitched up in short order, though Spall's wound required a good amount of care and attention; he wouldn't have full use of his left arm for several weeks, at least. Adebe did have a mild concussion, but there was little else she could do but rest.

Fortunately there was also food available for them, and they all ate ravenously. Once they were fed, stitched, and bandaged, Blake led them to the prison telegraph room to allow Spall to send a message to the Secret Service and the prime minister's office. They had to be made aware of recent events and to watch for Slattispoone. Once

ELEMENT

Spall's task was complete, they were escorted to the cable car, where Blake saluted them and shook their hands before wishing them luck with their impending hunt of Slattispoone.

"I hope you catch him, but I hope he puts up a fight when you do. He deserves a few well-placed bullet holes for everything he's done here."

"Yes, I would be only too happy to acquaint him with small amounts of lead at high velocity," Spall agreed. "Thank you for your rescue, Captain. I hope the next time we meet will be under better circumstances."

With that, the cable car moved off from the platform and out over the abyss of Isolation Crevasse. This time, Shaw didn't really care as much about his fear of heights; he was too tired. They had been through a lot in the past twenty-four hours, and the most depressing part was that they had been awake for it all. Within a few minutes, all five agents were asleep, and none of them stirred until they had arrived at the far end of the crevasse. The guards awakened the agents once the cable car stopped, and they were ushered up to the train platform. There were a few signs of a small battle near the train platform, with bullet holes and dark patches of dried blood on the floor. Clearly the guards had given Slattispoone's group a difficult time leaving. The thought made Shaw smile groggily as they were led to a bench in the small guardroom to wait for the train.

Shaw leaned against Saoirse and Adebe, and they were all asleep within moments. It seemed as though they had just closed their eyes when they were awakened once again for the train. Shaw looked over and could see several guards shaking Doctor Schlenker vigorously in an attempt to wake him. Shaw couldn't help feeling sorry for Schlenker; the man kept himself in decent shape somehow, but the ordeal he had just gone through in climbing the power conduit was unimaginable, and he was a good ten years older than Shaw. No wonder the guards were having such a hard time waking him up.

305

Finally Schlenker opened his eyes and stood with a groan. "Oh, bugger. I feel as though every muscle in my body has been replaced with hot lead. I could sleep for a month."

"I agree. This has been unexpectedly strenuous," Spall added.

Shaw looked at Spall, who aside from his left arm, which was in a sling, looked as fresh and well pressed as he always did. He even looked freshly shaved, which Shaw knew was impossible. Saoirse looked haggard, with tufts of hair coming out of her bun, and Adebe's tight black curls had erupted after the doctors examined the back of her head. The effect made her head look like a giant black pom-pom. Looking over at Schlenker, the doctor had clearly seen better days. He had a short growth of beard starting, the lines in his face were deeper and more pronounced, and his skin looked almost gray.

The train arrived as they walked onto the platform. They boarded the first-class coach and took their private cabin, stowing their now ragged-looking baggage before sitting down. Once the train began to move, they were all asleep within seconds.

The eleven hours of their return journey to Echo Cavern went blissfully quickly as the five agents slept off the effects of their adventure at the asylum. They slept right through breakfast, but Shaw and Spall woke Saoirse for lunch in the dining car while Schlenker and Adebe continued to sleep. Once back in their compartment, they all returned to sleep until they were awakened for dinner. They were nearing their destination, so all five rose (slowly and painfully) and took dinner together before preparing themselves for their arrival at Echo City. The food was delicious, and they wanted to get one last good meal in before they had to submit themselves to Mrs. Clary's culinary tyranny again.

"My father always said our stomachs needed an oil change every few weeks, but Mrs. Clary gives us one every meal," Shaw joked.

Doctor Schlenker laughed, and it was clear that his good spirits had fully returned, even though he groaned with every movement.

The train arrived at the cavernous copper interior of the Echo City train station shortly after the evening meal was finished. The five agents shambled out of the station and into a steam taxi, which took them back to Schlenker's home. Copperhead met them at the door with his usual hissing and clanking.

*Whistle.*

"Ah, Copperhead. I am so glad to be home. We have already eaten, so Mrs. Clary can take the evening off. We've had quite the adventure, and we all need baths. Would you see to it?"

*Whistle.*

"Yes, including Spall. Thank you."

"I won't be needing one here; I'll be heading back home right away," Saoirse said.

"Me too," Adebe added. "I plan to bathe and sleep for a week."

With that, and a short pause in Spall's direction (Shaw found himself thinking that Copperhead was glaring at Spall), Copperhead clomped away up the stairs to the rooms. Meanwhile, the agents made their way out back to Schlenker's lab, where they emptied their satchels and put their equipment away.

"I will have to make a report to the prime minister in the morning," Spall explained when they had emptied the last of their confiscated pistols onto a workbench. "Some of these weapons are clearly Trician manufacture; I hope Slattispoone doesn't have any other Trician weapons at his disposal. I have no doubt he will be making his preparations for leaving Echo City soon. He has to know we will be looking for him."

"We may be lucky in that regard," Schlenker said. "He may think we're dead, or still trapped down in that infernal crevasse. It's possible we could surprise him."

"Possible, but unlikely. We will have to assume that he will have agents watching our homes. He knows we are looking for Bergstrom's Fragment, and if he has that one, he will try to get any of the others we already have. He will also know that we do not have Bergstrom's Fragment and so will be looking to get it from him. He would be a great fool if we could surprise him now."

Schlenker looked at Spall. "I see what you mean, Spall. He is not a great fool, and that means we must be on our guard while we hunt him. He may be hunting us at the same time."

"Can we secure the Fragments we already have?" Shaw asked.

"Oh, yes; I took that precaution already," Schlenker answered. "They have been well hidden under lock and key for some months now. Only Copperhead knows their location so no one could get the materials from any of us using torture."

"An excellent notion, Schlenker," Spall congratulated him.

"Yes, fantastic. I often think about torture as well. And what happens when Copperhead breaks down and forgets where he put them?"

Schlenker looked blank. "I hadn't thought of that. My machines usually don't break down."

"Oh, good. Glad I checked. What other weapons are you afraid of? Those Black Hands you were telling me about?"

Spall nodded. "Yes, I fear Slattispoone may have access to them. There is no known defense against them, and our armor and weapons will be useless."

"Apparently even water won't cause them to short out," Adebe noted.

Spall sighed. "We shall have to address these issues later. I do not know about anyone else, but I require that bath."

They all agreed to continue their discussion later. Adebe and Saoirse left for their own homes, and the others made their way back to the house.

The combined greenish-blue light of the quake shield and the gas lamps illuminated the city, while numerous clock towers chimed the evening hours. Shaw realized through his exhausted daze that he could even hear the clock tower on the roof of the Steam Workers Guild nearby, which used a gigantic pipe organ rather than bells to sing the hours. He hadn't noticed it before; it was incredible how many things he was still experiencing for the first time, even after months in the underground. As he stumbled up the stairs to his room, he wondered how many more new and exciting things he would see and experience in the future.

Shaw undressed with some difficulty, his shoulder still screaming from the bullet wound. It had been about twenty-four hours since the gunfight, but it simultaneously felt like it had been twenty years or just ten minutes. *The human mind has a funny way of stretching or compressing time depending on the circumstances*, thought Shaw as he gingerly stepped into his bath, wincing at the hot water. He nearly cried out when the water splashed onto his fresh bandages, and he made a mental note not to allow his shoulder to sink below the water again. He sat and soaked for a while, allowing the hot water to relax his sore muscles.

He sat in the hot water, staring across the copper tub at the wall, paneled in embossed steel sheets like wallpaper. His eyes eventually settled on a shelf on the wall opposite him, which held a few towels and an electric fan. He was glad the fan wasn't plugged in; if it fell off the shelf into the tub, he could be electrocuted. That thought brought him back to the Black Hands of the Tricians. Apparently waterproof, Adebe mentioned. He pondered the problem for a while before finishing his bath and getting ready for bed, the thought of water pistols running in circles through his mind for some odd reason.

Spall was in much the same position as Shaw as far as getting into the tub. His left arm ached where the bullet had entered, and there was a fair bit of discoloration at both the entry and exit wounds. *I'll not have much use of that arm for some time*, thought Spall. He bathed and prepared for bed, grateful that Schlenker had always insisted that he keep a room with clothing and other necessities there for such an occasion. There had been many nights of helping Schlenker with various projects throughout the past few years, and Spall was glad to not have to make the trip home after a long session.

Schlenker enjoyed his bath for a considerable length of time, allowing it to ease the tension inside his aching, screaming muscles. He hadn't been this sore in years, and he certainly hadn't seen this much excitement in one day, at least not since he had first met Spall. Now *that* had been an adventure. They had always been the unlikeliest of friends: Spall the large, brooding hero type, and Schlenker the talkative genius. But they had accomplished some truly monumental tasks for the prime minister in the past, and they would accomplish more, Schlenker was certain. They would succeed in their quest to find all the Fragments, including Bergstrom's.

All three agents went to bed thinking of the remainder of their quest, and how they still had work to do in finding Slattispoone and retrieving the fourth Fragment. If they still could.

# 30

## The Hunt for Slattispoone

The next morning, after a generous helping of Mrs. Clary's porridge (which Spall muttered would be very effective at stopping bullets), the three agents reconvened in the lab, where Adebe was already waiting, looking quite a lot better, though she was still paler than usual. The concussion was going to take a long time to fully heal.

"The first place we need to investigate is Slattispoone's residence here in the city," Spall began. "I sent a telegram from the prison to the office to have agents posted at all train stations and all vehicular exits from this cavern to keep a watch for him. If he attempts to leave the cavern, we will know. We also have agents searching his house as we speak."

"Are we even sure that he and his goons came here?" asked Shaw. "Isn't there anywhere else to go from the prison line?"

Spall shook his head. "No. The prison is nearly the end of that particular line, and I am uncertain if you noticed, but there are no other exits from that tunnel. It was built that way purposefully to ensure that any escaped convicts would only have one way to go, which is right into this cavern, where they would be picked up quickly by the Echo Police or the Secret Service. No, Slattispoone is here, somewhere. Now we need to find out where he has gone to ground. He wouldn't have been able to get from this cavern to any areas controlled by Ünterreich very easily, at least not without us hearing about it."

"I agree," Schlenker added; "he must still be in our realm. The only ways to get through to Ünterreich are through the battlefield in Winterswijk or with the diplomatic embassy. We would have gotten word if he had attempted either route."

"So we focus on finding him here, then?" Adebe asked.

"Yes, the city is the only place where he could remain concealed for any length of time. The Tricians must have a safe house here somewhere. Likely two or more."

"How do you know that, Spall?" Schlenker asked.

"I would have several. In espionage, one must always have a backup of everything. Preferably numerous backups. It does not do to get caught."

"So how do we find a safe house here in the city? You told me there were close to two million people living here. They could be anywhere," Shaw observed.

"Indeed they could. We will have to make a visit to the head office," Spall said.

"We have a head office? Why is that something I don't know?"

"It never came up. I seldom go there. Schlenker and I prefer to work in the periphery of things."

"But aren't you the head of the Secret Service? Shouldn't you be at the office all the time?"

"No, just the head of the Special Branch, the members of which are here in this room, with one exception," Spall said, indicating the four of them. "I generally have very little to do at my office. We have hundreds of fine agents who will be able to assist us. Agent Muir is already there briefing several teams."

"I hope some of them know where to find a Trician safe house around here."

"As do I. Shall we?"

With that, the four Agents left Doctor Schlenker's home and traveled in Schlenker's steam car. Shaw couldn't shake the feeling of unease growing inside him. They had discussed the possibility that Slattispoone or his agents might be hunting for the Fragments in their possession, and yet they had made no attempts to hide or conceal themselves to make it more difficult for the Tricians to find what they were after. And here they were, driving openly through the streets of Echo City in Schlenker's bright stainless steel car, which was instantly recognizable, leaving Schlenker's house unprotected. As Schlenker said, even he didn't know where their three Fragments were hidden. But should they be captured or killed, the Trician agents might be able to search Schlenker's house at their leisure—though they might have to contend with Copperhead. *That would slow them down for a while*, thought Shaw with a smile. *I don't even know how anyone would damage him. He's hardened steel everywhere except the head, and that would still function even when filled with bullet holes, according to Schlenker.*

They passed crowds of people on their way to work, and Shaw was always surprised at the variations in the clothing and styles of the underground. Of course there was nothing like the variety of the surface world (and Shaw still felt a particular longing for the sight of a miniskirt); nevertheless, the fashion industry was alive and well in the caverns. There was a large use of synthetic fibers in the textiles, which had surprised Shaw at first, since this society had evolved before most synthetic fibers had been developed. Necessity is the mother of invention, of course, and the lack of daylight in the caverns for much of the twentieth century meant that plants and animals had become scarce and expensive. It made sense for the scientists to find alternatives to natural fibers. They seemed to have found similar products to nylon and rayon, but that was where Shaw's knowledge of man-made fabrics ended.

Shaw watched the passing crowds and wondered what sort of work everyone did down in the underground. There must have been the usual doctors, lawyers, police officers, firefighters, accountants, butchers, bakers, plumbers, carpenters. Though the last one, Shaw thought, must have been a very well-paid profession indeed, like a goldsmith on the surface. Every occupation would have a necessary place in the underground city. They even had professional athletes, although their preferred game of stone-ball still had Shaw intrigued. *I really have to sit down when this is all over and watch a few more games*, he thought. The one he had seen had been very exciting, and the fans seemed to be just as boisterous as any he had seen on the surface with any other game.

They arrived at a plain, nondescript steel-and-stone building in the government district. A glance up to the nearest corner revealed a sign marking it as Jade Street. It looked as though parking in this area was as problematic as it would be in the downtown core of any major city, despite the use of public transit. There were electric and steam cars parked along the street under the glow of the gaslights, with people coming and going everywhere. They finally found a parking spot around the corner from their destination and had to walk around the building to get in.

Once inside, the more or less featureless building showed its true nature. Inside the door were posted armed guards, who immediately stopped the four agents and demanded their identification. Once the guards were satisfied (Adebe got a wink from one of the female guards; the others recognized Spall and Schlenker immediately but regarded Shaw with suspicion), they were allowed to proceed past the entry foyer, which was polished marble like so many other buildings Shaw had seen. The seal of the Echo City Secret Service was inset into the floor in polished brass, and Spall instructed Shaw to avoid stepping on the seal as a sign of respect to the agency. As in the Government Spire, everything seemed to be made of polished stone. The floor gleamed, as did the walls and pillars; the interior of the building was much grander than the exterior.

They took a massive staircase up to the third floor, their footsteps echoing along the hallways (except for Spall's, which Shaw still found to be creepy for such a large man). Spall led them through a huge wrought-iron door that opened onto a large anteroom with a bronze desk. Shaw was delighted to see Saoirse sitting at the desk, typing on a large machine that looked to Shaw like a typewriter that had, against all natural laws and sanity, mated with a steam engine. There were gears and levers protruding at strange angles from slots and grooves in the brass casing, and the machine hummed loudly when it wasn't clanking away on a sheet of metal paper.

Saoirse looked up from her work and exclaimed, "Oh, Mr. Spall! I'm so glad to see you. I've briefed the teams as you requested, and they're getting themselves sorted out right now. Hawkesbury should be up soon to let us know when they're ready. Aside from that, I've left a stack of ironing on your desk for you to sign, and I need to reschedule a couple of meetings with the deputy directors. You've missed a few of them now, you know."

"Yes, every missed meeting saddens me more," Spall said as sarcastically as he could.

The others all chuckled. Clearly they all felt the same way about meetings.

"You've done well, Muir. Thank you for finishing up here. I hope your wound isn't too painful?"

"Not at all, sir." She glanced over at Shaw and blushed a little. "Not nearly as debilitating as yours and Ryan's."

Shaw nodded. His wound still ached abominably. He was thankful that aspirin had been discovered before the caverns had been settled. They didn't have ibuprofen or acetaminophen, but at least they had one painkiller that didn't knock a person out like morphine or other opiates.

"You've done stellar work, Muir. Now that you've returned to full duty, they will have a difficult time replacing you in this administration position," Spall added.

"Thanks, sir. I can't say I'll miss the desk."

"For now, we need to discuss our next steps in the office."

The five agents entered Spall's spacious office. It wasn't as impressive as the prime minister's or Warden Reichert's office, but it was still nicely appointed.

"Ironing? Does that mean paperwork?" Shaw asked.

"Yes, I suppose it does. Rather than paper, everything is printed on sheets of iron alloy. Where you have 'paperwork,' we have 'ironing.'"

Shaw smiled as he looked around the room. It looked like a beautifully paneled surface-world room, except instead of wood paneling, the room was finished in abraded copper. Even the desk matched the paneling and the bookcases. The floor tiles were made from dark green serpentine with flecks of gold. It was such a beautiful deep hue that Shaw thought it was a carpet when he first stepped into the room. The large window looked out onto the city, with a good view of the Government Spire and the beam from the quake shield. The gas lamps in the room gave off their customary warm glow, amplified by the copper walls. Spall motioned for the others to sit in four leather and wrought-iron chairs as Spall sat in the spacious chair behind the desk.

"Unfortunately, we will have to play a waiting game now. I had hoped Slattispoone and his Trician friends would have made their move before we escaped the asylum; however, this is not the case. They will be very cautious now, as I am certain they know we have returned and will be looking for them. We have agents all over the city now, especially around your house, Doctor. My hope is that they will attempt to break in and find the other Fragments. When they cannot find them, they will return to their hiding place and report.

With some luck and a great deal of skill, our agents will be able to follow them through the city to determine their location. If we can find Slattispoone, we may be able to find Bergstrom's Fragment. I am sure this will have answered a great many questions that were burning in your mind, Shaw. I know you were concerned with our overt movements through the city, especially in taking Schlenker's ridiculous automobile."

"It's not ridiculous. It's perfectly functional; I just added a few um, improvements." Schlenker defended his invention. "It just looks unusual because Copperhead sticks out so much when he drives it."

"It looks like a Shriner's car in a circus parade, Schlenker," Shaw added. He was met with blank stares from the others.

"They're old guys who drive around in tiny vehicles in parades," he explained. "I don't know what else they do, so don't ask for any more explanation than that."

"I think I've heard of them," Schlenker mentioned. "They're a gentlemen's league or club that does good works, correct?"

Shaw nodded. "Sounds about right," he said.

"Why drive tiny vehicles?" Spall asked.

Shaw shrugged, wincing at his shoulder.

"I sometimes think the underground is a madhouse, but compared to the surface, we are an island of sanity," remarked Adebe.

"You're not wrong," Shaw admitted.

Spall turned his attention back to Schlenker. "I hope they don't damage your property too badly, Doctor."

"Not to worry. Copperhead accidentally destroys many of my possessions every week. I doubt an army of Tricians could do more damage than he."

Saoirse was still worried. "What if they realize that Schlenker's house is a trap? What if they decide to just cut their losses and run back to Ünterreich without our Fragments? Where would that leave us?"

Schlenker spoke up. "We would be out Bergstrom's Fragment, it is true, but once we have all the others, we would only have to puzzle out the one piece. It may still take years, but if we had only one Fragment, we would need a second group of geniuses to work for decades to recreate the first success. That is where the Tricians would be if they left. I think they will want to improve their chances."

Spall nodded in agreement. "I think that as well. You may be correct, Muir. They may decide to cut and run, but I think this will be too important for them to just leave. The potential for energy and food production is too great for them to ignore."

"Plus the possibility of them developing it into a weapon," added Shaw.

"Yes, they would be salivating about that, I have no doubt. No, they will try something soon. And when they do, we will be able to find them," said Spall confidently.

They continued to discuss various scenarios and options for some time, stopping only for a quick tea break.

After an hour, there was a knock at the office door and a stocky man with dark features entered, holding a dented aluminum bowler hat in his massive hands. His nose was crooked and flat, and both ears were moderately swollen and knobby, reminding Shaw of the classic "cauliflower ears" exhibited by many prizefighters and professional wrestlers. He was definitely a person who had seen a fight or two in his time. No doubt he would fit in in a lot of nasty places. The man's face looked like a Picasso that had really let itself go. He stood to attention before Spall and nodded.

"Sir. I 'ave a report for yeh," began the agent in a thick Scottish accent.

"Very well. Thank you for joining us, Agent Hawkesbury. Do proceed."

"Well, sir, the agents were all in place as soon as we received yer message. There was no activity at Doctor Schlenker's residence until yeh arrived. Shortly afterward, an unidentified female subject was observed leaving the area in some 'aste. Agents Fawkes and Loxterkamp attempted to follow 'er; 'owever, she managed to lose them in the rail yards. She was clearly well trained in counterespionage, sir."

"I see. How was she able to lose Fawkes and Loxterkamp? They are two of our best agents."

"Classic rail trick, sir. She approached the rail yards and waited at the platform fer a train to approach. Once it was nearly to 'er position, she ran across the tracks in front of the locomotive to t'other side. Me men couldn't pursue until the train was gone. By then, she'd disappeared. I've already given 'em an earful, sir, saving you the trouble."

"That was kind of you, Hawkesbury. We are dealing with the best the Tricians have to offer, I fear. Many of them will be every bit as good as our agents. Perhaps better. This will be an excellent reminder to everyone to have our wits about us. Our people may even be attacked. Ensure that everyone has their weapons on them as well. They may be necessary all too soon."

"Yes, sir. I 'ave already seen to that. They're wearing their armor as well, though the bloody Tricians will probably be carrying their blasted Black Hands and shard guns. Those wolfram darts'll go right bloody through, and the iron gloves'll cook yeh from the inside out, armor or no."

"Wolfram? Is that the same as tungsten?" Shaw asked.

Hawkesbury turned and regarded Shaw with curiosity. Spall nodded at Shaw.

"Agent Hawkesbury, this is Agent Shaw. The man from the surface, if you recall."

Hawkesbury smiled at Shaw, and Shaw noticed quite a number of patches of gold where teeth should have been. He must have kept more than a few dentists in business all on his own. Shaw rose from his seat and they shook hands. Shaw's hand was crushed in a nearly inhuman grip. The man was a bear.

"Ah, yeh, the surfacer," Hawkesbury said. "Thought I recognized yeh. Glad to have yeh aboard. Anthony Hawkesbury."

"Ryan Shaw, but everyone calls me Shaw. Nice to meet you, Anthony."

"Call me Tony. The only person that calls me Anthony is me wife, and that's when I've committed some foul transgression. It 'appens a lot. Mr. Spall, 'ere, is a dainty flower in comparison to the missus."

Spall rolled his eyes as though he had heard far worse from this agent and had learned to ignore it as best he could. Hawkesbury was a fantastic agent in spite of, or perhaps because of, his many eccentricities.

Schlenker spoke up. "I believe you are correct, Shaw. It seems to me that wolfram was also called tungsten in some languages on the surface. It makes very effective projectiles for penetrating armor, and the Tricians have developed what we call 'shard guns,' which use an electromagnetic field to accelerate a wolfram dart at extremely high velocity. Their pistols aren't as effective as their rifles, but they can still penetrate our best armor at close range, with a perpendicular shot—"

"Thank you, Doctor," Spall interjected in an effort to cut off Schlenker before he got going. "As you were saying, Hawkesbury, your people are in position?"

"Yes, sir. They're still about, and they're bein' extra cautious now. We 'ave to assume we're bein' watched as well. Agent Davidson 'as 'is wife and kids out at the park across the street for a picnic. Best cover we could come up with under the circumstances. Nobody would assume a 'ole family made up of agents."

"Davidson doesn't have children," began Spall. "Unless . . . don't tell me that Agents Malcolm and Swan are dressed up as children."

"That they are, sir, and never a better lookin' pair of lads was seen outside o' school."

"You have dressed our two midgets up as school children?"

"Aye, sir. Nobody would expect it. 'Twas their idea, sir, and a terrific one it was."

Spall sat for a second while trying to absorb this revelation. "Agent Swan has a beard, Hawkesbury."

"Aye, and Malcolm sings bass in the police choir. I pointed those facts out to 'em, sir, but they were so keen, I 'ad to let 'em go through with it. I think their savin' grace will be the fact that the park is two hundred meters away. From that distance, they can still keep an eye on the Doctor's 'ouse, but anyone close to the 'ouse will just see a pair of filthy little bastards playing in the sand."

Shaw had been sitting in silence for some time, but he had to speak up. "We employ midgets as agents here?" he asked. He couldn't remember if 'midget' was an inappropriate word anymore. Apparently not in the underground.

"Of course, as long as they pass the entrance requirements. Agents Swan and Malcolm are both very good at being unnoticed," Spall answered. "Though I don't know how effective they will be while playing in the sandbox. I suppose we will have to find out."

"Aye, sir. If it's stupid, and it works, it's not stupid. That's what me mam always said, rest 'er."

"What if it is stupid and it *doesn't* work?" asked Spall.

"Well, sir, then that would be government policy, wouldn't it?"

Spall gave Hawkesbury a humorless expression before continuing. "Thank you, Hawkesbury. You may return to your duties. Notify us immediately if there is any activity."

"Aye, sir."

With that, Agent Hawkesbury turned and left the room, shutting the door behind him.

"If he was not such a good agent in his regular duties, I would have added him to our team long ago," Spall said.

"I just wish he'd stop trying to pinch my backside," Saoirse noted. "Every time I walk past him, he makes an attempt."

"I've given him *two* black eyes over the years," Adebe added.

"I punched him in the throat last time," Saoirse went on. "Maybe he'll figure it out."

Spall looked stern. "I will have a talk with him. That behavior is unacceptable, and he knows it."

Shaw, silent for the last few moments, had to bring the conversation back to the matter at hand. "So we're just going to sit and wait for the Tricians and Slotted Spoon to make a move? There's no other way to find their safe house?"

Spall shook his head. "I am afraid not. We have discovered a few of their safe houses in the past; however, they either know we have found them or have a protocol of moving safe houses at random intervals, because they never keep them for long. It has been some time since we found one."

"How would they get agents into the city anyway?" Shaw asked, looking at Schlenker. "Schlenker, you said they would have to sneak across the battlefield or through diplomatic channels. Are those really the only two ways?"

Doctor Schlenker nodded. "Yes, as far as we know. The battlefield—or, more accurately, the battle-cavern—would be far too dangerous, with too many sets of eyes. It would be far simpler to bring their agents through disguised as attachés to their embassy here. From there they must be obtaining false identification and credentials to disappear into our society. That would be how they managed to get so many of them employed at the asylum. How Slattispoone made his initial contact with them, I don't know; how he intends to escape to Ünterreich, I can't even speculate."

"Perhaps he attended an embassy soirée and became friendly with one of their people," Adebe mused. "In any case, we will need to continue our investigations elsewhere. We cannot sit here idle."

"Agreed," Spall said.

"So where are we going now?" Shaw asked.

"Let us have a look at Slotted Spoon's house, shall we?" Spall offered.

# 31

## Slattispoone Makes His Move

They made a few plans and checked their weapons and armor before leaving the office. The five agents walked to the basement level, which turned out to be a large parking garage. Shaw noticed that Schlenker's steam car was parked in a stall clearly marked "DEPUTY DIRECTOR, SPECIAL BRANCH."

"Why did we park down the block when we could have parked in here?" Shaw asked.

"We wanted our adversaries to know where we were," Schlenker answered. "We are trying to draw them out."

Shaw rolled his eyes. "Well, we're being pretty obvious about it. I was never trained as a spy, but a lot of the things you're doing are pretty elementary. They know we're after their Fragment, and they know we know they're after our Fragments. It's a game of chess, and we're in a stalemate right now. I seriously doubt they'll ever try anything while we're being so obvious."

"You are right; we are being obvious. Acting so overtly is also a gamble," Spall agreed. "But I suspect that their desperation for our Fragments will eventually draw them out into the open. My hope is that they might underestimate us and attack."

"I just hope we're not underestimating them," said Shaw.

"As do I," said Spall. "The longer they stay here, the better our chances of locating them. They will wish to find our Fragments and leave as soon as possible. I feel they will be willing to take the risk of attacking us, and soon."

"And if they do attack us?" Shaw asked.

"They will want us alive," Spall replied. "They cannot risk killing any of us; the information is too valuable. Should we be attacked and captured, plans are in place for our agents to come to our aid."

"Oh, good. Do you mind sharing this plan with the rest of us?" Shaw was a little bit perturbed that Spall's plan hadn't come up until this very moment.

Spall smiled his unnerving crooked smile that was nearly undetectable. He explained his plan to the others as Copperhead stood nearby, occasionally letting out a short hiss of steam and dripping on the concrete floor. Once Spall was finished explaining his plan, Shaw let out a loud sigh while staring at Spall with raised eyebrows.

"It's a good plan, except for the part that's *insane,*" he said.

"Which part do you feel is insane?" Spall asked.

"The whole thing," Shaw replied. "It hinges on us surviving their initial attack. What if we don't?"

"Well, my dear Agent Shaw," Spall answered, "we shall not care much if the rest of the plan fails then, shall we?"

Copperhead started up the impressive steam car and Spall got into the back with Schlenker. Saoirse and Adebe remained behind to organize the other teams of agents assembling in the parking garage. They would all have to be on their toes should the Tricians attack.

Shaw hesitated. "I just need to take care of something. I'll be right back."

With that, he headed off toward the restrooms, past the vehicle fueling and servicing bays. He returned a minute later, apparently satisfied.

"Okay, let's go."

The polished silver vehicle glided out of the underground parking area (*or is it underbuilding? The building itself is already underground,* thought Shaw), and they traveled along Jade Street toward the far side of the city. Shaw still hadn't grown accustomed to the directions underground—he had always unconsciously used the sun to orient himself on the surface. After only a couple of minutes, he was nearly lost in the streets of Echo City. Many of the main streets were straight, radiating outward from the Government Spire like spokes on a wheel. These were bisected every kilometer by circular ring roads; however, there were many times when a road had to split off at an odd angle or curve unexpectedly to avoid a large feature of the cavern, such as a gigantic stalagmite or pillar of stone. Copperhead was also turning at random to avoid the worst areas of traffic, and Shaw suspected that the mechanical behemoth had been given instructions to make any pursuit a little more difficult for their inevitable followers. A quick glance back, though, showed Shaw what he had been expecting. He could see several vehicles following behind at a discreet distance, but none of them ever got close enough to see who the occupants were.

"We're being followed," Shaw said.

"Yes, by our own agents. I expect an attack at any time," Spall said.

After some time of traveling, Spall nudged Shaw and Schlenker and said, "We are almost there."

Schlenker looked over at Spall and asked, "What do you expect we will find there—"

Suddenly, their vehicle was struck from the side as a huge transport truck sped out of an alleyway and collided with them. The impact spun Doctor Schlenker's vehicle around until it hit a curb, which caused the once-beautiful car to flip on its side. Copperhead was thrown from the open driver's compartment, rolling and landing much as one would expect a three-ton hardened steel mechanical beast to do. The next day, when the road repair crew arrived to fix the site of the impact, the foreman looked at the crater and wondered if perhaps the war had gotten bored and decided to happen to one particular spot on the outskirts of the city.

The three agents inside the vehicle were shaken up from the impact, but nobody seemed badly hurt.

"Ugh. I hate being right all the time. I don't think I need to tell you how much I hate your stupid plan, Spall! Next time, find a plan that doesn't involve me being rolled over in a steel death trap! Is everyone okay?" Shaw asked.

"I think so," Schlenker answered. "Where in all the hells did that come from?"

Spall groaned and crawled over the broken glass. He looked out through the shattered windscreen. "Ah. As I expected, the Tricians have paid us a visit, and we have company. Lots of it."

Shaw managed to free himself from some of the wreckage and look outside. There was a large group of serious-looking men and women converging on the mangled remains of their vehicle as others backed the steam truck away. Every one of them was armed with a Trician weapon. Shaw could hear the sounds of automatic gunfire somewhere nearby. It seemed that their security detail had engaged the Trician agents. The Tricians were clearly putting up an effective fight, however. After a few seconds, the shooting was over and the Trician agents once again began to converge on the wreckage.

One of the Tricians, clearly the leader, stood forward of the group and shouted to the occupants of the vehicle.

"Director Spall. Doctor Schlenker. Agent Shaw. We know you're inside, and we know you wouldn't normally come peacefully. Since you can easily see that we have you surrounded with no means of escape, and that our weapons could tear through your vehicle and your bodies with ease, I advise you to come out quickly and surrender quietly. Do so now and you will not be harmed further. Try my patience, or show any sign of aggression or defiance, and we will simply annihilate you where you sit and disappear. Your security detail has already been pushed back. You have no option but compliance."

Spall looked at his comrades, nodded to both in turn, and shouted back out the windscreen.

"Very well. We will come out one at a time. We will not resist."

Spall reached down and adjusted his shoe, which looked as though it had come loose in the crash. With that, Spall crawled out through the now empty driver's compartment and the windscreen into the street. Shaw could see him struggle to his feet and walk forward with his hands raised to the circle of enemy agents. Seeing Spall surrendering to such horrible people, the people who had supported Slattispoone in his treachery and filthy experimentation, filled Shaw with a hatred and loathing so strong it left a taste in his mouth. He clenched his jaw shut and reached for his steam gun.

Schlenker, ever the optimist, grabbed Shaw's hand and shook his head at his friend. "We must do this Spall's way," he whispered. "This may be the only opportunity we have of finding the Fragment that Slattispoone has. They are focused on us right now. They are probably not aware that we have means of communicating our whereabouts to our agents once we are at their safe house. Our people will rescue us when the time is right."

Schlenker began to crawl out of the vehicle, followed by Shaw. Once they had emerged from the vehicle, they both raised their hands in surrender and were immediately taken and bound with manacles. The Trician agents quickly searched them, finding their weapons with ease.

"What is this?" one of the Tricians asked, finding a second pistol, this one painted in bright colors, in Shaw's waistband. The Trician shook it and they could all hear the sloshing of the contents inside. "It's a water pistol!"

Some of the other Tricians laughed derisively at Shaw's choice of secondary weapon, which was indeed a water pistol. The Trician aimed and squirted Shaw in the chest, still laughing.

"Poor surfacer," another remarked. "Can't tell a real weapon from a child's toy. Let him keep it. See what good it'll do him when he meets the doctor."

The three agents were hustled into the back of the steam truck with the rest of the Trician agents, and they were all driven from the scene. Three Trician agents remained behind for several minutes, mingling with onlookers to ensure that nobody followed. They didn't see any sign of Secret Service agents, so they too disappeared into the growing crowd that had gathered to see what had happened.

The large crowd gathering around the site of the collision was amazed to see a large steel behemoth unfold itself from the rubble of what had lately been a (fortunately) vacant house. A behemoth was nothing to raise one's eyebrows in Echo City; however, this one was unique in that it had a head of polished copper. The head was somewhat dented, but it seemed to be functioning properly as the mechanical monster clawed its way out of the rubble with its massive shovel-sized hands.

If the metal automaton had possessed a face, it would have shown anger at having been tossed across a roadway by a truck. The behemoth stood on its feet, appeared to look around, then began to dig through the remains of what had been a very nice steam car, tearing it open like foil on a packet of candy.

Agent Hawkesbury had been following Schlenker's vehicle with Saoirse Muir and Ama Adebe, several minutes behind. He hadn't liked Spall's plan at all, but he didn't make the plans; he just followed them and complained about them when the boss wasn't around. There were too many opportunities for everything to go wrong and for Spall,

Schlenker, and Shaw to be seriously injured or killed. Hawkesbury didn't know what their operation was for, but he was certain it must be a vital one. Otherwise, why risk the director of Special Branch himself, their best inventor, and their newest agent all in one go? He had known the Tricians would take the bait, but what if they were able to simply disappear? The entire plan hinged on their finding the Trician hideout and rescuing their comrades.

Hawkesbury turned the corner in his government steam car and saw the wreckage of Schlenker's vehicle with Copperhead pawing through it. He simultaneously cursed the entire operation and rejoiced that the Tricians had made their move. He hoped that everyone had made it out of the wreck alive. He didn't know what the vehicle had looked like after the Tricians had stopped it, but now that Copperhead had decided to tear through it like holiday wrapping foil, it looked like it had been hit with an artillery shell.

"The Tricians made their move," Adebe said.

"Aye, that they 'ave," Hawkesbury admitted. "Quite the move as well."

"I hope everyone made it out alive," Saoirse said, worried in spite of herself.

Hawkesbury pulled the vehicle over and got out to survey the wreckage, hoping there wasn't anyone still inside. Glancing past Copperhead's bulk, he could see small spots of blood, but no bodies, and no sign of bullet holes.

"Ah, by Vulcan's 'ammer," swore Hawkesbury. "What in all the underground 'appened 'ere?"

Copperhead stopped and turned to "look" at Hawkesbury.

*Whistle!*

"A steam truck? What the bloody 'ell are they doin' with somethin' that size? They could be followed by a child!"

*Whistle!*

329

"Yeh, it was effective. I'll give 'em that. Ah, Johanssen! Where've yeh been? Give me some good news, lad! Were yeh able teh follow 'em?"

Agent Johanssen, a thin, bespectacled young man, had stepped away from a badly shot-up monocycle to report to his superior.

"No, sir. Myself and Agent Trenholm engaged the Trician agents immediately, but they were too many. They had some serious firepower, sir. We would've needed the military to force them back. They hit the doctor's vehicle and rolled it with a large steam truck. At the same time, they had some agents up on top of these houses open fire on us from above. We were fortunate that they didn't hit us. We couldn't do anything else, sir. They collected all three of our people and drove away. Both our vehicles were too badly damaged to follow, sir."

"Alright, I understand. Nothin' else ye could 'ave done."

Saoirse sighed. "Plan B it is, then."

"I'm not surprised," Adebe added. "Let's hope the Tricians can't detect the trail."

At that point, Copperhead had extricated what he had been searching for in the vehicle wreckage. He stood to his full height, expelled a large amount of steam, and turned to Hawkesbury, Saoirse, and Adebe.

*Whistle!*

Hawkesbury smiled his golden prizefighter's smile and glanced sidelong at Johanssen. "Not gonna be a problem. Let's get the other agents here on the double, lad!"

"What are we going to do, sir? How do we find them?" Johanssen asked.

"Well this gigantic steamy bastard's part 'o the plan, 'ere. Watch and learn, lad."

# 32

## A Trician Stronghold

The Trician fortress was a large house with very high ceilings. It reminded Shaw of an English mansion from one of the BBC period dramas one of his ex-girlfriends used to watch. It was well lit with electric lights rather than gas lamps, but the rest of the stone architecture was the same as every other house on the street. The huge entrance foyer they had been taken into was black marble with white marble trim and bronze electrical fittings. Shaw wasn't able to get a very good look at the rest of the house through any of the doorways, however, as he and his friends were forced to their knees after the front doors were heavily bolted. From the sound of the doors and the bolts, they would have a difficult time getting out, and anyone attempting a rescue would have an even harder time getting in. Shaw prayed that their fellow agents had managed to follow their captors, and that Spall had a contingency plan if they hadn't.

They heard footsteps approaching, followed by the sound of laughter. Slattispoone had been awaiting them. He entered the grand foyer looking none the worse for wear after his escape from the asylum and prison. The only obvious change was that he was wearing large metal gauntlets with thick wires running up his sleeves to a pack on his back. Electricity arced from fingertip to fingertip. The Black Hands crackled with power and were every bit as fearsome as Shaw had imagined they would be. Bright blue robes flowed around Slattispoone. He looked every bit the Trician leader he believed he was.

"We meet again, gentlemen! I must say I am impressed. I expected you to be trapped for a lot longer down there," Slattispoone gloated.

"The pleasure is all yours, to be sure," Spall sneered. "What did the Tricians promise you to turn traitor?"

Slattispoone smiled. "They kindly offered to help me continue my research. They have others working on similar projects, I understand, but the more the merrier. I was limited in what I could do to my patients here, with the inspections and oversight from the blasted prison. It was growing more difficult for me to keep things secret, especially with having to make the other doctors at the asylum 'disappear.' As it turns out, in Ünterreich I will be able to work unimpeded. I had no use for the information I extracted from Bergstrom, and I knew this pathetic government wouldn't look kindly on what I was doing. So I went to the Tricians. Easy as you like. But now, I'll need the information you already have so I may go to Ünterreich."

Schlenker coughed. "And what makes you think we have any other information?"

Slattispoone gave Schlenker an ironic grin. "I'm no idiot. Three of the other scientists settled here after building their star. I know full well that you already have their pieces of the puzzle. I need them, and you will give them to me."

Schlenker looked at Slattispoone with a defiant eye. "We don't seem to have them with us at the moment. Perhaps if you had invited us—"

Slattispoone fetched a backhanded slap across Schlenker's face, splitting the doctor's lip and drawing blood with his metal gauntlets.

E.B. Tolley

"I know you don't have them with you. But you will tell me where you have hidden them. Or you will watch your friends die. Slowly."

With that, Slattispoone turned to Shaw and lifted his metal-clad hands. Blue-white electricity shot from the iron gloves into Shaw's body. The jolt lasted only a second, but to Shaw it felt like years. Every muscle in his body contracted instantaneously and painfully, forcing the air out of his lungs and causing him to fall to the floor. He landed hard on his face, feeling his nose break and blood squirt from both nostrils. He wasn't sure if he screamed or not, since the sound of the electricity from the gloves was almost deafening, like tiny lightning. He lay panting on his face, trying not to choke on his own blood, feeling his muscles slowly begin to loosen from their electrical punishment.

Just as Shaw caught his breath, Slattispoone fired another jolt into him, causing his entire body to stiffen and twitch once again. The jolt was longer this time, perhaps two seconds, and the pain was unspeakable. Shaw was certain that he screamed this time, as he ground his own face into the floor while he thrashed. Finally the pain subsided, and Shaw caught his breath, coughing on the blood that was trying to run back through his sinuses. He could hear Slattispoone laughing. As he lay there panting and gagging on his own blood, he looked over Slattispoone's shoulder at the doorway behind his tormentor. Shaw could see the silhouette of another Trician agent, but he couldn't see the man's face; the light from behind the man was too bright. There was something that struck Shaw about the man. He couldn't put his finger on it, though, and in any case there were other more pressing matters to consider.

Slattispoone finished laughing. "There. Not a particularly powerful shot of electricity, but enough to get my point across, yes? So, Schlenker, do you want to continue to try my patience? Or do you feel like Agent Shaw here would care to ride the lightning for another few seconds? It's nothing to me."

333

Schlenker looked over at Shaw, who had turned his head to look at his friend. Shaw's nose was clearly broken, and his face was covered in his own blood. He was gasping for air, but his eyes had a look of defiance in them that was unmistakable. Schlenker sighed.

"Even if I tell you where to find the information, you will never escape from here, Slattispoone. By now our agents will be surrounding this place."

Slattispoone grinned in a slimy way and leaned forward into Schlenker's face. "Oh, we've had this planned since the beginning. Even if they manage to find this place, your agents will never find the exit to our little tunnel in the basement, nor will they be able to breach those doors behind you."

"You truly are a mastermind," Spall congratulated Slattispoone. "Though you haven't considered that our power here isn't limited to our agents."

Slattispoone giggled. "If you're referring to your pet behemoth—*slave*—I assure you, even that thing won't easily breach those doors. Not that any of your resources will find this place. All my agents have checked in, and they tell me that none of your people were able to track us. No, I think we are quite safe from your pathetic agency."

Once he had finished talking, Slattispoone fired a burst of electrical energy from his Black Hands into Shaw again with no warning or provocation. Shaw writhed on the ground, kicking his feet and thrashing his entire body as the electricity filled his body with fire.

"Enough, Slattispoone! He's had enough!" Schlenker yelled over the hiss and snap of the Black Hands' discharge. After several seconds, Slattispoone finished his demonstration of power and allowed Shaw to catch his breath.

"Has he? Afraid for your little surfacer, are you? Apparently not afraid enough to save him from further acquaintance with my Black Hands." Slattispoone sneered and gestured with the gauntlets, suggesting that he would like nothing more than to continue using them.

"You win, Slattispoone," Schlenker said. "We will give you the other three Fragments we already have."

"And the locations of the ones you don't have as well." Slattispoone grinned.

"Yes, the locations of the others too." Schlenker looked defeated as he glanced over at Shaw, lying nearly unconscious in a coagulating puddle. "Just let Spall and Shaw go, and I will guide you to the Fragments in my possession."

Spall looked shocked. "Schlenker, no! He will kill us all whether we give him the Fragments or not! You cannot—"

Slattispoone nearly lifted Spall off the floor with a burst from the Black Hands, sending him flying onto his back and writhing in agony.

"You will remain silent, *slave*! Regardless of what occurs here with the Fragments, you will suffer a very unpleasant and public death in Ünterreich. I hadn't planned on capturing you; however, returning you alive to Ünterreich will only solidify my standing in their upper nobility when I arrive! The slave who *dared* to escape, returned at last." Slattispoone turned back to Schlenker and fixed him with an icy look. "I grow tired of this game, *Doctor*. You have nothing to bargain with. You will not *lead* us anywhere. You will tell us where the Fragments are hidden, and then, when we have them in hand, I will consider allowing you and this surfacer to go free. The slave comes with me regardless. Now tell me what I wish to know, and I may spare your friends some agony."

Schlenker sighed and looked side to side at Spall and Shaw. Spall had slowly lurched himself back to his knees, and some small burn marks could be seen on his face, even through the blue tattoo. He was panting heavily but seemed to be in much better shape than Shaw, who still lay on his stomach, seemingly unconscious. The only sounds that could be heard were the occasional crackle of electricity from the Black Hands and the heavy breathing from Spall. Suddenly Schlenker smiled and began to laugh, a deep, hearty laugh of pure joy.

"What are you laughing at? Have you gone insane?" Slattispoone looked incredulously at Schlenker, who continued laughing for several seconds.

"Ah, my dear Doctor Slotted Spoon," began Schlenker, still chuckling. "I think you of all people would be able to tell whether someone is insane or not. I am merely laughing because the person who has the information you seek is arriving at this very moment."

Sounds had been steadily growing in volume from outside the house, and many of the Trician agents had been slowly becoming aware of them. The sounds were of heavy, metallic impacts on pavement, slowly getting closer. As the sounds grew louder, they could be felt as tremors in the ground as well. Slattispoone and the Tricians began to look around worriedly. Suddenly the impacts seemed to stop just outside the front door, followed by a loud metallic snap.

"What is that out there?" Slattispoone demanded.

"That . . . ," explained Shaw, gagging on his blood and sounding pitiful through his broken nose, ". . . is called a blunderbuss."

Spall and Schlenker threw themselves flat on the floor beside Shaw. Less than a second later, the front doors to the house imploded in a huge ball of fire and shrapnel that sailed over the three Echoan agents and cut many Trician agents apart where they stood. Others were thrown bodily across the room by the concussion; the lucky few who had been standing far enough from the doors were simply knocked off their feet. The room filled with smoke and debris, and most of the electric lights went out as the bulbs burst from the pressure wave of the blast. Slattispoone was thrown backward across the foyer, landing heavily on his back. The agent whose silhouette had caught Shaw's attention turned quickly and disappeared through an open doorway down the hall.

Ears ringing, his recently wounded arm once again singing in agony, Spall struggled up to his knees and began to search for the agent with the keys to their manacles. He had difficulty, as the room was in chaos with people shouting, debris still falling (some of which had recently been people, or parts thereof), and the smoke and lack of light. Finally he located the keys, still attached to the belt of the Trician who had handcuffed them. Unfortunately for the Trician, there was very little of himself left attached to his belt. Spall grabbed the keys and managed to free himself as Copperhead loomed through the now wide-open doorway, blunderbuss in hand. Shots began to ring out as the few Tricians still able to mount a defense took up their weapons and opened fire at the behemoth. Copperhead calmly reloaded his weapon as the Tricians' wolfram darts bounced harmlessly off his hardened steel body, leaving only tiny scratches and nicks. A few darts made their way completely through the copper dome of his head, but that didn't seem to faze the mechanical beast. He slid a new shell into the chamber of the small artillery gun and shut the breech with a now-familiar, and to the Tricians, fearsome, snap. Hearing the sound of the blunderbuss closing, the Tricians realized that the sound had historically been followed by a much louder sound, accompanied by fire and flying body parts. Many of them came to this realization just as Copperhead aimed and fired his weapon, filling the hall with a huge explosion.

Once the sound and smoke had died down, there were very few Tricians left in the building. Agent Hawkesbury, followed by Saoirse, Adebe, and the rest of the Secret Service agents began to flood through the opening in the front doors, opening fire on any enemies still foolish enough to attempt a defense. Spall was soon helped to his feet by his agents, as were Shaw and Doctor Schlenker. Their manacles were removed, and they were able to find their weapons among the debris and human remains. Agent Hawkesbury approached Spall with his golden grin.

"There yeh are, sir. Good thing the Doctor 'ere 'as his metal friend. Otherwise, we'd 'ave 'ad a terrible time gettin' through that door there, and we wouldn't 'ave found ye at all. 'Ow was 'e able to track yeh, anyway?"

Spall pointed at his left shoe. "Schlenker was kind enough to give me an ultrasonic transmitter that I fit into the heel of my shoe. It emits sound at an extremely high frequency, so high that people cannot hear it. Fortunately, Copperhead here can hear it like fireworks on Founding Day. It was simple enough for him to follow the sound to its source."

"Fantastic, sir. Yeh, 'e walked us straight 'ere. Good thing we 'ad 'im. They've gone and reinforced the entire place, and no mistake. That wee cannon took care of it right quick, though."

Spall felt his left arm gingerly and winced as a fresh jolt of pain shot up from the bullet wound. He had forgotten it was only a day since he had been shot in the asylum gunfight.

"Excellent. What is the situation?"

"Well, sir, we've taken the entire main floor, as well as the basement. Turns out when they excavated the basement they built a tunnel as well, but no idea where it comes out. Adebe took a few agents through to see where it goes."

"Does it look like anyone has gone through the tunnel recently?" Shaw asked, his nose still dripping blood as Saoirse helped him stand. "I don't see Slotted Spoon anywhere. He might have tried to get away once Copperhead minced all of his men."

"From what me men tell me, the tunnel is quite crude, but we canna tell if the rubble in front 'as been disturbed recently. I think yer Slotted Spoon fellow is still 'ere. We 'aven't searched the upper floors yet."

"Good. Consolidate our position here and search that tunnel just to make sure. I will find that Trician scum." Spall started toward the grand staircase.

"Shaw, Muir, and I are coming as well, and I think we could use Copperhead's expertise in opening doors," Schlenker spoke up. "Shaw looks well enough to be hunting Tricians," he added.

Spall looked at his comrades, one of whom was three meters tall and steaming. With the exception of Saoirse, who was standing there looking fresh with a pistol in each hand, all of them looked like they had been through a war lasting months, not minutes. Shaw's lower face was covered in his own blood, drying to a dark maroon around the edges. His suit was torn and burnt in several places, and there were electrical burn marks in several areas of exposed skin. Schlenker had cuts and scrapes all over, and his salt-and-pepper hair was wilder than usual. His spectacles were cracked and bent, sitting slightly askew on his narrow face. His clothing was in even worse shape than Shaw's, but he was nonetheless smiling in his cheerful, endearing way. Copperhead, though not necessarily a friend to Spall, was still a comfort to have. When storming a fortress, who better to have than a walking steam engine with several tons of armor plating and a handheld cannon beside you? He was battered as well, with scratches all over and most of his ridiculous butler's uniform torn off. There were holes right through his head, and some significant dents, but Spall was confident that Copperhead would still be able to "see" perfectly well. Despite their bedraggled appearance, Spall would not have wished for a better team to face Slattispoone.

"I would be glad to have you four beside me," Spall smiled his crooked half-smile. "Even you, Copperhead."

*Whistle!*

"Even with your filthy mouth, yes."

*Whistle!*

"Thank you, Copperhead. After you."

Copperhead hefted his small artillery piece and began to stomp up the stairs. Shaw couldn't help feeling glad that the stairs were made of solid stone. Wooden stairs, despite being prohibitively expensive, would have quickly, and literally, let Copperhead down. They all ascended the stairs behind Copperhead, using him as a shield in case there were more Trician agents.

They reached the top of the stairs to find a long hallway with doors leading off either side at regular intervals. Copperhead stopped, listening for sounds of life. The others also stopped, instinctively realizing what Copperhead was doing. His echolocator was so sensitive, it was no wonder that he was able to see into the front hall before firing his first shot through the door. He was able to see anything that made noise with his strange electronic brain, even through doors and walls.

After a few seconds, Copperhead pointed down the hallway at one of the doorways and began to clomp forward again, ignoring several doorways along the passage. He came to a large doorway he had pointed to on the right and leveled his weapon.

"Copperhead, wait," Spall instructed. "We need him alive, if possible."

Copperhead lowered the blunderbuss slightly and motioned for the agents to join him by the door. They gathered on either side of the doorway, and Spall motioned for Copperhead to open the door.

With a single hit from Copperhead's massive steel fist, the door smashed from its hinges and fell forward into the room.

"Copperhead, I rather suspect you're enjoying yourself," Spall observed. *Whistle!*

"And the swearing has to stop."

Slattispoone's voice, altered somewhat, came from within. It sounded like he was talking into a bucket.

"Gentlemen, I suspected that you would be up here directly. Please come in."

Copperhead leveled his blunderbuss again and stalked into the room, followed by the four agents. Suddenly Copperhead was hit by a huge bolt of blue-white lightning from the far side of the room. The electricity enveloped his entire body, arcing across every part. The blunderbuss dropped to the floor as Copperhead's body seized up. The bolt of electricity stopped, and Copperhead, hissing steam from several places, fell bodily face-first onto the floor. The house shook as the impact cracked the stone floor, and Copperhead lay in an immobile heap, smoking and steaming.

"Copperhead!" Schlenker started forward, concerned for his creation.

The others followed Schlenker forward, wary of the power they had just seen. Slattispoone had clearly turned up the Black Hands to full power, and the result was frightening. The blast that had leveled Copperhead would have burned any of the humans to a cinder.

As they came into the room, they could see that it was a music room or ballroom of sorts, with very little furniture and lots of light. Slattispoone was standing in the far corner, from which the shot of electricity had come. He was still dressed in his electric-blue robe, but underneath he was clad entirely in strange armor. The armor was built of overlapping plates of a grayish metal alloy in which no openings could be seen. The Black Hands attached neatly into the arms of the suit, and the electricity could be seen sizzling its way up the arms and onto the torso. Slattispoone's head was covered by a helmet with no obvious eye openings. The helmet came to a vertical knife-edge in the front and looked very solid.

"They've made you a Trician prefect, then," Spall growled. "I recognize the armor. They must have been very anxious to get Bergstrom's information from you to allow you to have that title and armor."

"Indeed so, slave. When I escape from this city, I will be welcomed as a hero. And you will all be dead!"

# 33

## The Surfacer Comes Through

Spall leveled his gigantic double-barreled revolver and fired several deafening shots at Doctor Slattispoone's head as the others fired their steam pistols. The shots ricocheted loudly off of the heavy armored suit protecting the Trician, and the four agents could then hear the sounds of metallic laughter from within the metal suit.

"Fire every bullet you have, slave. You'll never penetrate this armor! And now you die!" Slattispoone raised his hands, blue electricity arcing from iron fingertip to iron fingertip.

Shaw dropped his now empty steam pistol and drew out a much smaller and lighter pistol, aiming it at the armored Trician. Slattispoone laughed his hollow, metallic laugh again.

"And what do you think you are going to do with that? It's even smaller than your worthless steam gun!"

Shaw smiled and replied, "It's a water pistol."

Slattispoone laughed again. "Do you honestly think the Tricians couldn't create an ultimate weapon such as the Black Hands without

**342**

making sure they wouldn't short-circuit when doused with water? Go ahead, empty your little water pistol at me!"

Shaw pressed the trigger and was rewarded with a long stream that sprayed across Slattispoone's Black Hands and the front of the armored suit, soaking the blue robes. Slattispoone continued to laugh as the electricity arced across the gloves, seemingly unaffected by the liquid.

The laughter stopped abruptly when the liquid spontaneously ignited as it touched the electricity. In less than a second, Slattispoone's armored suit was engulfed in orange flames and blue electricity. The hollow laughter turned to screams as Slattispoone began to thrash about, attempting to quell the fire.

Shaw yelled at Slattispoone, "I never said it was full of water, you murdering bastard! It's pure ethanol!"

As Slattispoone spun and ran about the room, Spall grabbed Shaw with one arm and motioned to the others to head toward the exit.

Shaw resisted. "No, I want to see this! He deserves it!"

Spall stopped. "I want to see it as well, but that suit is a giant battery! What happens to a battery when it's lit on fire?"

They all looked at Spall, then at one another, then at the burning apparition that was rapidly becoming the late Doctor Slattispoone. All four watched him fall to the floor in a heap of flame and crackling electricity, then they turned and ran to the exit. They reached the doorway just before the battery pack on the armored suit exploded, sending pieces of armor, burning acid, and Doctor Slattispoone in all directions.

Shaw turned and looked back through the doorway at the grisly remains. "Well, that was . . . satisfying."

Schlenker joined Shaw in surveying the devastation. "Indeed so, my dear Shaw. It was a much-deserved end. Now we have a very unpleasant job to do, I'm afraid."

Shaw looked at his friend with a disgusted look. "We don't have to clean up this mess, do we?"

Saoirse pointed into the room. "I don't think Schlenker was referring to everything, but I notice that Copperhead is still lying where he fell, and he seems to have gotten some 'Slotted Spoon' on him."

Shaw looked at the giant metal heap that was the unconscious Copperhead and noted that there did seem to be a lot of surface that required cleaning.

"Is he … alright? That bolt of lightning stopped him pretty quickly," Shaw observed.

"Oh, he should be just fine; no doubt the shot of electricity just shut down his committee. He will need a new suit, of course. It is fortunate that he left his coat and hat at home. He will be much easier to scrub; I shall see if I can get him started back up." Schlenker gingerly stepped through the room, avoiding as much of Doctor Slattispoone as possible, especially those pieces that were still aflame.

While Schlenker worked on Copperhead, the others decided to avoid the dripping mess that Doctor Slattispoone had become and search for anything that might be Bergstrom's Fragment. Their search of the ballroom was fruitless, so they quickly began a search of the remainder of the upstairs rooms, joined by several other agents. Eventually they found a large library, which was mostly empty of books. It was clear that the entire house was used as a safe haven for the Tricians to use when necessary, as most of the rooms were sparsely furnished. The library was evidence enough that nobody spent much time there. In a desk drawer they did find several large leather-bound metal books. Browsing through these books revealed them to be Slattispoone's journals from his work in the asylum. A quick scan of one of them gave Shaw a chill and turned his stomach.

"Ugh, I think this is the journal where he recorded his experiments. Sickening."

"Normally, I would ask you to destroy that filthy thing," Spall began, "but in this case, we cannot afford to overlook anything. He had to have recorded Bergstrom's information in one of these books.

Schlenker will need to look through everything regardless of what we find. He will be able to use some of Slotted Spoon's research, I am sure."

"Hopefully some good will come of this research. I hate to think of what Slotty was going to do with it, or what he was working toward," Shaw said with a grimace.

"Indeed. It may be that none of the research will be useful for anything beneficial. We shall have to see."

Saoirse snapped her fingers at Spall and Shaw. "This journal here has notes from patient sessions, and it looks like Bergstrom's entry has a lot of notations. I will show this one to Schlenker. There are several entries that make little sense to me."

She looked over at Shaw's face. The blood was still covering most of his features, and his broken nose had swelled significantly. Even looking as badly as he did, she still thought he was handsome. She set the book down and walked over.

"Are you alright?" she asked, examining his injuries. "I didn't get a chance to ask you earlier."

"I'll live," Shaw answered, hoping he sounded tougher than he looked and felt.

Saoirse smiled. "I hope this book is the one we're looking for. It would be terrible if we all got injured for nothing."

"I hope that as well, Agent Muir," Spall said as Adebe entered.

"Sir, is everything under control here?" Adebe asked.

"Indeed. Slattispoone is down the hall. In a satisfying number of pieces. Have you and your team finished with the escape tunnel?"

"Yes, sir. Looks like they had it mined with explosives a short way down. Once they passed, they collapsed it."

"Prudent of them; I would have done the same," Spall observed, his brows furrowing in frustration.

They gathered up the books, which weighed five kilograms apiece, and walked back down the hall to find Schlenker still working on the blood-covered Copperhead.

Schlenker smiled his good-natured smile, which contrasted greatly with the overall ambience of the room. "Ah, my friends. I will be finished with Copperhead very soon. Another couple of minutes and he will be up and his usual cheerful self."

Spall gave Schlenker an ironic expression. "There are many words I would use to describe Copperhead, Doctor, but 'cheerful' does not spring to mind."

"Oh, Spall. You have no sense of humor. He's really quite fond of you. He just doesn't know how to show his friendship."

"Doctor, I have removed friendlier creatures from the bottom of my shoe."

"Ew!" Shaw interjected. "Spall, please don't elaborate. Doctor, we found a bunch of Slotted Spoon's asylum journals. Spall has one you need to have a look at."

Schlenker perked up immediately and began to flip through the proffered journal. After several minutes, he smiled broadly and began to move about excitedly as he read, heedless of the fact that he was walking through puddles of Slattispoone and tracking gore through the room. Finally he stopped pacing and looked up at the others.

"My friends, we have it! The entire fourth Fragment! It's all here! I have to give Slotted Spoon his credit; he knew how to interrogate a person! Some of the more technical terms are misspelled, of course. He clearly didn't have a background in experimental physics, but it's all here. He even got what Bergstrom knew of the other Fragments. Not much, but everything will help, especially if we cannot locate one or more of the other Fragments. This is what we have been looking for!"

Shaw breathed a huge sigh of relief and sat down on the floor in a small clear spot. He was incredibly happy knowing that the pain and suffering they had endured over the last two days had given them the result they had sought. His wounded shoulder still ached incredibly, and he wondered if the stitches holding everything closed had burst during his torture at the hands of the maniacal doctor. He had also noticed that Spall was avoiding using his wounded arm as much as possible. Saoirse seemed to be perfectly fine with her minor leg wound, and Adebe was working through her concussion quite well.

Doctor Schlenker spent some time working on Copperhead and eventually got the steel behemoth fired back up and on his feet and walking again. Copperhead picked up his massive blunderbuss and carried it outside into Echo Cavern, dripping as he went and followed by the team and most of the other Echoan agents.

A sizable crowd had gathered outside and were being held at bay by Echo City Police and Secret Service agents. Everyone, police included, seemed to be inspecting the not inconsiderable damage done by Copperhead during his unorthodox entry to the former Trician stronghold. The huge steel doors were in tatters (as close to tatters as solid steel could look), and hung limply from their hinges. Bodies, or pieces thereof, littered the front hall alongside numerous Trician weapons. The remnants of several small fires were apparent; however, most had burned themselves out since Copperhead had first announced himself at the front door.

The crowd began chattering excitedly as Shaw emerged from the building, and numerous reporters quickly approached, yelling questions at him and Schlenker. Shaw even had to face several questions from his old friend, Schmidt-Hess of the *Gossippeer*, but he was fortunate that the other reporters shoved Schmidt-Hess out of the crowd rather quickly. It seemed that Schmidt-Hess, with his disturbing fishlike features and steadfast adherence to garbage journalism, was not widely regarded even among his peers. The reporters seemed to take no notice of Copperhead, but Shaw saw that many of them gave Spall a furtive glance and edged away as much as possible. Spall didn't seem to mind, which made Shaw smile.

At one point, Mr. Withers even made an appearance, attempting to sell his questionable sausages from his little warming tray. It seemed that any sizable crowd in Echo City would attract the skinny little man, who would always succeed in selling his wares to the unwary. Shaw chuckled to himself and wondered if his life in the underground would always be this interesting.

# 34

## A Well-Deserved Rest

Shaw and Schlenker answered a few of the reporters' questions as police officers and Secret Service agents buzzed around the building. Spall was seen talking to the police watch commander, a very tall blonde woman who wasn't much shorter than the giant. Once his conversation with the watch commander was finished, Spall collected the others and they were ushered into a waiting police wagon. Copperhead, still looking like he had run a race through a slaughterhouse, couldn't fit into the steam wagon and followed behind in his usual lumbering, hissing gait, trailing shreds of his butler's uniform as they were transported to the Government Spire.

They were ushered into the prime minister's office immediately, though Copperhead was politely asked to wait outside, despite him having stopped off at a handy fire station along the way to fill his water reservoir and hose the majority of the gore off. The prime minister greeted them with a large smile and a firm handshake before sitting them down with their preferred drinks. Spall, of course, stood in his customary shadowy corner near the back of the room.

The prime minister finished his usual pleasantries, then grew serious. "Agents, if I can believe the initial reports, it seems as though you have had some successes in your quest. It also seems as though you have a lot of explaining to do. A near disaster at Wolf Station, the Isolation Asylum destroyed with what sounds like at least thirty-seven dead or missing patients and staff, and now a mansion full of bodies or, more accurately, pieces of bodies, as well as a small pile of Trician weapons. And the five of you look somewhat the worse for wear. Of course we will feed the press some believable story soon enough, but I will require the entire story from the beginning."

Shaw glanced over at Schlenker, Saoirse, and Adebe, who all nodded, then back at the nearly invisible Spall, who smiled his crooked smile and nodded quietly back at Shaw. Shaw turned around again to face Prime Minister Whitley and began the story of their investigation, beginning with their search for the fourth Fragment and finishing with their kidnapping by Doctor Slattispoone and the subsequent battle in the Trician mansion. Doctor Schlenker occasionally added a few details, as did the others, and within a few hours the tale was told and the prime minister was satisfied.

"Well, I must say you five have had quite the adventure. You managed to obtain the fourth Fragment, and you uncovered a ring of Trician spies at the same time. Not to mention the black desert and the Aztec city. How positively incredible. I will have to send an expedition to explore that cavern soon. I have just the person for it, actually. Any ideas on how it was built?"

Schlenker perked up. "Well, Prime Minister, I have pondered it for some time now, and I think it is very likely that what we found was once a vast city on the surface hundreds, possibly thousands of years ago. There was evidence of volcanic activity in the area, and I believe that the city was brought down in some great cataclysm. Then the earth swallowed it up whole and sealed it from above."

"I think you're right, Schlenker," Shaw began. "I remember reading years ago about some historical records or carvings that were found that had been written by one of those civilizations. They talked about massive earthquakes at one time that completely changed the land. Entire cities sank into the ocean; others disappeared into the ground. It just may have happened that these pyramids and other buildings were pulled down in some huge crack in the earth that closed over again."

"Hmm. Well, the best way to find out will be a full expedition. I will contact the university and have them form a scientific expedition, once I have scouts investigate first." Prime Minister Whitley jotted a note on a metal pad with a scriber. "I understand that you especially would like to be part of such an expedition, Doctor, but I am afraid you must remain on your current assignment."

Schlenker looked to be about to protest but thought better of it and shut his mouth. The prime minister smiled.

"I know how much you hunger for knowledge, Doctor. I also know how important you are to this current project, and how important this project is to all of us. You are the genius who will save these caverns, I have no doubt. But until you succeed, you must curb your curiosity and focus on the task at hand. Leave the ruins to lesser scientists for now."

"As you wish, sir." Schlenker looked crestfallen. "I must insist, though, that the expedition is made aware of the metal disk we mentioned to you. I have thought about it, and it may be that Bergstrom was killed just by touching it. I cannot be certain, of course, but his body was found a mere twenty meters from it. Anyone who goes to inspect it must take all precautions. There was also the matter of the manticores that tried to attack us—"

Prime Minister Whitley continued, "Of course. I will ensure that you are able to brief the expedition leaders personally, and you shall have full credit for the discovery of the giant manticores if they turn out to be a new species. Good. Now that's settled, it seems that you all still have three Fragments to find. They seem to be growing more and more difficult as well. Do you know where to find them?"

Spall stepped forward out of the shadows. "We do, sir. One is in Panthalassa. One is in Lille Danmark. The last is in Ünterreich."

Prime Minister Whitley stared at Spall for several seconds before rising and pouring himself a drink. He offered drinks to the agents and sat back down.

"I may have underestimated the difficulty, then. We haven't had any communications from Panthalassa since the tunnels flooded. Lille Danmark, as you know, has been sealed off and is considered under permanent quarantine. And I feel that you would be better off giving up the Fragment in Ünterreich for lost. Diplomacy is not going well, as you know, and your recent elimination of what I assume to be many of their best agents here will not help matters. You would have to infiltrate Ünterreich, find the Fragment, then escape without being detected, and you would have to do it alone. Our own spies in Ünterreich would not be able to break cover to assist you."

Spall nodded. "We are aware of the risks involved, sir, which is why we would never ask anyone else to perform these tasks. We shall recover what Fragments we can find, sir, and complete the mission to replenish Wolf's Star. We shall not fail, sir."

Prime Minister Whitley looked at each agent in turn. The agents looked at one another, and they all stood from their seats and joined Spall.

"We shall not fail, Prime Minister," Schlenker said.

"No failure while I'm breathing, sir," Adebe said.

"They can try and stop us, sir, but they'll end up just like the other Tricians we met today," Saoirse said confidently.

"And you, Agent Shaw?" Prime Minister Whitley asked, fixing Shaw with a calculating stare.

"If they say we shall not fail, Prime Minister, then we shall not. I'll do whatever's necessary to help them complete this mission, sir.

Though I hope they will warn me in the future before throwing me into bottomless pits."

Spall rolled his eyes. "It was not bottomless, Shaw. You would have found the bottom eventually."

The prime minister smiled. "It seems as though you have some team-building to work on, Spall. In the meantime, keep me informed of your progress. Have you decided which Fragment you will look for next?"

Schlenker cleared his throat. "Well, sir, I have not finished our submersible train for the journey to Panthalassa, and the operation into Ünterreich will take much time and planning. We will also have to study the contagion in Lille Danmark and test protective equipment before we will be able to breach the quarantine. I shall work on that problem as I complete the submersible locomotive, though I suspect we will be visiting Panthalassa next."

Whitley nodded. "I believe you, Doctor. If anyone can find a way to solve those issues, you can. I wish you all luck. You may go."

As they turned to leave with Spall, Schlenker stopped and faced the prime minister again.

"Sir, there is one last thing I must make you aware of before we leave."

Whitley smiled indulgently. "Go ahead, Doctor. What is it?"

Schlenker held up one of Slattispoone's heavy asylum journals. "I was looking through Doctor Slattispoone's journal here on the way over, and I found something about what he was working on for the Tricians. He refers several times to something called 'Osiris,' and I fear what I have read may be part of their plan to build some kind of super soldier."

"A super soldier?"

"Indeed so, sir. Slattispoone mentions that he was attempting to map areas of the human brain so that he could control it with electronic equipment of his own design. Or use the brain to control the equipment, like an impervious mechanical body."

"Like some sort of a human behemoth?" Prime Minister Whitley looked both shocked and disgusted. "Barbaric."

"I agree, sir. But think of the possibilities for the Trician army if they could succeed in placing a human brain inside a behemoth-like steel body. They would have an invincible army that would be able to walk right through our defenses."

"Yes. We will have to see if our agents can find out anything else about this project of theirs. If Slattispoone was working for them, there's no telling how many other brilliant scientists are doing the same. I will need a full report on your studies of Slattispoone's journals as soon as you can finish it, Doctor." Whitley sat back in his chair. "Was there anything else, Doctor?"

"No, sir. I will have a report for you as soon as possible. Thank you for your time, Prime Minister."

With that, the five agents left the prime minister's office and shambled their way out to the street to collect Copperhead. They were definitely a ragged looking group as they piled back into the police steam wagon and headed back to Schlenker's home, Copperhead marching slowly behind.

They were driven back to Schlenker's home, stopping to drop Adebe at her home, then Saoirse. At her front door, Saoirse gave Shaw a hug and a small kiss on the cheek.

"I'm so glad you weren't too badly hurt," she said, looking sympathetically at Shaw's swollen nose and blood-covered shirt. "Things could have been much worse."

"Yeah, they could," Shaw agreed. "I'm glad you came to the rescue, though. My hero."

Saoirse blushed and her blue eyes sparkled. She turned and opened the door, releasing a string of what Shaw assumed were Irish swear-words from the elderly Mrs. Muir somewhere inside. Saoirse turned back with a little embarrassed smile and closed the door.

Shaw, Schlenker, and Spall arrived back at Schlenker's and once again had to recuperate from numerous injuries and some delayed shock.

As he tended to his badly abused face in the bathroom mirror, Shaw was amazed at how much his new life in Inner Earth had surprised him. Years as an army engineer, followed by more years as a police officer, had never held as much excitement (and danger) as the last week had. As he dropped off to sleep, trying to think of Saoirse Muir rather than the ache in his shoulder and face, his mind kept returning to what had happened in the Trician mansion. Despite the positive outcome, there was still something wrong that was nagging at the back of his mind. He couldn't quite put his finger on it, though.

The next few weeks saw the five agents recovering quickly from their injuries, in spite of Mrs. Clary's cooking. Shaw was once more able to use his arm, as was Spall, though both of them would never have told anyone how much their injuries really hurt. Saoirse and Adebe were regular fixtures at Schlenker's house now, assisting with different projects in Schlenker's lab. Adebe, as it turned out, was quite adept at electronics, and took to understanding the inner workings of Shaw's smartphone more quickly than anyone else. Saoirse, after unearthing some of Shaw's sketches of aircraft, had started building small wooden gliders, making them more and more intricate as time passed.

One day, after working for some time on a project he wouldn't reveal to anyone, Shaw took Saoirse by the arm and led her out through the garden and into Schlenker's house. Sitting Saoirse down in the front parlor on a comfortable sofa, he stood before her, smiling.

"Ryan, what's going on?" she asked, a little nervous.

"Oh, just a little surprise I made for you," Shaw answered.

Sitting on the wrought-iron tea table in the center of the room was a large metal sphere atop a short pole mounted on a base. The pole was at an angle and had a simple gear mechanism attached to it.

Shaw saw her looking at the object and continued to smile. "I first got the idea when you stopped by that night in the garden and found me feeling sorry for myself."

"You were still grieving, Ryan; your mood that night was perfectly understandable."

"I know. I'm not ashamed, but I don't think you know how much it meant to me to have you there. I wanted to repay your kindness."

"Ryan, you don't have to—"

"I know that too," he interrupted. "But I made this for you anyway. Close your eyes."

Saoirse gave Shaw a questioning expression but did as he requested.

Shaw smiled and walked through the room, turning off all the gaslights. With the door shut, the room was completely black. He flipped a switch on the object.

"Open your eyes," he said.

Saoirse opened her eyes, and the universe was waiting for her.

Everywhere she looked she saw a thousand tiny pinpoints of light. Stars, planets, constellations, nebulae; everything appeared before her in a slow, graceful arc across the room. Just as her disbelieving eyes focused on one feature, they were drawn to another and then another.

In her life, Saoirse Muir had beheld many of the most incredible natural sights the underground had to offer. Entire caverns, like mammoth geodes, filled with crystals the size of buildings, perpetual flames of every color roaring out of gas vents, bioluminescent gardens, and even animals that defied description. Gigantic migrating fungi, gossamer thin, that slowly filled themselves with gas and eventually began to float lazily across their caverns until they settled in a new spot to feed on the minerals there. Stone amalgamations of such size and beauty they could scarcely be believed.

All of those sights paled in comparison to the vision of the night sky that Ryan Shaw had conjured for her in Schlenker's parlor. Without even being aware of it, Saoirse stood, transfixed. She held out her hands, staring at her palms as the stars themselves danced across them.

The human mind cannot fully comprehend something endless. Existing in a linear fashion through time, humans are constrained to the thought that everything has a beginning and an end. The nearest one may come to perceiving endlessness is to look up into the night sky.

For citizens of the underground, endlessness is even more impossible to perceive. Caverns, huge as they are, still have clearly defined boundaries. A "bottomless" chasm, even one as immense as Isolation, still eventually has a bottom.

What Saoirse experienced in those few moments after Shaw turned on the star projector was forever indescribable by her afterward. In those few moments, Saoirse perceived infinity.

She stood in stunned silence for so long she thought her heart had stopped. After what felt like forever, Saoirse realized that she was weeping. Wiping the tears from her eyes, she suddenly beheld Earth's moon, impossibly huge and bright and round, slowly rising toward the ceiling. Her breath caught in her throat as she sat back onto the sofa and began to sob.

Shaw sat next to her on the sofa and put his arm around her, saying nothing, letting her take it all in. Eventually she was able to gather herself. She turned to Shaw, and in that moment, she knew she loved him.

"Ryan . . . I . . . don't have words . . . ," she choked out. "I . . . I don't deserve it."

"You deserve far more than this," he said.

"Ryan, I gave you a hug. You gave me—" Here she almost started to sob again but caught herself and took a breath. "You gave me the whole sky. The whole universe."

Saoirse embraced Shaw and held him close for a long time as she looked over his shoulder at more constellations as they moved across the embossed copper wall plating. They sat holding each other for several minutes, Saoirse mesmerized by the slowly revolving night sky.

"Oh, I've made your collar all wet," she apologized, leaning away from Shaw and wiping her eyes once again.

Shaw just sat and smiled. "I can change my shirt," he said, "but that's not important. I think I'm ready to ask you out now."

Saoirse smiled, her beautiful blue eyes red and swollen and her nose running. She pulled out a small pocket handkerchief and did her best to clean her face up as the stars continued their dance across every surface, including the two of them.

"I was ready for you to court me when I first met you," she said, still sniffing.

"Is that a yes?"

She leaned in and kissed him quickly.

"What do you think, surfacer?" she asked, smiling coyly.

Shaw smiled and held her hand, saying nothing. He just sat and looked at her. In the few months he had been in the underground, he had faced many challenges, not the least of which were the challenges within himself. He had accepted that his old life, his old world, his old self, were gone forever. He had to make a new life and a new self in this new world. If courting Saoirse was the best step he ever took in Inner Earth, Shaw felt he could still be perfectly happy in the underground.

"How did you build this?" Saoirse asked, looking more closely at the device.

"Well, it's the best I could do, considering. I got a few of the constellations more or less the right shape, but that's about it. All the stars are just random tiny holes drilled in the globe, but the Moon and the nebulae were tough. I painted them on glass and fit them into bigger holes. I ruined a lot of Schlenker's drill bits, and it took a few tries with the electronics to get the light inside to work properly. I'm no artificer, but I'm actually proud of how it turned out. Schlenker helped with the gear mechanism to make it turn, and Spall helped with the metal globe, but they didn't know what the whole project was going to be. I wanted you to be the first one to see it. I'm glad you like it."

Saoirse wiped her eyes. "You made me cry, you bastard. Of course I like it."

Shaw laughed.

Shaw and Saoirse weren't sure if they were violating any code of conduct regarding fraternization within the Secret Service, but they didn't care if they were. In any case, Spall didn't seem to mind as long as they stayed professional while they were working.

After a week of courtship, they tried introducing Shaw to Saoirse's mother; however, they decided it would be best to meet at Schlenker's house in the future after Saoirse's mother became confused and tried to serve tea. It turned out that, thanks to the tea cozy, the teapot was wearing more than Saoirse's mother was.

"I really do apologize, Ryan. I'm so embarrassed," Saoirse said after she had bustled him out of the house.

"Don't mention it, Saoirse. She probably doesn't know it isn't teatime," he said with a smile.

Saoirse laughed as they walked to Schlenker's.

# 35

## Prefect Fromm

Prefect Fromm sat in his blue ceremonial robes on a bench that looked like it was made of solid gold. He knew it wasn't *solid* gold of course. Such a thing would have been truly extravagant, and certainly worthy of the council chamber of The Galvanus, Lord Trician and ruler of Ünterreich and its dominions, but gold as a metal was heavy, expensive, and impractical. It would not have taken long for the benches to bend under their own weight. No, these benches were surely cast steel with a heavy plating of pure gold. Regardless of their actual construction, though, they were undeniably uncomfortable.

He and Bondarenko had been recalled immediately to Ünterreich following the debacle at the Echo safe house. He knew he would be called to task regarding the many failures of his agents, but it would be simplicity itself to hang everything on Bondarenko. The ex-top-agent's corpse was already an incandescent vapor. To fail an operation on such a massive scale was to take a very short walk and a very long drop into the river of magma that flowed around the city. Fromm didn't think it came as much of a surprise to Bondarenko.

The doors to the chamber, two stories tall and each plated in several tons of gold, swung open without a sound. Two slaves, dressed in the crimson robes of those who directly served The Galvanus, finished pushing the doors wide and then immediately produced linen cloths and polished their handprints from the gold. It did not do to displease their lord.

"Prefect Fromm," said an unusually tall Asian woman, dressed in the same color as the slaves but in a much more elegant manner, and devoid of the stark tattoo that marked the silent servants who discreetly made themselves as invisible as possible.

"Chancellor Kim," Fromm replied, bowing before his superior.

"His lordship will see you now," Kim said emotionlessly.

Fromm entered the round room, feeling incredibly small and unimportant. In stark contrast to the opulent appointments of the anteroom and the main doors, the room was built entirely of black marble. The only color was the deep red marble floor and the red tapestries that hung around the circumference of the dehumanizingly large chamber.

He approached the center of the room, stopping at the bottom of the raised dais there. Atop the dais was a massive black throne built from the same marble as the walls. Fromm always thought the throne should look more impressive, with carved electricity picked out in gold or something like it, but it was smooth and, to his thinking, plain.

The Galvanus stood in front of the throne, crimson robes open to reveal a suit of jet-black armor. He watched Fromm approach, his deceptively young gray eyes studying the older prefect keenly.

Fromm bowed before his ruler, lower than he had for Chancellor Kim. It did not do to displease his lord.

"Prefect Fromm," The Galvanus said.

Fromm straightened up and stood before the Lord Trician and ruler of Ünterreich, waiting for him to speak.

"I am displeased."

The Galvanus raised one hand, and the air in the chamber was instantly filled with blinding white and blue electricity from the raised Black Hand. The power was so intense that Fromm was lifted bodily and thrown across the room, striking the far wall with a bone-rending thud. He fell lifeless to the floor as The Galvanus continued to fill the air with raw electricity that earthed itself into the quickly disintegrating form that had been Prefect Fromm.

After only a few seconds, Fromm had been reduced to a pile of ash and scorched, splintered bones. The Galvanus lowered his hand and the display of power was over. He sighed contentedly.

"How disappointing. I had high hopes for Fromm. Not as high as the hopes he no doubt had for himself, but higher than this," he said to no one in particular.

Several slaves entered and silently began to sweep up Fromm's remains. As they departed with the late prefect, they passed Chancellor Kim.

"Throw that into the river," she ordered. The slaves bowed and hurried outside toward one of the many bridges crossing the river of magma to carry out their task. It did not do to displease their lord.

The Galvanus sat on the throne, betraying an impatient expression. He usually controlled his emotions far more carefully, but in this instance there had been too many failures to ignore, not the least of which was the fact that his protégé had actually been responsible for much of them. He turned to Chancellor Kim.

"Send Raker in, would you?"

Kim bowed and left the room through the massive doorway.

# 36

## An Unsettling Revelation

The five Echoan agents of Special Branch were working on various small projects in the laboratory. Schlenker was finishing up with Slattispoone's old journals, ensuring that he had gotten every last detail of the fourth Fragment. Spall was at the forge with his sleeves rolled up, hammering out a large knife of some kind from a piece of tool steel. Saoirse and Adebe were attempting to construct a new blunderbuss for Copperhead, this one with a repeating mechanism. His single-shot weapon had proved quite useful, and they anticipated that a semiautomatic one would be even more so. Shaw was sitting at the rolltop desk, working on a crude drawing of a nuclear submarine cross-section. Next to him was a stack of ironing, consisting of notes and report fragments from their recent adventure. On top was the final sketch that Shaw had worked on with Schlenker, showing the face of the spider driver from the attack at Wolf Station. Shaw thought it was perfect, but it still bothered him for some reason. He repeatedly glanced back at it while he was working, and had done so ever since the incident in the Trician stronghold. It was beginning to frustrate him.

"You're very quiet today, Ryan," Saoirse said, breaking the silence. All they had heard for the last hour was the repeated pounding of Spall's hammer on the piece of steel he was working on.

"Oh, just thinking."

"About your drawing? Do people really travel about in such contraptions?" she asked.

"Oh, yeah. Submarines are very common in the military. But that's not what I was thinking about. I keep looking back at the face of this spider driver, the one who was in the attack at Wolf Station. I can't shake the feeling that I know him. I'm not sure from where, but I do. I think he was the one agent I couldn't quite see in the Trician safe house while I was getting electrocuted by Slattispoone."

"The one you told me about? Why do you think it was the same man?"

"Just call it instinct, a hunch, intuition, whatever. I'm pretty sure it was him. Aside from that woman who danced with Spall, Etheridge, this man and that guy, what was his name? Ivan something?"

"Ivan Bondarenko."

"Yeah, him. Those three were the only people I didn't see in that place. The other two agents I recognized from the Wolf Station attack were found dead after Copperhead led the rescue in the safe house."

"Are you certain that you're not just *wanting* it to be him?" Saoirse put her hand on Shaw's arm and smiled.

"Maybe I am. Who knows how many Trician spies there actually were in Echo City at the time of the attack. We killed a few at the asylum—"

Shaw abruptly stopped talking and began to stare intensely at the sketch. Saoirse looked at him, concerned.

"What is it, Ryan? You're scaring me." The look on his face was causing Saoirse some alarm.

"Schlenker, Spall! Come over here!" Shaw's voice projected the intensity that was displayed on his face. Schlenker and Spall both immediately stopped what they were doing and quickly walked over to the desk. Shaw turned and showed them both the sketch.

"I've figured out who this is. Imagine him with much shorter hair, and no beard or mustache. It'll make things easier if you imagine him wearing an orderly's uniform from Isolation Asylum."

Schlenker gasped. "By Vulcan's hammer! We had him! We had him!"

"Henry the orderly," Spall said, his eyes narrowing.

# 37

## Agent Raker

"My Lord Galvanus," Agent Raker said, bowing before the black throne. Gone was the orderly's uniform, replaced by a black suit that fit him much better.

His was a nondescript face, neither handsome nor homely. His hair, eyes, and physique were all average, standing out not a whit. He was the sort of person that someone could see and immediately forget; he existed in the background. Bondarenko and Etheridge were both memorable in their own ways and were excellent agents, or at least Bondarenko had been prior to his swimming adventure in Ünterreich's incandescent river. Etheridge was untouchable, at least for the time being, her grandfather being who he was, but she still stood out, relying on her undeniable beauty and charm to disarm her opponents.

Raker was a born espionage agent. He had always been invisible; quickly overlooked or, if noticed, quickly forgotten. He was still surprised that The Galvanus had noticed him in the first place and had taken such an interest in his training. His lordship had made it clear that he had high expectations. Up to now, he had always delivered. Up to now.

The Galvanus regarded his protégé coldly.

"Raker. I am displeased."

Raker nodded. "I have no excuse, Lord. I clearly underestimated the Echoans."

"Clearly."

Raker swallowed. "I beg only for a chance to face them again, if your lordship will allow."

The Galvanus considered for a few moments. Normally, he would quickly and cheerfully make an example out of those who failed him, as Fromm had discovered only minutes before. Raker was different, though. He could see the potential in Raker. The cold-blooded desire to destroy the enemies of Ünterreich, the complete disregard for his own advancement. Raker didn't care about gaining status or power. He just wanted to watch Echo City burn. It was refreshing. Raker deserved another chance to make that happen.

"I have decided that you shall have another opportunity to impress me," The Galvanus said at last. "Do not imagine that I am blind to your recent failures, or that I was not tempted to have you join Fromm and Bondarenko. Those who fail me are rarely afforded a second chance. Be aware of what a blessing this is."

"I am keenly aware of this blessing, Lord. I thank you."

"Yes. You are aware of the locations of the remaining scientists?"

"Indeed, my lord. Before he attacked the Echoans, that ignorant prig Slattispoone provided me with a copy of the Fragment information he got from Bergstrom. This included the locations of the others the Echoans haven't found yet."

"Where are they?" The Galvanus asked, displaying some interest despite himself. The prospect of re-creating the Echoans' artificial star was too important an opportunity. The potential use as a weapon to annihilate Echo City and the filthy Republic was tantalizing.

"One of them is right here in Ünterreich," Raker began. "We are searching for this Professor Turgeneyev or his relations now. One is in Panthalassa, and one in Lille Danmark. I already have teams working on submersible craft to reach the underwater city, and I have ordered the collapsed tunnel to the ocean to be reopened. Both of those projects will take some time, of course. I have another team studying the contagion in Lille Danmark, and once they discover what is causing it and how to counter it, we will be able to enter that cavern as well."

The Galvanus nodded. He had made the right decision, it seemed. If he had acted on his earlier impulse to incinerate Raker, he would have likely set back the operation considerably. It sounded like things were well in hand. The only uncertainty lay in the Echoans. That wretch Spall and his pitiful team had proven themselves to be formidable opponents. He was certain Raker would not underestimate them again. Nor would The Galvanus.

"Excellent. You are dismissed."

Raker bowed deeply and left.

# 38

## A Surfacer No More

"I'm willing to bet he's the Tricians' top agent," Shaw said. "I'm certain he's the one I couldn't see clearly at the safe house. He was probably pulling the strings the entire time. He must have been Slattispoone's handler."

"No doubt you are correct," Spall added.

"But why would he let you explore the asylum and discover Slattispoone's activities?" Schlenker asked. "If he was a Trician agent, he would have noticed you leaving. Wouldn't he want to keep things a secret as long as possible? Why allow the confrontation to happen?"

Spall considered. "There was an armed agent waiting for Agent Adebe and myself in the hospital. They must have planned to separate us and kill us one or two at a time. That would have bought them at least a little time. Once we began to enquire at the prison, they must have known their game was up. They knew we would be coming to investigate, and they would have had to make their getaway regardless of the outcome. Adebe and I are fortunate we were able to subdue the agent in the hospital. They would have ambushed the rest of you much more easily."

"But why not just seal us in the confinement room when we went down to look for Bergstrom in the black desert?" Shaw asked. "He could have left us to die and just say we were in the asylum when it collapsed."

"He must have decided to keep us alive to see if we would be of use to him. He wanted the other Fragments, after all," Adebe said.

"He's clever, I'll give him that much," Shaw said. "Now what? Do you think there's a chance we might be able to find him?"

"No." Spall answered. "He will have changed his appearance by the time he was a block away from the safe house. If he is as clever and well trained as we think he is, he will be invisible. I have no doubt that he has been here in Echo for some time, and I would not be overly surprised to find that he has been orchestrating the activities of our very own anarchists here as well."

"If he was at the safe house, though," began Saoirse, "how did he escape? Copperhead cut most of them to pieces with his first shot."

Shaw turned to Saoirse. "He turned and ran for that tunnel of theirs as soon as he heard Copperhead's approach. He's not dumb, that's for sure."

"Definitely not," Schlenker agreed.

"All we can do now is disseminate as many pictures of him as possible throughout the Service," Spall added. "Shaw, I will need you to coordinate that with your sketch artist here."

"Consider it done."

A few more weeks rolled by. The agents were all once again in top shape, their injuries healed. The entire Secret Service was looking high and low for Henry the orderly, but the Special Branch knew it would prove fruitless. Thus, they had returned to their various projects.

Schlenker, Adebe, and Copperhead were working on what the doctor called "Schlenker's Incredible Self-Contained Submersible Track Navigating Steam-Electric Locomotive," and everyone else called "That Heap in the Back Corner." Spall, Shaw, and Saoirse were putting their heads together to build a prototype electric Gatling gun, after Shaw had described the use of miniguns in warfare on the surface.

"Why in earth would you call it a 'minigun'?" Saoirse asked when she first looked at Shaw's rough sketch. "It's so large and heavy."

Shaw frowned in thought for a moment. "I think it's because the first electric ones were big, designed for aircraft. 20 mm, I think. They would have weighed hundreds of kilos. When these smaller versions were developed, they called them miniguns. I know it sounds silly."

"Well, it makes a *bit* more sense now."

Shaw and Saoirse were holding hands, which Shaw felt was a big step for them, considering she had introduced herself to him by revealing that she had kicked her previous boyfriend in the unmentionables. They would take their lunch breaks in Schlenker's back garden, enjoying each other's company in the soft variegated glow of the bioluminescent vegetation. Shaw had finally begun to feel like he was home rather than just a visitor. He had even come to dislike being called "surfacer." The word felt as though it excluded him from the rest of society. He was now an Echoan.

Saoirse smiled when he told her that.

"Well, Shaw. What do you think of our Inner Earth so far?" Saoirse asked as they were joined by the others one afternoon.

Shaw thought for a moment before answering. "Well, I'm stuck down here forever, so I may as well enjoy it. You're here, and that helps more than I can say. Plus I can make an awful lot of money writing about the surface and 'inventing' some things. I think I like it just fine. There are a few movies from the surface I think will do well down here, if I can recreate them."

"Absolutely! I want to hear more about this *Star Wars* you told me about," Schlenker said. "I have never seen stars, you know, aside from that miraculous star-globe you built for Miss Muir."

"Despite the fact that you would fit right in with the Astronomers Guild," Spall added drily.

"So, Doctor," Saoirse began, "do you think we'll be able to find the other Fragments?"

Doctor Schlenker thought for a moment before replying. "I hope so, Miss Muir. There will be many obstacles in our way for the last three Fragments, and even my usual optimism has to be tempered by the facts. There is one thing that we must do before we attempt to find any of the other Fragments, though."

Spall raised an eyebrow. "What is that, Doctor?"

Doctor Schlenker smiled his infectious smile. "Adebe and Copperhead are outnumbered. Spall, Schlenker, Shaw, Saoirse. We need to find someone for our team whose name starts with a different letter."

Even Spall laughed a little at that.

# ACKNOWLEDGEMENTS

This work would not have been possible without the support of far too many people to list here, so I'll keep this as short as I dare.

My children, Odin, Thorin, Linnea, and Aksel, who asked for me to make up an epic bedtime story for them.

My wife, Kallie, for encouraging me to take my copious notes and write the story.

My mother, novelist Diane Stringam Tolley, who was my first editor and provided amazing feedback.

My father, Grant, who gave me endless support and encouragement.

Novelist Alison McBain, who had coffee with me and started my journey to publication.

Steve Eisner and everyone at When Words Count for the astronomical amount of feedback and coaching.

David LeGere and everyone at Woodhall Press for taking a chance on a first timer.

To those here and to everyone else involved in one way or another, I will be forever grateful.

# ABOUT THE AUTHOR

E.B. Tolley is new to writing, and Beneath a Sky of Stone, a story which grew from a bedtime story told to his children, is his first published work. He is a Police Officer and former Army Engineer, currently working as a Forensic Firearms and Ballistics analyst. Tolley lives in Beaumont, Alberta, Canada, with his wife and four children.